Love With the Proper Husband

"I am terribly sorry, my lord." Gwendolyn pulled her hands from his. "But I will not marry you."

"Oh but you will, Miss Townsend, because you see, I will not give up." Marcus got to his feet and stared down at her. It was most intimidating. "I have almost a full three months to persuade you to change your mind, and do not doubt that I will."

She stood and glared up at him. "I shall not change my mind."

"I will be at your door every day and every night. I shall do everything in my power to convince you to marry me, and I will not give up until the day I have completed thirty years of life.

"There is only one way to truly get me out of your life, Miss Townsend, and that"—he smiled slowly in a wicked and far too suggestive manner—"is to marry me."

VICTORIA ALEXANDER

Love
With The
Proper Husband

AVON BOOKS
An Imprint of HarperCollinsPublishers

This is a work of fiction. Names, characters, places, and incidents are products of the author's imagination or are used fictitiously and are not to be construed as real. Any resemblance to actual events, locales, organizations, or persons, living or dead, is entirely coincidental.

AVON BOOKS
An Imprint of HarperCollins*Publishers*
10 East 53rd Street
New York, New York 10022-5299

This book is dedicated
with gratitude and affection to
Chuck and the boys:
Terry, Joe, Tom, Jim, Dan, and Marcus,
who inspire me and make me laugh
and give me the tiniest glimpse
into the totally incomprehensible minds of men.
Thanks, guys!

Prologue

Spring 1820

The delight in male children is strictly in fulfilling one's responsibility and having them in the first place because, unfortunately, at some point they become men.

The Duchess of Roxborough

"And so, ladies, I propose we do something beyond simply complaining and hoping for the best." The Duchess of Roxborough cast her brightest smile around the gathering of ladies in the parlor at Effington House.

Helena, the Countess of Pennington, sipped thoughtfully at her tea and glanced around the fashionably decorated parlor to see the reaction of the dozen or so other women present. They were all friends, or at least acquaintances. Indeed, she'd known most since her come-out season, which happened far too many years ago now to note without a visible shudder of dismay. Beyond that, each and every lady there had a son or daughter of marriageable age. And at one point or another, Helena had heard each and every one despair of ever getting said child to agree to a suitable match.

"I'm a bit confused, Your Grace." Marian, Viscountess Berkley, drew her brows together.

Marian had been a bit confused for as long as anyone had known her but was so delightfully pleasant, no one particularly minded. In truth, when she was very young and very blond and very flirtatious, Helena quite suspected Marian had actively perfected her state of innocent confusion to the level of art.

"Your son and daughter are both married," Marian said. "I don't quite understand why you should propose this—what did you call it again?"

"The Ladies' Society for the Betterment of the Future of Britain." The duchess's voice rang in the room, and Helena was certain she saw Her Grace's chest visibly swell with pride.

A murmur of approval washed through the crowd. And why not? It was indeed a grand name. And far better than anything with the words *meddling* or *interfering* or, heaven forbid, *matchmaking* in it.

"And I propose this, Lady Berkley, precisely because I no longer have to worry about my children making suitable matches, but I am, as we all should be, concerned about future generations. Indeed, it could well be considered our patriotic duty. Besides, there are a number of young people throughout my family who are making no particular effort to marry. I find it quite distressing. In addition"—she flashed a wicked grin—"I think it will be great fun."

The ladies laughed and nodded their approval.

"I am simply suggesting we take our children's destinies in hand and do all within our power, with the help of one another, to find suitable matches for them, whether they wish it or not."

"It's past time my son wed," a lady somewhere behind Helena murmured.

Lady Heaton pursed her lips. "One more season and my daughter will be firmly on the shelf. And I shall be stuck with her forever."

"Probably because she greatly resembles her mother," Marian said under her breath to Helena.

"Shhh," Helena whispered, stifling a grin and her agreement.

"We are a clever lot," the duchess continued, "and we certainly have the skills among us to assist one another, should it be necessary, with various and assorted ideas—"

"Plots, schemes—" someone said.

"Plans, tactics—" another added.

Voices raised with excitement. "Strategies, intrigues!"

"Exactly." The duchess beamed. "It may be that, in certain cases—I think of them as projects—members of the society need do little more than lend moral support to one another. In other, more complicated projects, it might be necessary to actively take matters in hand to assist each other."

"Surely you're not suggesting those of us with daughters trap some gentleman into a situation by which the only honorable solution is marriage?" Lady Dawson said with a note of horror in her voice.

"Of course not, although I for one would at least consider such a suggestion under the appropriate circumstances." The duchess paused thoughtfully. "And how old is your daughter now?"

"Nearly two and twenty, Your Grace." Lady Dawson smiled weakly.

"As old as that," the duchess murmured.

On one hand, the duchess's proposal was outrageous: turning their children into the projects of a society determined to see them wed. Still, Helena knew full well the marriages of a fair number of the women present had been arranged by their families, and most of those had turned out well. Indeed, it was rather a pity that such things had fallen out of favor. In some respects the duchess's society would simply be arranging matters in a tried-and-true method. Upholding a time-honored tradition, as it were. Honoring the heritage of their country. Why, who could possibly argue with that?

"I needn't mention, should we decide to go forward with this, secrecy is of the utmost importance." Her Grace's tone was firm. "This simply will not work if any of the children become aware they are the target of an organized effort." She shook her head. "They can be quite stubborn when they suspect interference on the part of a mother. I believe they get it from their fathers."

There was a general murmur of agreement.

Helena already had an idea of sorts that would serve well to get her son to at last accept his familial obligations and marry. It had begun as an odd, chance thought but had dwelt in the back of her mind, becoming more solid each time she turned her attention to it. She simply hadn't the courage to carry it through. Now, however, with, at the very least, the moral encouragement of the society behind her . . .

"Your Grace." Helena rose to her feet. "I think the Ladies' Society for the Betterment of the Future of Britain is an outstanding proposal, and I should like to do my part." She squared her shoulders. "Therefore, I am more than willing to offer my son as the society's first project."

"Excellent, Lady Pennington." The duchess favored her with a brilliant smile. "I daresay you won't be sorry. Now, do you have any prospects in mind for him?"

"I not only have prospects." Helena grinned. "I have a plan."

Chapter One

*Men are untrustworthy, disloyal swine who
care for nothing save their own pleasures
and the perpetuation of their line.*

Gwendolyn Townsend

No good ever came of a summons from a solicitor.

Gwendolyn Townsend stiffened her already ramrod straight posture and ignored the urge to pick at the worn cuff of her pelisse. She was the daughter of a viscount, and regardless of her current circumstances, she would not be intimidated by a mere solicitor. Furthermore, she was not at all pleased to be kept waiting. She ignored as well the fact that, in spite of her lineage, she was nothing more than a governess at the moment and an unsuccessful one at that.

No good ever came of a summons from a solicitor.

It was harder to ignore the long-forgotten warning that had surfaced in her mind with a vengeance and refused to let her be. It had echoed in the back of her thoughts ever since the letter from her late father's man of affairs, Mr. Whiting, had at long last reached her in New York. And why shouldn't it? She'd heard the servants at Madame Chaussan's Academy for Young Ladies say it often enough through most of the first sixteen years of her life, and indeed, hadn't it always proved true?

The last time Gwen had had anything whatsoever to do with a solicitor had been five years ago when Mr. Whiting's nephew, taking up his uncle's business, had informed her she was penniless. She still recalled that moment—the discomfort of the young man, a scant few years older than she, at his announcement, and the sympathy in his brown eyes. She remembered the look in his eyes as clearly as she remembered his words.

"Miss Townsend, forgive me for keeping you waiting." A gentleman of distinguished appearance stepped into the room and crossed to her chair. Gwen knew his name, but they'd never had occasion to meet before now. He extended his hand, and she accepted it cautiously. "Your appearance is something of a surprise. I did not expect you for several days yet."

"I thought it best to return to England at once."

"Of course." He withdrew his hand and nodded toward the door. "You remember my nephew, Albert?"

Only now did she note the younger man standing by the open door, a decidedly apologetic expression on his face. There was no sympathy in his eyes today but an odd look nonetheless.

"Of course." She smiled politely and waited. If there was one thing, and indeed there might well be only one thing, she had learned through seven positions of employment, it was how to give the appearance of patience.

Mr. Whiting took his place behind his desk and nodded dismissively at his nephew. Albert started toward the door, then abruptly turned back. "Miss Townsend, please accept my most heartfelt apologies."

At once she recognized the look in his eye as guilt.

He stepped closer. "This is entirely my fault, and I cannot tell you how truly horrible I have felt since the error was first discovered. I have been most concerned about your—"

"That's quite enough, Albert," Whiting said firmly.

Error? Gwen's gaze slid from Albert to his uncle and back.

"What error?" she said slowly.

"It was a mistake." Albert shook his head. "Quite inexcusable, and I shall never forgive—"

Mistake?

"Albert." Whiting's voice cut through the room.

Albert ignored him. "Miss Townsend, please understand I consider myself at your service from this moment forward. Should you need anything whatsoever, up to and including the benefits that can only be derived from marriage, I should be honored to offer my—"

"Albert," Whiting snapped. "I will take care of this. I'm certain you have other duties to attend to."

Albert hesitated, then nodded. "Of course, Uncle." He squared his shoulders and met her gaze. "Again, Miss Townsend, my apologies."

He left without another word. Gwen stared after him. A hundred myriad thoughts swirled through her mind, but not one made any sense.

Whiting cleared his throat. "Miss Townsend, I—"

"What mistake?" Her gaze snapped to his.

Whiting paused as if considering his words. He was distinctly ill-at-ease, and for the first time since her father's death, a glimmer of what might have been hope surfaced within her.

When she'd received Whiting's letter she'd been curious, of course: it was accompanied by an already paid passage back to England. But he'd said nothing more than that there was a matter of importance regarding her family that required her immediate return. She'd been only too glad to bid her employers and their annoying offspring goodbye and had sailed on the first ship home.

"Mr. Whiting?"

She'd assumed Whiting's summons had to do with the signing of papers regarding her father's estate or the transfer of ownership of his property, matters she'd assumed as well had been settled long ago. Still, whatever it was, it was significant enough, in Whiting's eyes, to provide her with a way back to England, and that was all she really cared about.

Now, looking at the solicitor's obvious discomfort, coupled with his nephew's abject apology and strange proposal of marriage, Gwen realized the "matter of importance" was far more significant than she'd imagined.

"Miss Townsend." Whiting folded his hands on the desk in front of him. "My nephew should never have informed you of the state of your finances in the manner in which he did. Nor should he have said anything whatsoever so soon after your father's demise."

Gwen's heart sank.

"It was most thoughtless of him and—"

"Mr. Whiting, as much as I appreciate your sincere,

albeit long overdue apology on the behalf of your nephew, it scarcely necessitated having me transported across an ocean. Even so, I am most grateful for the passage home. I can only imagine you provided it as a way to ease your conscience regarding the abrupt nature of the disclosure of my financial status on the day following my father's death. Still, it is exceedingly kind of you.

"I would offer to reimburse you but such an offer would be pointless as my finances are little better today than they were five years ago. In addition, I have absolutely no difficulty in accepting both your apology and your funding of my return to England. You may tell Albert I appreciate his offer of marriage as well. Now." She rose to her feet. "Unless there is something more—"

Whiting stood. "If you please, Miss Townsend, I beg your indulgence. There is a great deal more. However, this is extremely awkward and most difficult. In many ways I feel as if my nephew and I have, well, very nearly ruined your life."

"Ruined my life? That's scarcely possible." She met his gaze squarely. "You, of all people, are well aware of the status of my father's estate. His title, his home, and his land were entailed and as such were the legacy of his only living male relative—a distant cousin I have never met. As I was not born male"—she bit back the tide of bitterness that swelled in her at the words—"I could not inherit his home, *my* home. This is a fact, Mr. Whiting. One I have known always. Your nephew's pronouncement came as no surprise, even if his timing and his exact words were not as politic as they might have been."

For the first time since entering his office she smiled,

if a bit ruefully. "Circumstances of nature and the legalities of men ruined my life, although I daresay I scarcely feel entirely ruined. I have my name and my reputation, and I shall find some way to support myself."

"Yes, well"—Whiting's voice was gruff—"that may not be necessary."

"No?"

"Please." He gestured at her chair, and she retook her seat.

Whiting settled back in his chair and drew a deep breath. "When my nephew informed you of your financial circumstances, he was not as experienced in such matters as he is now—"

She waved his words away. "Another apology is not necessary."

"Do allow me to proceed, Miss Townsend, this is not another apology." He huffed. "What I am trying to say is that Albert's inexperience five years ago led him to make certain assumptions based on what he knew of your father's affairs. He was correct, but only insofar as those issues he was versed in. He was not aware, as I was, that your father had made certain provisions for your future."

"Provisions?" She held her breath. "What kind of provisions?"

"He did not leave you with nothing."

For a moment, the world tilted about her. Her perfect posture failed, and she collapsed back in her chair feeling much like a sail suddenly bereft of wind.

"Are you all right, Miss Townsend?" Whiting leaped to his feet and started around the desk toward her.

He did not leave you with nothing.

"Quite." She shook her head to clear it and waved him away. "Do go on."

"Very well." Whiting studied her carefully, then returned to his seat. He glanced at the papers on his desk. "Upon the birth of each of his daughters, your father set up accounts to provide you both with incomes in the event that you were unwed upon his death. When your sister married against his wishes, he abolished her account."

"Of course," Gwen murmured.

She couldn't remember the last time she'd thought of her sister. Louisa was thirteen years her senior and had fallen in love with a daring, dashing, adventurer when Gwen was very young. Louisa had married against her father's wishes and left with her husband to travel the world, severing all ties with her family. At least that was Gwen's understanding from what little she'd heard through the years. She'd wondered on occasion about this sister of hers that she barely remembered. Where she was and what she was doing. And if she ever thought of the younger sister she'd never really known.

"As I was saying, the annual income is not extensive but will allow you to live modestly. In addition, his legacy to you includes a small house in the country, near the village of Pennington."

"An income and a house." She stared in disbelief for a long moment. "An income and a house?"

"There's more. Shall I go on?" Concern colored his face. "Are you certain you're all right?

"I don't know." She shook her head. *An income and a house?* "I don't believe I am." At once the absurdity of it all struck her, and she laughed.

"Miss Townsend?"

"Oh, do wipe that look off your face, Mr. Whiting, I am not going mad. It's simply . . ." She pressed her fingers to her temples, trying to fully absorb the import of his words.

She could not possibly explain to this relative stranger the relief, no, the joy of finding salvation where none is expected. A thought struck her, and any amusement vanished. "Why was I not informed of this before now?"

"Miss Townsend, as I explained, Albert was—"

"Albert be damned." Abrupt, unrelenting anger pulled her to her feet. "You are the man my father trusted to handle his affairs, not your nephew. The fault here, Mr. Whiting, is yours and yours alone!"

"Indeed it is. And I accept it. It is precisely why I paid for your passage home." He too was on his feet. "My mistake was sending an inexperienced boy to begin handling the details of your father's estate. I had no idea he would leap into it to the extent he did. He was not charged with informing you of anything whatsoever. In truth, I sent him to Townsend Park in advance of my arrival to do nothing more than begin sorting through your father's papers, quite within the jurisdiction of my responsibilities as his executor. I joined Albert the next day, but you, my dear young woman, were already gone."

"What did you expect? My fears had all been realized. My father was dead." She swiveled and paced before the desk, her words as much for herself as for him. "Yes, I'd spent much of my life away at school and I barely knew the man, but still he had always existed. I always knew he was *there*. And he did treat me kindly if without extreme affection. I had no reason to think he didn't have some feeling for me, and I cared for him as well. I did not realize how much until he was gone. I was quite distressed by his passing.

"In addition, I was about to be tossed out of my home. I was, in your nephew's words, a penniless orphan with no prospects and no future save throwing myself on the mercy and generosity of a heretofore unknown cousin."

She stopped and met his gaze. "I had long ago determined that in this world, the only one you can truly count on is yourself. My parents were both dead, my sister long since gone; there was nothing to keep me at Townsend Park. You can scarcely blame me for leaving." She stepped closer. "Every day of my life I was all too aware that should my father die when I was not yet wed, I would have nothing and no one to depend on but myself. And that, Mr. Whiting, is precisely what I did."

"And made it damnably hard to find you in the process," Whiting snapped. "I tried, Lord knows how hard I tried. It took months to track you from Townsend Park to that blasted Frenchwoman's house here in London—" He narrowed his eyes. "How did you manage that, *penniless orphan* that you were?"

"I had some resources," she said loftily. She had, for years, saved whatever spare money had come her way.

He snorted. "No doubt. By the time I found your Madames Freneau and de Chabot—and I should at some point like a detailed accounting as to precisely how you know a woman of her dubious reputation—"

"Mr. Whiting, Madame de Chabot is Madame Freneau's sister-in-law. Madame Freneau was my teacher and remains my dearest friend. And both ladies have been exceedingly kind to me." Given Mr. Whiting's obvious disapproval of Madame de Chabot, it was scarcely necessary to mention Gwen had been staying with the women since her return to London two days ago. The man had control of her finances after all. Still . . . "Furthermore I do not owe an accounting to anyone, least of all you. I am not some errant child straight from the schoolroom—"

"Aha!" He glared. "But that was precisely what you were at your father's death. You were barely sixteen years of age, and I was named your guardian as well as executor of his estate. And, I should point out, the administrator of your income until such time as you marry."

"I have no need of a guardian now. I am of age."

"Nonetheless, I am still in control of your income and shall remain so until the day you wed or the day I die. Now." He leaned forward in a distinctly menacing manner. "Sit down, Miss Townsend."

She started to protest, then thought better of it and sat.

"By the time I managed to discover where you had resided in London, you had fled to America." His eyes narrowed. "Imagine my surprise to discover I was no longer trying to find the sixteen-year-old daughter of a British lord but a twenty-year-old governess. A Miss"—he glanced at the papers before him—"no—a Mademoiselle . . . Fromage. Fromage?" He raised a brow. "Cheese?"

"Don't be absurd," she muttered. "It was Froumage."

"I see. Regardless, you did indeed manage to stay one step ahead of my efforts to locate you." Again he glanced at the papers. "Your first position, in Philadelphia, lasted no more than a few months. Following that, you accepted a new position in Boston, again your employment was brief, as were your subsequent positions in Baltimore, Trenton, Philadelphia again, until your most recent in New York, where at long last, you stayed in one place long enough for my agents to catch up to you." He glared. "It would have been far easier had you not continuously changed your name. The last one was . . . what?"

"Piccard," she murmured.

"I'm assuming this was to avoid bad references?"

She sighed in irritation and gazed innocently at nothing in particular, taking care not to meet his gaze. "My character is not overly suited to the position of governess. A deficit that was only enhanced by the tendency of Americans to produce remarkably ill-mannered and spoiled offspring."

At once it struck her that she would never have to be in that position again. She snapped her gaze back to Whiting's, an odd note of awe in her voice. "I won't ever have to do that again, will I?"

"As I said before, Miss Townsend, the income is extremely modest, sufficient for your needs as an unmarried woman but nothing more. You will not be able to live in the style of Townsend Park, but no"—he smiled—"you will not have to seek employment of any kind."

For a long moment Gwen savored the sound of his words. Of all the things she had expected when she'd received his letter, this was not even imagined. Her anger had faded, wiped away by the dawning realization of her change in circumstances as well as her acceptance that the last five years were as much the result of her own impulsiveness as of Albert's error.

"Well, then, Mr. Whiting"—she flashed him a genuine smile and stood—"where is my money?"

He rose to his feet and looked at her with a fair amount of amusement. "I am not finished, Miss Townsend. There's more."

"More?" She plopped back in her chair and stared with astonishment. "More money?"

Whiting laughed, and she had the good grace to blush.

"Forgive me for sounding so . . . so mercenary, but"—she leaned forward—"in the span of a few short minutes I have gone from having nothing to having something, modest though it may be. And the thought of having more, well, it's somewhat intoxicating."

"No doubt." Whiting tried and failed to hide his amusement and once again resumed his seat. "However, while this has the potential to provide you with increased"—he cleared his throat—"*finances*, I'm not sure . . ." He paused and studied her carefully. "Right now you have an income that will continue until you marry. When you wed, contingent upon my approval of the match, there are funds that have been reserved for a respectable dowry as well as the settlement of a substantial sum upon you personally. You will never have to worry about money again."

"Never again worry about money?" She shook her head. "It is an interesting idea if a bit difficult to grasp at the moment. However"—she chose her words carefully— "in order to achieve that freedom from financial want, I should have to sacrifice my own personal freedom."

"My dear woman, we are speaking of marriage, not prison."

"Is there a great deal of difference, Mr. Whiting?"

"Most certainly," he said with the indignation reserved for those who dare to question the principles of crown and country and other respectable institutions.

"Oh?" She considered him carefully. "Are you married?"

"That is neither here nor there."

She raised a brow.

He sighed. "No."

"Have you ever been married?"

"No. Nonetheless." His tone was staunch. "It is a desirable state, much to be preferred by women."

"Not this particular woman." She shook her head firmly.

"Miss Townsend—"

"It's quite simple, Mr. Whiting. What I have seen of marriage through my life does not endear the institution to me." She met his gaze directly. "For the upper classes, marriage is for no other reason than to cling to titles and property. My mother died when I was very young while trying to give my father a male heir—the only true purpose of their union. My sister's marriage estranged her from her family and friends. I have no idea where she is, nor has she ever made any effort to contact me."

An uneasy look crossed Whiting's face. "Miss Townsend—"

She held out her hand to quiet him. "Mr. Whiting, do allow me to finish. Even if what I have seen in my own family did not dissuade me from the bonds of holy wedlock, what I have witnessed in the households of my employers has certainly done so." She drew a deep breath. "I freely admit I am not an overly competent governess. In point of fact, with one or two exceptions, the children in my charge were not especially fond of me, and I confess, their lack of affection was returned. However, that was not the only reason I took leave of my employments."

She paused, not entirely sure how to say this. There was, and had been from the beginning, the strange feeling that perhaps all that had befallen her was somehow her fault. That she had not coiled her dark red hair tightly enough against her head, or she had not chosen clothing appropriately dull enough to conceal what to her dismay was an overly lush figure, or she had not been subservient enough to avoid the attention of men who saw an unmarried woman in her position as fair game for their lecherous pursuits.

"In my first position, the head of the household, the father of my charges, believed my duties extended beyond attending to his children to attending to his own"—she grimaced—"*needs*. Suffice it to say I refused and left his employment at once."

"Damnation," Whiting murmured.

"I chose my second employer as carefully as he chose me. Unfortunately, I did not extend my scrutiny to his acquaintances, and there was a nasty incident late one evening when I rebuffed the advances of a houseguest who made his way to my quarters." She shuddered at the memory of awaking in the night to groping hands and demanding lips. And fear. "I managed to discourage him with the help of a chamber pot."

"Good God!" Whiting stared in horror. "Were you all right?"

"I escaped with my virtue intact; however, my employment did not survive." She shrugged. "There were other instances in other positions and in each and every one, the gentlemen involved were married, yet that state did not deter their lecherous advances. At the very least, I should expect fidelity from a husband"—she shook her head—"and I have yet to meet a married man who understood that concept."

"Actually, Miss Townsend," Whiting said slowly, "your father made arrangements for a specific husband."

"Did he?" For a moment she stared in disbelief. Then she laughed. "Mr. Whiting, if nothing else, this is most amusing. And gratifying as well to know that my father did indeed think enough of me to make such arrangements. Very well"—she grinned—"who did he have in mind?"

"The Earl of Pennington." Whiting shuffled through the papers on his desk. "Your father and the old earl were great friends in their youth. They agreed to a marriage between you and his son if you were both unwed when the boy reached his thirtieth year. It's detailed in a letter signed by both men and delivered to me, as I also handled the earl's affairs."

"And?"

"And the thirtieth anniversary of his birth is fast approaching and he is not married."

"I see." She thought for a moment. "Tell me, Mr. Whiting, do I lose my income, or my house, if I do not wed this earl?"

He shook his head. "You forfeit nothing whatsoever. At least nothing you already have. It's an exceedingly unusual arrangement as such things go. The old earl decided it was fair to allow his son to choose his own bride, yet he was only willing to give him so long to do so."

"Until he was thirty."

"Exactly." Whiting nodded. "Your father, given your sister's unsuitable marriage, was not quite as willing to let you choose your husband but bent to the wishes of the earl in light of what would be a most favorable match for you. Besides, when the earl's son turned thirty you would be one and twenty and if you were not yet married—"

"I too would need assistance," she said dryly.

"I am glad you understand." He picked up and discarded several papers, then found the one he wanted. "Here is where it becomes awkward."

"Only here?"

He ignored her. "The earliest you and the young earl were to be made aware of this arrangement was three months before his birth date. Once you were informed, the only way to receive the dowry I mentioned previously, and the settlement, is to marry according to your father's wishes."

"So"—she chose her words carefully—"if I had married as late as this morning, or if I had accepted Albert's proposal just a few minutes ago, I would have received this substantial settlement. But as of this moment, the only way to get that is to marry this thirty-year-old gentleman who cannot find a bride on his own?"

Whiting frowned. "I would not have put it quite like that but yes, that is essentially accurate."

"Is he fat, Mr. Whiting? Or ugly? Does he have too much stomach and not enough hair?"

The solicitor pressed his lips together in disapproval. "Most certainly not. The earl is quite handsome but beyond that, he is considered a match much to be desired."

"Not for me. I shall have to do without the handsome, desirable earl. I shall be quite happy to live on my modest income, which is far better than I had ever hoped for, in my new house near the village of"—she started—"did you say Pennington? As in the Earl of Pennington?"

"Indeed I did. While your property is less than an acre, it does abut his."

"How very clever of my father. What a pity I did not know him better. Nonetheless, I will not marry a stranger even for a substantial settlement." Once again she got to her feet. "Now then, Mr. Whiting . . ." The look on his face pulled her up short. "There is more, isn't there?"

He nodded, and she sighed and sat back down.

"This is not at all pleasant and I'm not entirely sure how to say it." Apprehension creased Whiting's forehead. "Miss Townsend, it is with deep regret that I must inform you of the deaths of Mr. and Mrs. Loring, your sister and her husband."

The words hung in the air, so unexpected Gwen could not comprehend them for a long moment. Without warning, pain sharp and relentless stabbed through her, and she nearly gasped aloud. She had never known this woman, this *sister*, who had never made any effort to contact her. Why should Gwen care about Louisa's fate now?

"... drowned as I understand it, a shipwreck I think, but that information was rather vague. Somewhere in the South Seas, Polynesia, perhaps, or ..."

But she did, far more than she had ever dreamed she would.

"... more than a year ago now, however ..."

Perhaps it was because as long as she had a sister somewhere, Gwen would never be truly alone in the world.

"... the children were not ..."

Now she was.

"... taken in by missionaries, I believe, then finally sent on to England ..."

Children?

Gwen's attention jerked back to him. "What children?"

"Your sister's children." He glanced at his papers. "Three of them. Girls." He looked at her. "I gather you didn't know she had children?"

Perhaps she was not alone after all. "What has become of them?"

"They are currently residing in the country"—reluctance sounded in his voice—"with your cousin. At Townsend Park."

"They are well taken care of, then," she said slowly,

her calm demeanor belying the turmoil inside her. Townsend Park. Home. How ironic that her sister's children were now living in the very place their mother had left without a second thought.

"It would appear so." His manner was noncommittal. Too much so.

She narrowed her eyes and studied him, but his expression matched his tone. In the back of her mind she noted this very characteristic probably made him an excellent solicitor.

"What are you not saying, Mr. Whiting?"

"It's not my place to say anything, Miss Townsend."

"I suspect that will not stop you."

"Very well. Save for your cousin, a remote relation if I recall correctly, you have no family. It would be most appropriate for you to call on your nieces and make their acquaintance. Ascertain for yourself their state." His tone remained aloof, but his gaze was intense. "Besides, regardless of one's courage or strength or self-reliance, it is exceedingly difficult to travel through life alone. Especially for young women."

Her chin shot up, and she glared. "I have managed my life thus far entirely on my own and quite adequately as well."

"That is debatable, Miss Townsend. However"—he heaved a long-suffering sigh—"the question is not so much one of your life and future, but of that of these girls. They are your only family, but much more importantly, *you* are all that they have."

Chapter Two

Sons or husbands, young or old, men in general haven't the least understanding of what they are supposed to do until we tell them.

Helena Pennington

"Don't know why you didn't have the blasted man come to see you." The indignant voice of Reginald, Viscount Berkley, drifted up the stairs. "Bloody inconvenient, if you ask me."

Marcus Holcroft, the eighth Earl of Pennington, bit back a grin and glanced over his shoulder at his friend. "I don't recall anyone asking you."

Reggie muttered something Marcus didn't quite catch, and he chuckled.

"Come now, Reggie, it's hardly an inconvenience. We were on our way to the club anyway, and this is but a few blocks from there. Besides, Whiting's note said he had a matter of some urgency to discuss."

"Precisely why he should have come to you. Something havey-cavey about all this," Reggie said darkly.

"Nonsense."

Even as he brushed aside Reggie's warning, Marcus had to admit the summons from the man who had long served as his father's solicitor and, in the seven years since his father's death, as his own, was, at the very least, unusual. Whiting was not a man prone to rash impulse or undue emotion. Yet his missive betrayed an urgency at odds with the solicitor's character, and Marcus could not ignore a nagging sense of unease. Far better to visit the man at once and discover what was afoot than waste time worrying about it.

"I daresay it's nothing more than the requirement of a signature on one official document or other." Marcus reached the third floor and glanced back at his friend. "Probably something involving a bit of property near Holcroft Hall that I have my eye on. The old dower house, actually. My father sold it years ago and I have been trying to get it back. I am in hopes that Whit—"

"Sir! If you please—"

An irate feminine voice assaulted his ears at nearly the same instant he smacked into a short but surprisingly firm female form. Marcus jerked his attention back to where he was going in time to reach out and steady the woman he'd just walked into.

"Pardon me, miss, I—"

"Unhand me at once!" Beneath her now askew hat, she glared up at him, blue eyes flashing, a blush of anger coloring a porcelain complexion, lips full and ripe. For a moment he could do nothing but stare down at her.

"Is your hearing as faulty as your ability to place one foot in front of the other?" She slapped his hand away.

"You have my abject apologies." Marcus moved

back and swept an exaggerated bow. "I should be well advised to watch my step in the future in the event yet another determined female should plow headlong into me."

"I was scarcely the one doing the plowing. You were looking where you had been rather than where you were headed." She straightened her hat and narrowed her lovely eyes. "Your sarcasm, sir, is neither necessary nor appreciated."

"Really? How exceedingly odd," he said in the droll manner he had honed through the years to a fine art. "I usually find sarcasm second only to wit in both need and appreciation."

She stared, obviously suspicious as well as annoyed, and he tried not to laugh. It was apparent the young woman was trying to decide if he was merely impolite or actually deranged.

"Forgive him, miss." Reggie nudged him aside and tipped his hat. "He fancies himself a great wit. Truth is, he hasn't been the same since he was the victim of a horrible hunting accident last year." Reggie leaned toward the woman, who eyed him with equal amounts of curiosity and trepidation. "You see, he was mistaken for a buck. Shot right in the—"

"Sir!" Shock rang in the lady's voice but Marcus swore he saw what might be the tiniest glint of reluctant amusement in her eye.

"That's quite enough," Marcus said mildly. "And patently false as well. I can assure you I have never been shot in any part of my person, neither accidentally nor deliberately."

"I find that exceedingly difficult to believe." The

young woman's forbidding and vaguely familiar expression was unchanged, but now Marcus was certain she was, however unwillingly, amused. "I would not be at all surprised to learn more than a few shots have been directed at your person, for the arrogance of your manner if nothing else."

Reggie laughed. "She's got you there, old man."

"Indeed she does," Marcus said coolly.

Reggie grinned at her as if they were coconspirators. "Any number of people would like to shoot him, miss. It was no more than an entertaining fancy on my part that someone actually had."

"My friend is easily amused." Marcus stepped aside and nodded cordially. "I fear we have detained you far too long. Again, my apologies, miss."

"Certainly." She lifted her chin, marched past them, and proceeded briskly down the stairs.

Marcus watched her with his usual sense of appreciation for the sway of attractive hips and toyed with the passing notion that there was more to this woman than met the eye. Not that it was any of his concern, of course.

"She's unaccompanied, Marcus." Reggie's gaze lingered on the figure rapidly vanishing down the stairwell. "Not so much as a maid with her. Odd, don't you think? She's well spoken enough, obviously a woman of quality."

"Yes, but her cuffs were frayed," Marcus said thoughtfully. "And her gown is sadly out of style."

"Ugly as well. Too—"

"Proper? Stiff? Dull?"

"Exactly." Reggie nodded. "Seems a pity. I'd wager

there is a fetching figure beneath that drab gown and an intriguing story behind those eyes. She could well be the victim of dire circumstances beyond her control. And sorely in need of assistance, even rescue. Why, I should probably see—"

"You most certainly should not." Marcus took his friend's elbow firmly, steered him away from the stairs and down the corridor toward the solicitor's office.

Viscount Berkley, Reginald, *Reggie*, was Marcus's closest friend and his oldest. Their country estates were in the same county, and the men had grown up side by side. In many ways they were as alike as brothers. In others they couldn't be more dissimilar.

Reggie had the most annoying tendency to imagine himself in the manner of a knight of old, rescuing fair maidens and damsels in distress. Most times the lady in question neither wanted nor needed the proffered rescuing and always Reggie offered his heart along with his assistance.

As for Marcus, he was certainly no rescuer of helpless females but he'd always had a fondness for mysteries and a corner of his mind lingered on the enigma presented by a pair of fetching eyes, a nicely rounded derrière and an air at odds with the obvious circumstances of her existence. It had been his experience that only women born to his own station in life ever met a gentleman's gaze with the unflinching directness she'd displayed and even then, such women were exceedingly rare. In truth, the only other women he could recall ever speaking in so firm and direct a manner to him had been those entrusted with his care as a child. His mother, of course, nursemaids, governesses—

He chuckled. "I daresay your damsel in distress is more than capable of taking care of herself. In truth, I would wager a considerable sum the lady in question is used to navigating far more treacherous waters than even those presented by being unescorted on the streets of London. I suspect she's accustomed to dealing with that most unpleasant form of life,"—he pulled open the door to Whiting's outer office and grinned at his friend—"children."

A scant two hours later, mysterious women, firm-spoken governesses, and helpless maidens were the last things on Marcus's mind.

"It's absurd, that's what it is," Reggie declared for perhaps the hundredth time, his level of indignation growing with his consumption of Marcus's excellent brandy. "I cannot believe—"

"I can." Marcus's tone was wry. "My father always did have an interesting way of giving me just enough rope to hang myself."

"Enough rope?" Reggie held out his again empty glass.

"Figuratively speaking, for the most part." Marcus shrugged and refilled the viscount's glass. The two were ensconced in the spacious library at Pennington House, the London residence of the Holcroft family and the earls of Pennington for the last two centuries, and the two friends' personal sanctuary throughout the years of their majority. "What he has done now, without my knowledge, of course, is to allow me what he considered a reasonable amount of time—"

"Thirty years?" Reggie peered over the rim of his glass. "That would be the rope?"

"Exactly. A sufficient amount of time, in the eyes of many, to select a bride of my own choosing. That I have failed to accomplish that thus far means I now forfeit the right to do so." Marcus leaned back against the edge of the desk and sipped at his brandy thoughtfully. "As much as I do not relish the idea of such a choice being taken from my hands, I must admit the way in which it has been done is remarkably clever."

"Is it?"

"If I had known of this deadline for matrimony I might well have selected a wife on the basis of suitability alone. Position, finances, that sort of thing. My father, you see, was something of a romantic. Affection, even love if you will, would never have been a possibility if I had known of his plan. He was a great believer in engagements of the heart." He chuckled. "Oh yes, he was exceedingly clever. I might have to perpetrate the same hoax on my own son someday."

"See here, Marcus, I thought you were bloody angry about all this."

"I was. No, I still am, but my ire is tempered with admiration." He blew a long breath. "In truth, Reggie, he's reached out from the grave and grabbed me by the—"

The door to the library slammed open and the dowager Countess of Pennington swept into the room like an unrelenting, ill wind.

"Marcus Aloysius Grenville Hamilton Holcroft, are you or are you not going to marry this girl?"

Reggie sprang to his feet in an interesting mix of terror and courtesy. The widow of the seventh Earl of Pennington often had that effect on those who did not see through her behavior, generally everyone except her late husband and her son. "Good evening, my lady. As always it is a pleas—"

Lady Pennington waved him quiet and halted a few feet from her only child. "Well? What's it to be?"

"Good evening, Mother," Marcus said mildly. He was eternally grateful he had not inherited his mother's tendency toward overly dramatic displays of passion. "I see you have heard the news."

"Of course I have heard. I was here when Mr. Whiting came by this morning with the horrible tidings. You, needless to say, were as usual nowhere to be found."

"Imagine that." Marcus tried not to smile at the accusation.

He loved his mother, as any good son should, but much preferred her at a distance. The mansion in London and Holcroft Hall in the country were large enough, and mother and son's individual interests varied enough, to allow them to cohabit peacefully during those months of the year when it could not be avoided. He had long considered the purchase of a town house of his own, although, in truth, even when they were both in residence, their paths rarely crossed. Marcus thought, and he suspected his mother agreed, that was for the best.

"If you had not squandered your life thus far you would be married by now and, with any luck, already have an heir." Lady Pennington glared as if Marcus's failure to wed and reproduce was part of a grand scheme to deny her life meaning and fulfillment. "Now you have no choice."

"Apparently not," Marcus said.

"You do not seem overset at the prospect." His mother studied him suspiciously. "Why on earth not?"

Marcus shrugged as if the idea of marrying a woman he had never so much as seen was of no consequence whatsoever and not one of the most infuriating prospects he had ever encountered. One from which he could see no means of escape.

"Your distress is sufficient for both of us." He sipped casually at his drink.

"My distress is entirely appropriate given the dreadful nature of the situation." Her eyes widened in dismay. "You do realize the consequences if you do not marry the Townsend girl, do you not? You will lose your entire fortune, every bit of it."

"Yes, but I shall retain my title and the estate as well as this house."

"Neither a title nor an estate is of any significance if you cannot keep them up," she snapped. "And what of me, Marcus? Didn't Mr. Whiting explain that I too will lose everything? All that your father left me? Funding, I should point out, that has allowed me to live without impinging on your resources. It has allowed me to live independently for the most part." She paced to and fro across the width of the library. "I have not had to depend on your finances for every little thing. I have been able to make my own decisions, and you have been able to make yours. In truth, when I look at my friends who are completely dependent on their families for survival, I am eternally grateful for your father's foresight."

"As am I," Marcus murmured.

Reggie edged toward the door. "Perhaps I should take my leave—"

"Stay right where you are, my lord. *Reginald.* Even though I daresay you are no better than he is. I know your own mother has quite despaired of you ever doing your duty and finding a suitable wife. Still, I do need someone to help him see that he has very little choice in this matter." She forced a pleasant smile. "And you are apparently the best I can do."

"Glad to help." Reggie smiled weakly and glanced longingly at the brandy decanter on the desk.

Lady Pennington's gaze followed his. "Oh, do fill your glass, my boy, and one for me as well. The situation fairly screams for spirits of some sort although something stronger than brandy is probably appropriate. I have been most distressed since I heard of all this and have had to face the most dire of fates."

Marcus bit back a grin.

His mother's gaze caught his. "You think I'm being overly dramatic, don't you?"

"Perhaps a bit."

"Only a bit?" She sank down on the sofa with a sigh and accepted a glass from Reggie. "Perhaps I am not being dramatic enough. It has come as quite a shock."

"You didn't know about this plot of Father's, then?" Marcus studied his mother carefully.

She stared at him. "Of course not."

Marcus wasn't sure whether to believe her. His parents had always struck him as being extraordinarily close, more so than most husbands and wives. Theirs was obviously a love match. It was exceedingly odd that

his father would not have shared something this significant with his wife. "He never mentioned this arrangement he had entered into?"

"Not a word," she said blithely.

"Oh?" He raised a brow.

"Do not look at me like that, Marcus. I tell you I had
no idea." Her tone was firm. "First of all, I would never
have approved of such a thing. I find the very idea of an
arranged marriage distasteful and positively medieval.
And secondly, had I known of your father's plan, I
should have told you long before now."

"To allow you to pick out your own bride." Reggie
nodded.

"Exactly." She cast his friend an appreciative smile.
Reggie fairly swelled under her approval and beamed
back at her.

"Damnably decent of you, Mother."

"I think so." She nodded in a smug manner and
sipped at her brandy. For a moment she looked far
younger than her eight and forty years and rather vulnerable as well. Ridiculous idea, of course. Helena, the
dowager Countess of Pennington, was anything but vulnerable. She'd been very much his father's partner as
well as wife.

From the moment Marcus had recognized that as a
young boy he'd been rather pleased by the concept and
vowed to forge a similar relationship with his own wife.
The difficulty was in finding a woman who possessed
the qualities of intelligence and competence necessary
for such a position, as well as charm, passion, and,
preferably, a fair face and figure. A woman who could
capture his heart and his mind. In short, the perfect

wife. A creature even he admitted could not possibly exist.

Of course, what he wanted no longer mattered.

"Did you look at this letter your father signed?" Lady Pennington studied her son. "Was it legitimate?"

"It appeared so." Marcus nodded. "I know father's signature as well as I know my own, and I have no doubt as to the authenticity of the letter. However, it simply laid out the bones of the agreement. Whiting had other documents detailing the fine points of this marriage bargain."

"And did you examine those as well?" she said, a curious note in her voice.

Marcus waved away the question. "I glanced at them. It scarcely seemed necessary to do more. My fate is apparently sealed."

"It might well be wise to have another solicitor look at it all." Reggie's manner was thoughtful. "Another eye might find a way out and—"

"Nonsense, Reginald, it would simply prolong the inevitable," Lady Pennington said with a sigh. "Besides, Mr. Whiting has always acted in the best interest of Marcus and his father. Indeed, he has been of great assistance to me in the years since my husband's passing."

"I trust Whiting implicitly." To Marcus's knowledge, the man had never done anything that was not aboveboard, nor had his counsel ever been ill-advised. "If there was a graceful way out of this, I do not doubt Whiting would have found it already."

"That goes without saying." His mother sipped her brandy. "Of course, neither Lord Townsend nor your father could foresee the depths to which his daughter might fall through no fault—"

"What depths?" Marcus's brows pulled together.

"Oh, that does not bode well," Reggie murmured.

"It's not nearly as bad as it sounds," she said lightly.

"What depths?" Marcus said again.

"I must say it *sounds* exceedingly bad," Reggie said under his breath.

"Indeed it does. What depths, Mother?"

"It was actually a terrible error according to Mr. Whiting. Miss Townsend was erroneously informed as to the nature of her finances after her father's death and was compelled to seek honest employment as a governess." Lady Pennington's gaze met her son's, and a challenge gleamed in her eyes. "I certainly think no less of her for that. For taking her fate in her hands. Do you, Marcus?"

"Not at all, Mother." He couldn't suppress a wry smile. His mother was unusually egalitarian about such things. No doubt because she too had faced financial difficulties as a girl, and she too had taken charge of her life. "You seem to have considerably more information than I do about my intended bride. Just how long was your chat with Whiting?"

"Long enough. I simply know the right questions to ask, and I daresay, Marcus, you were probably far too stunned by Whiting's revelation to ask anything about the girl herself." His mother settled back in the sofa. "I do hope her circumstances do not shock you."

"I doubt I should find much of anything shocking at this point," he said slowly. Without warning, the image of a mysterious woman of quality with the unmistakable tones of a governess and flashing blue eyes popped into his head. "Is Miss Townsend aware of this arrangement?"

"Not as of this morning. Mr. Whiting said he had sent for her but was uncertain as to when her ship would arrive, probably later this week." She paused for a moment. "She is coming from America."

Reggie winced.

The picture in Marcus's mind vanished.

"Do not look like that, Marcus. The girl is English, after all. Her parentage is impeccable, and I am certain her character has only been strengthened by her trials."

"No doubt." A new picture emerged in Marcus's mind. One of a woman stout and sturdy with the unyielding disposition of a no-nonsense governess and a strong, irresolute character. God help him.

Lady Pennington eyed her son cautiously. "Even so, you have not yet decided to marry her, have you?"

"No." Marcus shook his head. "And I am not sure I can make that decision until I meet the woman."

"It may well be worth giving up your fortune," Reggie said sagely, "should she prove to have the look of a draft horse about her."

Lady Pennington shot Reggie a sharp glance, and he immediately turned his attention to the brandy in his glass. "Don't be absurd. One can make do with an unattractive wife. It is far more difficult to survive without funds. Especially when one has responsibilities." She rose to her feet. Reggie stood at once. "You would do wise to remember that, Lord Berkley."

"Yes, ma'am," Reggie mumbled, and Marcus stifled

a smile. What was it about certain women, or rather certain mothers, that turned competent men, regardless of titles or age, into stammering schoolboys?

She turned to Marcus. "And you, my dear son, would be wise to remember that without the fortune your father left us, we shall be hard-pressed to maintain the estate. The tenants will manage, I suppose, although there will be no more funding for the agricultural improvements you are so fond of.

"We shall have to economize in ways we have never imagined. At the very least, this house will have to be sold. Many of the servants will have to be let go, and much of Holcroft Hall closed up. All except what we need to live there permanently, of course. Needless to say, I will no longer be able to travel or to enjoy my own interests.

"Still, the decision is entirely yours. Marry the girl or not. I would never be a party to forcing you into marriage against your will, no matter how suitable the match or how long past due your starting a family is. No, you do what you think is best." She heaved a heartfelt sigh and cast him a brave smile.

"Some good shall come of it in any case. Why, we shall be able to spend much more time with one another." She stepped to him and patted his check. "We shall face the future together, you and I, mother and son. Together . . . for the rest of our days."

Her gaze met his, the look in her eye as innocent as if she was not issuing him a challenge or perhaps a threat. Lady Pennington then squared her shoulders in a noble and courageous gesture and sailed from the room like a warrior valiantly facing whatever would lie ahead. She closed the door firmly in her wake, and for a long moment neither man said a word.

"Very good, Mother," Marcus murmured.

Reggie stared at the door. "She wouldn't really do that, would she, old man? Spend all that time with you, I mean."

"Good God, I hope not." Marcus downed the rest of his drink. Surely his mother didn't want that any more than he did? He knew there were men who were especially close to their mothers, he simply did not know one he particularly liked or respected. And he had no intention of joining their ranks.

She had been after him for years now to choose a bride and start a nursery. Given that, he was not at all confident that her threat was an empty one.

"It certainly puts wedding a stranger into the proper perspective." Marcus blew a long breath. "And places poverty in an entirely different light as well."

"Not true poverty," Reggie said and settled back in his chair. "After all, it's not as if you will be turned out to beg on the streets."

"No, I suppose not. We shall only face that genteel type of noble poverty, despairing and quite pathetic. The kind that takes men like us, good sorts, really, with no bigger vices than overindulgence in spirits or gaming or women, and makes us hunters of fortune. Chasing after eligible brides for no better reason than their wealth can save the way we are accustomed to living or rescue the heritage of an honorable name or—"

"Or keep our mothers from invading our lives." Reggie saluted him with his glass.

"Indeed." Marcus raised his own glass and shook his head. "What in the name of all that's holy am I going to do about this?"

Berkley swirled his brandy and grimaced. "My advice would be to drink a good deal."

"Thank you. I have already considered that."

"I also think"—Reggie drew a deep breath and met his friend's gaze—"you should marry Miss Townsend."

"Et tu, Brutus?" Marcus raised a brow.

"You don't appear to have many options. Besides, it's not as if you'd be giving up a great deal. I daresay the model of female perfection you have spoken of in the past does not exist. And even if it should, well"—Reggie shrugged—"it might do you no good. There's every chance you would not recognize it."

"What?"

"You are unfailingly calm, cool, and collected. You have never come close to the altar, nor have you ever made a fool of yourself over a woman. You, old man, have never been in love, at least not so I've noticed."

"Are you saying I'm cold?" Marcus stared in disbelief. "Unemotional?

"Not at all. But you may be too cautious for love. Too rational. Perhaps even too intellectual. You think about things far and away too much. Your mind has always ruled your heart. You have a firm idea of what you want and you will allow nothing less than that perfection to serve. On the other hand, I—"

"You fall in love in the blink of an eye."

"Indeed I do."

"And have had your heart broken how many times?"

"Far too many to mention." Reggie grinned in an unrepentant manner. "And each and every heartbreak well worth it. The anticipation, the high emotion, and best of all, old man, the untold possibilities. It is like tumbling over a precipice with the sure and certain knowledge that you can fly."

"I have been close to that precipice." Marcus ignored the defensive note in his voice. He certainly had nothing to be defensive about.

Reggie snorted. "But you've yet to take the plunge. Admittedly you have approached the brink on occasion. I distinctly remember a few years ago and a quite delectable widow."

"Pity her dead husband chose to return to life." Marcus winced at the memory. Who would have imagined that after nearly a half dozen years, a man thought to have died in Spain would miraculously return to life?

"And then last year," Reggie continued. "I believe you were becoming more than a bit smitten with Marianne Shel—"

"Lady Helmsley now, Reggie," Marcus said firmly. "And I believe you too were more than a bit smitten."

Marcus had long ago admitted to himself that he had indeed come close to falling in love with the charming bluestocking. It was both poor luck and bad timing that the young woman was already in the process of falling in love with one of his oldest friends, the Marquess of Helmsley. Marcus found himself in the odd position of taking part in a bizarre but successful plot to convince her to marry Helmsley.

Marcus shook his head. "Love has eluded me, old man, and I daresay it always shall. You may be right: I may be far too cautious for such emotion. Perhaps I have learned my lesson from watching you. Indeed, you may well have taught me love is to be avoided at all costs."

"Nonetheless, we do make an interesting pair. One who hesitates to engage his emotions at all and the other who throws caution to the winds of chance. Unsuccessfully." Reggie laughed, then sobered. "If you do indeed believe that love is to be avoided, why not marry this Townsend chit?"

"What if she's ugly?"

"Close your eyes."

"What if she is a foul-tempered termagant?"

"Precisely why men have mistresses." Reggie shrugged. "There are worse reasons for marriage than your father's wishes and the salvation of your fortune."

"I suppose so, although offhand I can only think of one.

"Oh?"

"Judging strictly from your example, of course, the most complicated, the most fraught with peril, and therefore possibly the worst reason is indeed"—Marcus grinned—"love."

Chapter Three

*In all things regarding men save money,
quality is always better than quantity.*

Colette de Chabot

"Lord Pennington?"

Marcus leaped to his feet and tried not to gape at the angelic vision in shades of pink and white who floated into the overly fussy parlor.

Whiting had directed him to this town house with assurances that Miss Townsend was in residence here at the home of a former teacher. Obviously, given the location in a fashionable enclave of London, a teacher with excellent personal finances. Still, the woman approaching him was unlike any teacher he'd ever seen or imagined.

He stepped forward. "Miss Townsend?"

The enchanting blond creature laughed. Or rather she emitted a sound similar to the tinkling of delicate glass bells. Delightful and utterly feminine.

She held out her hand like an offering and tilted her head to gaze up at him in a manner that would make even the most hard-hearted of men weak in the knees. He raised her hand to his lips.

"No, my lord, I am not your Miss Townsend." A slight French accent clung to her words like a caress.

"Pity," he murmured against her silken skin.

She laughed again, and the sound rippled through him. He straightened and attempted to gather his senses. He could see now that she was older than Miss Townsend, perhaps Marcus's age. Not that it mattered in the least. She was ageless and exquisite. "Forgive me. You must be Madame Freneau, then."

"No, my lord, but you are considerably closer." An amused voice sounded from the doorway, and a second lady joined them. She too was fair-haired and attractive but she did not have the same air of ethereal sensuality as the first woman. "I am Madame Freneau."

She stepped to him and extended her hand. He dutifully brushed his lips across it. "Madame."

"This is Madame de Chabot, my late husband's sister." A wry smile quirked the corner of Madame Freneau's mouth. "But I see you have already met."

"Indeed we have," Madame de Chabot said softly as if she and he shared some intimate secret.

"Indeed," Marcus echoed, unable to pull his gaze away. "I can see now you are no teacher."

She laughed. "In that you are wrong, my lord. I have taught a great many a great deal."

Was there an offer in her words, or did he just wish there was? He stared with a mix of mild surprise and sheer delight.

"I am the teacher," Madame Freneau said firmly, and at once Marcus realized how impolite he must have sounded.

"My apologies, Madame," he said, flustered by his odd behavior.

This was not at all his usual demeanor. Why, he'd never been flustered in his life. Obviously the revelation about his father's estate, coupled with his own reluctance to do what was necessary, plus the unexpected appearance of a tempting confection in pink and white had addled his mind. Nor could he remember being addled before. Ever. Not by circumstances and certainly not by a woman—no matter how unexpected or enticing she might be. "I did not mean to imply—"

Madame waved away his comment. "An explanation is not necessary, my lord. I quite understand. No doubt you expected me to be ancient and forbidding. The specter of former teachers does tend to be both." She smiled with amusement. "And you could not possibly have expected the presence of my sister-in-law."

"Even so"—he pushed aside all thoughts of temptresses with foreign accents and adopted his most collected manner—"I have been most impolite, and I do beg your pardon."

"I think he is quite charming," Madame de Chabot said in an aside to the other woman, but her gaze lingered on Marcus as if she were determining his assets and his deficits.

"We shall see, Colette." Madame Freneau's voice was thoughtful.

"Is Miss Townsend at home, then?" Marcus had sent a note requesting a meeting but had been too impatient to wait for an answer. Now that he had decided he had no choice but to wed the lady, he wanted to proceed with the arrangements as soon as possible.

"While she was not expecting you"—Madame's voice carried a chastising note, and immediately he could well believe this lovely lady had once indeed been a teacher—"I am certain she shall be down momentarily. If you will excuse us?"

"Certainly."

"Come along, Colette," Madame said. "We shall see what is keeping Miss Townsend."

Colette cast another assessing glance at him, and without thinking, Marcus stood a bit taller and raised his chin a notch higher. She nodded in apparent satisfaction. "He might well be suitable for our Gwendolyn after all."

"Hush, Colette," Madame said firmly. "That is entirely up to her."

Colette raised a shapely shoulder in a casual shrug. A moment later he was again alone in the too feminine parlor.

Up to her?

Marcus had never considered the possibility Miss Townsend might be as reluctant to marry him as he was to marry her. How absurd. The woman had been a governess, after all. He expected she would jump at the chance to wed.

And, all modesty aside, he was considered something of a catch. His title was impeccable. His fortune, at least for the moment, was more than respectable. His reputation was no worse than that of many of his friends and considerably better than most. He was a witty conversationalist and a droll observer of life, and there was scarcely a social event where he was not merely welcome but desired. In addition, he was considered above average in appearance. Indeed, while he was not an Adonis, some might well call him handsome.

Only the most bizarre of circumstances brought him to this moment when he waited to propose marriage to a woman he had never met. A governess, for God's sakes. Regardless of his mother's own beginnings in life or her assertions about character building, the last thing he wished for in a wife was experience as little more than a servant. He was not nearly as democratic as his mother. Still, it could not be helped.

Well, he'd marry the chit and thereby maintain his fortune. She would provide him with an heir, and a second for good measure. Once that was accomplished, he saw no reason why she should not live her own life and pursue her own interests. He certainly intended to.

Their marriage would be little more than a legal contract. An arrangement for the benefit of them both. Marcus's wealth would remain firmly in his hands. He would support Miss Townsend in the manner and style expected for the Countess of Pennington, and according to Whiting, she would receive a sizable income from her father's estate for her personal use to boot. She would want for nothing either financially or socially.

These were his terms, and he had no doubt that any woman in her right mind would accept them. It was not what he had hoped for in marriage and certainly not what he'd ever wanted, yet he'd had the opportunity to find a woman who would fit into his dreams and desires and had failed. Now there was no choice.

Up to her.

He snorted in disbelief. It was most definitely not up to her. This marriage, and all that went with it, was up to him. Why on earth wouldn't she say yes?

Damnation, he was the blasted Earl of Pennington and she was a barely solvent governess. What woman on earth in her position would not want him and all he offered?

He heard voices in the hall and turned toward the door, plastering a pleasant smile on his face and bracing himself for whatever might appear. If indeed she was stout and sturdy with an unyielding disposition, he could bear it. He had responsibilities to his tenants and those whose livelihoods depended on him as well as to his family. Even to his ancestors, who had left their land and heritage and good name in his hands.

He blew a resigned breath. No, losing his fortune was not an option. He had to do what was best for everyone, personal preferences aside. Not that he felt especially noble about it at the moment. This was simply his duty, and he would live up to the obligations imposed upon him by tradition and birth. No matter how dreadful it—she—might be.

The door opened and the soon-to-be Lady Pennington stepped into the room.

Marcus's heart thudded.

Her gown was out of fashion, ill-fitting, of a faded gray color, but could not hide the promise of a shapely figure. Her hair was a dark red, the color of fine mahogany, bound up in an untidy knot as if it were desperate to break free. The top of her head would reach just to his chin. Her gaze met his. Her cheeks flushed and her blue eyes widened in shocked recognition that mirrored his own.

He stared for a long moment, and a feeling that was entirely too giddy for a man of his studied sophistication swept through him. It was an odd mix of amusement and irony and relief and . . . gratitude. And far too powerful to fight.

And he couldn't stop the spread across his face of a grin of truly foolish proportions.

"Good Lord, it's you!" Gwen stared in disbelief. This was Lord Pennington? The arrogant, sarcastic, and admittedly somewhat handsome man on the stairs was Lord Pennington? Her Lord Pennington?

Not that she had given him a second thought, of course.

Besides, at the moment, he appeared more insane than attractive.

"Why are you looking at me like that?" she said cautiously, wondering if it was too late to retreat to the corridor. "And why are you grinning like a lunatic?"

"It is only that I feel quite mad with relief." He strode to her, took her hand, and raised it to his lips. His gaze never left hers. It was most disconcerting. "It is a true pleasure to meet you at last, Miss Townsend."

"Is it?" She pulled her hand away. "Why?"

"Why?" He raised a brow. "I should think that would be obvious."

She shook her head. "Apparently not."

"Forgive me." The earl's forehead furrowed. "I assumed Mr. Whiting had informed you as to our connection."

"He told me of an arrangement between our fa-thers," she said slowly.

"Excellent." He nodded, and the grin returned to his face. It was somewhat crooked, and if his dark hair were a bit ruffled instead of perfectly in place, he would look more like a mischievous schoolboy than a gentle-man of nearly thirty. She suspected it could be quite en-gaging under other circumstances. This, however, was not one of them.

"Then we can proceed with the arrangements at once. I will secure a special license, and we can be wed by the end of the week."

Shock stole her voice, and for a moment she could do nothing but stare. The man was indeed every bit as ar-rogant as she'd thought at their first meeting and far more high-handed than she'd ever expected. She had no intention of marrying any man let alone this one. And even if she were interested in marriage, she would much prefer to be asked rather than issued a command.

"Miss Townsend?"

"I fear you have me at a disadvantage, my lord." She fixed him with a steady stare, the kind she'd perfected to intimidate children even if it had never especially worked. "I cannot be certain from your words but is this a proposal of marriage?"

"A proposal?" Confusion colored his face, then his ex-pression cleared. "Of course. How could I have been so thoughtless? You would expect that. Any woman would, regardless of the circumstances. I simply assumed . . . Well, it scarcely matters now, I suppose, but I do apolo-gize. Allow me to start over."

He took her hands in his and looked slightly ill at

ease. "I suppose I didn't think of it because, well, I am not especially polished at this sort of thing. I have never been in this position before. This is my first offer of marriage."

"How delightful to know you do not suggest marriage to every stranger you bump into."

"Indeed I do not." His eyes twinkled with amusement. "My dear Miss Townsend." He cleared his throat and met her gaze. "Would you do me the great honor of becoming my wife?"

His eyes were the darkest shade of green, cool and inviting like the depths of an endless garden pool, and for the briefest fraction of a moment, Gwen wanted nothing more than to fall into the promise they offered. Nothing more than to stare into those eyes forever. An odd fluttering settled in her stomach, as unsettling as the feel of his warm fingers wrapped around hers.

"Thank you." She drew a deep breath and pulled her hands from his. "But I must regretfully decline."

"Decline?" He stared as if she were speaking in a foreign tongue. "What do mean, decline?"

"I mean"—she clasped her hands together primly—"unless I am mistaken about the definition of the word, what I mean is, well, no."

"No?"

"No." She cast him her most pleasant smile. "But I do appreciate the offer."

"You may well appreciate it, Miss Townsend, but perhaps you do not fully understand it." His eyes narrowed, and a shiver of apprehension skated down her spine. Between his intense expression and the way he towered over her, he appeared just a bit dangerous and surprisingly more attractive. "I am not proposing an illicit arrangement, nor am I suggesting some temporary liaison. I am offering you my name, my title, my fortune, and my property. In truth, I am offering you a future."

"Why?" she said without thinking.

"Because of the arrangement between our fathers, that's why. Promises were made and should be kept. My father gave his word, and I have no recourse but to honor and abide by it."

"How very flattering." Her tone was dry.

"Obviously I did not phrase that well. It seems I am not phrasing much of anything well today." He drew a deep breath. "I wish to abide by it. Very much so."

"Really? You wish to wed a woman you don't know? How unusual."

He ignored her. "Nonetheless—"

"Your sense of honor is impressive, my lord. But regardless of your feelings, I feel under no obligation to abide by an agreement that was made without my consent. However, I do applaud your willingness to do so." She smiled dismissively. "Now then, you may consider your responsibility to your father and mine discharged, and you may resume your life without guilt. Good day."

Gwen nodded and started toward the door, at once relieved and a bit deflated. Not that she wanted to marry him, of course. She'd never even met the man. Still, aside from that guilt-spurred request from Albert, she'd never had an offer of marriage before either and suspected she would never have another. Besides, in spite of his arrogance, the earl was rather more pleasant, in manner and appearance, than she'd anticipated.

And not at all what she'd expected in a man who could not find his own bride.

She reached the door and turned. He stood exactly where she had left him.

"My lord?" She waved toward the opening. "I believe our discussion is at an end."

"On the contrary, Miss Townsend, our discussion is just beginning," he said mildly.

"I don't see that there is anything more to talk about. You asked me a question. I answered said question. Therefore"—she gestured once again, a bit more vehemently—"good day."

"A few minutes ago I thought it had become a very good day indeed. Now I see I was mistaken." He strode past her to the door and closed it firmly.

"What do you think you're doing?" She straightened her shoulders and stared up at him, determined to stand her ground even if it left her entirely too close to him. "Open that door at once. It is not at all proper for us—"

"For a woman who flits around London unaccompanied, I am surprised to hear that particular protest from you."

"I most certainly do not . . ." She paused. "If you are referring to our last meeting, I had a carriage waiting. Therefore I was not unaccompanied."

"There was no one with you when we met." His pointed words belied his casual manner. He strolled past her as if he had nothing of significance on his mind beyond the perusal of Madame's overly feminine parlor. "Regardless of how many carriages you had waiting, your behavior was most improper. Even scandalous."

"I would hardly call it scandalous. I am quite used to being unaccompanied."

"Perhaps in America such lack of decorum is acceptable," he said coolly. "Here, however, it is not."

She resisted the urge to snap at him. "I scarcely think it matters. No one knows me here. My father was not active in society, and he died before I could have a season. I have been out of England for a considerable length of time, and only a handful of people in London are even aware of my existence. I have no family to shelter, no position to protect."

"Ah, but you soon will have. As the Countess of Pennington, you will have no end of social obligations and responsibilities, and through them all, your every move will be watched and remarked upon." He picked up the figurine of an ugly pug dog and studied it. "In the beginning, of course, there will be a great deal of curiosity about you for the very reasons you have mentioned: in spite of your parentage, you are a virtual unknown. Friend and foe alike will be alert for any hint of impropriety, any modicum of inappropriate behavior."

She stared for a moment, then laughed in spite of herself. "Simply as a point of information, you should know my behavior is always impeccably proper. I pride myself on it. However, if you are trying to further your suit, this is not the way to do it. And it scarcely seems worth the effort, especially as I have no desire for position or—"

"What of family?" He looked at her sharply. "Do you not want family of your own? A husband and children?"

The sister she never knew and the nieces she'd never met immediately came to mind, and she pushed the thought firmly aside. She had not yet decided what, if anything, she should do in their regard, and as for children in general . . . "I am not particularly enamored of children, nor do they seem especially fond of me."

"Well, we do not have to have more than a handful," he said blithely. "In truth, two will be sufficient, both male, of course."

"Of course." She should have expected as much. In this he was no different from any other man with a title. "And no doubt they would be as stubborn as their father." She crossed her arms over her chest and studied him. "I have turned down your ever so gracious proposal. An offer that absolved you of any further responsibility, as even the most stalwart advocate of arcane principles of honor would agree, yet you persist in believing a marriage between us is possible."

"Not merely possible"—he flashed her a knowing grin—"but inevitable."

"Nothing is inevitable, my lord, beyond the rise and set of the sun, the change of seasons, and other attributes of nature."

"And what makes you think that you and I are not as inevitable as nature? That we are not as fated to spend our lives together as the stars are fated to light the night sky. Or as the day is destined to follow the dawn?" His words were as offhand as if he were speaking of nothing of any consequence, but there was an intriguing gleam in his eye.

"I would scarcely call a plot hatched by our fathers to ensure the continuation of our—or more specifically *your*—family line to be fate." Still, it was a surprisingly lovely idea, the possibility that he and she could be destined for each other. Lovely and completely farfetched.

"Really? You do not think the fact that you quite literally fell into my arms before we even knew of this arrangement to be an indication of destiny?"

"Oh, that is good, my lord." She applauded with polite sarcasm. "Excellent strategy. Taking what is essentially no more personal than a business arrangement between misguided fathers and molding it into something mysterious and romantic. How did it go again? Ah yes." She rested the back of her hand against her forehead and adopted a dramatic tone. "My dear Miss Townsend, we are fated to be together. Our destiny is written in the stars. It is . . . inevitable." She straightened. "Well done indeed."

Thank you," he said modestly. "I thought it was quite good myself."

"Still, I must point out I did not fall into your arms. You walked into me and nearly knocked me off my feet."

"Knocked you off your feet?" He raised a knowing brow. "And does that not say fate to you?"

"It says only that you were not paying attention to where you were going. It is nothing more than mere coincidence that we both chose to visit Mr. Whiting on the same day at the same hour—"

"Some would say there is no such thing as mere coincidence."

"—and chanced to cross each other's path."

"No such thing as chance."

"That's utter nonsense and you know it." She shook

her head. "Honestly, my lord, I do not know why you persist—"

"Why won't you marry me?" he said abruptly.

"Surely that is obvious."

"Not to me."

"Then I shall add obtuse as well as stubborn to your list of character flaws. Very well." She heaved a long suffering sigh and counted off the reasons on her fingers. "First—I don't know you. Second—I resent having my future determined by men, especially men long in their graves. And third—I have no desire to wed."

"Ever?" He raised a brow. "Or just not to me?"

"Both." She braced herself. Mr. Whiting certainly showed no understanding of her desire to remain unmarried. She didn't doubt Pennington would share the solicitor's opinion. "If a woman is not interested in children—"

"And you are not interested in children?"

She hesitated and he pounced.

"Aha!" He smiled in a smug manner, and she added *infuriating* to the list. "All women want children. It is a facet of their nature."

"Perhaps." Gwen was willing to concede this particular point, as she had often wondered if her dislike of children had more to do with those she had had in her charge than any lack of maternal instincts on her part. Still, the desire to procreate had yet to stir within her, and she was not certain it ever would. "Children aside, I do not see marriage as a desirable state for a woman."

"Why on earth not?" His tone was indignant, as if her distaste for marriage was a personal insult.

Impatience swept through her. "I scarcely need explain my reasoning to you."

"As your intended, I believe I have a right to know," he said in a lofty manner.

"What I *intend* toward you at the moment has nothing whatsoever to do with marriage but is indeed just as permanent." She tried to keep her tone firm, but his persistence was as amusing as it was irritating. She had never matched wits with a gentleman before and it was remarkably stimulating. "Lord Pennington, the only true benefit of marriage to a woman is financial. I have no need of marriage as I have a modest income, nowhere near yours, I imagine, but sufficient for my needs."

His gaze flicked over her gown. "Extremely modest it would appear."

Any sense of amusement vanished. "I have just learned of my financial state and have not yet had the opportunity to put any of my funding to good use in the purchase of a suitable wardrobe."

"That too is a relief."

"Too?" She studied him carefully. "What do you mean, *too?*"

"Well, I simply meant . . ." He paused, obviously searching for the right words. He looked exceedingly uncomfortable, and she hadn't so much as a twinge of sympathy for him.

"Yes?" she prompted.

"Come now, Miss Townsend, you know full well what I meant." His gaze roamed over her once again. Entirely too intimate and speculative and approving. For a moment she had the most disconcerting feeling he saw her entirely without the benefit of clothing. "I was prepared for someone not the least bit attractive. Someone rather overbearing in appearance. You are a most pleasant surprise. I am extremely fond of red hair."

She ignored the rush of heat to her cheeks. "As flattering as that is, my lord, it's neither here nor there. Now then, we were speaking of the reasons why women choose to—"

"What of love, Miss Townsend?" His tone was mild but his gaze was intense. "Affection? The sort of emotion that keeps poets putting pen to paper. Surely you believe there are woman who marry for benefits far more esoteric than finances?"

"Certainly." She raised her chin and met his gaze directly. "I simply think love, affection, emotion are ridiculous reasons to tie yourself to a man for the rest of your days. Marriage is a cage, and love is nothing more than a baited trap."

"Really?" He studied her intently. "You have given this a great deal of thought, then?"

"Some." She shrugged. It had long ago dawned on her that it wasn't simply marriage that destroyed women's lives but love. Love that made them follow a man to the ends of the earth or destroy their health in pursuit of a son or ignore infidelities by spouses who had sworn to love them forever and ignore as well the pain they wrought. "Enough to know I have no desire for it."

"Then this is perfect." He grinned. "You do not love me. I do not love you. Oh, admittedly I fully expect to experience a certain amount of lust toward my new wife. Toward you. Indeed, even now—"

"Stop it at once!" In spite of herself, she wanted to

laugh. He was most amusing. "You are incorrigible. Do you never take no for an answer?"

"Never." He moved toward her.

"What are you doing now?" She stepped back.

He stopped in front of her, a scant few inches away. His gaze slipped from her eyes to her lips then back, and she could have sworn he'd physically touched her. "As you are not interested in love or fortune I thought I should demonstrate the benefits of lust in a marriage."

"Surely you do not intend to . . . to . . ." She swallowed hard and stared up at him. "Kiss me?"

"No, of course not," he said softly. Once again his gaze lingered on her lips. "I had not even considered it."

"You're lying."

"I most certainly am not," he murmured, but she would have wagered her entire inheritance he was. "My dear Miss Townsend, when I intend to kiss you there will be no doubt in your mind."

"There is none now." She would not have thought it possible but his eyes were an even deeper green than before.

"Have you been kissed before?"

"Not willingly."

"Oh?"

"I have had the attentions of men forced upon me on occasion," she said before she could stop herself.

Concern crossed his face, and any ardor that might have crept up on her unexpectedly vanished.

"Does that bother you?" she said rather more sharply than she wished.

"It bothers me that any gentleman would force his attention upon an unwilling female. I can only hope you were not harmed." Sincerity sounded in his voice, and she realized he was a rather nice man, all things considered. Still, he was not, nor would be ever be, her betrothed.

"Not at all. I learned precisely how to deal with unwanted attention." She placed her palm squarely in the center of his chest and firmly pushed him away.

He grinned and stepped aside. "Surely there was more to it than that?"

"Of course." She swept past him and crossed the room, putting a safe distance between them. Gwen marveled that he didn't realize how very close she came to allowing him to kiss her, and worse, to kissing him back. She had never known such an impulse before and was not entirely sure how to deal with it now.

She reached the fireplace, then turned back to him. "However, it did not seem necessary at the moment. You strike me as the kind of gentleman who accepts that when a lady says no, no is what she means. You would be surprised how many gentlemen, who consider themselves honorable, have few qualms about disregarding that when it comes to women in their employ."

"Men are disgusting beasts," he said firmly.

She ignored the amusement in his eye. "Indeed they are."

"However, there are those of us, exceptions to the disgusting beast rule, who would never force our attentions on an unwilling female."

"Good."

"In addition, there are those of us, again not in the disgusting beast category, who have yet to meet an unwilling female."

She snorted in disdain. "Come now, my lord, you have never met a woman who did not particularly wish to kiss you?

"Never." He shrugged casually.

"You are as arrogant as I thought when we first met."

"And as charming, I hope." He wagged his brows rakishly, and she choked back a laugh. "However, you are mistaken in one thing, Miss Townsend." He folded his arms over his chest. "In the matter of our marriage, you have said no over and over today, yet I do not, nor will I ever, accept it."

"Why not?" She heaved a frustrated sigh. "You are as annoying as any child I've ever met and just as difficult to understand."

She turned on her heel and stepped to the window, trying to sort out the contradictions that made up this man before her.

"I have given you a most graceful way out of this. No one could hold you at fault for not honoring your father's promise. Lord knows you've tried. Admirably too, I might add. And it's not as if you have anything to gain save honor and my dowry, although that's scarcely worth mentioning to a man of your means."

He cleared his throat. "Miss Townsend, there is something—"

She waved him silent. "I, on the other hand, would derive great benefit from this match. I would acquire a tidy personal fortune, not to mention sharing in your wealth." An odd thought struck her, and she turned back to him. "Your finances are substantial, are they not?"

"They are," he said carefully, "for the moment."

"For the moment?" At once the truth slammed into her. "Good God, you're penniless, aren't you? You need this marriage. My dowry and my pathetic little income."

"A minute ago it was a tidy personal fortune."

"A minute ago it didn't matter."

"Regardless, I am not broke." He huffed and refused to meet her gaze. His voice was low. "Yet."

"Yet?" For a long moment she stared at him. The truth was obvious, and she was appalled she hadn't seen it before now. She chose her words with care. "I stand to inherit a fortune if we wed. How much do you get?"

The look on his face was confirmation. He resembled any one of her charges when caught doing something he shouldn't. "I would not have put it so bluntly—"

"How much, my lord?"

"In truth, I don't get anything besides a wife, of course. And the benefits of that are yet to be determined. I simply don't lose what I have." He blew a resigned breath. "If we do not marry, I forfeit my entire fortune."

"I see," she said slowly. His determination to marry her now made sense.

"Miss Townsend." He moved toward her. "This is not my choice. I would gladly live in poverty for the rest of my days rather than force either of us into a marriage that is not to our liking."

"I doubt that." She huffed in disbelief. "I have been poor, and it's not the least bit enjoyable."

He ignored her. "Even though I myself am more convinced than ever that we have been brought together by the hand of fate—"

"Yes, yes, fate. Destiny. Written in the stars and so

forth." She rolled her gaze toward the ceiling and sank onto the sofa. "Please, just go on."

"You should know my motives are not completely selfish. I am not the only one affected by this. There are people who depend on me." He ran his hand through his hair, and she realized she was right. He did indeed look like a boy with his hair ruffled. "Tenants on the estate, and small armies of servants, and my mother, who will lose her fortune as well if we do not marry.

"The village of Pennington itself depends on my patronage as it depended on the patronage of my father and his father before him. Beyond that, I have not been miserly with my wealth. I give generously to a great number of charities." He stopped and glared at her. "Do you have any idea how many orphans through the years have been named after me?"

"Pennington seems rather a mouthful for an orphan," she murmured.

"Don't be absurd. They've been named Marcus, of course." He shook his head. "Can't imagine naming an orphan Pennington."

"Marcus." The name rolled nicely on her tongue.

"I know this is my problem and not yours." He cast her a pointed glance. "Although a wife should share in her husband's troubles."

"Perhaps, but I am not going to be your wife."

Once again he continued as if he hadn't heard. "It is all my fault, I know that. I should have found a wife years ago. But it's not nearly as simple as it seems, you know."

"Not even for someone as charming as you?"

"No, indeed." His pacing continued without pause.

"Oh, certainly you would think with all those fresh young faces trotted out every year for the season like cattle at Tattersall's it would not be at all difficult to select a bride. Admittedly there are any number with respectable families or acceptable dowries. Indeed, there are many who are attractive as well, and some even have a modicum of intelligence. But I don't think one should choose a wife as one selects a new mount, with an eye simply toward teeth and bearing and breeding. Do you, Miss Townsend?"

"Not at all." The man was positively mesmerizing in his passion, and she could not tear her gaze from him.

"Of course not. It makes no sense. Yet that is essentially what is expected. But for good or ill, I did not do it. I did not take my pick of any season's offerings, and I certainly could have. Did I tell you I am considered quite eligible?"

"You may have mentioned it."

"Good. You should know what you're getting."

She opened her mouth to protest, then clamped it shut. He would pay her no heed right now anyway. He was distinctly reminiscent of a boulder rolling downhill faster and faster.

"In truth, I find this whole concept of a marriage mart most distasteful. And do you know why, Miss Townsend?"

She widened her eyes and shook her head.

"It's too . . . businesslike. Too impersonal. Don't you agree?"

She nodded.

"Damn it all, Miss Townsend, I realize it is not readily apparent but I have something of a sentimental streak in me, although admittedly I don't show it. Indeed, my friends think I have no sentiment in me whatsoever simply because I do not wear my heart on my sleeve."

"Do they?"

"They do. It is most annoying." He nodded firmly and paused. A wry smile lifted the corners of his mouth. "Perhaps if I had ever talked to them the way I'm talking to you they would think differently of me. Good Lord, I have never spoken about such things with anyone before, let alone a woman. The circumstances we find ourselves in must be wearing more heavily on me than I had suspected."

"Apparently."

"And what of you, Miss Townsend? We—or rather I—am in this mess because neither of us has wed. You are extraordinarily pretty and—"

"Extraordinarily?" She thought of herself as somewhat attractive but not *extraordinarily* pretty. In point of fact, she thought she was rather overdone: the color of her hair was too intense and her hips and bosom too round for her stature. To have a man like Pennington describe her as extraordinarily pretty was quite the nicest thing anyone had ever said to her.

"Extraordinarily." He nodded firmly. "I cannot believe you have not had the opportunity to marry before now."

"I was a mere governess, Lord Pennington. The opportunities for marriage were limited. Besides, I have explained—"

"Yes, yes, forgive me. I forgot for a moment. Marriage is not something you aspire to. Still, if you were married at this point, I could keep my fortune." His face brightened. "Maybe it's not too late? If you won't marry me, we can have you married off to someone else in no time. I know my friend Lord Berkley, the gentleman I was with the other day, would marry you in a moment. He was quite taken with you, and as it does seem there is rescuing to be done here—"

"That's enough, my lord. I have no intention of marrying anyone, let alone this friend of yours. Besides, if I were inclined to marriage at all, I would most certainly marry you." She knew the words were a mistake the moment they were out of her mouth.

Before she could utter a word of protest, he crossed the room, bent on one knee at her feet, and grasped her hands in his.

"My dear Miss—do you have a given name?"

"Gwendolyn."

"Gwendolyn." He nodded with approval. "It's lovely. Gwendolyn and Marcus. They sound perfect together. See, I told you it was fate."

"It most certainly is not." She tried to pull her hands free, but he held tight.

"Save me, Gwendolyn." His tone was as intense as his gaze. "Save those people who depend on me."

She stared down at him for a long moment. It would be rather easy to give in and agree to marry him. And she suspected it would be equally easy to care for him. Perhaps love him. Far too easy. But love would lead to no good. She would not tread the path of her mother and sister and all the women who'd gone before her to give their love to a man only to see their lives cut short or their hearts shattered.

No, aside from all the other reasons why it would be absurd to marry this man she'd just met, the best reason of all for running as far away from him as she could was love.

"I am terribly sorry, my lord." She pulled her hands from his. "But I will not marry you."

"Oh but you will, Miss Townsend, because you see, I will not give up." He got to his feet and stared down at her. It was most intimidating. "I have almost a full three months to persuade you to change your mind, and do not doubt that I will."

She stood and glared up at him. "I shall not change my mind."

"I will be at your door every day and every night. I shall do everything in my power to convince you to marry me, and I will not give up until the day I have completed thirty years of life.

"The retention of my fortune is far too important to far too many people. There is only one way to truly get me out of your life, Miss Townsend, and that"— he smiled slowly in a wicked and far too suggestive manner—"is to marry me."

Chapter Four

On occasion men, and what they provide,
are a necessary evil that can be borne as long as a woman
expects nothing beyond what is offered.

Gwendolyn Townsend

It was exceedingly odd to stand in the grand parlor at Townsend Park as nothing more than a guest, although Gwen had never particularly felt like anything other than a guest even when she had ostensibly belonged here.

Townsend Park had been the home of her father and his father before him and so forth, back half a dozen generations or more. A legacy come to a screeching halt when Gwen had been born a girl. She had been sent away to school the moment she had been deemed old enough, and in truth, Madame Chaussan's Academy was more of a home to her than this place had ever been.

She'd spent the occasional holiday here and the brief month of her father's illness, but she lacked the attachment to the place born of childhood memories or happier times. If her mother hadn't died or if her sister hadn't left, Gwen's life might have been different. She might well have been brought up here rather than sent off to the strangers at Madame Chaussan's. Strangers like Madame Freneau, who ultimately became not merely teacher but friend and family.

Little had changed here in five years. The furnishings had been rearranged, the rooms seemed a little smaller somehow, and the butler was new to her, but all in all it was quite as she remembered it.

"Miss Townsend?" A stern-faced, older woman with a proprietary manner and a dress duller than Gwen's, although of considerably better quality, stepped into the room.

"Yes?"

"I am Miss Hilliard, *Lord* Townsend's sister."

"Lord Townsend?" For a moment, Gwen's father's face flashed in her mind. She pushed away the image, and the odd ache it carried. "Of course, Lord Townsend. My cousin. Then you—"

"A cousin as well. Distant, of course." The woman sniffed as if the connection was distasteful.

Gwen bit back the urge to comment on how fortunate it was that there was such distance between them and forced a polite smile.

"Is my cous—Lord Townsend at home? I should like to pay my respects." It was a lie, of course. She had no desire to pay anything near respect to the man who had, however legitimately, taken what should have been her birthright. Still, she did harbor a bit of curiosity about the new Lord Townsend. He probably greatly resembled his sister, right down to the mustache.

"He is not. In truth, he has been abroad for nearly a year now. But I understood you were here to take charge of your nieces." Miss Hilliard's lip curled upward in distaste.

"I am here to visit them," Gwen said slowly.

She had no intention of taking the girls but was reluctant to admit that to this sour-faced relation. Miss Hilliard's manner reminded Gwen of any number of people she had met in recent years who, because of circumstances or birth or wealth, considered everyone else beneath their notice.

In point of fact, Gwen was not at all certain what had compelled her to make the two-hour trip from London to Townsend Park. Perhaps it was Mr. Whiting's implication that Gwen's needs were not as important as those of her nieces and a subsequent touch of remorse on Gwen's part. Or a desire to discharge herself of such guilt and any familial obligation, much the same way Pennington had discharged himself of any obligation to his father. Or perhaps it was some heretofore unacknowledged wish to know her family. What remained of it, at any rate.

"I have never met my nieces." Or perhaps it was nothing more than simple curiosity.

"Well, you shan't like them. I don't see how anyone could." Miss Hilliard's forbidding manner deepened if possible. "They are heathens, each and every one. Quite uncivilized. In addition, they are undisciplined, ill-mannered, and willful. Poor breeding, no doubt." The woman sniffed again. "I would not have taken them in at all but my brother insisted, at least for now. Apparently he was acquainted with their father and feels some sort of obligation. Beyond that, Adrian is the head of the family and he considered it his duty, especially as no one seemed to know your whereabouts. He takes his responsibilities in a most serious manner."

She pursed her lips in a disapproving manner. "Of course, he was off on his travels by the time they arrived."

"But he does intend to offer them a permanent home at Townsend Park?"

"I really cannot say," she said primly. "I would encourage him to find them a suitable home elsewhere, and I daresay once he meets them he will agree. We are usually in accord on such matters."

"No doubt," Gwen murmured. The image of Lord Townsend as a masculine version of his sister, complete with forbidding frown and petulant crease across his brow, intensified.

"However, now that you have returned from your . . . travels"—once more Miss Hilliard sniffed disdainfully—"you will cer—"

"Are you unwell?" Gwen said abruptly. "Are you chilled? Perhaps catching a cold?"

Her cousin drew back in surprise. "Not at all. On the contrary, I feel quite"—her eyes narrowed in understanding—"well. Thank you for asking. Now then, I think—"

"I should like to see my nieces." Gwen adopted her best governess demeanor. "At once, if you would be so kind."

"Of course." Miss Hilliard stepped to a bellpull and

gave it a vicious yank. Her gaze stayed firmly on Gwen as if she was afraid the younger woman would steal the silver if not watched every minute.

A leaden silence fell in the room. Gwen's mind was far too occupied with the possible fate that had befallen her sister's children at the hands of this most unpleasant creature to waste any efforts at polite conversation. While Gwen had never particularly liked children, at least not the children in her care, she did feel an odd sort of responsibility toward these girls. They were, after all, the only family she had, if one excluded Miss Hilliard and her brother.

Still, the children were well taken care of here. Their wants and needs were attended to. No doubt the new Lord Townsend, regardless of his similarity in nature to his sister, would make certain they would be properly educated and provided with decent dowries when the time came. All things considered, this was the best place for them.

"I warn you, cousin, regardless of what you expect you will not find it here," Miss Hilliard said.

"I scarcely need your warning, *cousin*." Gwen met the other woman's gaze firmly. "I expect nothing more than to make the acquaintance of my sister's children."

"Well, I shall be most relieved to have these hellions off my hands. Ungrateful little beasts. Although how you, as an unmarried woman, intend to care for them is beyond me."

Gwen heaved an annoyed sigh. "I have no intention of caring for them. You have already provided them with an excellent home and I have no—"

"We don't want to go with you anyway." A voice sounded from the doorway, and Gwen turned.

Three pairs of accusing eyes glared at her. Gwen stared back, struck by the altogether startling sensation of looking at herself in various stages of childhood.

They were stair steps of a fashion, ranging in height according to age. The three were remarkably similar in appearance, all with hair in varying shades of red, much like Gwen's own. The tallest was obviously the oldest at fourteen. It was apparent from the look on her face that she was the one who had spoken, equally obvious that she had a great deal more to say, and not at all far-fetched to assume what she had to say would not be the least bit pleasant. The next tallest, most likely the twelve-year-old, was in the middle, the youngest at age ten stood beside her. This would be much easier if Gwen could remember their names. They were all named for various Christian virtues but Gwen couldn't remember which ones.

Regardless of the nature of their names, there was scarcely a hint of anything even vaguely resembling virtuous qualities in the malevolent looks they leveled at her. At the moment Gwen doubted they were called Pleasance or Tolerance or Kindness. She had seen looks like that from children before.

They quite despised her.

"The choice is not up to you," Miss Hilliard said in an unyielding manner, then turned her gaze to Gwen. "Decisions must be made as to their future. However, we shall discuss it later. For now, I will leave you alone for your . . . visit." She cast a disapproving glare at the girls. "I'm sure it shall be most informative." She turned and marched from the room, snapping the door shut behind her.

As if of one mind, all eyes followed the older woman's departure, and Gwen realized the girls disliked Miss Hilliard even more than they disliked her. At least they had that in common.

They turned their attention back to Gwen, and she knew shared dislike would not be nearly enough.

"Are you Aunt Gwendolyn, then?" the oldest asked coolly.

Gwen nodded. "Indeed I am. And you are?"

The girl hesitated, as if she wasn't certain revealing even that much information was wise.

"You can tell her *that*." The middle girl sighed. "Her name is Charity, and this is Hope." She nodded at her younger sister. "I am Patience." Patience smiled politely and flicked her gaze over Gwen in that dismissive manner perfected by girls some time after their tenth year, when they start assessing every other woman with a critical eye. "Did you know you look a little like our mother?"

"Except she was pretty," Hope added. "Very pretty."

Patience studied Gwen thoughtfully. "She's pretty. Just not *very* pretty."

"Or"—Charity's eyes narrowed—"I daresay very nice."

Gwen started. "I am quite nice. Or at least I can be."

Charity snorted in disbelief.

"But you're right about one thing." Gwen's gaze shifted from one sister to the next. "You're not being fair. We've only just met. You've not given me the opportunity to be nice or anything else."

Hope planted her hands on her hips. "Why should we?"

"Indeed." Patience crossed her arms over her chest. "It's not as if you deserve it."

"Nonsense. I have done nothing whatsoever to warrant not deserving the opportunity to be, at the very least, friends." Gwen cringed to herself at the note in her voice.

She was speaking to these girls, the only family she had, in the same collected, firm manner she had always spoken to the children in her charge. In her *governess* voice, intended to display authority tempered with kindness. Gwen had never mastered it and knew full well she sounded hard instead of firm, and cold rather than collected. She tried again. "Now what, precisely, are you are talking about?"

"We're talking about where you have been since Mama and Papa died and why you haven't come for us." Resentment flashed in Charity's eyes and she fairly spit the word. "*Precisely.*"

"Mama said if anything happened to her and Papa, you would take care of us," Patience said.

"But I've only just learned of your existence," Gwen started. "I couldn't possibly have—"

Hope paid her no heed.

"Sisters are supposed to take care of one another. That's what Mama always said. It's what sisters do. It's what *families* do." The trio nodded in unison.

"She said grandfather no longer counted as family

because he didn't like Papa and Papa was her family."
Charity glared as if that was somehow Gwen's fault.
"And therefore we should not expect that he would
like us."

"Besides." Hope's glare matched her older sister's.
"He's dead. Like Mama and Papa. Only they're in
heaven and he's probably in—"

"That's quite enough," Gwen said sharply in her best
no-nonsense governess manner.

"Hell." Defiance rang in Charity's voice.

"Hell," Patience said firmly.

"Hell." Hope nodded. "Where he shall burn forever
in retribution for his sins."

All three glared at Gwen, challenging her to rebuke
them for their language. She'd seen that look before on
the faces of children in her care. Children whose sole
purpose in life was to drive their current governess
stark, raving mad.

She certainly could not handle these children as she
had handled those even if, in truth, the vast majority of
the time she'd been at their mercy rather than in
charge.

"You're not being fair to him either, you know,"
Gwen said slowly, realizing the irony of defending her
father. "He wasn't a bad man. But he did not approve of
your mother's choices and she defied him."

"Nonetheless, we don't like him." Charity's voice
was cool. "And we don't like you."

A horrible and familiar sense of helplessness gripped
Gwen. Was there anything more frightening on the face
of the earth than angry and defiant children? She'd been
scarcely more than a child herself when she'd fled home

and taken her first position. She'd had no more idea what to do with children then than she did now. And if truth were told, each time she was compelled to leave a job it was with a fair amount of relief and a grim determination to do better the next time. She never had.

From the moment her father had died, Gwen had faced every insurmountable problem, be it poverty or unsuitable employment, with the same solution. The panic that never failed to surge within in her could be quelled by only one thing.

Escape.

And panic seized her now.

"Very well." She straightened her shoulders. "That's that then."

"What do you mean?" Suspicion sounded in Charity's voice.

"Well, you said it yourself: you don't like me. And it's quite obvious you're unwilling to make any effort to change that nor are you willing to make the tiniest effort to encourage me to like you. And thus far, well, I don't." Gwen shrugged. "It seems to me we are at an impasse. I only came here to ascertain for myself if you were being well cared for."

She studied them for a moment, then nodded. "You are adequately clothed and do not appear to be starving. Therefore I shall take my leave." She turned and started toward the door, ignoring a twinge of guilt and an odd touch of regret.

"I told you she wouldn't be any different than old Pickleface," one of the girls said behind her. "She doesn't want us either."

"No one does, do they?" Hope said, or at least Gwen

thought it was Hope. She might not be able to recognize the child's voice, but the note of resignation was all too familiar.

For a moment the years vanished and Gwen was once again a young girl in this very house. A girl who could not help but hear the whispers of the servants about what a shame it was that His Lordship had had daughters instead of sons. And what a waste that all His Lordship had would go to a distant relation rather than his own flesh-and-blood son. And wasn't it a pity that there was no boy to carry on His Lordship's name.

And wasn't it wise of His Lordship to send the girl off to school to learn what she would need for a suitable match someday because, if truth were told, daughters weren't good for much else.

If truth were told, daughters, *girls* weren't particularly wanted.

Gwen wasn't particularly wanted.

She doesn't want us either.

Gwen's throat tightened, and an ache she'd thought long since put to rest returned with a vengeance. Surely it was only the result of being back in this house.

No one does, do they?

It might have been little more than Gwen's impulsive nature. Or some long-buried sense of familial connection or responsibility or even affection. Or perhaps it was simply that the pain in the girl's voice was a far stronger bond than sisters or family or blood.

Abruptly Gwen turned on her heel and considered them, realizing they were as scared as she. Probably more so. She stepped briskly to the sofa and sat down, pulling off her gloves in a deliberate manner, nothing more than a ploy to gain a moment to marshal her thoughts and make sense of her feelings, far too tumultuous to understand at the moment. The only thing she was certain of was that for the first time in her life, she was not alone. The fate of someone other than herself lay in her hands. Even if those others were children.

She drew a deep breath. "Do you like living at Townsend Park?"

"It's a lovely house with wonderful grounds," Charity said staunchly.

"But do you *like* it?" Gwen wasn't sure why it mattered, but it did.

"It's quite the nicest place we've ever lived." Patience's voice was cool.

Gwen sighed. "Very well then, if you're happy, I can scarcely—"

"No!" Hope shot a panicked glare at her sisters, then stepped toward Gwen. "We're not at all happy. We hate it here. It's horrid. Truly, truly horrid. No one, not even the servants, talks to us. Pickleface constantly looks at us as if she's just eaten something nasty."

"Oh dear," Gwen murmured, wondering how some of her charges might have described her and suspecting it was no better, and possibly a great deal worse, than Pickleface.

"Yes and do you know what else?" Patience sank on the sofa beside her. "She sniffs. All the time. Not like the sniffles but like she's smelling something the rest of us can't see. Something really nasty."

"Like a dog." Hope plopped onto the sofa on Gwen's other side. "Did you know dogs are remarkably good at sniffing? They have excellent noses."

"I had heard that somewhere," Gwen murmured.

"She doesn't like us." A vague edge of surprise sounded in Hope's voice. "And she says . . ." Hope's bottom lip trembled.

"She says . . ." Patience slanted a glance at her older sister, then drew a deep breath, her words coming in a breathless rush. "She says we're a dreadful inconvenience and a terrible burden and when her brother returns he shall probably send us away." Patience's eyes glistened. "One at a time."

"One at a time?" Gwen drew her brows together. "What do you mean?"

"She means we won't be able to stay together," Charity said sharply. "Pickleface says no one will take three girls, particularly girls who are as old as we are."

Hope sighed. "She says girls of our age are costly to maintain. Dresses and seasons and dowries and all sorts of things."

"We won't go, you know." Patience crossed her arms and settled deeper into the sofa. "We've already decided."

Gwen didn't like the sound of that, not that she blamed them. "Exactly what have you decided?"

"We're going to run away." Patience grinned in a smug manner. "We're going to the Friendly Islands. Do you know where they are?"

"Of course." Gwen nodded. "Polynesia."

"We visited there once with Mama and Papa." Hope paused. "Before they were eaten by cannibals, of course."

"Cannibals?" Gwen studied the child. "I thought

they were—" Three challenging gazes met hers. "Never mind. Do go on."

"The Friendly Islands are very pretty and we quite like the name." Hope nodded eagerly. "We shall live on the beach in little huts and catch fish for our supper."

"Running away never solved one's problems," Gwen said without thinking. Admittedly, while she spouted the time-honored advice, she'd never paid any heed to it herself. Still, who should know better than she the truth of it? "Besides, I suspect you need a fair amount of money to get to the Friendly Islands. Do you have a fair amount of money?"

"I hadn't thought of that," Patience murmured.

"I have." Determination sounded in Charity's voice. "And we won't need money. We shall stow away on a ship and it won't cost us anything at all." She slanted Gwen a triumphant look.

"I daresay that is clever." Gwen pulled her brows together. "Dreadfully uncomfortable though, I should think. You would have to hide throughout the entire voyage. Where does one hide on a ship bound for the Friendly Islands?"

"In the hold," Hope said firmly. "With the cargo."

"There are plenty of places to hide," Patience confided. "We know all about ships. We've been on them before, you know. A great deal actually."

"Of course you have. The three of you are far better traveled than most people I know. If you are willing to hide for weeks—how long does it take to get to the Friendly Islands anyway?" Gwen widened her eyes innocently.

"It took eight weeks, I think, to return to England," Charity said, her manner cautious as if she trusted neither the question nor Gwen's reason for asking.

"Eight weeks? My goodness. That's a long time to stay hidden." Gwen considered the trio curiously. "Will you bring food along with you, then?"

The girls traded glances.

"Of course," Hope said stoutly. "Lots of food. In our bags."

"Don't be absurd." Charity sighed in the universal manner of older sisters. "We shall have to take food from the galley when no one is looking."

"We can't steal food." Patience stared at her sister. "That would be a sin."

"We'd go to hell," Hope said matter-of-factly.

"Stealing food when you're hungry is not really a sin." In spite of the firm note in Charity's voice, Gwen suspected she too was uneasy at the idea of deliberate sin. "We shall be fine, and when we get to the Friendly Islands we can live on fish."

Patience nodded. "We do like fish."

"But not all the time." Hope wrinkled her nose.

"I see," Gwen said slowly. "You seem to have given this a great deal of thought. I suppose I should wish you well, then. And do try not to get caught." She shook her head in a forlorn manner. "I dare not think what would happen to you should you get caught."

Suspicion pulled Charity's brows together. "What would happen?"

"Well, when I was on board ship, I heard whenever they caught stowaways they would"—Gwen paused dramatically for added effect—"throw them into the sea."

A collective gasp went up.

Charity scoffed. "I don't believe you."

The two younger girls exchanged glances and Gwen pressed her point home. "Well, of course I could be mistaken. It's simply what I was told while I was on board ship. It could have been nothing but a seaman's tale told for the entertainment of naïve travelers. Yes, I'm certain it was nothing more than that.

"Of course"—she thought for a moment—"I have never seen a stowaway for myself, which is probably due more to the fact that most people do not choose to travel in that manner and not to the possibility that those that do end up as food for sea creatures." Gwen smiled pleasantly, as though the idea of being food for sea creatures was not the least bit terrifying to anyone, let alone three potential stowaways.

"You don't scare us in the least. I daresay we would never get caught. I would make certain of it." Charity looked from Patience to Hope and back to Gwen. "Admittedly we're not ready to go quite yet. We don't know everything. We are still making plans. And we are extremely flexible. Perhaps we won't even go to the Friendly Islands after all. Perhaps we shall simply go to London. I can't imagine it would be all that difficult to get to London from here."

"Not at all. It's a scant few hours away. What an excellent idea." Gwen nodded. "London is a wonderful place. The school I attended as a girl is in London, although it's been closed for some time now. In fact, I am staying in London with a lady who was a teacher of mine. Where will you reside when you get to London?" She widened her eyes innocently.

Patience shook her head. "We don't know."

Hope shrugged. "Haven't any idea."

"I told you we are not yet ready to go," Charity snapped. "I will determine where we shall stay when the time comes."

"Of course you will. You do strike me as an extremely competent young woman." Gwen cast her a pleasant smile and was gratified to see the tension in the girl's face ease slightly. "Still"—Gwen shook her head regretfully—"without money you shall be forced to sleep out of doors, in the alleys, or perhaps you might find a stable."

"With horses?" Patience's eyes lit.

"And dogs?" Hope said eagerly. "What fun."

"Indeed." Gwen nodded. "Of course stables do tend to attract other, less desirable creatures, but surely that won't bother you."

"What kind of creatures?" Apprehension sounded in Hope's voice.

"Oh you know, the usual sort of thing," Gwen said blithely. "Mice at the very least and I should think rats—"

"Then we shall sleep outside," Patience said quickly.

"Certainly you could but"—Gwen drew her brows together—"well, there are rats outside as well. And all manner of unpleasant people." Gwen shook her head. "No, I don't think that will do. The best answer is for you all to get some kind of employment. Perhaps as house or scullery maids."

"That was my plan all along." Charity smirked.

Patience and Hope traded uneasy glances. Patience met Gwen's gaze. "Aren't we a bit young for that?"

"Indeed you are, but"—Gwen heaved a heavy sigh—"I'm afraid we are back to that same question of money. Without it, one has very few options. Why, I myself had to face being without funds when I was scarcely older than Charity. It's not at all pleasant."

Hope frowned. "Then what are we to do?"

"We could come live with you." Challenge rang in Charity's eyes, and her unflinching gaze met Gwen's.

From the moment Gwen had turned and stepped back into the room—no—from the moment she'd heard that never forgotten note in Hope's voice, she knew it would come to this. And knew as well it was the right thing—the only thing—to do. These girls were all the family Gwen had left in the world. Her nieces had lost so much already, how could Gwen allow them to lose one another? Besides, how could she let any girls—let alone these girls—grow up knowing they weren't especially wanted? Grow up as Gwen had.

"Indeed you could." Gwen's gaze never left Charity's. "Although I cannot guarantee how we shall get along."

Patience snorted. "We shall certainly get along better with you than we do with Pickleface."

"We should get along better with *anyone* than we do with Pickleface," Hope said pointedly.

"Well then . . ." Gwen drew a deep breath, wondering how someone who did not especially like children now had three in her keeping. Forever. "It is decided."

"Wonderful," Patience said with a wide grin.

"We shall have a grand life together." Hope beamed. "And perhaps we could have a dog as well."

"Do not think this means we are going to like you." The relief in her eyes belied the note in Charity's voice.

"It doesn't?" Hope's brow furrowed. "Not even a little?"

"Not at all," Charity said.

"You cannot tell me what to do just because you're the oldest." Patience glared at her sister. "I shall like her if I want to, and you can't stop me." She shot an apologetic glance at Gwen. "Not that I intend to, you understand."

"It's really not necessary to like me," Gwen said quickly. "I understand completely." Of course she did. The girls had felt abandoned by her and she could not fault their resentment.

"We shall, however, feel a certain amount of gratitude toward you," Charity said grudgingly. "And we shall endeavor not to be rude or impolite."

Gwen nodded. "I can ask for nothing more."

"In return . . ." Charity straightened her shoulders. "We shall not expect you to like us."

"I expect her to like me," Patience murmured.

"Everyone has always liked me," Hope said under her breath.

"That seems entirely fair. However . . ." Gwen thought for a moment. "I do reserve the right to like you should that unlikely event occur."

Hope and Patience shared smug smiles, and Gwen was hard-pressed to stifle her own. "Is it agreed, then?"

Charity nodded slowly. "Yes."

"Excellent." Gwen nodded with satisfaction.

Her gaze slid from one girl to the next, and the oddest sense of affection stirred within her. She'd never felt anything near affection for children before. Of course, she'd never been around children that were, for all intents and purposes, hers. Perhaps that was the difference. She'd certainly treated them differently. Abruptly Gwen realized that, except for the first few minutes, she hadn't really treated them as she'd always treated children. She'd treated them more like, well, people. People she might possibly, in spite of herself, care about. The strangest idea popped into her head that perhaps this would be as much a solution for her as for them.

Raising her nieces would give her future purpose. Certainly she hadn't been much of a governess, but that didn't mean she wouldn't be an acceptable aunt. Why, wasn't she already off to an excellent start? Saving them from the separation planned by the wicked Pickleface? Rescuing them from the need to run away and possibly be tossed into the ocean as food for fish? Or eaten by rats in the gutters?

They would indeed have a lovely life together. Gwen would make certain they never felt unwanted or unworthy or unnecessary. She would provide them with an excellent education, and when they were old enough, give them the season she'd never had. Not specifically with an eye toward marriage, but that would be entirely up to them. Who they married and whether they married at all would be their choice. She would make sure of it. It would simply take determination and dedication and . . . money.

She sucked in a hard breath.

"Have you changed your mind?" Hope said with concern.

Charity frowned. "You look rather ill."

"Like you're going to lose your dinner." Patience peered at her closely.

"No, no I'm fine. Of course I haven't changed my mind." Gwen smiled in what she hoped was a reassuring manner but her heart had plummeted to the pit of her stomach, and Patience's concern wasn't at all far-fetched. "Indeed, we should be off as soon as possible. Get your things together and I will speak to Pic—Miss Hilliard."

"Are you sure?" Patience said, apprehension pulling her brows together.

Any second thoughts Gwen might have had were swept away by the look on Patience's face, and the identical look on Hope's and even Charity's. "I have never been so sure of anything before." She rose to her feet. "Go on now. And do hurry."

Patience and Hope leaped up from the sofa and raced from the room. Charity too started toward the door, then stopped and turned to Gwen.

"We really are grateful," she said with a slight nod, then turned back and followed after her sisters.

These girls needed her, Charity perhaps most of all. It must be exceedingly difficult to try to start a new life at her age with two sisters to care for. It had been exceedingly difficult for Gwen, who had been both older and unencumbered when she had found herself on her own. No one had needed her before. How different her life might have been if someone had.

"Take care, Charity," Gwen said softly. "You may find yourself liking me in spite of your best intentions. And I may well like you. Quite a lot."

She smiled after the girl, then drew a deep breath. It was all very well to conjure dreams of the future out of thin air, but real plans had to be made.

The legacy her father had left her would take care of her own needs and, in truth, she'd been dependent on wages for so long, simply not having to work for the money was a luxury in itself. But realistically, it was not overly substantial. And while it would provide nicely for one person and perhaps two extremely thrifty people, it certainly would amount to only bare survival for four.

It would take a great deal of money to support a family of four, let alone provide for dresses and seasons and dowries. Gwen simply did not have the finances. But she well knew where she could find it.

Whether she liked it or not, the means to the future was within her grasp.

All she had to do was marry it.

Chapter Five

*Even the most intelligent of men
rarely knows as much as he thinks he does.*

Francesa Freneau

"What you need is a plan of action," Reggie said once again, as if the simple saying of it would magically provide such a plan. The viscount lounged on the sofa in an indolent manner, a precariously tipped glass of brandy in his hand.

"We've determined that." Marcus rested his hip on the desk and swirled the liquor in his glass.

Indeed, that was all the men had determined. They had planned to spend the evening at their club but instead still lingered in the library at Pennington House. Thus far they'd agreed on nothing other than the need to come up with a course of action to entice Miss Townsend into marriage. Just what that should be remained annoyingly elusive.

"And with Miss Townsend, it must be a good plan. The stakes are exceedingly high, and she is no fool."

"A good plan is always difficult. However, an adequate plan is possible." Reggie sipped thoughtfully at his brandy. Both men had years ago agreed decisions of any magnitude could not properly be made without endless glasses of decent liquor. "I find flowers work well."

Marcus snorted. "That's scarcely a plan."

"No, but it's a start. A prelude to a plan, so to speak. Soften her up for the real thing and all that." Reggie thought for a moment. "Although it may not be enough in this case."

"No, it's not nearly enough. Still, in the belief that it couldn't possibly work against me, I have done my best to fill her residence with flowers since our meeting yesterday. I have had them delivered and indeed brought them myself today but she was not at home."

Reggie frowned. "I didn't think she knew anyone in London."

"Neither did I." Marcus did think Miss Townsend's absence rather odd, especially as Madame Freneau had politely but firmly declined to answer his casual query as to Miss Townsend's whereabouts. Still, it was probably not at all important, and Marcus set it from his mind.

"At any rate, I have thus far deluged her with blossoms, a remarkably expensive proposition, I might add. I have already spent a small fortune."

"Excellent. You don't want her to think you cheap. You might as well spend it while you have it, I say." Reggie shrugged. "I do."

Reggie had never been at all hesitant to shower the

current object of his affections with flowers or whatever else he deemed suitable. Not that it had ever done him a great deal of good, as he tended to select women who not only needed rescuing but were more often than not completely unsuitable or already had their affections engaged elsewhere. Reggie pursued love with a rash, single-minded determination and gave his heart as easily as he tipped his hat. Marcus viewed that same emotion with a cautious eye and a protective attitude.

Still, in spite of their differences, both friends had the unfortunate gift of setting their sights on the wrong women, and both harbored a desire for love. Only their ways of seeking it varied. But Marcus had long ago realized, even if Reggie never would, that such desire was at once overly romantic, highly impractical, and quite improbable.

"Poetry is a nice touch as well." Reggie's brow furrowed thoughtfully. "They like it if you write it yourself."

"I do not now, nor shall I ever write poetry," Marcus said in a lofty manner.

Reggie laughed. "You say that like it's quite disgraceful."

"Not at all. I simply realize my limitations."

"Helmsley writes poetry."

"Helmsley writes bad poetry and everyone who reads it knows it."

"Yes, but I'd wager it's that bad poetry that won him the hand of his lovely wife." Reggie grinned. "It's the sentiment, Marcus, not merely the words that touch a lady's heart."

"Nonetheless, I—"

"You could try someone else's poetry."

"Are you suggesting I borrow something of Helmsley's?" Marcus raised a brow. "I daresay neither he nor his wife would appreciate my absconding with his words, no matter how bad they may be."

"Don't be absurd." Reggie grimaced. "I doubt if Helmsley's poetry would have the same effect on a woman who wasn't already in love with him. However, I was going to suggest a few of Lord Byron's words. All that *she walks in beauty* nonsense." Reggie raised his glass. "It can be most effective when used correctly. And women do seem to love it."

"Women seem to love *him*," Marcus said wryly.

"He's always been scandalous. That dashing, even dangerous image, coupled with his poetry, makes him rather irresistible, I suspect. Thank God he's out of the country."

Reggie thought for a moment. "Perhaps that's been our problem all along. We are simply not rakes or rogues or scoundrels."

"Yet our reputations are not spotless."

Reggie scoffed. "Petty infractions. Youthful high spirits. Nothing of true significance. Nothing to make a woman wonder how exciting dipping her toe into the waters of our dangerous characters would be. We are altogether far too respectable." He leaned forward in his seat. "Perhaps what we need is to be involved in a scandal of epic proportions."

"Given this a great deal of thought, have you?"

"The circumstances you find yourself in have had the strangest effect of forcing me to reconsider my own life. And I find it rather disappointing." Reggie fell silent, obviously pondering his now recognized wasted years. At last he heaved a heartfelt sigh. "However, I suppose that discussion will have to wait for another night. Our first order of business is the arrangement of your life. Right now we must determine how to encourage Miss Townsend to consent to marriage."

He shook his head. "I confess, I don't understand her reluctance. You have everything any woman could ask for. In truth, Marcus, you are an excellent catch."

"Only for a woman interested in marriage." Marcus blew a long breath. "And unfortunately, Miss Townsend is apparently the only woman on the face of the earth who is not."

"We have to make it look exciting then. We have to make *you* exciting. Yes, of course, that's the answer." Reggie downed his drink and sprang to his feet. "You have to change, Marcus. Become a rogue, a rake, a scoundrel. Seduce virgins. Dally with married women. Flout convention."

"I'm not sure I have enough time for that," Marcus said wryly.

Reggie ignored him. "Embroil yourself in a good, juicy scandal. Your name on every gossip's lips and in every woman's heart. Why, look at what happened to that Effington chit. She ran off and wed a near stranger who then croaked, practically before the ink was dry on the marriage certificate. Everyone is still talking about that, I tell you."

"Somehow I don't think marrying the wrong person, whether they survive or not, is the way to attract Miss Townsend."

"Probably not." Reggie thought for a moment.

"Still, there are no end of things you could do. Adopt a wicked grin and a wickeder look in your eye." Reggie flashed his idea of a wicked grin, and Marcus tried not to laugh. "Sweep her off her feet, Marcus. Be mysterious. Women always want what they can't have. Be aloof. Dangerous. Be"—Reggie smiled slyly—"forbidden fruit."

"Forbidden fruit?" Marcus laughed. "I daresay, as I am pursuing her and it is my fortune at stake, I am scarcely the stuff forbidden fruit is made of. Rather I am all too readily available and ripe for picking."

"Ah well, then, it was just an idea." Reggie plopped back on the sofa and held out his glass for a refill. "Do you think that's a flaw in their characters? Women, I mean? The men they seem the most taken with are the ones I wouldn't let alone in a room with my sister for so much as the blink of an eye. A crowded room at that."

"No doubt one of many flaws, Reggie. I am not certain trying to study them with an eye toward rationality is at all possible." Marcus grasped the decanter beside him and reached forward to refill Reggie's glass. "However, what makes men superior is that we can turn their flaws to our advantage. The chinks in their armor are to our benefit."

"Does your Miss Townsend have flaws?"

"Every woman has flaws. Miss Townsend is no different. Thus far, I can confidently say she is stubborn and opinionated. She is overly independent, annoyingly outspoken, and has the oddest views on marriage and the relationships of men and women. Although, I believe if any woman could take care of herself, Miss

Townsend would be the one. In addition, I understand she can be quite impulsive as well. And worst of all"—he grinned—"I suspect she is nearly as clever as I am."

"Pity. Still, I assume you are not allowing a few minor defects to dissuade you. You are still determined to marry this termagant, are you not?"

"She and her attitudes are a blasted inconvenience, but my resolve is unshaken. What choice do I have? I have three months until my birth date, and I shall spend every day of that in pursuit of her until she relents or I am impoverished. In truth, though, now that I have met the lady"—Marcus grinned—"the prospect of marriage to her is not unappealing."

"I cannot believe your luck. In spite of the fire in her eyes"—Reggie returned his grin—"she did have the face of an angel."

"Both the face and the fire make her a most interesting challenge. I'm surprised to find I am quite looking forward to it." Marcus wasn't entirely sure he wanted to confess just how much he was looking forward to it, either to Reggie or to himself.

He had conceded that Miss Townsend—Gwendolyn—had had the oddest effect on him and had spent the day since their meeting trying to determine why.

Certainly she was pretty, and he would be eternally grateful for that, admitting to himself that he was shallow enough to wish for a pretty wife. But he had seen prettier, indeed had had prettier cast their eyes in his direction. It was not Gwendolyn's appearance, although he had always had a particular fondness for red hair, that intrigued him. No, it was something entirely different. Her manner, perhaps; her attitude, indeed; even her mind.

He had met clever women before, of course. The two women in his past to whom he had nearly given his heart were clever. And pretty. But Gwendolyn was unique among women of his acquaintance. She had something they did not; yet at the moment, he had no idea what that something was. Perhaps it was simply knowing his future was in her hands, and his attraction to her was nothing more than a concession to the inevitable, a means of accepting what he had no choice in. In a convoluted way, that did make sense.

"You're rather passionate about a woman you just met," Reggie said mildly. "I don't believe I've seen you quite this animated since Lady—"

"Nonsense."

"Denying the obvious?" Reggie studied him for a moment. "How very interesting."

"Don't be absurd," Marcus said firmly. "If I exhibit any passion at all about Miss Townsend, it's only because I have worked myself to a minimal amount of enthusiasm for that which I cannot avoid."

Reggie snorted. "You can protest all you want, old man, but don't forget: I know you as well as you know yourself. In spite of your reluctance to engage in displays of emotion, or indeed to admit you have emotions, I would wager a great deal that this woman has intrigued you to an extent I have rarely seen you exhibit."

It was pointless to deny it: argument would only strengthen Reggie's belief. Besides, Marcus was indeed intrigued by Miss Townsend. *Gwendolyn.* When had he started thinking of her by her given name?

"It seems to me, Reggie, if you have no choice in the matter of who your bride will be, it's far better to be intrigued by the woman than repulsed by her."

"No doubt. I should think—"

Without warning, the door to the library opened and the subject of their discussion swept into the room, Godfrey, Marcus's butler, fast on her heels.

Marcus straightened, and Reggie at once got to his feet.

"My lord," Godfrey said quickly, "I attempted to explain to the lady that she could not simply—"

"I told him it was all right." Gwendolyn's cool gaze met his. "That you would wish to see me."

"Which I could scarcely believe, my lord," A scandalized note sounded in Godfrey's lowered voice. "She is unaccompanied." In Godfrey's estimation, no respectable lady would go anywhere without accompaniment.

"I have a driver," she said in an overly sweet manner.

"It is quite all right, Godfrey. Miss Townsend is indeed"—he cast her an amused smile—"expected."

Godfrey hesitated but was too well trained to protest. "Very well, my lord." Godfrey slanted her a suspicious glance. "I shall be nearby if you require my assistance."

"Never fear, Godfrey." Reggie grinned. "I shall remain to protect His Lordship should it become necessary."

Godfrey's lips pressed together in a firm line, as if he doubted Reggie's ability to do much of anything. Reggie often had that effect on the servant. Godfrey nodded in a respectful if reluctant manner. "As you wish, my lord." He stepped to the door and closed it firmly behind him.

"What, precisely, does he think I will do to you?" Miss Townsend said mildly.

"It's hard to say with Godfrey." Marcus smiled. "He has been with me since I was a boy and is exceedingly protective."

"However, you are in excellent company. He has never trusted me in the least." Reggie stepped forward.

"With good reason, my lord?" Miss Townsend's eyes widened innocently.

"One can only hope." Reggie laughed. "You were right about her, Marcus."

"Were you?" Miss Townsend's brow lifted. "Right about what?"

"Miss Townsend," Marcus changed the subject, "may I present my friend Lord Berkley."

"Miss Townsend." Reggie took her hand a bit too eagerly and lifted it to his lips. His gaze met Gwendolyn's in an altogether too personal manner. "How delightful to see you again."

"Is it?" she murmured, staring at Reggie with a bemused look on her face, as if she'd never had her hand kissed before. Why, hadn't Marcus kissed her hand just yesterday? Her reaction hadn't seemed nearly as profound then.

"Indeed it is." Reggie's voice was low and overly warm.

Odd how Marcus had never before noted the flirtatious—no, the *intimate*—manner in which Reggie greeted female acquaintances. For a moment he had the most remarkable urge to thrash his oldest friend in the world. Surely he wasn't jealous? Or possessive? What nonsense. Still, he didn't like the look on Reggie's face or, for that matter, the look on Gwendolyn's.

"Then is what Lord Pennington said to me true?" she asked.

"It all depends on what he said."

"He suggested *you* would be happy to marry me and absolve him of the necessity to do the deed himself." She smiled pleasantly. "Would you?"

Marcus winced to himself.

Reggie's eyes widened, and he dropped her hand as if it were on fire. "Well, I . . . that is . . . I should . . ."

"It was a momentary impulse on my part," Marcus said quickly. "And quite ill-advised, I might add. My apologies to you both." He sounded rather stiff, but he couldn't seem to help himself.

Reggie cast him a curious look. "Apology accepted. Although"—he bowed in a courtly manner—"Miss Townsend, I should be honored to marry you if only to save you from the hands of Lord Pennington. He is a rake, a rogue, and a scoundrel. He has been embroiled in escapades and scandals far too numerous to mention." He lowered his voice confidentially. "He is exceedingly dangerous."

"Really?" Gwendolyn considered Marcus for a moment. "He does not look particularly dangerous."

"My dear young woman." Reggie shook his head. "The stories I could tell you would shock you to your very core."

"Berkley"—a warning sounded in Marcus's voice—"I don't think—"

"You mean stories about Lord Pennington being mistaken for a buck and shot?" Her tone was mild, but there was an amused twinkle in her eye.

"Exactly like that." Reggie grinned. "Only these are even better."

"That's quite enough," Marcus said firmly. "I doubt Miss Townsend is here this evening for the purpose of hearing stories about my exploits, real or imagined."

"Although I did rather enjoy the one about him being shot." A true smile lifted her lips, and Marcus was struck by what lovely lips they were. He hadn't seen her smile like that before. It lit up her face and deepened the blue of her eyes. And warmed something deep inside him.

"I could tell it again if you'd like." Reggie's tone was a touch too eager. "And this time it will be much more amusing."

"No," Marcus said. "But I'm certain Miss Townsend appreciates the offer."

"Indeed I do." She paused for a moment as if to gather her thoughts or perhaps her courage. "However, that is not the offer I am here to discuss."

At once the mood in the room sobered.

Marcus nodded. "I did not think so."

"I assume nothing has changed?" Gwendolyn started to remove her gloves, as if she planned on staying for a while. Marcus wasn't sure if that was good or bad. "You still wish to marry me?"

"Indeed I do, Miss Townsend. I have no choice." Marcus groaned to himself at the formal note in his voice and his overly cool manner. This was not at all the way to press his suit.

Reggie cast his gaze toward the ceiling.

She pulled off one glove, then slowly removed the other. "As much as ours is an unusual match, it is still disconcerting to hear the truth stated in such an unequivocal manner."

Blast it all. "I am sorry, Miss Townsend. I did not mean—"

"An apology is not necessary." Her gaze met his. She was as controlled as he, and he could read nothing in her eyes. "You are entirely right: you have been given no choice in the matter. Therefore I would suggest"— she drew a deep breath—"we discuss the terms of the arrangement."

"Terms, Miss Townsend?" He didn't especially like the sound of that. "What do you mean by *terms?*"

"Terms. Expectations. Conditions. Provisions and so forth. Of our"—she swallowed hard, and he wondered if the coolness of her manner was due to nerves and the significance of the moment—"marriage."

Relief swept through him, and a touch of something unexpected. Not joy, surely, but a certain pleasure nonetheless. Abruptly he wondered if the nonsense he'd spouted to her about fate might well have some veracity after all. Perhaps this was meant to be.

"Well, I say, congratulations to you both." Reggie beamed as if this were a love match and not an arrangement more akin to business than affection. "And, as you both have a great deal to discuss, I shall take my leave."

"You needn't go," Marcus said quickly.

"You could be of some help," Gwendolyn added.

"I would offer my assistance, of course, but I have

just this moment remembered an appointment I must keep." Reggie stepped to the door, pulled it open, then glanced back at Gwendolyn and grinned. "Do be careful, my dear, he is exceedingly dangerous." He turned and stepped into the hall. "Take care, Godfrey. You'll soon have a new mistress." The door snapped shut behind him.

An uncomfortable silence settled between them. Marcus had no idea what to say now. Or what to do. She looked as ill-at-ease as he.

"Would you like a brandy?" he blurted.

"That would be lovely," she said with obvious relief.

He moved to the desk, selected a clean glass from a silver tray, filled it, then refilled his own. He was grateful for the activity and the respite from conversation. He turned toward her. She'd taken off her hat and was smoothing her hair away from her face.

"Oh dear. I do hope you are not going to chastise me again for a lapse in decorum. As I told you yesterday, I have always been exceedingly proper in behavior and attitude. However . . ." She wrinkled her nose in a charming manner that made her appear entirely too young and far too innocent. "I know hats are a necessary evil, correct and all that, but I simply hate wearing them." She dropped it onto the sofa, as if daring him to protest.

"Then we have something in common. I am not fond of wearing hats myself." He stepped toward her. "Besides, this shall soon be your home, and you should feel free to behave as you like here. Within reason of course."

She cocked her head. "Within reason?"

"I should hate to scandalize Godfrey." He handed her the drink. "It's very good brandy. I hope you like it."

"I'm certain I shall." She eyed the glass with a skeptical smile. "Although I have never had brandy before." She took a swallow and gasped. "It's very"—her voice was choked—"intense."

"Yes, I suppose it is." He grinned.

Her eyes watered, and she clasped her hand to her throat. "And extremely warm."

"That too."

"Still . . ." She took a second, far more cautious sip. "It does have a not unpleasant taste."

"Not at all unpleasant."

She licked her lips and nodded thoughtfully. "Quite pleasant, really. Don't you think?"

"I do." Without thinking, he leaned forward and lightly brushed his lips across hers. "Very pleasant."

She caught her breath and stared up at him. "Why did you do that?"

He grimaced. "I'm not sure. I am not usually given to impulse but—"

"But you have not been in this position before."

"Which position." He stared at her lips, slightly parted, full and firm and tasting delightfully of brandy.

"Marriage?"

"Ah yes." He lifted his gaze to hers. "I should apologize again."

"For kissing me?" Her eyes were wide, and her breath was shallow.

"Yes," he said softly. "We met only yesterday, yet it seems I am always apologizing to you for my behavior."

"You needn't." She lifted her chin slightly and leaned imperceptibly closer. "Not for this."

"I can't." He wanted to kiss her again. "Not for kissing you." Pull her into his arms and kiss her senseless. "I would not mean it." And lose his own senses in the process.

For an endless moment he could do nothing but stare into her eyes, and he saw his own unforeseen desire mirrored there. And, unexpectedly, apprehension or perhaps fear as well. And he realized that too was a reflection.

"Yes, well . . ." He stepped away and resisted the urge to run his hand through his hair, the moment broken, the tension between them shattered.

"Yes, well . . ." She uttered a short, awkward laugh. "Indeed." Gwendolyn pulled a long swallow of her drink.

"Take care with the brandy, Miss Townsend, it is extremely potent for one who is not used to it." His manner was again cool and remote, and as much as he regretted it, he wasn't at all sure it wasn't for the best at the moment.

"Thank you, Lord Pennington." She smiled politely and drew a deep swallow of the liquor. She too was now brisk and impersonal, and once again he both regretted it and was grateful. "Perhaps we should now discuss the terms of our arrangement."

"*Marriage*, Miss Townsend, not merely an arrangement," he said firmly. "This is to be a marriage, which implies any number of things that indeed we should resolve."

"I quite agree." She marched to the sofa and perched primly on the edge, the vision of stiff propriety somewhat spoiled by the glass of brandy in her hand and the tendril of red hair that had freed itself from the knot on the top of her head. "You may begin."

"I may begin?" He shook his head. "I think not. You are the one who insisted on laying out the terms of this marriage." He set his glass down, crossed his arms over his chest, and propped his hip on the desk. "You should be the one to begin."

"Very well. First of all"—she took another sip—"as you know, I will acquire a tidy personal fortune when we wed."

"Just how much is tidy, Miss Townsend?"

She hesitated.

"Come now, I have no designs on your money."

She downed the rest of her brandy. "One hundred thousand pounds."

He blew a low whistle. "That is tidy."

"That money is to be mine and mine alone," she said quickly.

"Once we wed, what's yours is mine, Miss Townsend." His tone was mild. "It's the law, the way of the world."

"I don't care." Her defiant gaze locked with his. "You are to have no say over that money, and I shall not make an accounting of it to you. Not now or ever. And I further wish Mr. Whiting to draw up an agreement specifying this."

"And if I do not agree?"

"Then there will be no marriage." She smiled

smugly. The woman had the upper hand in this game, and she well knew it.

"Very well. As this marriage will ensure the stability of my own fortune, I will have no need for your hundred thousand pounds." He shrugged. "It is, in truth, a pittance in comparison with my resources."

Her eyes widened. "Really?"

"Really. And as my wife, you will certainly share in my wealth even if you refuse to allow me to share in yours." It was interesting to note the play of expressions across her face. Not greed as much as awe and even perhaps relief. Not surprising. She had spent the last years of her life with very little. It must indeed ease her mind to realize she would not have to worry about money ever again.

"Imagine that," she said under her breath and upended her glass, only to discover it empty.

He grabbed the decanter, crossed the room, and filled her glass, firmly ignoring the voice in his head that said this was a mistake. He did not want her foxed.

"Thank you," she murmured, staring into the glass. "It really is extremely tasty." She looked up at him. "I believe it's your turn. For terms, that is."

"Ah yes." He returned to his perch on the edge of the desk. He had, of course, already considered the conditions of their arrangement, but that was before he'd met her. He was expecting a marriage of convenience for them both. Once she had provided him with heirs, they could both live their own lives. He was no longer entirely certain that was what he wanted. Still, it was a place to start. "We need to discuss children."

"Of course," she said coolly, but there was an odd look in her eye. "You shall want sons, I assume."

"Absolutely. Two should do nicely."

"I see." She took a gulp of her drink. "When?"

He started. "I had not considered when. Soon, I should think."

"And what of girls?"

"What of girls?" he said slowly and studied her closely. Even though she showed no outward appearance of inebriation, it was probable the brandy was taking its toll.

She heaved an annoyed sigh. "What if we have girls?"

"Frankly, Miss Townsend, I have not considered that question either. It's heirs that I am concerned with."

She narrowed her eyes. "You don't like girls, do you?"

"I have never given them any particular thought."

"Of course not." She got to her feet in a surprisingly steady manner, straightened her shoulders, and glared at him. "I am a girl."

He bit back a grin. "Yes, indeed, I can certainly see that."

"Do you like me?" she said in a lofty manner.

"I'm afraid I do."

She tilted her head and stared at him. "Are you really? Afraid, I mean?"

He nodded. "I really am."

"Why? Shouldn't I be the one who is afraid of you?"

"Possibly." He paused. "Are you?"

She narrowed her eyes. "Absolutely not."

He laughed. "Why not?"

"Well . . ." She paused. "Because you are an adult, I suppose. And I quite consider myself equal to you."

"Do you?"

"I do indeed."

"I can't imagine you being afraid of anything."

"What a very nice thing to say. Inaccurate but nice." She sipped her drink and considered him. "I have always been rather afraid of children."

"I doubt that that is at all uncommon, Miss Townsend. I suspect many women are fearful of bearing children."

"Oh, I'm not talking about that." She waved away his comment. "Although that does not sound especially pleasant. My mother died in childbirth." Again she paused. "Did you know I was a governess?"

He nodded. Between Whiting and his mother, he knew most of the details of her life thus far.

"I was not a very good governess," she said wryly. "Children do not seem to like me. Even my own ne—charges were not fond of me." Her brows pulled together thoughtfully. "I think they sensed my fear of them."

"Why on earth would you fear children?"

"I have tried to determine that myself." She shrugged. "I can only think it was because I was scarcely more than a child myself when I took my first position. In truth, I had no experience with children, no idea what to do. I believe I expressed my fears by being too harsh and rigid in my treatment of them." Her questioning gaze caught his. "Does that make any sense at all?"

"It seems quite logical to me."

"It does, doesn't it?" She nodded in agreement. "I

have recently discovered that treating children as rational beings rather than completely foreign entities seems to elicit a far better response."

What was she talking about? "I should think so, although admittedly I have had no experience with children myself."

"And you don't like girls. That does make things awkward." She heaved a sigh and wandered toward the fireplace. A dark, old-fashioned portrait of the seventh Earl of Pennington hung above the mantel. "Is that your father?"

"Yes." Marcus joined her and stared up at the painting. The artist had managed to capture his father's character well: the expression on his face was firm but not unkind. And there was a hint of a smile in his eyes.

"Do you miss him?"

"Indeed I do." Marcus had quite liked his father and never doubted the affection was mutual. Even now, in the situation his father had placed him in, he was hard-pressed to resent the man who had always done what he thought best for his son. "Do you miss yours?"

"I did not know him well enough to miss him." She continued to stare up at the painting. "He wanted sons and had only daughters. It was a great disappointment to him. He sent me away to school when I was very young, and I saw him only infrequently." Her manner was matter-of-fact, as if she was relating facts that had nothing to do with her.

"You said daughters. Do you have sisters then?"

"One, but she married against my father's wishes and went off with her husband to wander the world in search of grand adventures. I did not know her at all."

She sipped her drink. "She's dead now. Eaten by cannibals, I believe."

"Good God! Cannibals?"

"Something like that. It's of little consequence." She shrugged. "She's dead and I am quite alone."

He stared at her profile for a long moment. She was so dispassionate, as if having a sister eaten by cannibals, or whatever; a mother dead in childbirth; and a father who seemed to care nothing for her was not at all unusual. His heart twisted for her.

"Not quite alone," he said quietly. "Now you have me."

She laughed. "Whether you want me or not." She turned her gaze toward him. "I cannot believe marriage to a woman you do not know would be your preference."

Without thinking, he took her hand and pulled it to his lips. "You, my dear Miss Townsend, have become my preference."

"Because, as you have so plainly stated, you have no choice."

"I was mistaken," he said firmly. "I do indeed have a choice. I can choose to ignore my father's decree, forfeit my fortune, and make my way in the world on my own. It would not be easy, but I do not doubt I could do it. Isn't that precisely what you did?"

"And it was not at all pleasant." She pulled her hand from his. "I was forced to find employment that I was neither prepared for nor suited to. I was little more than a servant and completely dependent on the whims of others for my keeping and for wages that amounted to next to nothing. If you believe nothing else I say to you for the rest of our lives, believe this." The corners of her lips quirked upward. "Poverty, my dear Lord Pennington, reeks."

"Then by all means, we shall avoid it." He laughed, and she joined him. It was an odd moment of accord, and he wondered if they had just taken the first steps toward a life together.

"Now then." She returned to the sofa and seated herself. "We should continue with the terms. In addition to my income, I have a small house in the country which shall remain mine alone."

At once the feeling of unity vanished. "Am I to understand what is yours is yours, and what is mine is to be yours as well?"

She thought for a moment, then nodded. "That sounds accurate."

"But not at all fair."

"I will give you children. *Sons.*" There was a slight note of disgust in her voice, and given her history, he could well understand it. Still, his understanding made it no less irritating. "It seems exceedingly fair to me."

"Fair or not, there is more involved in the duties of the Countess of Pennington than the breeding of children." He followed her and settled back on the edge of the desk. "I shall expect you to run my households in an efficient manner. You will be provided with a suitable allowance for household and personal needs. Clothing and whatever other sorts of things women require. In addition, my position demands a certain amount of entertaining, and that shall fall to you as well. And you will be required to behave in a manner suitable to the office of my wife."

"We wouldn't want to scandalize Godfrey."

"Godfrey is the least of my concerns. As the purpose of this, in truth most, marriages is the continuation of my family line, until such time as heirs are provided"— he narrowed his eyes—"I shall expect complete faithfulness, fidelity, and loyalty."

"As shall I," she said primly.

He raised a brow. "Most women do not expect that from their husbands."

"Then most woman are fools."

"Perhaps." In truth, he had no problem with that particular term. "Agreed, then."

"I do reserve the right, however, to come and go as I please. Within reason, of course."

He shrugged. "As long as you remain faithful to me, I have no objection to that. Indeed, I have never particularly wanted a wife who would not have a certain amount of independence in her spirit."

"Then, Lord Pennington, we may well suit after all." She cast him a brilliant smile, and again he noted how it transformed her face. And how pretty she really was. "And I believe this evening's business is concluded."

"Not entirely." He straightened and stepped toward her. "I do not relish the thought of my wife calling me by my title. Regardless of the circumstances of our union, it is indeed a union, and a lifetime one at that. I would much prefer to be called by my given name."

"Very well, Marcus. And you may call me"—she looked up at him with a distinctly teasing look in her eye—"Miss Townsend."

"As you wish, *Miss Townsend*." He laughed,

plucked her again empty glass from her hand and set it aside, then held out his hand and helped her to her feet. She swayed and he caught her in his arms. "My dear Miss Townsend, you are indeed foxed."

"I most certainly am not," she said with a weak attempt at indignation. She drew back and grinned up at him. "I do feel remarkably . . . confident, but I am not inebriated."

"Have you ever been inebriated?"

"I have drunk enough wine in my life to know what inebriated is." She smiled smugly. "And this is not it."

Her acquaintance with wine explained why the brandy had not overwhelmed her. He was at once pleased and a tiny bit disappointed, although he was far too honorable to ever take advantage of a drunken Gwendolyn.

"Now, I think you should kiss me." She closed her eyes and raised her chin.

"Should I?"

"Indeed you should." She waited, then opened her eyes. "Well?"

"Well what?"

She sighed. "You told me I would know when you wanted to kiss me."

"And do I?"

"Yes, you do." She flashed him a wicked smile that would have done Berkley proud.

"Very well, then." He chuckled and lowered his lips to hers.

"I have never truly been kissed before," she said, her lips a scant breath from his. There was a tremulous note in her voice at odds with the forthrightness of a moment ago. She rested her hands on his chest as if to push him away, or perhaps to pull him close. "Not when I wanted to be."

"And do you want to be kissed now?" His lips brushed against hers.

"I think . . . yes." Her words were little more than a sigh.

"Very well then." His lips met hers gently, tentatively. He gathered her closer against him and deepened his kiss. Her lips opened slightly beneath his, and he felt her relax against him.

She tasted of brandy, sweet and warm and inviting. Her lips were pliant, welcoming. Without warning, desire swept through him for this stranger, the woman he would spend the rest of his days with. He wanted her here and now and . . . yes, even forever.

She moaned, a sensual sound deep in her throat, and her hands slipped upward to wrap around his neck, her fingers cool against his flesh. An odd shiver raced down his spine. An ache of wanting, of need filled him, and he crushed her tighter against him, the curves of her body molding to his. Intriguing and irresistible.

And for the third time in his life he tottered on a precipice wondering if with this woman he would have the courage to fly or if caution would hold him back. Dimly, in the back of a mind already fogged with desire, a familiar voice screamed for him to take care. In truth he did not know her at all. He could indeed bed her, but it was too soon for more. He could not give her his heart as easily as he gave her his name. He did not have that courage yet.

Slowly he raised his head and stared down at her.

Her eyes opened, and her gaze met his. "I believe, my lord . . . Marcus . . ." Her blue eyes were dark with newly awakened passion and understanding. Her voice was breathless. "I have now been truly kissed."

"It was my pleasure, Miss Townsend." A lingering passion still edged his words.

He cleared his throat and released her, well aware if he did not let her go now he would kiss her again and again and make her his before the night was out. Given her response to his kiss, he did not doubt she would be willing, even enthusiastic. But he suspected that would not be the way to begin life with this particular woman. Besides, it was apparent the brandy had indeed affected her.

He stepped away, and her eyes widened, her knees buckled, and she sank back onto the sofa. She gazed up at him with surprise. "Oh dear."

"I must say, my kiss has never had quite this effect on a woman before."

"Have you kissed many woman?"

He ignored her. "Although I suspect it's probably the brandy. I did warn you."

"But I feel so confident. As if I could do anything. Not the tiniest bit inebriated. Do you know I was quite nervous about coming here?"

"Were you?"

She nodded in a deceptively sober manner. "I have never told a man I would marry him before." Her brows pulled together thoughtfully. "Although I have been asked . . . once."

"Oh?"

"It's of no importance." She shrugged off the question.

Marcus wondered if this previous proposal was indeed insignificant or something she'd simply prefer not to discuss. Had her heart been involved with this other man?

"I suppose I should go," Gwendolyn murmured. She got to her feet, immediately tumbled backward, and giggled up at him. "This is quite embarrassing."

"Have you ever lost your composure before, Miss Townsend?"

"Not that I can recall. Nor have I ever . . . giggled." Her brow furrowed. "There have been moments, though, when I could not control . . . well . . . life, as it were."

"And what did you do then?"

"I left." She grinned. "As I shall do right now." She rose to her feet in a slow and careful manner. "There. I am quite all right."

He tried not to laugh. "But can you walk?"

She frowned. "Oh dear, I will need to do that, won't I? To get to my carriage."

"Not at all." He stepped to her, scooped her into his arms, and started toward the door.

"Are you taking me to my carriage, then?"

"I would rather take you to my bed," he murmured.

She gasped, then giggled again. It was an altogether delightful sound. "But we are not married yet. Indeed, if it's two sons you want, I should think I shall be in your bed no more than twice anyway."

He snorted. "Not if I can help it."

She snuggled against him, and the muscles of his stomach tightened. "My, you are dangerous after all."

"And getting more so by the moment," he muttered. He reached the door, shifted her in his arms, and managed to pull it open. "I have already arranged for a special license. I am nothing if not determined and optimistic. I shall make further arrangements tomorrow, and I think the day after will be an excellent day to wed."

A gasp sounded from the shadows of the corridor. Godfrey, no doubt. Marcus was in no mood to deal with him at the moment.

"Do you, Marcus?"

"If that meets with your approval." He glanced down at her. "Take care, Miss Townsend, it will soon be too late to turn back. For either of us."

"Well, I do want my money as soon as possible." Her smile belied the mercenary nature of her words.

"My lord, may I be of some assistance." The butler appeared out of nowhere.

"Call for my carriage, Godfrey. I am accompanying Miss Townsend home."

"Very well, my lord." Godfrey's tone left no doubt of his opinion of any woman His Lordship carried around like a sack of flour. He started off, then turned back. "Forgive me, my lord, I could not help overhearing. Am I to understand you intend to"—Godfrey paused as if struggling to say the word—"*marry* this young woman?"

Gwendolyn giggled.

"Yes, Godfrey, I do."

"I see." Godfrey drew a deep breath. "Then I assume she is the daughter of—"

"Viscount Townsend. Yes, Godfrey, this is the woman my father arranged to be my bride." Marcus heaved a resigned sigh. "But you know all about this, don't you?"

"It is my business to know, my lord."

Marcus was not surprised. Godfrey always knew everything.

"Good evening to you, Godfrey," Gwendolyn said politely.

"And you, miss." Godfrey's lips pressed together. "She will need a bit of work, my lord, if she is to be a countess."

"She will do fine, Godfrey. This is entirely my fault," Marcus said firmly. "Now then, the carriage."

"Yes, my lord. It will be at the door in a moment." Godfrey vanished into the corridor.

"I have a carriage waiting." Gwendolyn waved in the general direction of the front entry. "Somewhere out there."

"I cannot possibly let my future wife leave unaccompanied in this state."

"I am not in a state, Marcus, I am simply confident. I have no idea why my legs won't work," she said loftily.

"Nonetheless." He grinned in spite of himself. "Consider it one of my terms."

"You are extremely nice," she said under her breath. "It will be exceedingly difficult to dislike you."

"Why do you want to dislike me?" His question came too late. She was already dozing against him.

It was an odd thing for her to say, yet what that had passed between them thus far was not a bit odd? Perhaps she was as cautious about love as he was. The question now was why.

Marcus had watched Reggie break his heart too many times to count and had come close enough himself to that emotion to at least taste the possibility of pain. Had Gwendolyn had a similar experience? With the man who had once offered to marry her? Had she known love with him only to have her heart crushed?

Or worse—his jaw clenched at the thought—did she love someone still?

Chapter Six

*Even if a man is chosen for the
right reasons, fortune, title, power, we will
always love them for the wrong.*

Francesca Freneau

"It sounds so . . . inconvenient and awkward," Gwen said under her breath. "And not at all appealing."

She gingerly lay back against her pillow and adjusted the wet cloth over her eyes. Any noise at all, even that of her own voice, reverberated in her head. It was already midday, and she hadn't yet found the strength to move from her bed. Indeed, Gwen thought she'd have to feel considerably better simply to die.

"My dear girl, it is extremely appealing." Colette perched at the foot of her bed. "And a great deal of fun."

Madame Freneau—Francesca—sat in a chair beside the bed. The women were kind about the ill effects of last night's brandy but insisted on what they saw as their responsibilities, in the absence of Gwen's mother, to educate her as to wifely duties and the pleasure a woman could derive from them. It was rather hard to believe.

"Exciting?" Gwen shuddered. The details of the marriage bed were not a complete shock: the girls at Madame Chaussan's had discussed such matters late at night amid a great deal of giggling. Still, it was surprising to note how much they had. "I cannot imagine that would be exciting."

"With the right man it can be wonderful." Madame— Gwen never could think of her by her given name— smiled, and Gwen wondered if she was thinking of her husband.

Madame had been married only a few years before her French-born husband had been lost at sea. She was not yet twenty at the time. To support herself, she'd become a teacher at Madame Chaussan's Academy and a substitute mother to countless young girls boarded at the school. For whatever reason, Gwen had always been one of her favorites.

"I'm certain Lord Pennington has a fair amount of experience in these matters," Madame said gently. "At least from what Colette has been able to determine."

Gwen groaned. "Is he really dangerous, then?"

She could hear the smile in Madame's voice. "Not unless he continues to ply you with brandy."

"He did not ply me. I plied myself."

How could she have been so stupid? The effects of too much drink were all too apparent in most of the households she'd worked in. How could she have behaved so improperly? And revealed so much? She remembered each and every dreadful word. Of all her regrets about last night, one of the biggest was that she had obviously not consumed enough to forget exactly what she had said. "How can I ever face him again? Surely he thinks I'm nothing but a drunken sot of a bad governess."

Colette laughed. "Nonsense, Gwendolyn. I am certain he thinks nothing of the sort."

"You didn't see me. I was . . ." She could barely think about the evening, let alone discuss it. "I was either quite rude to him or horribly forward. I *asked* him to kiss me." She buried her face in her hands, cloth and all. "He probably thinks I'm not merely a drunken sot of a bad governess but a drunken sot of a bad governess with no manners whatsoever and questionable morals."

"Come now, my dear." Madame patted her on the back. "It's not that bad. He was quite charming when he brought you home. Even rather amused, I think. After all, you're the woman he's going to marry."

"Because he has no choice," she wailed, then winced.

"I have never seen you like this." Concern sounded in Madame's voice. "Of course, it has been five years . . ."

Gwen lifted her head and met her teacher's gaze. "I have never *been* like this. I have taken care of myself and run my life since my father's death. I was not a very good governess, but I was extremely competent when it came to my own survival. I found employment. I avoided scandal. I was at all times quite proper and extremely well mannered. And now look at me." Her lower lip quivered. "I am on the verge of tears, and I never cry. I feel worse than I ever have in my entire life.

And the man I will spend the rest of that life with thinks I am a drunken sot."

"It does sound exceedingly bad when you put it that way," Colette murmured.

Madame cast her a quelling glance. "Don't be absurd. I daresay Pennington will never mention the incident. I doubt he would ever cause a woman deliberate embarrassment. He seems an honorable and decent sort."

"Is he?" Gwen sniffed and struggled to sit upright, trying not to moan. It was past time she stopped coddling herself. She looked at Colette. "What have you learned about him?"

"Quite a bit and all of it good." Colette smiled in reassurance.

If anyone could find out anything about anyone in London, Colette de Chabot could. The widow of a very wealthy man, the French exile had lived in England for more than a decade and retained only the slightest of accents. Colette was allegedly the mistress of a powerful English lord. Someone well positioned in the government or a high-ranking military officer perhaps. Possibly even royalty. Gwen had never asked, and neither Colette nor Madame had ever offered the information. All Gwen really knew was that the gentleman and Colette had been together when she'd first met her teacher's sister-in-law five years ago and were still together today.

Colette took Madame in after her school closed its doors, sending its students to their respective homes. It was a scant month before Gwen's father died. Colette was a few years older than Madame, and while the two women couldn't be more different in their attitudes toward life, they meshed together perfectly and truly considered each other sisters, not merely sisters by marriage.

"You already know his family is quite respectable, his title is unblemished, although"—Colette lowered her voice in a confidential manner—"there was talk of piracy some generations back."

"I believe it was privateering," Madame said with a long-suffering smile. In spite of their affection for one another, each saw the past histories of their respective countries with distinctly different eyes.

Colette brushed away the correction. "I should think that depends entirely on whether you are the pirate or the innocent victim. Regardless, it was far too long ago to worry about. As for Lord Pennington himself, his fortune is quite impressive."

Gwen nodded. "I was fairly certain of that."

"It is always sensible to wed wealth, my dear. You would be wise to remember that for the next marriage. As for this one . . ." Colette thought for a moment. "Your Lord Pennington apparently had a somewhat misspent youth, although not overly so. Nothing that would tarnish his good name for any length of time or linger in society's memory. Indeed, from my inquiries, it was difficult to find anyone who remembered anything specific, just a vague impression of overly high spirits and mildly scandalous behavior. Nothing at all unusual, really.

"As for His Lordship today, he is considered something of a wit. Cool, sophisticated, a man of the world. And as you already know, he is not unattractive."

"Not at all." His green eyes and crooked smile flashed in her mind. "Then he is not especially . . . dangerous? A debaucher of women and all that?"

"Debauchery is exceedingly difficult to hide, word does tend to get out, and I have learned nothing of that sort. As for dangerous . . ." Colette laughed. "*Mon cher*, all interesting men are dangerous, it's what makes them so interesting. And I think your Lord Pennington is extremely interesting."

"And I am going to marry him." Gwen blew a long breath and plucked absently at the coverlet.

Aside from sheer embarrassment and a heartfelt desire to die, her impending marriage dominated her thoughts. Her stomach lurched in a manner that had nothing to do with brandy. "Tomorrow."

"You have not had time to get any new clothes since your return." Madame always was exceedingly practical. "We shall have to find you something appropriate to wear. You can purchase a new wardrobe after the wedding."

"Madame." Gwen met the older woman's eyes. "What am I to do?"

"I thought you had decided the only way to support your nieces is to marry the earl." Madame studied her. "Have you changed your mind?"

"No. But . . ." Gwen wrinkled her nose. "I did not mention them to Mar—Pennington."

Colette laughed. "He shall discover them soon enough when they are living in his house."

"He does not like girls. He was very firm about that. At least I think he was very firm." Gwen rubbed her forehead carefully. "I couldn't bring myself to tell him. I was afraid he would change his mind about marrying me and I would not get the money I need.

"He is not overjoyed at the idea of marrying a woman he does not know, although I do think he likes me a bit. Furthermore, were it not for the people who depend on him for their living, I am not at all certain he wouldn't ignore his father's wishes and thereby give up his fortune. I found his attitude rather admirable if not especially intelligent. He has never been poor, you know."

Madame considered her for a moment. "I assume you have given some thought to what you shall do with the girls"

"Actually, I have." Gwen drew a deep breath. "Once I am married, I will have my own money. I intend to hire a staff, for the house in the country. They shall live there, and I will visit them as often as possible. It won't be for very long," she said quickly. "I plan to tell Pennington about them when the moment is right. However"—she sat a bit straighter— "until he can welcome them without restraint, I shall not say a word. I will not allow them to live anywhere where they are not wanted."

Colette and Madame traded glances.

Gwen drew a deep breath. "I am sorry about last night. It was their first night with me and I certainly did not intend to abandon them. All I had planned was to speak to Lord Pennington, then return here. Are they very upset with me?"

Colette sighed. "They do not seem overly fond of you."

"You must understand, my dear," Madame said

quickly. "They have been through a great deal since the deaths of their parents. They have been shuffled around the world, not knowing where they would land, until they ended up with your cousin. And apparently she was not overly pleased to have them show up on her doorstep."

Colette sniffed in disdain. "A vile woman, no doubt."

"That's of no significance now." Madame's tone was firm. "The point is, their mother filled their heads with talk of how they should take care of one another. How *sisters* should take care of one another. Extremely wise on her part, I should think, given what I understand about the rather adventurous life the family led. At any rate, the girls fully expected their mother's sister to come to their rescue, and you did not." Madame shrugged. "Regardless of the fact that you neither knew of your sister's death nor of their existence, their resentment of you is quite understandable."

"Of course," Gwen murmured. "How stupid of me not to have realized that."

"Not at all," Colette said staunchly. "Your sister has had no contact with you from the time she left home. You could not be expected to feel any obligation to her whatsoever."

"Nonetheless, I should have—"

"Gwendolyn," Madame said firmly. "What has passed is past. All that matters now is what you do from this moment forward. And you must start by telling Lord Pennington."

"Absolutely not." Gwen shook her head. "Not until we are married and I am firmly ensconced as his wife. I will not risk his sending them away."

"But the power at the moment is in your hands." Colette frowned. "Do you not understand that? If you demand he allow these girls to live with you as a condition of the marriage, he will have no choice."

"I won't do that." Gwen struggled to find the right words, but her thoughts made very little sense. "I have already made certain I have control of my inheritance as well as my house. I cannot demand more of him. He is, well, *nice*, and probably deserves better than what he is getting. Besides, if I bring them into a house where they are not wanted, they'll grow up thinking . . . they'll feel . . ."

"As you did, my dear?" Madame said gently.

Gwen nodded. "If I can do nothing else for them, I can do that much."

"Very well. We suspected that would be your decision." Colette glanced at her sister-in-law. Madame nodded. "Therefore we have decided the girls shall remain here with us until you feel Lord Pennington is amenable to their presence."

"That's very kind of you, but I could not possibly—"

"Of course you can," Madame said with a smile. "In truth, their presence will liven up our lives. I quite miss being around young girls. They were delightful last night and far older than their ages. We chatted and played cards together."

"I owe them a great deal of money," Colette said under her breath. "Nonetheless, they are charming, and we shall get on quite well together."

"But"—Gwen pulled her brows together—"what of your . . . friend? Won't he object?"

"This is my home and I shall do precisely as I wish

here." Colette waved offhandedly. "As it happens, he is unavailable for a time, and I am quite at a loss for something to fill my idle moments."

"Besides . . ." Madame placed her hand over Gwen's. "I feel this is the least I can do for you. Since the moment I learned of the mistake that caused you to set out on your own, I have regretted my part in it. I should never have helped you find that first position that took you to America. I should have known better."

"Don't be absurd." Gwen covered Madame's hand with her own. "I would have found some other means of escape. Indeed, my actions were both impulsive and stupid but you are not to blame."

"Still . . ." Madame sighed. "If I hadn't provided my assistance, your life would have been much different. Mr. Whiting would have located you much sooner. Why, you might even have had a season and—"

"Forgive me, but did you not just say what's done is done and we should go on from here?" Gwen's voice carried a teasing note. "You should follow your own advice."

"I have told her that on any number of occasions," Colette said loftily. "As well as offering her the benefit of my wisdom. She is barely eight and twenty and I think she should be married again herself."

Madame's eyes sparked. "Just as I think you would do well to follow that wisdom yourself and stop wasting your life on a man—"

"If you're certain then, about allowing the girls to live here," Gwen cut in. This was obviously an ongoing debate between the women and just as obviously had no resolution.

Colette huffed. "On that, we are agreed."

A wonderful sense of relief filled Gwen. Her nieces could not be in better hands than Madame's or more interesting hands than Colette's. Their generous offer lifted a load off Gwen that had settled hard on her shoulders yesterday afternoon and set her course firmly toward marriage with Marcus. She beamed at the dear ladies. "I am most grateful. I have no doubt they will not be with you for long. Pennington seems to be rather surprisingly nice; did I say he was nice? He is very nice."

Colette considered her carefully. "Are you falling in love with this man? Already?"

"Or"—Madame eyes narrowed—"*could* you fall in love with this man?"

"I have not fallen in love with him. I have just met him," Gwen said to Colette, then turned to Madame. "And furthermore I have no intention of falling in love with him. Love is a horrible trap for women, and I shall do all in my power to avoid it. I do, however, think we can have an excellent relationship built on respect and the kind of affection one feels for a very good friend."

"You are so young." Colette laughed. "And so foolish."

"I am not foolish." Indignation sounded in Gwen's voice. "I am . . . practical."

Madame grinned. "I do wish you luck in your practicality but I will warn you: love is not something one can either avoid or attract. It sweeps upon you unexpectedly, like a midsummer storm."

"Catching you in a grip of iron and velvet," Colette

said, "filling your heart with emotion you never dreamed of."

"With joy and sometimes sorrow." An odd, dreamy look crossed Madame's face. "A small price to pay for the glory of being one with another human being. Of sharing his thoughts and his feelings. Of knowing, with him, you are whole, as you have never been before. He is the missing part of your soul."

"Love brings you to life." The look on Colette's face matched Madame's. "One is never more aware or alive than when one is in love."

"And you know you cannot live without him." Madame's voice was soft. "And you know as well you would gladly die with him. Or for him."

Gwen stared at the women, both caught in their own thoughts, one obviously remembering what she had lost, the other what she still had.

"That's all very well and good," Gwen started, "but I have no intention—"

A knock sounded at the door and it immediately pushed open. Hope poked her head in. "Are you awake yet?"

"At last." Gwen forced a weak smile.

"Capital." Hope bounded into the room, followed closely by Patience. A reluctant Charity trailed behind. "We brought you something." Hope stepped to the bed and pulled forth an open bottle she had hidden behind her back.

"Champagne?" Madame raised a brow.

Colette peered at the bottle. "Very good champagne." She slanted the girls a chastising look. "*My* very good champagne."

They ignored her.

Hope settled on the bed beside Colette. Patience perched on the arm of Madame's chair and handed her a glass.

"Papa said there is nothing better for the day after one has had a great deal to drink than champagne," Patience said, taking the bottle from Hope and filling a glass.

Gwen forced a light note to her voice. "What makes you think I had a great deal to drink?"

Charity snorted. "We saw you come in last night."

"We were watching from the parlor." Patience handed Gwen the glass. "That gentleman carried you into the house. We thought it was extremely gallant of him."

"Yes, I suppose it was," Gwen said weakly and took a cautious sip.

"Who was he? He was quite handsome." Hope grinned. "And very dashing."

Gwen looked at Madame, then Colette. Neither said a word. It was up to Gwen. "That was Lord Pennington. My"—she was hard-pressed not to choke on the word—"betrothed."

"How lovely." Patience's eyes lit with excitement. "Is he rich? He looks rich."

Gwen nodded. "He is quite wealthy."

"Will we all live together, then?" Hope asked.

Again Gwen looked to her friends for assistance, and again none was forthcoming. She took another sip of the wine and drew a steadying breath. "Lord Pennington, while a very nice man, is not prepared at the moment for all of us."

"Oh." Hope's expression fell.

"Dear." Disappointment showed on Patience's face.

"Then what is to become of us?" Charity said sharply.

"Charity," Madame said in a no-nonsense voice.

Charity blushed and muttered at the floor. "That was rude of me. I am sorry."

"It's quite all right." Gwen smiled at her. "I understand life has been most unsettled for you. And now I have dragged you here—"

"We like it here," Patience said quickly. "The food is very good and Madame Freneau and Madame de Chabot are great fun."

Hope leaned forward in a confidential manner. "They're not very good at cards though."

Colette snorted.

"Then would you mind terribly staying with them for a bit?" Gwen looked at Hope. "It shouldn't be for too long, I hope." She turned to Patience. "Just until I can get Lord Pennington used to the idea of a . . . a family." She met Charity's resentful gaze. "I will not leave you. I promise."

Suspicion shone in the older girl's face. "Do you?"

Gwen nodded. "I do."

"Swear it." Charity's gaze was unflinching, and Gwen realized how important this was if they were to have any sort of future together.

"I swear it."

"Then you must do the blood oath," Patience said firmly. "It's the bond that ties us together, and should anyone break it"—her voice lowered dramatically—"there will be hell to pay."

Madame raised a brow.

"Well, there will." Patience huffed.

"A blood oath?" Gwen grimaced. "I'm not sure I'm up to a blood oath."

"Oh, we don't use blood." Hope rolled her eyes as if no one would be so silly as to think blood was actually involved in a blood oath. "That would hurt rather a lot."

"Then what do we use?" Gwen was almost afraid of the answer.

"Spit. It's the next best thing to blood." Patience spit on her index finger and held it up. Her sisters followed suit. All three held up their fingers. "See."

"One can scarcely avoid seeing," Colette murmured.

"Your turn." The challenge in Charity's voice echoed the challenge in her eye.

"Very well." Without pause Gwen spit on the index finger of her free hand and held it up. "Now what?"

"Now we all rub our fingers together." Hope cast Colette a pointed look. "All of us."

Madame bit back a smile, promptly spit on her finger, and held it up.

"I am not making any sworn promises here." Colette folded her arms over her chest. "I see no reason why I should have to spit on anything."

Hope leaned forward and whispered something in her ear. Colette sighed. "Very well then." She spit and showed her finger. "I hope you are all quite happy now."

"Now we have to each touch our finger to someone else's." Patience touched Gwen's, then turned to Colette. "Until everyone has touched everyone else and all our blood has mingled. And repeat after me." Patience lowered her voice dramatically. "I promise by all the blood in my veins that I shall never break this oath or suffer the dire, horrible, consequences. Forever."

The gathering repeated the vow and continued the ceremony in an appropriately solemn manner until everyone had shared her "blood" with everyone else.

Colette promptly whipped out a kerchief, wiped her hand, and passed it to Madame. "Well, that was indeed an unusual experience."

"And calls for a celebration," Madame said thoughtfully. "I believe Cook is baking something delightful, and I daresay it might be ready for sampling."

At once, Patience and Hope slid off the bed and headed toward the door.

Charity started after them, then stopped. "I didn't think you would do it. I thought you were too . . . stiff to be any fun."

"To be quite honest, neither did I. I have always been exceedingly stiff." Gwen grinned. "But I suspect we shall all be doing any number of things in the future we do not anticipate."

Charity cast Gwen a grudging smile and followed after her sisters.

"That was a most auspicious beginning." Madame cast a smile at her former student. "You have said what a bad governess you were, yet seeing you with them I am hard-pressed to believe it."

"It's different with them." Gwen thought for a moment. "Charity was right, I have always been extremely stiff with the children in my charge. I have never been able to understand them. But with these three, I feel as if we are somehow bound together."

"It's the blood." Colette stared at her finger with disgust. "Blood is always the tie that binds."

"And love," Madame added.

"Love?" Could Gwen indeed love these girls? She wasn't sure she could love anyone and wasn't sure she wanted to. Love was a frightening proposition and was not a guarantee of faithfulness or security. It would not prevent abandonment by choice or fate or death.

"And speaking of love," Colette adopted a brisk tone, "we must get back to serious matters. You are to be married tomorrow and it will not do if you are not thoroughly prepared, as it were."

Gwen downed the remaining champagne, acknowledging that while the wine did indeed make her feel better, the topic of discussion left her almost as queasy as the brandy. Still, it could not be avoided. And it was probably a good idea to know not only what she should expect from him but what he might expect from her.

What he might *like* from her.

Abruptly she remembered the altogether remarkable sensation of his lips on hers. The amazing warmth of his body against hers. The way her own seemed to melt against him of its own accord. The delightful ache that rose from somewhere deep inside her and washed away all rational thought and urged her to cling to him. And demand more.

At once she understood exactly what Colette and Madame had been trying to explain about intimacies and the pleasure one could find. And understood as well she wanted to know more.

"Gwendolyn, are you listening?"

"Yes." Gwen nodded slowly. "And I believe I have a number of questions." She smiled with the memory of how lovely his touch had been and the realization that it was just a taste. "And a great deal to learn."

Chapter Seven

No matter how clever or sophisticated a man may appear,
he is merely clay waiting to be shaped
by the hand of a superior woman.
It is, however, best not to let him know this.

Helena Pennington

"You look lovely, my dear." Lady Pennington beamed at her new daughter-in-law. "I must tell you again how delighted I am to welcome you to the family."

"Thank you, Lady Pennington," Gwen murmured, struggling against the dreamlike sensation of being caught in an irresistible current of events and people.

It had been a scant few hours since the late-morning ceremony at Pennington House had forever transformed Gwen from Miss Townsend to Lady Pennington. Marcus had seemed almost as nervous as she for the most part until she had been officially pronounced his wife. Then his gaze had met hers, he'd smiled wryly and brushed a kiss across her cheek, pausing to whisper into her ear, "There is no turning back now . . . Miss Townsend."

He'd said her name as if it were a term of endearment, and an odd excitement skipped down her spine.

She'd scarcely exchanged more than a word or two with him since. While the wedding itself was private, with only Madames Freneau and de Chabot, Lady Pennington, and Lord Berkley present, shortly after the ceremony an endless stream of callers had begun, flitting through the grand hall and gracious rooms of Pennington House. They'd come alone or in couples, at first staying only long enough to wish the newlyweds well, but now the visitors lingered and the large parlor would soon overflow. Even Marcus looked surprised at their number. Many were apparently friends of Lady Pennington's, and Gwen suspected the lady had discreetly encouraged them to meet and welcome Marcus's new wife. Most she had met thus far were quite nice. She had been introduced to Lord Berkley's mother as well as the Duchess of Roxborough and Lord and Lady Helmsley. Others were equally pleasant but made no effort to hide their curiosity.

And why should they? The Earl of Pennington was an outstanding match, and it was only natural that there would be a great deal of speculation about the virtual stranger who had ended the career of this most eligible bachelor.

"Oh no, that won't do at all. You mustn't call me Lady Pennington. It's far too formal and there are two of us now. Two Lady Penningtons that is." Marcus's mother thought for a moment. "You could use my given name, Helena, although that doesn't seem quite right either, does it? Or you could always call me"—she paused and seemed to hold her breath—"Mama."

"Mama," Gwen said carefully, placing the emphasis on the second syllable in the French manner as Lady Pennington had. She'd been so young when her own mother had died she had no real memory of her. "I should like that."

"Wonderful." Relief flooded the lady's face, and she beamed. "I never had a daughter, you know, and I am quite looking forward to having one now. I think we shall get on famously together." She hooked her arm through Gwen's and led her toward a small group standing near the windows on the far wall. "Granddaughters would be lovely as well."

"Lord Pennington does not seem overly fond of the idea of daughters." Gwen grimaced. "However, he is quite enthused by the prospect of sons."

"Of course he would be, my dear. All men in his position are. Still, I do suspect he would like daughters as well. He was my only child, and I've always thought it a great pity. He's quite delightful on those family occasions when he's around children. Nothing more than an overlarge child himself now and then."

Gwen stared. "Are we speaking of the same Lord Pennington?"

The older woman laughed. "It is hard to believe, I know. For whatever reason, my son has developed an overly cool, too droll, and rather aloof way of looking at the world that, while entertaining, serves to put a bit of distance between him and others." She paused thoughtfully. "His public demeanor is distinctly different from his private manner. I do hope he will share that part of himself with you. Lord knows, he doesn't share with me."

Perhaps he already had. Gwen remembered his impassioned address on the night he'd proposed and his confession that his friends thought him unemotional and too collected. But there were those moments, in the brief time they'd shared thus far, when he retreated behind an amused and remote façade. Of course, Gwen too had a public manner far different from her private self.

"I should warn you, Gwendolyn, sons grow up and go their own way, disregarding your wishes or advice. However, I have heard daughters are daughters all of their days." She squeezed Gwen's arm affectionately. "And I am so pleased to have one now."

"I am pleased as well, my lady." Gwen forced a pleasant smile and wished she didn't feel quite so awkward. But aside from Madame and Colette, she'd never been freely offered affection from anyone before. Affection that asked nothing in return. It was most disconcerting.

Marcus's mother studied her for a moment, then smiled her son's wry smile. "Oh dear. I see you have a great deal in common with my son. This is indeed an interesting match."

"I have no idea what you are telling her, Mother, but I am certain I would not like it." Marcus appeared at Gwen's side. "However, I would like to steal my bride"—he said the word smoothly, as if he had practiced—"for a few moments, if you have no objections."

"Marcus." Lady Pennington's brow furrowed in admonishment. "There are any number of people here who would like to meet her. She is, after all is said and done, the new Countess of Pennington."

"She is, after all is said and done, my wife," Marcus said firmly, and took Gwen by the arm. "I've been told the garden is in bloom, and I should like you to see it." He steered her toward the door.

"It is lovely but you have never been especially interested in the gardens. I don't see . . ." His mother's exasperated sigh lingered behind them. "Do try not to keep her too long."

A muscle in Marcus's jaw ticked and his voice was low. "Wouldn't want to do that."

He led her out of the parlor, along a grand corridor, and through a gallery lined with portraits of what she assumed were previous Earls of Pennington and their assorted progeny, and into what was apparently a conservatory, although she had no idea precisely where she was in the grand house. And he did so at a speed that precluded any attempt she might make at conversation.

"Do you really want me to see the gardens?" Gwen struggled to keep up with him.

"Yes, of course," he said absently, practically pulling her along behind him. "They're lovely."

"Or so you've been told." She tried, and failed, to match her pace to his. "You certainly don't strike me as the type of man who is especially given to the appreciation of nature."

"I have a great appreciation of nature." His tone was as brisk as his stride. "I quite like the out-of-doors."

"As do I." She gasped.

"I find it easier to breathe freely with the skies overhead and the earth beneath my feet. In point of fact, while I do spend a great deal of my time in town, it is, in truth, the countryside I prefer. Do you—" He glanced down at her and stopped so abruptly she nearly smacked into him. "I say, are you all right?"

"Quite, no thanks to you." She glared up at him. "I realize your need to *breathe freely* might well overcome all other considerations, but you cannot drag me along at breakneck speed and expect me not to feel a bit of a strain. You are considerably taller and considerably faster and—"

Without warning he laughed.

"What on earth is so funny?" She planted her hands on her hips. "I see nothing amusing about being hauled through your house—"

"Your house as well now," he said with a grin.

"Even worse," she snapped.

"I do apologize if I have been overly eager to escape the crowd we have found ourselves besieged by."

A footman she hadn't noticed stepped forward from the shadows to pull open a door Gwen hadn't noted either.

Marcus directed her toward the exit. "I simply assumed you too needed a respite."

She stepped past him and onto a broad flagstone terrace. It was thoughtful of him to consider her, even if, for whatever reason, she wasn't ready to acknowledge such thoughtfulness at the moment. It was just so blasted *nice* of him. "It was something of a crush, wasn't it? I admit, I was rather surprised and indeed somewhat—"

"Overwhelmed?" He smiled in a too knowing manner and tucked her hand in the crook of his elbow.

"Perhaps." She gazed up at him coolly. "A bit."

"Well, I admit I was more than a bit overwhelmed myself. I suspect the inundation here was my mother's doing. Most of those who have so coincidentally descended on us this afternoon are friends of hers." He guided Gwen toward the edge of the terrace and steps leading down into a formal garden. "Don't look behind you."

"Why? Is someone following us?"

"Only with their eyes." He glanced back at the house. "There are any number of people, my mother prime among them, discreetly peering at us from the parlor windows."

"Really?" She resisted the urge to check. "Why?"

A corner of his mouth quirked upward, and at once she knew the answer. Heat flushed up her face. "Oh my."

"However"—his hand slipped down her arm to firmly grasp her hand—"while this garden is not especially large, it is designed so that those seeking privacy from observation need simply descend the stair and follow the path along the wall of the terrace to a secluded niche protected by marble guardians. It comes in quite handy at balls and soirées and the like for intimate assignations."

"And you have firsthand knowledge of this?"

His grin said more than mere words and was most annoying.

"So are we seeking privacy, my lord?" There was a slight flirtatious lilt to her voice, and she wondered where on earth that had come from.

"We are," he said without hesitation and started down the steps, his fingers firmly entwined with hers. She had no choice but to accompany him. And no desire to do otherwise. "We have a great deal to talk about."

"I see. So the privacy you seek in the gardens is for nothing more than discussion?"

He ignored the question. "Have you noticed how few of our callers have expressed surprise at the news of our nuptials?"

She nodded. "And those who have do not seem especially sincere."

"They are dreadful actors, one and all." His brows pulled together thoughtfully. "It is probably of no significance, but as it has been less than a week since the need to marry surfaced and no more than two days since you agreed to do so, it strikes me as exceedingly odd that the majority of my mother's acquaintances are not so much as mildly surprised by our abrupt and unexpected wedding."

They reached the foot of the stairs and started down the walkway. "Does it matter?"

"Probably not." He continued on until the path curved away from the wall, then abruptly widened to a circular alcove sheltered by high, clipped hedges.

A stone bench sat positioned toward the back of the alcove, concealed behind a life-sized marble statue of three women with arms entwined. They stood on an oval-shaped base rising a good three feet above the ground. It was an extremely large piece overall, carved in the classic Greek style and quite lovely. She gazed up at the towering figures whose own eyes were cast modestly downward and couldn't help but wonder what the mythical trio of Muses or Graces or something equally as whimsical thought of the activities that apparently took place here right beneath their noses.

"My, this is private," she murmured, peering around the statue. Two people could easily remain hidden behind it, lingering on the bench unobserved.

"Do you mind?" A wry half smile lifted his lips. "Being alone here? With me?"

"Not at all." She pulled her hand from his and stepped toward the statue as if there was nothing more in the world she wished to do than study the work. As if she hadn't the slightest desire to put a bit of distance between them. As if she was not aware of every breath he took. "I suspect we shall spend a great deal of our time alone together in the future." Her voice remained aloof, remote, but there was the oddest fluttering deep in her midsection.

"No doubt." He too stepped closer, as if he too wished to study the ladies in their classical poses and marble gowns. Was his interest as feigned as hers? "Do you like it?"

She started. "Being alone with you?"

"I was talking about the statue," he said lightly.

He had the decency not to look at her or crack so much as the slightest smile. Her cheeks burned, and she was grateful for his courtesy. He studied the figures before him, his brow furrowed in a considering manner. "What do you think?"

"It's lovely, of course." She ran her hand over the carved folds of the gown of the nearest figure. Smooth and cold against her fingers, still oddly warm from his touch. "Is it original? From ancient Greece, I mean?"

"I doubt it, but it could be, I suppose." Marcus shrugged. "It's been here as long as I can remember."

"And you are nearly thirty. That is ancient," she said, again surprised at the teasing note in her voice. What was wrong with her? In spite of her resolve to show him nothing more than courtesy and perhaps a cordial friendship, she was definitely flirting with the man.

The unbidden memory of his lips on hers flashed through her mind, and she cast him a surreptitious glance. His gaze remained fixed on the statue, and she stifled an oddly disappointed sigh. He was right; she would know when he intended to kiss her, and it was obvious he had no such intentions now.

"Indeed." He nodded in a somber manner. "Miss Townsend?" He glanced curiously at her. "What were your intentions?"

I intended to allow you to kiss me. She pushed aside the abrupt and shocking thought. "What do you mean?"

"Regarding your life. If you did not wish to wed, what were your plans?"

"My plans?"

"Surely you had some thoughts about your future? Some sort of course of action as to how you would spend the rest of your days?"

"Why no," she said, as surprised to hear the words as he. "I don't believe I did."

He raised a brow.

"Oh, don't look at me as if I were an idiot, Marcus."

Impatience sounded in her voice. "As hard as this may be to believe for a man of your nature, since the death of my father I have scarcely thought further than the next day or the next position. I never particularly considered the future, in truth, I never had the luxury of time in which to do so, and I suppose I never really suspected there was much of a future to consider."

He folded his arms over his chest and leaned back against the statue. "What do you mean by *a man of my nature?*"

Her hand rested on the marble a scant inch or so from him and she resisted the urge to rest it on his arm and instead let it drop to her side. "I simply meant a man as confident, as reserved as you are."

He started to say something but she waved him silent. "Oh, I have not forgotten your comments the other day as to your sentimental streak, although I'm not entirely sure I believe it." She considered him for a moment. "I cannot imagine you being swept away by emotion for more than an instant or two. Nor can I imagine you not having your life perfectly laid out for you. Planned down to the tiniest detail."

He stared for a moment. "I believe, Miss Townsend, you may well have insulted me."

"It was not my intention."

"That's something at any rate," he muttered. "Down to the tiniest detail, you say?"

"Yes."

"Then apparently I planned"—his eyes twinkled with amusement—"you and I."

"Of course not, that was—"

"Fate, Miss Townsend," he said firmly. "More and more I believe you and I were destined to come together."

"That's nonsense, my lord, why would you think that?"

"We could start with your history. A simple mistake on the part of an inexperienced solicitor, and you are off for parts unknown and a life completely foreign to the one you expected to lead. You thereby sacrificed a proper season and any number of opportunities to meet suitable matches and marry long before we met."

"But I had no desire to wed," she said primly. "Therefore the possibility—"

"May I continue?"

She sighed. "I daresay I can't stop you."

"I, on the other hand, had any number of chances to marry, yet I did not. Why?"

"Because you find the usual process of choosing a wife too businesslike and impersonal?" she said sweetly.

"Ah, the joys of having a wife who listens to her husband." His tone was wry. "And better yet, to have a wife who will throw your statements back at you. I can see I am in for a good time of it."

"Thank you, my lord." She grinned.

"As you have so thoughtfully pointed out, I have found the usual methods not to my taste. Nor have I been lucky, or unlucky enough given my observation of Berkley's experiences, to fall under the spell of love. Therefore, when the moment came that you entered my life and my father's bizarre plot was revealed, I was free to marry you." He flashed a smug smile. "Fate."

She laughed in spite of herself. "I scarcely think a series of random events equates fate."

"Fate is a series of random events, or seemingly random events, that culminate in a specific outcome. In this case, you and I." Triumph colored his face. "I believe we are fated to be together. It is somehow right. Even proper, as it were."

She shook her heard. "I believe that's the most—"

"There's more. Would you care to hear it?"

"As it is so very entertaining, even if total absurdity." She lifted a shoulder in a casual shrug, refusing to reveal so much as a hint of her intrigue with his claim. "Please do continue."

"Very well." He straightened and paced before the statue. "When you originally told me you had never planned to marry I wondered what plans you did have for your life. Now that you have confessed you had not considered your future, it is clear to me that our marriage is the best course of action for you. Certainly our fathers thought so. It may even perhaps be what you were always meant to do."

"Is it?"

"Indeed it is. However, fate aside, I am not so foolish as to believe that what happens from here on is as destined as the forces that have brought us together. I strongly suspect the future now is up to us."

"Really? So fate brought us together but may not necessarily keep us together."

"Something like that."

"How inconvenient."

He glanced at her. "I assure you it made a great deal of sense when it first came to mind."

She bit back a smile. "I'm certain it did."

"At any rate, this brings me to the point I wish to make."

"There was a point?"

He stopped and met her gaze. "I have a proposition for you."

"A proposition?" She tilted her head and studied him cautiously. "We are already married. I can't imagine what kind of proposition you have in mind."

"It's quite simple. I propose that you, that we, do our best to make our marriage a successful one. In addition to our previously agreed-upon terms, I shall do all in my power to be a thoughtful and considerate husband."

"And I?"

"You shall strive with equal fervor to be a good wife and fulfill your position as my countess. If, after a specified amount of time, we find we do not suit well enough to continue we may both go our separate ways."

Her breath caught. "Divorce?"

"No, no, I am sorry, my dear, but I could never agree to divorce. The scandal would be detrimental to both our futures as well as to our"—he cleared his throat—"children."

"Our sons," she said wryly.

He nodded. "What I had in mind was more the type of arrangement so many couples seem to be content with. You will retain your title and position always but we will simply live separate lives."

"I see," she said slowly, a heavy lump settling in the pit of her stomach. "It does seem like a, well, plan for the future. How long a period do you have in mind?"

"I was thinking five years would be a suitable amount of time."

"Five years," she murmured. "It seems at once like a lifetime and yet not long at all."

His expression brightened. "Ten years, then?"

"An entire decade?"

His brow furrowed. "You think it's too long?"

"Perhaps seven and a half years would be better," she said, the lightness in her tone belying the weight in her stomach. They'd scarce been married a day and already he was talking about living separate lives. Not that that wasn't exactly what she wanted. He had simply thought of it first.

"A compromise." He grinned. "I can agree to that."

"Excellent." She clasped her hands behind her back and circled the statue in a slow and deliberate manner. She waited until he was hidden from her view, then drew a deep breath. "I do wonder, though, if I am not now the one who should be insulted."

There was a long pause. His voice was somber. "It was not my intention."

"I didn't think it was. Still, a proposition such as yours is not precisely what a lady wishes to hear on the day of her wedding."

A soft curse sounded from behind the statue. "Miss Townsend, I—"

"Do you know how ridiculous *Miss Townsend* sounds?" she said in a sharper tone than she intended.

There was another pause. "You wanted me to call you Miss Townsend."

"But I'm not Miss anything anymore. I'm"—she swallowed hard—"Lady Pennington."

"Do you want me to call you Lady Pennington, then?" Confusion sounded in his voice. Vaguely endearing, actually.

"No, of course not." She heaved a heavy sigh. "You may call me Gwendolyn now. Or Gwen. We are, after all, man and wife."

"Gwendolyn." Her name drifted lightly on the breeze. "It's beautiful and it suits you. Still, I think I much prefer"—she could hear the smile in his voice— "Miss Townsend."

"My lord." She huffed and started around the statue toward him. "Marcus." She reached the point where she thought he was and stopped. He was nowhere in sight. "Marcus?"

"We are going round in circles. Perhaps not the best way to begin a marriage." His voice sounded from the opposite side of the statue, precisely where she had been a moment before. His voice sobered. "But stay where you are for a moment. This might well be easier to say without having to gaze into those lovely blue eyes of yours."

"You think my eyes are lovely?"

"I think everything about you is lovely. I think"—he paused and his voice was firm—"I am an extraordinarily lucky man."

"Do you?" Her heart thudded in her chest.

"I do. And I further think that you, and marriage to you, might well be the best thing to happen to me."

"Yet you propose the end of the marriage before it has even begun," she said without thinking.

"I only did so because this arrangement is more to my benefit than yours. I thought it only fair that you have . . . that you know . . . well . . . blast it all, Miss Townsend. *Gwen.* I am not good at this."

"Of course, you have never done it before." She couldn't help but smile. She noted he seemed to make her smile a great deal.

"If my proposal is not to your liking . . ." His voice drew closer.

"No, wait. Don't come any closer. You're right. It's easier to speak one's mind about such matters without being face-to-face." She paused to gather her thoughts. "And I think you're right about your proposition as well. This is a marriage neither of us planned, although I for one am willing to make the best of it."

"Are you?"

"Yes." She nodded firmly, more for herself than for him. "I have given it a great deal of thought in the last few days. I don't know if indeed it is right and proper or fated but it may indeed be the best thing. For both of us. For now anyway. And I am willing to try exceedingly hard to be a good countess and"—she lifted her chin— "wife."

"But will you allow yourself to like me?" Marcus's voice sounded right behind her.

She jumped and swiveled sharply. "Not if you constantly sneak up on me."

"It seemed like a good idea. And I have only snuck up on you once." The corner of his lips quirked upward in that charmingly crooked manner of his.

"Once is enough, thank you."

"So you will give me seven and a half years, then?"

"Not at all, Marcus." She met his gaze directly. "I will give *us* seven and a half years."

"I quite like the sound of *us*." He glanced upward at the figures towering over them. "And I think they approve."

"Do you? Why?"

"Because this is probably all their doing." He nodded at the marble women towering over them. "Do you know who they are?"

"Muses? No," she said quickly. "There are three of them. The Graces then? Their Greek names escape me, but they were Splendor, Good Cheer, and I can't remember the last."

"Mirth," he said with a grin. "You're right about the names but these are not the three Graces."

"No?" she said cautiously, wondering what he was up to now.

"No. These are the daughters of the Goddess of Necessity." He nodded at the statue. "The figure on the left is Clothos, the weaver of life. In the middle is Lachesis, who measures life, and this is Atropos, who cuts the thread of life and thereby ends it. These, my dear, are the Fates."

"I should have known." She pulled her brows together. "Did you plan this?"

"Not I." He looked upward significantly. "However, they—"

She laughed. "Marcus, stop it at once." Her gaze met his. Amusement lingered in his eyes. "You are like a dog with a bone. Honestly, you simply will not . . ." The look in his eyes changed, deepened, and gave her pause. The deep green of his gaze simmered, delightful and dangerous. She caught her breath and said the first thing that came to mind. "What else do you think they have planned for us?"

"For the future?" His gaze slipped to her lips and back to her eyes. He had moved closer, so close she could touch him easily. Her lips could meet his without the least bit of effort.

At once she thought of the advice Colette and Madame had given her about what would happen in his bed.

Too late to turn back, Miss Townsend.

It no longer seemed as distasteful or inconvenient as it had initially. Indeed, there was an intense yearning growing inside her to feel his flesh naked against hers. It was a thought at once shocking and exciting.

"We should probably return to the parlor," he said softly. "They will be wondering where we have gotten to. And wondering as well . . ." His gaze again drifted to her lips, and she leaned forward slightly, hoping, wanting him to take her in his arms. He drew a deep breath and straightened. "Precisely what we have been up to."

"Of course," she murmured, brushing aside a distinct touch of disappointment.

He took her hand and started toward the house, then abruptly turned and pulled her hand to his lips. "I am rather looking forward to the next seven and a half years." His gaze bored into hers. "And quite looking forward to tonight."

"As am I," she said, more to herself than him.

He flashed her a quick grin, then started back along the path, her hand still in his.

Gwen couldn't quite hide a bemused smile, no doubt due to nothing more than all his talk about fate and their marriage being right and proper. It was silly, of course, but what if he was right? It was no more un-likely than anything else that had happened to her in re-cent days. The oddest thought struck her that this virtual stranger might well be all she'd ever wanted and never known she'd wanted until him.

She wondered if it was indeed fate, right and proper.

And wondered how he would feel when he learned about the secret she kept from him.

And wondered as well why she cared.

Chapter Eight

*A man never knows more than
a woman wishes him to.*

Helena Pennington

"What am I supposed to do now, Reggie?" Marcus's low tone echoed the questions muddling his mind, and he paced the width of the library.

The viscount was the last guest still lingering at the end of an endless day filled with far too many people casting far too many speculative looks and knowing glances, and far too little time—indeed, no time at all after their brief moments in the garden—to spend alone with his wife. The afternoon had turned to evening, and an impromptu wedding dinner celebration with a discreet handful of people.

His mother had taken the opportunity to gently begin advising Gwendolyn about the behavior expected of a countess. If asked beforehand, Marcus would have said he would much prefer to run screaming into the night naked rather than bear witness to such an exchange. But much to his surprise, both Lady Penningtons seemed to reach a silent understanding he was not privy to. Nor, he suspected, would any man be privy to it. There was an obvious and immediate bond forged between the woman who had always wanted a daughter and the woman who had never known a mother. Marcus was pleased, of course, yet it was most disconcerting to note more than one private smile shared between the two of them. Amusement he strongly suspected was at his expense.

He'd had precious little opportunity yet to share much more than a mere smile with his bride. Her eyes had met his now and again through the course of the day, across the crowded room, and later the dining table. They had exchanged a few lighthearted comments, a bit of casual banter, but always in the presence of others. She visibly relaxed as the day progressed, and in spite of her years in service, was not the least bit intimidated, displaying natural wit and effortless grace. Marcus was both pleased and awed. She was so much more than he had expected, or hoped for.

Yet, for him, she remained as difficult to decipher as an unknown language. He had absolutely no idea what was going on behind those lovely blue eyes. What were her thoughts? Her plans. Her desires.

"I suspect you should do what any man on his wedding night does." Reggie sprawled in his usual chair and watched Marcus with undisguised amusement.

"That's not what I was speaking of, and you well know it, but now that you've brought it up. . . ." Marcus blew a frustrated breath. "I have never had a wedding night. Never had a bride. And I certainly have never—"

Reggie snorted. "You most certainly have.

Marcus cast him a withering look. "As I was attempting to say, I have never shared my bed with a woman who has never been with a man. Damn it all, Reggie, I have never made love to a virgin."

"Never?"

"No."

"Surely when you were just beginning?"

"Just beginning?"

"In your youth?"

"Never." Marcus's voice was firm.

"Are you sure?"

Marcus considered the question, then shook his head. "As certain as a man can be."

"What about your, you know, the first time you—"

"My uncle's mistress?" Marcus laughed. "I daresay she might have dressed as a virgin on occasion; my uncle had notoriously unique if relatively harmless tastes, if you recall, but there any resemblance to virginity ended."

"You never told me she was your first." Reggie's eyes narrowed. "In fact, I distinctly recall you saying—"

"Implied, Reggie. I never *said* anything. At any rate, I was a mere boy at the time. I can scarcely be held accountable for what I might have led you to believe. In truth, I don't remember what I said at all."

"I remember," Reggie said darkly. "I remember my feelings of jealousy as well. She was exceedingly—"

"She was indeed." Marcus smiled in spite of himself. "She was quite . . . creative."

"Creative." Reggie emitted a sound somewhere between a groan and a sigh, the same painfully envious sound he'd made every time this particular topic had come up since their youth. Marcus wondered if Reggie would ever notice the story became more embellished with each telling. And the lady in question more creative.

"Very well, then." Reggie's brow furrowed. "Let me think. There was also a housemaid . . . pretty, fair-haired. You remember, she worked at the manor the summer before we started off to school. Wasn't she—"

"As she seduced me, with skills far beyond her years, I scarcely think so."

"You'll just have to do your best then, old man," Reggie said. "It would be much easier if your Miss Townsend was experienced but I daresay you wouldn't like that either."

"Of course I wouldn't," Marcus said sharply. "Unmarried women are expected to be—"

"Everything we're not." Reggie grinned wryly. "Not that I would change it, but it does seem rather unfair."

"Perhaps, but such is the way of the world. We did not make the rules; however, we do have to abide by them. Miss Townsend, Lady Pennington, my *wife* has, with a few notable exceptions triggered by dramatic events in her life, followed those rules.

"I have no doubt as to her virtue." Marcus brushed aside the disquieting idea that perhaps he was wrong. No, if he was confident of nothing else about Gwen, he was confident of her innocence. "She thinks if we are to have two sons we shall only need to make love twice."

"That does sound virginal. You have your work cut out for you."

"Yes, well, I simply do not want her to . . . that is to say . . ." Marcus blew a long breath. "Never mind."

Reggie laughed. "I'm not sure I have ever seen anything quite as amusing as you at this particular moment."

"Your support is duly noted."

"Come now, Marcus, it's a seduction, the same as any other. Perhaps a bit slower, with an eye toward gentleness, but I am certain you can do it."

"Your confidence is overwhelming. However, I would be most appreciative if we could simply drop the subject."

"Of course." Reggie paused, and a wicked gleam flashed in his eye. "Twice you say?"

"Enough!"

Reggie laughed and Marcus ignored him. "As amusing as that may well be, her attitude about children concerns me."

"Oh?"

"She's continually mentioning sons, heirs."

"You do need an heir."

"Yes, of course, but it strikes me as exceedingly odd that she would disregard daughters the way she has."

"Given her position in life, losing everything because she was female and unable to inherit, it seems logical to me that she would not be interested in daughters."

"I hadn't thought of it that way, but you could be right."

"Considering her past, perhaps she doesn't realize that you would be amenable to daughters." Reggie raised a brow. "Are you?"

"Certainly but . . ." Marcus paused. Reggie's assessment of Gwen's attitude made a surprising amount of sense. Marcus was annoyed he hadn't thought of it himself. "I may well simply avoid the subject of daughters altogether for the time being. It's of no consequence at the moment, I suppose."

"I would think you have more than enough on your plate for tonight." Reggie smirked.

"Indeed." Marcus barely noted his friend's comment, his thoughts already returning to his new wife.

Gwen's virginal state was enough to give any man pause about the night to come. Still, it couldn't really account for the nervous churning of his stomach. There was far more to consider than the mere bedding of a virgin. "She is quite remarkable, you know."

"Is she?" Reggie said mildly. "In what ways other than appearance?"

"Oh, certainly she is pretty, but Lord knows, pretty girls are not all that difficult to find."

Reggie blew a disbelieving breath.

"She took her fate in her hands when she refused to become a poor relation and live off the charity of her cousin. I grant you, fleeing the country to take a position as a governess is not the most prudent thing to do. And she obviously has a tendency toward impulsive behavior when cornered."

"Like a fox?"

Marcus continued without pause. "Yet the more I am with her, the more I find her character admirable."

"Do you?"

"She is strong-willed and determined—"

"Stubborn and opinionated?"

"—and has a great deal of courage, yet she is really

rather vulnerable. I have thus far only seen mere glimpses of these assorted aspects of her nature. It is a confusing but intoxicating picture."

"Intoxicating?"

"Perhaps that was the wrong word," Marcus lied. *Intoxicating* was precisely the right word. "Perhaps *intriguing* is a better word."

"I find it interesting to note all these now sterling qualities were what you called flaws but a few days ago."

"Did I?" Marcus shook his head. "Are you sure?"

Reggie studied him curiously. "Very sure."

What could Marcus have been thinking? Gwen's qualities were as much strength as weakness and made her the complex creature she was. Oh, certainly he had no idea what was on her mind from one minute to the next, although she had revealed a few clues as to who she was and how she felt and why she saw the world as she did. Bits of a puzzle he had yet to fully make sense of. Still, even if he did not agree with her, he could not help but admire her convictions.

"It's past time for me to be off." Reggie got to his feet. "While I appreciate your hospitality, I have things to do, as do you."

"Yes, of course," Marcus murmured. Gwen was already upstairs, probably in her room. The room adjoining his. Was she waiting for him? Wondering what it would be like when he at last took her in his arms. In his bed. Was she nervous? Scared? Eager?

"I must say, Marcus, you have quite shattered my few remaining illusions tonight. I never thought to see you in such a state."

"What state?" Marcus pulled his brows together in annoyance. "What are you talking about?"

"You. You're not at all your normal self. You're distracted. Preoccupied. Your thoughts are anywhere but here. You're behaving quite as if you are in the throes of some heretofore unknown emotion." Reggie shook his head and sighed in an overly dramatic manner. "If I didn't know better, I would think you had lost your heart to"—he tried and failed to hide a grin—"your inconvenience."

"Then it is good for both of us that you know better," Marcus said firmly.

"Do I?" Reggie studied him thoughtfully. "What I know is that you have always been far and away too cautious when it comes to matters of the heart. I have often wondered if it's truly your nature or simply because you have always had, I don't know, a choice, I suppose, when confronted with the possibility that your emotions might become involved. An escape, as it were.

"You have no escape now. You have a wife."

Marcus snorted. "That's absurd."

"Perhaps. It's an observation, nothing more. Take it as you will." Reggie shrugged, strode to the door, and pulled it open. "You told me it was my example that taught you love was to be avoided at all costs. If so, I did you a grave disservice."

"Reggie—"

"However, I do have a piece of advice that may well come in handy now."

"You've never given me advice before."

"I've never found myself in the odd position of knowing more than you about any particular subject."

Reggie cast him a wry smile. "Listen well, old friend. Close your eyes, ignore that voice of sanity ringing in your head, and jump off that precipice." He chuckled. "The fall is glorious."

"And the landing?"

"Oh, the landing can kill you. But the risk is worth taking. As is anything worthwhile in this life."

"I may fly then?" Marcus chuckled skeptically.

"You may indeed. Even a brief flight is magnificent. And if you're very lucky, you may not land at all. I must say, I quite envy you at the moment." Reggie's gaze was abruptly serious. "Sooner or later, I have always landed." With that, Reggie turned and stepped from the room, closing the door softly behind him.

Marcus stared after his friend thoughtfully.

Was there the least bit of truth in Reggie's charges? Of course not. What the viscount saw as Marcus's long-awaited foray into love was no doubt little more than his attempt to sort out the conflicting nature of the woman he had married. His alleged emotional state was nothing more than the perplexity any man would feel when trying to understand any woman. And Gwen was not just any woman: she was clearly unique. And she was his wife.

Oh, certainly he liked her. A great deal actually. She was a mystery begging to be solved. He'd always been fond of mysteries, and she was an excellent challenge. Confusing and baffling and—abruptly he realized he was fascinated as he had never been by a woman before. Or by any mystery.

And realized as well that seven and a half years might not be long enough.

Chapter Nine

A man is always less charming than he
thinks he is, never as irresistible as we lead him to believe,
and completely captivating in his ignorance.

Colette de Chabot

Gwen wasn't entirely sure what she should be doing at this point. Or what she was expected to do. Or, well, anything.

She pulled aside the drapes covering the tall window in her bedchamber and stared into the night and the dark London streets below. All she knew for certain was that she could not recall ever having been more apprehensive, or more filled with anticipation, in her life.

Where was Marcus anyway? Not that it mattered. He and Berkley could stay ensconced in the library for the rest of the night for all she cared. It would certainly make things easier if he did not insist on his—she swallowed hard—marital rights tonight.

Not that she wasn't willing to acquiesce to his wishes, of course. It was her duty and very much a part of their arrangement. At least for the next seven and a half years.

She let the drape fall back into place and turned away from the window to study the room that was now hers. It was spacious and well appointed, in a style that was vaguely feminine but not overly so. It was warm and cozy tonight but would be bright and pretty in the light of day. She quite liked it even as she realized she could change it to suit herself. She could do just about anything she wished. She was Lady Pennington now.

Lady Pennington.

She shook her head in disbelief. Was it only a week ago that she'd returned to England at Mr. Whiting's summons? Hardly seemed long enough for a life to change so completely. She was no longer destitute. She had taken on the responsibilities of her nieces, of *children*, for goodness' sakes, and she was hiding them from—in truth, deceiving—her ... *husband*. Marcus was her husband and he would be here any moment. And he would want ... would expect ... would demand.

No! She drew a deep breath and released it slowly, until the panic rising within her eased and the desire to blindly flee from the room and the house and possibly the city itself abated. The very thought was ridiculous. Marcus was a reasonable, logical man. And everything she'd seen of him thus far indicated he was thoughtful and kind as well. Why, that absurd business about how long they should live as man and wife was for her benefit alone. Gwen knew full well, even in this modern age, a man could do exactly as he wished and a wife was completely at the mercy of her husband.

Beyond that, more and more she was convinced Marcus was a good man. He had married her more for the sake of those who depended on him than for himself. He had agreed to all her demands and asked for nothing but faithfulness and loyalty in return. If she were confident of nothing else about her new husband, she was certain Marcus would never demand his rights or her favors or anything else from her she did not freely wish to give.

Maybe, indeed, he was not just good but wonderful. He made her smile when she least expected it, and he was perpetually saying things that called for an apology. Rather charming, actually. In truth, she suspected she quite unsettled him. Much as he unsettled her.

And when he kissed her or his hand touched hers or she met his gaze across the room, something quite remarkable happened in the pit of her stomach and warmed her cheeks and stole her breath.

Perhaps he wasn't coming at all? Perhaps he had decided to forgo consummating their marriage? She admitted she was wrong a moment ago when she'd thought he could stay away and she wouldn't care. She did care. Very much so.

Or perhaps he was waiting for her to come to him?

She started toward the door on the far wall. The maid who had helped her change into her nightclothes had said it led to a dressing room that separated Marcus's room from hers. The girl had also told her, with a knowing wink, that Marcus had dismissed his valet for the night.

If he wasn't in his room, it would do no harm to look. If he was . . .

The door seemed to swell in front of her, its proportions distorted like an image in a poorly wrought mirror. It grew fat and tall and towered over her. A portal menacing and threatening and dangerous and . . .

Nothing more than a figment of her overwrought imagination.

The door was wood and brass-trimmed and just a door. There was absolutely nothing to be afraid of. Not from Marcus. Not from herself.

She squared her shoulders, grasped the door handle firmly, and pulled it open. Madame, but more Colette, had well prepared her for what was to come tonight. She was nervous, of course; that was to be expected. But she absolutely was not afraid. Indeed she was, well, if not eager exactly, at least intrigued.

She stepped into the dressing room. The door to his room was ajar.

"Marcus?" She waited a moment, then slowly pushed his door open.

His room was bigger than hers although not substantially so. A lamp was lit on a table between two comfortable-looking chairs arranged before a fireplace, and cast a dim, comforting glow. There was an armoire on one wall and a clothespress on the opposite side of the room. The furniture was dark and heavy, and even in the faint light glowed with polishing. There was the vaguest scent of lemon oil in the air and something familiar she couldn't quite place. All in all, it was a decidedly male room.

At last her gaze drifted to the bed. To the place of her downfall. Her ruin.

Nonsense. It was just a bed, as the door was just a door, and an exceedingly old bed at that. Probably more than a hundred years or so. There was nothing frightening about an old piece of furniture.

Regardless of how many Pennington brides had been deflowered there.

She pushed the thought firmly from her mind and strode to the bed. It was massive and solid in appearance, with four posters, too thick to encircle with her hands, rising upward to meet a carved wood frame. Heavy velvet hangings draped down from the canopy. The bed had a presence all its own and dominated the room as it now dominated her thoughts.

Still, the closer she came, the less overwhelming it seemed. She trailed her fingers lightly over the silken coverlet, noting an overstuffed feather bed lay beneath it. It wasn't the least bit intimidating. In fact, the bed now looked rather comfortable. Welcoming, even. Possibly inviting.

It was probably some sort of trick to get past her defenses. Still, if a woman was about to lose her virginity, comfort was certainly to be wished for.

She glanced toward the door. If Marcus was coming, surely he would be here by now. The oddest touch of indignation seized her. How could he do this to her?

She scrambled up onto the bed with some difficulty. It was an exceptionally high bed, and she was too impatient to look for bed steps, although Marcus was tall enough that he certainly wouldn't need them. She flung herself forward and sank into the mattress face-first.

Gwen rolled over, sat up, and spread her lace-trimmed nightrail around her. The gown was a gift from Colette and quite the nicest thing she had owned in years. Indeed, even the dress she'd worn today was borrowed. She would have to indulge in some serious purchases now that she had the funds.

She surveyed the room and grinned. She could quite get used to this business of being a wealthy countess. And get used to this bed as well. She lay back and stared at the canopy above. This was the most comfortable bed she'd ever lain on. Possibly the most comfortable bed in the world. The mattress enveloped her in a soft, cushiony caress. Quite delightful.

How much more delightful would it be with Marcus by my side?

The thought was not as startling as the realization that she really wasn't reluctant to share Marcus's bed, this bed, and everything that entailed. In truth, thanks to her friends, and the nature of the man she was just beginning to know, she'd started to, well, look forward to it. At least a bit.

Now all she needed was the gentleman in question.

She struggled to sit up but seemed to sink rather than rise, the feather bed an omnipotent beast threatening to pull her back into its depths like the sea sucking down a drowning man. She huffed with annoyance. Apparently this bed meant to keep its victims as long as possible. Getting out was as difficult as getting in. She managed to scoot to the edge of the mattress and dangled her slipper-shod feet over the side. As much as she knew the drop to the floor was probably no more than a foot, she was not eager to take the plunge.

"Well, this is an unexpected pleasure." Marcus's voice sounded from the door.

Gwen started at the sound and promptly slid off the side of the bed. She grabbed at the covers to stop her fall but succeeded in nothing more than pulling everything down with her. She landed with a soft thud. The silken coverlet drifted over her head.

"Are you all right?" Marcus's voice drew closer.

"Quite." She wasn't the least bit all right. Her bottom stung a little. Worse, she was mortified. What must he think, finding her in his room? In his bed?

"Would you like some assistance?" His tone was casual, as if he were offering to do nothing more than help her from a carriage, but she could hear the smile in his voice.

"No," she said in her haughtiest manner. "It is most kind of you to offer, though."

She didn't want his help, and she had no desire to pull the cover off her head and face him. She'd rather sit there pretending nothing was wrong than see the amusement in his green eyes. Besides, he was probably thinking all sorts of dreadful things about her character and her lapses in judgment, and beyond that, he'd ask why she was in his room in the first place. An excellent question for which she had no particular answer.

She pulled her hand free of the fabric and waved at him. "Do not feel obligated to remain here on my account. Feel free to go about your business. You may leave if you wish."

"I'm not going anywhere." He chuckled. "This is, after all, my room."

A moment later she felt him settle onto the floor beside her. This was getting more absurd by the moment. She would have to do something.

There were only two choices. She could pull off the cover and make some sort of inept excuse as to why she was on his bed. Or she could pretend she was not sitting on the floor, under a coverlet, with only her arm visible.

"So," she said brightly, deciding delusion was better than honesty. Now that her arm was exposed, she wasn't quite sure what to do with it except wave it casually. She must look like a complete lunatic. This whole thing was so annoyingly awkward. And humiliating. "How is Lord Berkley tonight?"

"Excellent. May I ask you a question?"

"No."

"No?"

"Absolutely not."

"I see." He paused, and she could well envision the grin on his face. "Well, that does pose a bit of a dilemma, then, doesn't it?"

"I don't see why."

"You're right." He laughed. "This is delightful. I never thought I'd be spending my wedding night sitting on the floor beside a heap of bedclothes and a disembodied arm. It will be an excellent story to tell our children one day."

"You shall not tell a single soul about this, Marcus," she snapped. "Or I shall—"

"You shall what?" He caught her hand and pressed his lips against it. A thrill of excitement shot up her arm.

She heaved a resigned sigh. "You're not going to make this easy for me, are you?"

"That would not be nearly as much fun." He paused, no doubt trying to hold back laughter. "Not like, say, watching you succumb to the effects of brandy."

"I shall never drink brandy again." She pulled off the cover and grimaced. "And I should be most grateful if you took it upon yourself to make certain I don't."

"Perhaps we should have included it in the wedding vows."

She cast him a grudging smile. "That would have been most appreciated."

He laughed, leaned close, and brushed his lips against hers. Then he got to his feet, grabbed her hands, and pulled her up to join him. The coverlet fell to the floor. Marcus's gaze slipped over her in a slow, deliberate manner, as much a caress as if he'd touched her. Her gown covered her from neck to toe but she had not realized before quite how sheer the material was. And well appreciated, judging by the look in her husband's eye. She shivered with anticipation.

"Are you cold?" His hands slipped from hers, and his fingers trailed lightly, absently over her forearms. His touch was warm through the light fabric.

"No. I am really rather warm." She met his gaze and held her breath. Would he kiss her now? There was no doubt in her mind that he wanted to. She could see it in his eyes and wondered what he saw in hers. And what she wanted him to see.

He stared down at her for a long moment, then swiftly twirled her around and drew her back against his chest.

"What are you doing?"

"Call it an experiment of a scientific nature." He wrapped his arms around her. "The essence of scientific experimentation is repetition. I am repeating an experiment begun today. The continuation of the one we started this afternoon."

"I had no idea you had an interest in science."

"I have an interest in all sorts of things," he said

loftily. He rested his chin on the top of her head and tightened his embrace. It was quite, quite lovely.

"I'm trying to determine if indeed it is easier, at times, to talk to someone without facing them. Do you mind?"

"No," she said cautiously. "What do you want to talk about?"

"Reggie thinks I'm in love."

Her breath caught. "Oh?"

"I have never been in love although I have come exceedingly close on two occasions. Both times, the ladies involved developed interests elsewhere."

"I see." She drew a deep breath. If he could be honest, so could she. At least about this. "Everyone I've ever cared for has left, through death or their own pursuits. Except Madames Freneau and de Chabot, of course."

He was silent for a long moment. "You have not had an easy time of it."

"I could have had a much easier time of it had I been, I don't know, wiser, I suppose." She relaxed against him. It was indeed remarkably easy to talk freely when one was not face-to-face. Especially with the comfort of a man's arms around you. "I have a horrid tendency to believe I can solve my problems by running from them."

"Can you?"

She shook her head. "No. If I have learned nothing else, I have learned that."

"Am I a problem?" His voice was low, intense.

"I haven't decided," she said lightly.

He spun her around and pulled her into his arms. "And when will you make that decision, Miss Townsend?"

"I'm not sure." She raised her chin and wrapped her arms around his neck. "Perhaps you can help me decide, Lord Pennington."

He raised a brow. "And how will I do that?"

She reached upward and touched her lips to his. He didn't move, and she pressed her lips harder against his. He didn't so much as twitch. This was pleasant, but she knew full well there should be a great deal more happening beyond the simple touching of lips. Certainly there was a great deal more happening when he had kissed her. Of course, brandy had been involved then. Was she doing this wrong? She remembered something Colette had mentioned, and while it had sounded distasteful at the time, it seemed rather exciting now. She opened her mouth and flicked her tongue over his lips.

"What was that?" He grabbed her shoulders and thrust her away from him.

She winced. "You didn't like it."

"Oh no, I liked it. I liked it quite lot," he said quickly. "I just didn't expect it, that's all."

"I knew this was a mistake." She pulled out of his grasp and moved out of reach. "Do you think I'm a tart now?"

He smiled wryly. "I very much fear you aren't."

"Would you prefer I was a tart, then?"

"It would certainly make this easier," he murmured.

"For both of us." She wrapped her arms around herself and drew her brows together. "I have never done this before, you know, and you could be a little more understanding."

His mouth dropped open and he stared. "I was being

understanding. For God's sakes, I was being bloody restrained. I didn't want to scare you. I didn't want to go too quickly or—"

"There's no fear of that now, is there?" She cast her gaze toward the ceiling. "I'm not a child, Marcus, I do know what to expect."

"Do you?" His brows drew together skeptically.

"I've been thoroughly instructed on precisely what will happen," she said in a haughty manner. "And how to respond."

"Have you indeed." His voice was choked as if he was struggling to keep back anger. Or laughter. "And what"—he could barely get out the words— "do you expect? Precisely."

She thought for a moment. "First, you are supposed to kiss me, quite a lot really, and not just on the mouth, until my knees are weak and I melt against you."

"Until your knees are weak, you say?" He crossed his arms over his chest and leaned against the bedpost. "I think I can manage that. Then what?"

"Well . . ." She paused to gather her courage and forced an unconcerned note to her voice. "Then you should sweep me into your arms and carry me to your bed."

"Seems a bit premature to me." He shook his head thoughtfully. "Are you certain you haven't left something out?"

"I don't think—"

"I know." He aimed his finger at her. "Your clothes. You've forgotten all about them. At some point we need to take them off, and mine as well."

"I don't think Madame de Chabot ever mentioned clothes. Perhaps she assumed we would already be disrobed?"

"Of course." He smacked his forehead with his palm. "That's the answer. I should have thought of that myself."

She narrowed her eyes and studied him. "You're making fun of me."

"Never." His voice was solemn, and she didn't trust him for a moment. "Please, do go on. After I carry you to the bed?"

"Then there is more kissing and a great deal of . . . well . . . you know . . . whatever." She glared and planted her hands on her hips. "I don't know why I am telling you this. No doubt you know far more than I what happens next."

"No doubt." He studied her with ill-concealed amusement. "You have given this a great deal of thought, haven't you?"

She sighed. "I have thought of little else."

"As have I." His voice was low and echoed deep inside her. "But"—he shook his head—"while the steps you have detailed are adequate, I'm not certain they're entirely to my liking."

She stared in astonishment. "Why not?"

He shrugged. "Far too cut-and-dried for my taste. I prefer things a bit more . . . spontaneous."

"Spontaneous?" She huffed. "How can things be spontaneous? You and I both know what's going to happen here. It's not entirely a surprise."

"You never know," he said under his breath and started toward her.

Without thinking, she backed up. "What are you doing?"

He grinned and walked past her, loosening his cravat. "Where are you going?"

"I am getting ready for bed." He pulled his cravat free and stepped into the dressing room.

Good Lord, was he taking off his clothes? Now? With the lights on? No matter how prepared she was, she was certainly not prepared for the sight of a naked man. Mercifully, he was hidden behind the half-open door. For a moment she considered escaping back to her own room. Of course, that would entail going through the dressing room.

Besides, that would never do. She was resigned to this. No. She wanted this. Wanted him. She wasn't sure why or when it had happened, but at some moment between their first brandy-laden kiss and now, something inside her had changed from mere resignation to an odd, aching need. She wanted to have him kiss her again and again and altogether more thoroughly than he had thus far. She wanted to lie in his arms and wanted her knees to grow weak beneath his touch and wanted to feel all the things Colette said he would make her feel.

She wanted her husband.

The door to the dressing room swung slowly open, and she clapped her hand over her eyes.

Marcus's laugh echoed in the room. "What are you doing now?"

"Nothing. Not a thing." She waved her free hand. "Do go about your business."

"That's the second time you've told me to go about my business. Very well, I will."

She heard the soft footfall of bare feet circle past her and couldn't help but peek from between her fingers. She gasped and dropped her hand. "You're wearing a dressing gown."

He raised an amused brow. "Indeed I am. What were you expecting me to be wearing?"

"I expected you . . ." Her gaze reluctantly roamed over him and her mouth went dry. His shoulders were broader than she'd realized, indeed he was taller and handsomer in a decidedly roguish sort of way than she noticed before. In truth, he was much more *male* than she'd imagined and quite impressive. The robe was open nearly to the waist, revealing his throat and a significant portion of his chest, his *naked* chest, to close at the tie at his waist. Her gaze quickly skipped that portion below his waist—she wasn't quite ready for that— to the hem hitting at his calves and the bare legs below. "You're naked under that, aren't you?"

"Indeed I am." His tone was casual, as if they were involved in nothing more than lighthearted conversation in a parlor somewhere and not in his room with little more than a few scraps of lace and silk separating his body from hers. "I find the wearing of clothing, particularly during warm weather, as annoying to my pursuit of a good night's sleep as you find the wearing of hats. Now then." He nodded toward the bed. "I warn you, I am going about my business as per your request. I am taking my robe off now and getting into my bed. You might want to cover your eyes again to avoid my offending your maidenly sensibilities."

"You haven't offended my sensibilities," she scoffed. "I was simply giving you some privacy."

"Really?" He worked at the knot at his waist. "And here I assumed you were apprehensive at the sight of a naked man."

"Don't be absurd," she said stoutly. "I have seen naked men before."

"Oh?"

"Statues and sculptures and the like. Greeks and Romans primarily." She tried to look anywhere but at him. "Museums, you know. Full of statues."

"Indeed. Plenty of naked men there." He chuckled and turned his back to her. "Last warning, Miss Townsend."

Her chin jerked upward. "Lady Pennington, if you please."

"As you wish, *Lady Pennington*." His robe slipped off his shoulders to fall in a puddle of silk at his feet.

She bit her lip and stared.

He was exceedingly well sculpted.

The muscles of his back and buttocks were firmly defined, and his skin seemed to glow in the dim light. She had the immediate urge to run her fingers over those muscles, warm herself on his heated flesh. He climbed into bed as if she weren't there.

"What are you doing?" Indignation sounded in her voice, and she stepped toward the bed.

He rolled onto his back, clasped his hands behind his neck, and studied her. "I am going to sleep. It's been a long and rather tiring day," he said, reaching for the bedcovers.

"You're going to sleep? Just like that?" She moved closer. "No kissing? No melting of my knees? No . . . whatever?"

He thought for a moment. "I don't believe so."

"Don't you want me?" She stared in disbelief.

"Indeed I do. Quite a lot, actually." His voice was wry. "I'm rather proud of myself for my restraint thus far."

"Then"—she flung her arms wide—"take me!"

He shook his head. "I think not."

"Marcus!" She scrambled up onto the bed to kneel beside him, noting in the back of her mind how indignation and, indeed, impatience swept aside any trepidation. "Why not?"

"You've taken all the fun out of it. As if making love involves nothing more than following a step-by-step instruction booklet." He considered her thoughtfully. "I don't want you in my bed because you have no other choice. Because this is your duty."

"That's not why I'm here. I want this." She laid her hand on his chest. "I want you."

"Do you?"

"Yes. And I shall prove it." Before she could think better of it, she threw her leg over his to sit straddling his hips. She cast him a wicked smile. "If you shall not take me, I shall be compelled to take you."

"Really?" He gazed at her in amusement. "And how precisely do you plan on doing that?"

"With the help of my step-by-step instructions you made fun of." She drew a breath for courage and stretched out on top of him, ignoring the feel of his delightfully hard body beneath hers and grateful that, for now, they were separated by layers of bedclothes. Her face was inches from his. He watched her, his hands still laced behind his neck, a slight smile playing over his lips. "First . . ." She brushed her lips across the hollow of his throat and was gratified to feel his body tense under her.

"This is the kissing part?"

"Um-hm." She kissed his throat and ran a trail of light kisses up his neck to the line of his jaw. It was rather nice kissing him like this. Indeed, with every touch of her lips to his warm skin, she wanted to kiss him more. The curious fluttering she'd noted the last time they'd kissed started again within her. Delicious and demanding.

She reached the corner of his jaw and moved her mouth to nibble at the lobe of his ear. He sucked in a hard breath. She murmured against him. "Madame de Chabot says men quite like this sort of thing."

"Does she?" His voice was slightly strangled, as if he couldn't quite get the words out. "What else does she say men like?"

Gwen shifted to look into his eyes, sliding her body slightly over his with a seductive skill she didn't know she had. At once she felt the distinct evidence of his arousal beneath her and realized she wasn't the least bit frightened but rather excited. "She says they like this."

She cupped his face in her hands and met his lips with hers. His mouth opened to hers, and for a long moment she did nothing but taste him. He tasted slightly of brandy and perhaps vanilla, and she recognized it as the scent that lingered in his room. And tasted as well of heat and desire. She deepened her kiss, and felt him shift and his arms wrap around her, pulling her tighter to him. His tongue found hers, and a delighted shock surged through her and caught at her breath.

He snagged her gown and pulled it upward until the evening air whispered over the backs of her legs. His hands found her bare flesh and his fingers teased along her legs and higher until he cupped her buttocks in his hands. And still her lips clung to his and she fell into a glorious abyss of sensation that was as yet no more than a promise. She pulled her mouth from his and moved to sit up, once again straddling his hips, his arousal hard beneath the covers underneath her.

"Now what?" His breath was labored.

"Clothing, I should think." She yanked her gown over her head and tossed it aside. In some lone, still rational part of her mind, she noted her distinct lack of modesty but she no longer cared. Some demon far more powerful than mere maidenly reserve had her in its grasp and she wanted, she needed . . . more.

"Excellent." He gasped and his hands grasped her waist, then trailed slowly upward to caress her breasts.

She moaned and her head fell back. His hands moved over her breasts, and his thumbs toyed with her nipples, now hard beneath his skillful touch. And she wondered that she had ever had the least bit of hesitation. And wondered as well how much sheer sensation she could endure. And what an amazing endurance it was.

Without warning he sat up and caught her in his arms, his mouth meeting hers with a demand and an urgency that could not be denied. An urgency she shared and reveled in. He shifted and kicked off the covers and entwined his legs with hers, his lean, hard body pressed tight against her. He pulled his lips from hers and kissed her throat and the side of her neck to a point she never suspected was at all sensitive just below her ears. His voice was low and labored. "There is no turning back now, Miss Townsend."

"Lady Pennington." She could barely gasp out the words. "If you please."

"Oh, I please." His words panted against her skin. "Lady Pennington. Gwen."

His hands and his mouth roamed over her as if she were an unknown land and he an ardent adventurer. He explored and surveyed and discovered and she could not touch him enough, taste him enough, feel the searing heat of his body against her mouth and her hands enough. His hand slipped between her legs to touch that part of her she had never given much thought to. A shock of pleasure so intense it arched her back shot through her, and she cried out.

"Marcus!" She gripped his shoulders tightly. "That is . . . I don't . . . oh my . . ."

"Not part of your instructions?" His voice was thick with passion.

"Perhaps it was mentioned." Her voice was little more than a whisper. Marcus certainly knew what he was doing. She wondered that women survived such exquisite pleasure. Raw and intense, it spread in hard waves from his touch through every inch of her and stoked a burning need deep inside. A fire growing ever hotter and higher.

She struggled for breath and clutched at him. "I fear I may be a tart after all."

"Thank God," he murmured, his lips again claiming hers.

He swept her into a spiral of increasing sensation and with it swept away all rational thought. She existed only in the touch of his hand, the feel of his lips, the reality of his body pressing against hers.

She felt his fingers slick and wet slide into her and marveled that it was not at all unpleasant but somehow right and proper and yet not nearly enough. She throbbed against his hand and yearned, burned for more.

He removed his hand and at once positioned himself between her legs. He hesitated, and she stared into his eyes, darkened with the desire she shared.

"Gwen, this might be—"

"I know and it doesn't matter. I want"—she drew his lips back to hers—"you."

He reached between them and guided himself into her with a slow, gentle pressure. She knew full well there could be pain and no longer cared. It seemed a small price to pay for such pleasure. He entered her, filled her, and she noted that he had not seemed quite this large with the covers between them. Still, it was an odd sensation but not bad. Not bad at all. He paused and she realized he had reached what Colette had called *la barrière de l'amour.* He drew back, then thrust forward hard and fast and unrelenting. A sharp pain stabbed through her. She sucked in her breath and clenched her teeth. She felt distinctly impaled, and it hurt.

"Perhaps I'm not a tart after all," she said with an odd squeak in her voice.

"Bloody hell, Gwen, I am sorry." He swallowed hard and stared at her. "We can stop if this is too—"

"No, it will be fine in a moment." There wasn't the least bit of conviction in her voice. "I think." Colette had been right about everything else, and Gwen prayed she was right about this too.

He lay inside her for a long moment and the pain eased. She moved tentatively beneath him, and it seemed to help. He started to slide gently back and forth within her, and it helped a great deal. The fire that had been building inside her rekindled, and she matched her movements to his. It helped a great deal indeed. In truth, it was rather remarkable.

He thrust faster and harder, and she arched upward to meet his body with her own. To welcome. To consume. What vague pain still lingered melded with this unimagined, newfound pleasure and added to the intensity of their coupling. Her existence expanded to obliterate the rest of the world and shrank to nothing beyond wild joy and pure sensation. He stoked the fire that seared within her ever hotter and ever higher, and she wondered if one could die from absolute pleasure and welcome the glory of it.

Without warning the flames within her burst in waves of hot, unimagined bliss, and she cried out and dug her fingers into his shoulders and felt him shudder with her.

It lasted forever and was far and away too brief.

Still, in some part of her mind not fogged with sensation, she vowed she would not, she could not allow the passion and intense emotion of what was not nearly as inconvenient as she had thought, and far more wonderful than she had been told, overwhelm her. Not to let all this mean more than it was. It was passion. Lust. Nothing more than that.

It was certainly not love.

Even now she was determined not to love him. Not to give up that last vestige of control over her own life.

And it would be so easy to love him.

But women in love were fools, and she would not join their ranks no matter how much she wanted to.

Still, she couldn't help but wonder if seven and a half years with this man would be nearly long enough.

Chapter Ten

A man's previous experience is important only insofar as it guarantees he knows what he is doing. And guarantees as well that he does it with a certain amount of skill. Such things may be improved with practice but simply cannot be taught.

Colette de Chabot

"You did that very well." Gwen rested her chin on Marcus's chest and gazed up at him. Starlight drifted in from the windows with the breeze to cast a luminous glow on her face and reflect in her eyes. "Or at least, given what I was told to expect, I think you did that very well. I was quite impressed."

Marcus tried not to sound as smug as he felt. Or as satisfied. "Thank you. I do what I can."

"I daresay you have a lot of experience."

"Some," he said cautiously.

She quirked a skeptical brow.

"Some," he repeated firmly. In his experience it was never wise to give one's current lover too much information about one's previous lovers.

"With many women?" Her manner was offhand, belying the danger lurking in her words.

"Some." Nor was it smart to reveal how many previous lovers there were. Women were exceedingly strange about information like that. If, in their estimation, a man had too few lovers, his nature was in question. Too many and his character was at stake.

She widened her eyes innocently. "A great many?"

"I have never particularly considered it *a great many*, although I do think *a great many* itself is rather vague."

"How many then? Exactly?"

"First of all, my dear Lady Pennington, a gentleman does not reduce such things to something as impersonal as statistics. In addition, it is neither proper nor honorable either to keep some sort of tally or to reveal it. Furthermore, such things are never discussed with ladies, particularly one's wife."

"Really?" She shook her head thoughtfully. "I should think a wife would be the one lady you could discuss such things with."

"Then your thinking would be wrong," he said in a firm tone he hoped clearly conveyed the end of this particular topic. Not that he was confident she would pay any attention.

Even in the faint light he could see the gleam in her eye. "Then what is appropriate to discuss with a wife?"

"I'm not entirely certain, never having had a wife before." He tightened his arms around her and rolled over to trap her beneath him. "This, I should think"—he nuzzled the base of her throat—"is always an appropriate subject for discussion."

"Is it?" she murmured. "What else?"

"Oh, I don't know. This perhaps." He ran a line of light kisses up to a point just beneath her ear he had found was exceptionally sensitive, and earned a shiver from her for his troubles. He couldn't resist a satisfied grin. "And possibly this—"

"Marcus." She nudged him up and met his gaze, the starlight reflecting the far too serious gleam in her eyes. "I need to arrange for new clothes. An entirely new wardrobe really. All of my clothes are dreadful, you said so yourself."

"Did I?" He stifled a sigh of disappointment, rolled to his side, ignored the growing stiffness between his legs, and propped his head in his hand. "When did I say that?"

"Perhaps you didn't say it exactly but you definitely implied it."

"Did I?" he said, idling tracing a line with his finger from her throat to the valley between her breasts and the point where the sheet prevented further exploration.

"I shall need funds. I believe you mentioned an allowance."

"Yes, of course." He slipped his finger beneath the sheet and ran it lightly over the swell of her breast. "We shall arrange for whatever you want in the morning."

"Excellent." Her voice was a shade unsteady, and he tried not to grin. She was not as unaffected by his touch as she might have him believe. "I do appreciate it."

"You are now the Countess of Pennington." He pushed the sheet lower to reveal her breasts and leaned close to take her nipple in his mouth. He murmured against her skin. "You should dress accordingly." He took her nipple gently between his teeth, and she gasped softly, the sensitive flesh puckering and hardening under the flick of his tongue.

Her voice had a breathless edge. "Your mother said she would help me."

He heaved a resigned sigh and lifted his head. "Did she?"

"Yes." Gwendolyn cleared her throat. "I believe we shall get along quite well."

"My mother has never been adverse to spending money, especially when it is not hers." He eyed her curiously. "I gather you do not intend on spending your own newfound fortune?"

"Don't be absurd, Marcus, I am saving my money for"—she hesitated—"the future. Yes, that's it, I'm saving my money for the future," she repeated firmly.

"Your future is assured," he said mildly. "The biggest threat to my fortune has vanished with our wedding. However, this whole incident has made me reassess what plans I have made for the future, at least in terms of finances. I have already begun looking into a number of excellent investments that should serve to strengthen the Pennington fortune well into the next generations. I shall not be caught in a trap like this one again."

"A trap like having to marry me?"

He winced. "I have done it again, haven't I? I did not mean it that way at all. I simply meant, I do not want to ever again find myself in a situation where I have no choice." He leaned close and brushed his lips across hers. "In truth, this is rather a lovely trap."

"Thus far it is indeed much better than I anticipated." She smiled in that smug manner of women who have been well and truly satisfied.

"Indeed it is," he murmured and gathered her closer.

"Was he right?"

Marcus stifled his growing excitement and forced a casual note to his voice. "Was who right about what?"

"Lord Berkley. Was he right about . . ." She shook her head. "Never mind. It doesn't matter."

"Right about what?"

"It's not important." Her tone indicated that it, whatever it might be, was indeed important. Still, it could certainly wait until morning.

"Very well then." He ran his hand along the curve of her hip. Her skin was warm and silken and inviting. His fingers drifted to the cleft between her legs.

She sucked in a short breath. "I should warn you I do not plan on falling in love with you."

He ignored her, his fingers teasing the damp curls between her legs. "Yes, yes, I know, you've mentioned that. Love is a trap for women."

Her legs parted and her breath was labored. "In spite of the fact that this was really quite, um . . ."

"Exciting?" He delved deeper to touch that part of her only he had known. "Then I gather lust between us is acceptable? Passion, desire, that sort of thing."

"Oh my, yes. Lust. Passion." She struggled to get out the words. "Very exciting. And I think perhaps we should do it again."

"Do you?" His fingers slipped over her, already wet with desire. He shifted to press his erection harder against her heated flesh and bent to nibble her shoulders

"Oh, absolutely. Without hesitation." Her words were barely more than a sigh, and he sensed her struggle to maintain a coherent thought. "Marcus, you should not fall in love with me either."

"As you wish." His words whispered against her skin. "Would it relieve you to know I have planned nothing of the sort?"

"Yes, goodness . . ." She swallowed hard. "Actually it . . . would . . ."

"Your shoulders are quite delectable." He increased the rhythm of his fingers, and her body tensed beside his.

"Is that what you told Lord Berkley?"

He smiled. She absolutely refused to let go of anything. "Berkely's shoulders aren't the least bit delectable."

"Of course not." Her voice was barely audible, and she rocked slightly against his hand. She was very close to losing control completely. "So then, we are agreed. Lust is acceptable—"

"Preferable even." He raised his head to watch the play of emotion on her face.

"However, love is to be avoided." Her eyes were closed and her lips parted and she looked as if she were waiting for something quite wonderful.

"Agreed. However, I should warn you I do rather like you."

She arched upward. "Do you?"

"Indeed I do." He pulled her to lie on top of him and slid gently into her. "Quite a lot, I should think."

She planted her hands on either side of his head, pushed herself up, and stared down at him. "Do you? Why?"

"I'm not entirely sure." He grasped her waist and began to slowly thrust upward. She moaned and bit her bottom lip. "But it seems a good idea, to like the woman you have married."

"A very good idea," she said under her breath and matched her movements to his.

"Very good indeed." He moved in an easy, deliberate manner.

She was tight and slick and enveloped him in heat and sensation. He resisted the urge to move faster, to thrust harder, his restraint deepening his need, her desire. He shifted her until she sat upright upon him, and slid his hands up to curl around the underside of her breasts. Her eyes were closed, her mouth slightly open, and an expression of exquisite tension shadowed her face. Watching her react to his every move, every touch, and her discovery of passion increased his own. His thumbs flicked over her nipples, and she uttered something that might have been a moan or a sigh. It echoed through her and into him, and his restraint snapped.

He pulled her down on top of him and rolled over to pinion her beneath him. She arched upward and wrapped her legs around his hips. He thrust into her, and she met his increasing demands with her own. He could feel her throb around him, feel himself pulse within her. Joined together as one, he no longer knew where he ended and she began. Faster and harder they rocked together until she tightened around him and spasms shuddered through her and through him and his senses shattered with the release of his body.

And he marveled at the intensity of this physical act

that he had always enjoyed, yet never had it seemed so complete before. So all consuming and perhaps perfect. So right.

And wondered as well if it wasn't merely his body involved but his heart.

Some time later she slept curled against him. The nicest warmth spread from her body to his and crept into his soul. It struck him that this woman was a perfect fit. Not simply physically, although she was altogether more passionate and eager than he had expected or even hoped for, but in something of a spiritual sense. It was a ridiculous concept, as if all that nonsense he had spouted about fate and what was right and proper was the truth and not the ramblings of a man desperate to save his fortune and future.

Still, fate was an exceedingly odd thing. It could well be that she was indeed his destiny. After all, hadn't he been too cautious about love up until now to risk marriage? Or his heart?

It would be very easy to allow her to slip into his heart. He already liked her, perhaps more than liked her. In spite of his promise to avoid love, he wondered if it could be avoided. If it had already struck.

Probably not. He brushed off the disquieting idea. The last thing he needed was to love a woman who had made it very clear she had no intention of loving him. Love on one side alone would lead to nothing but pain. Reggie was proof of that. Still, they would have a good life together. He would make certain of it.

He hadn't told her, but the purpose of the investments he'd mentioned was not merely to make sure his fortune would not be threatened again, as it had been by his father's edict. The difficulties Gwen had faced after her father's death had made him acutely aware for the first time of the unfairness of life when it came to women. No daughter of his would ever be placed in such a position. Gwen had the oddest view of daughters and didn't seem at all inclined toward producing any, but even she could not guarantee they would have only sons. However, Marcus could, and would, guarantee their children, all their children, would be provided for always.

He wondered when, or even if, he should tell her he would rather like a large family. He brushed a strand of dark hair away from her face and smiled. They would have an exceedingly good time producing that family. In truth, they would have an exceedingly good life together. At the moment he didn't doubt that they would be together far beyond a mere seven and a half years. Admittedly he was still wrapped in the warm flush of their lovemaking, but right now anything seemed not only possible but probable.

Was she his fate?

He didn't know, and it scarcely mattered. She was his now, and with luck would be his forever. He could thank his father and hers for that. And no doubt thank as well the mythical Fates that watched over the hidden spot in the garden that they had been brought together. That neither of them had found love before now. That he had been left no other choice but to pull her into his life as his wife.

Abruptly an odd thought struck him. He knew precisely why he had married her, but had no idea why she'd married him. He'd had no real choice, but she had originally turned him down. He'd been so pleased when she'd changed her mind, he'd never considered why she had done so. Certainly it could have been to get her inheritance, the funds she now said she was saving for the future. But she hadn't given that a moment's thought when she'd first refused his suit and claimed to be quite content with her modest income. What had changed?

Without warning, the idea flashed through his mind that perhaps she needed her own private funds not for herself but for someone else. Had a past love perhaps returned to her life? Was he demanding money from her for whatever reason, or worse, was she planning on leaving Marcus for another man? Was it possible that she—

Good Lord, what had happened to him? His imagination had never been so active. In truth, he'd never thought himself particularly imaginative at all. This was complete and utter nonsense, and he firmly pushed aside the preposterous notion of another man in Gwen's life. It was no more than his own history with women that would make him think something so farfetched in the first place. She'd done nothing to indicate such a thing, or to indicate she was hiding anything from him whatsoever.

Still, she had said his proposal was not the first time she'd been asked to marry . . .

Ridiculous. The very idea was absurd. Gwen was intelligent and well used to running her own life, yet he did not for a moment believe she would deceive him.

Of course, in truth, he did not know her well. And

she did insist on keeping control of her money as well as some house she owned somewhere.

Gwen sighed in her sleep and snuggled closer against him. He tightened his grip around her and resolved to ignore his unsettling thoughts. The real problem had nothing whatsoever to do with her but with him. He'd been so reluctant to fully care for a woman that now that he was in the position where caring, indeed even loving, was a possibility, he was doing what he could to protect himself from the likelihood of pain. Inventing fanciful reasons to maintain his reserve rather than allow himself to surrender fully to the emotion that would tug at his heart if he let it.

Not that he had done so yet but perhaps it was time. There were worse things in life than falling in love with one's wife. He already liked her. More than he had ever liked a woman before. And she would be so very easy to love.

It was a question of trust. He had to trust his wife. And even more difficult, he had to trust himself.

Chapter Eleven

Men are especially endearing when
they are foolish, which is much to their favor,
as they are foolish a great deal of the time.

Francesca Freneau

Gwen gazed at her reflection in the tall pier mirror at the top of the stairs and couldn't resist a smile of satisfaction. She looked rather pretty in this new gown, the first of many expected to arrive at Pennington House over the course of the next week or so. Possibly even extraordinarily pretty. Marcus thought so at any rate, and that was all that really mattered.

In the four days since her marriage, Gwen had come to the startling realization that, for perhaps the first time in her life, she belonged. She wasn't an outsider in her own home, and in truth, Pennington House already felt like home. Indeed, she not only belonged somewhere but to someone. To a family. To Marcus and his mother and her nieces. She was wanted and it was wonderful.

She'd never imagined happiness like this. Real, true

happiness. She could see it in the reflection in the mirror. Her skin glowed and her eyes were bright and she had the most absurd grin on her face. And she had an insane desire to laugh at the most inappropriate times. Her step was light, as was her heart. It had nothing to do with her new clothes, as fetching as they were, and little as well to do with this new life she had somehow stumbled into. The blame or the credit for this absurd sense of happiness could be placed squarely on the shoulders of her new husband.

Marcus.

Even the mere mention of his name brought a silly, dazed sort of smile to her lips. He was perhaps the most wonderful person she'd ever known. He was thoughtful and considerate and made her laugh more than she thought possible. Beyond that, he treated her as if she were important, of value. As if her thoughts and her words and her opinions mattered to him. And when he took her in his arms, the entire world consisted of nothing more than the two of them.

She liked Marcus a great deal. Of course, she liked his friend Lord Berkley, who seemed to be around rather a lot, as well, but that was entirely different. She liked Berkley as she would any friend, not that she had had any male friends before. She thought him quite amusing and found nothing more enjoyable than observing the sometimes quite astute and always humorous exchanges between Berkley and her husband. The two men were as close as brothers, and she was relieved that Berkley appeared to approve of her. And relieved as well that she enjoyed the pleasure of his company.

But her liking for Marcus was entirely different. She

liked her husband as precisely what he was: her lover. However, she was not in love with him, nor did she ever plan on loving him. She did, however, feel a certain amount of fondness for him. If she was anything, she was, well, in lust with him. Yes, that was it exactly. She was in lust. It was a powerful, overwhelming, and all too delightful feeling.

She gave a final nod to the image in the mirror and started down the stairs, ignoring the mild soreness and stiffness that was a direct result of the last few nights. One of the maids had informed her she had a caller waiting in the parlor, and she assumed it was one of the endless numbers of people wanting to make the acquaintance of the new Countess of Pennington. The Countess of Pennington. She bit back a grin.

She certainly didn't feel like a countess even though everyone treated her as such, from callers to merchants. Her status in the world had taken a sharp upswing, and it was both startling and great fun. Lady Pennington—Helena—*Mama* had taken her to her own modiste and cobbler and milliner and so forth and so on until Gwen had lost track of the shops and fittings. It was exhausting, yet she'd found there was nothing quite as stimulating as being wrapped in swaths of fine silk in vibrant colors to see which best brought out the blue of her eyes. Or shown gloves so soft they fit like a second skin. Or fitted for shoes so supple they molded to her feet. Shopping had provided an excellent excuse as well to visit the girls every day.

Her brows drew together at the thought of her nieces. While with every visit they seemed to like her more—or Patience and Hope seemed to like her more—

Charity simply tolerated her—every visit also served to emphasize her ongoing deception. Oh certainly, she had not actually mentioned the girls to Marcus, therefore she was more than willing to argue she'd never actually lied to him, even if not revealing their existence, indeed, hiding them with Madame and Colette, would probably be perceived by him as, at the very least, deceit. And it certainly felt like a lie.

She planned to tell him. Indeed, she'd begun nearly every day of their marriage thus far with the firm intention of telling him. The more she knew him, the more she believed, or perhaps hoped, he would welcome them into his home. But what if she was wrong? After all, how well did she really know him? And as open as Marcus had been with her, there were moments when he became cool and reserved. When there was a look in his eye she couldn't read. A question she couldn't answer. That, more than anything else, kept her still for now. There would be time enough later to tell him all. For the moment, the girls were well taken care of and really quite happy.

As was Gwen.

She reached the bottom of the stairs, crossed the wide entry to the parlor, and cast a blinding smile at the footman waiting to open the doors a beat ahead of her arrival. She sailed into the room and pulled up short at the sight of Mr. Whiting's nephew.

"Albert?" she said without thinking, then shook her head. "Forgive me. It's Mr. Whiting, isn't it?"

"Actually it's Trumble," Albert said apologetically, twisting his hat in his hands. "Mr. Whiting is my mother's brother."

"I see." She eyed him curiously. "Well then, Mr. Trumble, how may I help you?"

"I heard, that is I was informed . . ." Albert's brow furrowed. "I understand you have taken the drastic step of marrying the Earl of Pennington."

She laughed. "I daresay it wasn't all that drastic, Mr. Trumble, and yes, I did marry the earl."

"Oh, please do call me Albert." He stepped toward her eagerly. "We have shared rather too much to be so formal with one another."

She stepped back in surprise. "That would be entirely inappropriate, *Mr. Trumble*, and quite improper as well. Beyond that, we have shared nothing more than a dreadful mistake on your part that adversely affected my life. It's scarcely the stuff friendships are based on."

"I did offer to marry you," he said in a chiding manner.

She stared in disbelief. "As something of an afterthought, if I recall. You certainly made no such offer five years ago when I could have benefited from such a proposal."

"I know, and I have regretted it each and every day since." He ran his hand through his hair. "I should have prevented you from taking the impulsive actions you deemed necessary, but by the time I had realized marriage was the only thing that would, in truth, save you from dire poverty—"

"The poverty you and you alone had determined was my lot," she said pointedly.

"I know." He heaved a heartfelt sigh. "I have berated myself endlessly for my mistake. Indeed, I did all in my power to help my uncle find you."

"That's all very well and good, Mr. Trumble but"—
she narrowed her eyes and considered him—"the past is
over and done with and I have put it behind me. I have
accepted the apologies of both yourself and your uncle,
and there really is no more to be said on the matter.
Therefore, I do wonder precisely why you are here today."

"I am here, Miss Townsend—"

"Lady Pennington," Gwen said firmly.

"Of course, Lady Pennington." Albert squared his
shoulders and lifted his chin in the manner of any man
facing a firing squad. "I am here to reiterate the offer of
assistance I made in my uncle's office. I wish you to
know you may call on me at any time, for any reason. I
shall now and always be at your service. It is the least I
can do."

"I do appreciate it, Mr. Trumble, but"—she cast him
a skeptical smile—"it's not necessary."

"Oh, but it is." Albert's tone was resolute. "If not for
you, then for my own piece of mind."

"Very well then, I accept your offer. Indeed, it is most
gracious of you." It really was exceedingly nice of him
even if Gwen doubted she would ever have need of his
assistance. "Now then, if there is nothing else." She
started toward the door. "Do give my regards to your
uncle."

"Actually, Lady Pennington, there is more." Albert
said staunchly.

"Yes, there would be, wouldn't there? You are certainly following in your uncle's footsteps," she said under her breath, then favored him with a patient smile.
"Please go on."

"It's about your nieces."

Gwen held her breath. "What about them?"

He paused, obviously uncertain how to proceed. "Apparently your sister's husband was not without financial resources. Were you aware that he owned the ship they were traveling on?"

"No."

"Your nieces may be the recipients of a substantial inheritance."

"I was not told of any inheritance."

"We have just learned of the possibility. My uncle received some rather vague information regarding the situation and he is even now looking into it." A reluctant note sounded in Albert's voice. "There may be a question as to your legal right to guardianship."

"Mr. Trumble." Gwen clenched her fists by her side and forced a firm tone. "These girls are my family, my only family. I am their closest living relative. I will not allow them to fall into the hands of anyone more interested in their money than their happiness. Any inheritance they may have is of no importance. I have the funds now to ensure they are provided with an excellent future. And I will not relinquish them without one bloody hell of a fight."

"Lady Pennington!" Albert's eyes widened with shock. "Such language!"

Gwen didn't care. She stepped toward him in a decidedly menacing manner. "You tell your uncle I expect him to serve my interests, and those of my nieces, with the thoroughness and dedication he served my father. He has my blessing to do whatever he deems necessary to get to the bottom of this matter and resolve it in a satisfactory manner. Are we quite clear on this, Mr. Trumble?"

"Indeed we are, my lady." Albert studied her for a moment. "I see now my offer of assistance may be misplaced. You are not quite as helpless as I had believed."

"I have never been helpless." She smiled coolly. "Impulsive and unwise in my actions, perhaps, but never helpless. However, Mr. Trumble"—she straightened her shoulders and met his gaze directly—"*Albert*, I shall indeed feel free to call on you should circumstances warrant it. And I am most grateful for your offer."

"Excellent, Lady Pennington." Albert looked as if he wanted to take her hand but thought better of it. "Then I shall bid you good day." Albert nodded and strode from the room.

Gwen waited until the parlor doors closed behind him then collapsed onto a sofa and buried her face in her hands.

What was she to do if someone tried to take the girls from her? Granted, she hadn't even known of their existence a scant few weeks ago and indeed, when she had first learned of them she'd had no desire to do anything beyond ensure they were well cared for. But now all had changed. She still wasn't sure why it had happened or how.

All she knew was that Charity, Patience, and Hope drew her back to her own childhood and reminded her with heart-wrenching clarity of the desperation of children, of girls, who knew full well they were not wanted. It was a bond between them that was stronger than even blood. And she would not fail them.

Would Marcus help?

With every passing day she was confident he was a good man, but men were notoriously blind when it came to the plight of females. And notoriously single-minded when it came to the gender of children.

She wanted desperately to be able to count on Marcus. To depend on him and share what was fast becoming a burden. It was no longer simply a question of his acceptance of them but of keeping them in her life. Still, in spite of everything she knew, or thought she knew about him thus far, she did not know him well enough to trust him.

She raised her head and gazed unseeing across the room. Until she was certain of his feelings, she could neither tell him about the girls nor rely on his assistance. In this, as in much of everything else in her life, she would have to depend on herself and herself alone.

She was older and, she hoped, much wiser than that girl of sixteen who'd taken her fate in her hands and fled her home to make her own way in the world. She freely admitted she hadn't been particularly successful at it, but she had survived, and the lessons she'd learned along the way would serve her well now.

Now she would restrain her panic and her immediate impulse to take the girls and steal away into the night. Now she would be patient, as contradictory as that might be to her very nature. She would not simply take Albert's word this time but would wait until Mr. Whiting determined what this vague threat might in truth be.

If, at some point, there was no other choice, she would not hesitate to take her nieces, her family, and run, perhaps back to America. She was certain Colette and Madame would help now as they had five years ago, but more importantly Gwen now had the financial means to do whatever was necessary. To go far away from Pennington House and the dear lady who insisted she call her Mama and the amusing Lord Berkley who was fast becoming her friend and . . . Marcus.

A sharp pain stabbed through her at the thought of leaving him, of never seeing him again. Never hearing his laugh, never lying in his arms. An ache formed in the back of her throat. This business of being in lust with a man might be nearly as dangerous as loving him. She swallowed hard and got to her feet. Thank God, she had resisted love. How could she leave him at all if she loved him?

She needed to see the girls at once, if only to assure herself they were still safe. Besides, Colette and Madame needed to know of the possibility of problems. She comforted herself with the idea that Albert had been very wrong before and could well be wrong again.

Patience, Gwen.

She pulled open the door and came face to face with her husband and Lord Berkley.

She started in surprise. "Marcus."

"Gwendolyn, my dear. You are looking remarkably lovely this afternoon."

He looked rather remarkable himself. She hadn't seen him since this morning, and judging by his apparel, he'd been out riding. The cut of the jacket emphasized the breadth of his shoulders, the tight fit of his breeches molded to the curves of his thighs, and a now familiar sense of desire swept through her. Blasted lust. He brushed a kiss across her cheek and strode past her into the room, Lord Berkley a step behind.

Berkley took her hand and lifted it to his lips. "Good day, Lady Pennington. That dress quite becomes you."

"Thank you, my lord." She smiled with the pure pleasure of a woman unused to casual compliments who now found them quite enjoyable. "But you should really thank my husband. He is receiving the bills."

"Bills that are starting to stream in with the insistence of a flood," Marcus said wryly.

"But well worth it, old man." Berkley grinned.

"In fact, I was just on my way out," Gwen said lightly. "I have yet another fitting, and I fear I shall be late."

"My mother is keeping you busy, then?" Marcus said.

"She's been wonderful. I confess I am quite unused to dealing with the myriad details of what she insists are the minimum wardrobe requirements of the Countess of Pennington." She shook her head. "I had no idea. It quite boggles the mind."

"I can well imagine." Marcus studied her in an offhand manner. "Godfrey mentioned that you had a caller."

"Nothing of significance." She waved dismissively. "A messenger from Mr. Whiting's office. A minor detail about the terms of my inheritance."

"Oh?" Marcus raised a curious brow. "Something you'd like me to handle for you?"

"Not at all," she said a shade too quickly. "I was assured it's not important. Well, I must be going."

"Of course." Marcus nodded. "You wouldn't want to keep my mother waiting."

She smiled and started toward the door, then impulsively turned on her heel, crossed the room to him, and threw her arms around him, pressing her lips to his. For a moment he hesitated, then his arms wrapped tightly around her and he kissed her back. Hard and with unexpected ferocity, as if he sensed her need to cling to him and shared it. For a moment she lost herself in his embrace.

Berkley cleared his throat, and a hot blush washed up her face.

She drew her head back and stared up at her husband in horror. "I do apologize, my lord, I don't know what came over me."

Marcus gazed down at her with his slightly crooked smile. "Nor do I, but I have no complaints." He kissed her quickly again and released her. "I believe you said you were late."

"Yes, of course." She cast a quick glance at Berkley, who gazed back innocently. "Good day, my lord."

Berkley nodded. "So it appears."

Gwen forced a weak smile and fled the room. Good Lord, what had possessed her to exhibit such sheer wantonness in front of Lord Berkley? Certainly she had become rather wanton in recent days when it came to the privacy of the bedchamber. And indeed, there were moments when she wondered how she could survive the long hours when she was not in Marcus's bed. And yes, aside from the sheer pleasure of his touch, she had found comfort and security and even peace when he held her in his arms. But to throw herself at him as if they would never be together again . . .

As if they would never be together again.

No. She refused to consider such a thing. If and when the time ever came that she had no choice but to leave him she would deal with it, but much could happen between now and then. It was far too soon to worry.

She noted in the back of her mind how quickly happiness could vanish. Replaced by a heavy, awful weight in the pit of her stomach and an ache lingering somewhere in the region of her heart.

"Well, that was certainly impressive." Reggie chuckled. "I knew things we're going well but not that—"

"I spoke to my mother this morning." Marcus stared thoughtfully at the closed door. "She's pleased Gwen is taking the acquisition of a new wardrobe to heart and noted she has been absent from the house a great deal in pursuit of it. My mother also said she regrets not accompanying her on most of these errands. Odd, as I was under the impression my mother and my wife were spending most of their time together. In addition, my mother apologized for not being able to meet Gwendolyn today. Some sort of gathering with her friends."

Reggie shrugged. "Either your mother or your wife was obviously mistaken about their plans."

"Possibly. I also ran into Whiting yesterday. He didn't mention any problems."

"She said it wasn't important. Perhaps it just came to light today."

"Perhaps," Marcus murmured. "Still, Godfrey indicated Gwen's caller insisted on speaking to her personally. Rather impertinent for a simple messenger, don't you think?"

"Not in the least." Reggie's brows pulled together. "What are *you* thinking?"

"Nothing really." Marcus knew full well how ridiculous his suspicions would sound, especially as they were based on little of significance.

"I know you as well as you know yourself, old friend. And I know when you have something on your mind." Reggie studied him curiously. "It has to do with your wife, doesn't it?"

"It's nothing," Marcus said with a firmness he didn't feel. "I have simply begun to wonder if she is keeping something from me."

"I suspect most wives keep a great deal from their husbands."

"I suppose."

"I should think you have little to worry about with a wife who would kiss you in a manner that curled my toes from halfway across the room." Reggie chuckled. "Forgive me, but I didn't seem to note anything even remotely secretive about her behavior. Would that I, when the time comes, have a wife as passionate in her nature."

"Her passion is not in question."

"Then what is?"

"You will think me insane."

"Probably."

"Have you wondered, in this past week, why she consented to marry me?"

"No." Reggie shook his head. "I assumed, once she'd thought about it, she agreed for the usual reasons. You have wealth, a respectable title, and you're not entirely ugly. In truth, you're an excellent catch. The woman could scarce do better. Unless, of course, she married me," he said with a grin.

Marcus ignored him. "I really don't know her, Reggie. Oh, certainly I know her background. What her life has been like these last five years. Her ancestry, that sort of thing. I know she claims not to desire love—"

"You never told me that."

"I don't tell you everything." Marcus gestured dismissively. "It scarcely matters except one does wonder why a woman as lovely and intelligent as she would not have married long ago."

"She was a governess, Marcus," Reggie pointed out. "In truth, little more than a servant. I daresay suitable matches for ladies of breeding rarely come along when one is forced into such a position."

"But what if she had found someone?" Marcus knew how ridiculous he sounded but couldn't seem to stop himself. "What if indeed there was some man she'd pledged her heart to." He turned and paced the room. "Someone who had tossed her aside without a second thought. Someone who was now back in her life."

"Marcus—"

"You said it yourself, women are always fascinated by men who are no good for them. It would explain why she is so set against love. Oh, certainly she claims love is a cage or a trap or some such nonsense."

"You have never especially seen the merits of love yourself," Reggie said mildly.

Marcus continued without pause. "What if this man now demanded money from her? Or worse, wanted to take her away. What if—" He swiveled toward his friend. "What if I lose her?"

"Why do you care?" Reggie said carefully.

"Bloody hell, man, what kind of a question is that? She's my wife."

Reggie stared at him for a long moment. "You're right, I do think you're insane."

"I knew you would and I daresay you're right." Marcus strode to the nearest chair, collapsed into it, and blew a long, frustrated breath. "My mind seems to have gotten hold of this admittedly absurd idea, and it's like the refrain to a tune you cannot abide, yet it plays over and over in your head until you're quite mad."

"I know of the two of us, I have never been the one with the most rational way of looking at the world, but in this particular instance, apparently mine is the clearer head." Reggie settled into a nearby chair and leaned forward. "First of all, you must admit everything you've cited is no more than mere speculation. The facts, as you have detailed them, are easily explained away. In truth, your interpretation is one of the most fanciful I have ever heard from anyone, let alone you. You are assuming the worst on the basis of next to nothing. There are a dozen innocent explanations for everything you've mentioned."

Reggie leaned back in his chair and studied him intently. "The question now is why you have done so."

"She's my wife," Marcus muttered.

"A wife you didn't particularly want. A blasted inconvenience, I think you called her."

"I want her now."

"I see." Reggie's voice was smug.

Marcus narrowed his eyes. "What, precisely, do you see?"

"You won't like it." A warning sounded in Reggie's voice.

Marcus heaved a resigned sigh. "Probably not. But my displeasure has scarcely stopped you before."

"Very well." Reggie considered him thoughtfully. "First of all, I see a man in the throes of irrational jealousy."

"I most certainly am not."

"You most certainly are. If I behaved as you are now, you would be the first to point it out to me. With a great deal of glee, I might add." Reggie raised a brow. "Shall I continue?"

Marcus shrugged. "As you wish."

"Oh, I do wish. I am rather enjoying this." Reggie flashed a grin and then sobered. "This jealousy of yours is based on nothing of substance, and I suspect has much more to do with incidents in your past than in your present. The only times you have truly grown close to a woman, she has ultimately been involved with someone else. While there is no real evidence that the same thing is happening with your wife, your previous experience has made you wary. You are now prone to suspicion where there is, in truth, nothing suspicious at all."

"I know that." Marcus clenched his jaw. "I have already, in a calm and intellectual manner, thoroughly examined my suspicions and have furthermore tried, and failed, to lay them to rest. My head understands this is sheer nonsense, but what I"—he thumped his chest—"*feel* will not let the matter be."

Reggie grinned.

"What?" Marcus snapped.

Reggie's grin widened. "Welcome to my club, old man."

"I am not in love with her." Marcus's tone was firm. Reggie snorted.

"I like her a great deal." Even as he said the word, Marcus cringed to himself at the defensive note in his voice. "Indeed, I even care for her. There is a certain amount of . . . affection. But it is not love."

"What makes you think so?"

"For one thing, from my observation, every time you have been in love you have been quite miserable," Marcus snapped.

"Are you so very happy?" Reggie said mildly.

"This is entirely different." Marcus glared for a moment then blew a long breath. "What am I to do now?"

"Ah, the eternal question." Reggie chuckled. "I suppose you could always try talking to your wife. Asking her straight out about your suspicions."

"I couldn't possibly do that." Marcus shook his head. "She would think I did not trust her, and that does not strike me as a good way to begin our life together. Besides, we agree my fears are no doubt groundless. Still, I feel I should do something."

"Then why not take her away from London for a time? You could go to the country. She hasn't seen Holcroft Hall yet."

"I could do that," Marcus said slowly. "Of course, the season is just getting under way. She's never had a season, you know. We have already received a fair number of invitations. I did think she would quite enjoy the upcoming festivities."

"But given your current state, would you?"

"No, not in the least. I fear I might well view every man who so much as asked her for a dance with unwarranted suspicion." Marcus drummed his fingers on the arm of the chair. "Gwen would probably like the estate, don't you think? It's her home now and she should see it. And the countryside is lovely at this time of year." Marcus thought for a moment. "Besides, I could take the opportunity to pursue the acquisition of the dower house. Whiting still hasn't managed to strike a deal for its purchase. When I was last there it was vacant but perhaps someone in the village can direct me to the owner and I could approach him myself."

"It's the perfect answer, then. You will have your new bride to yourself and your fears will be set to rest once and for all." Reggie leaned forward. "I am confident, Marcus, that your concerns are groundless. One has only to look at the lady to see how much she cares for you. I would wager my entire fortune this woman who claims no interest in love has already fallen over the precipice of that uncertain emotion." Reggie settled back in his chair and grinned. "As have you."

"Nonsense," Marcus said with a certainty he did not feel. If this was love, this unpleasant, unsettled tension lingering in his midsection like a poorly digested meal, he had been right to step cautiously around it in the past. This couldn't possibly be love.

But what of Reggie's observation of Gwen's feelings? Could she be in love with her husband? Certainly the look in her eye when she gazed at him was warm, and there was obviously already affection on her part. Admittedly, on his as well. But love? The idea was not nearly as offsetting as it had once been. Indeed, the very suggestion that Gwen might love him touched something deep inside him.

And if Reggie was right about Gwen's feelings, could he be right about Marcus's as well? At the moment Marcus wasn't entirely certain how he felt about anything beyond keeping Gwen in his life.

Whether Reggie was right or wrong, about either Gwen's emotions or Marcus's suspicions, she would soon be far removed from anyone who might try to take her away. And Marcus could concentrate his effort on determining if indeed, in spite of his resolve, love had caught him unawares.

And hoped it would not destroy them both.

Chapter Twelve

*There is nothing more charming than those moments
when a man who is supremely confident of his own nature
falters and a woman knows it is to her credit.*

Francesca Freneau

"So, what am I to do?" Gwen nervously prowled the perimeter of Colette's parlor.

Madame sat in a chair calmly working on her embroidery. "Nothing."

"Nothing?" Gwen pulled her brows together in frustration. In the past, Madame's unrelenting serenity in the midst of turmoil had always served to calm Gwen's own nerves. Until today. "What do you mean, nothing? I have to do something. I can't just wait until—"

"You can, my dear," Madame said coolly, "and you shall. You must cultivate patience, Gwendolyn."

"I thought I had." Gwen sighed. "At least when Albert—Mr. Trumble—at first told me there might be some problem with my guardianship, I was determined to keep my wits about me. But that was earlier today and now I cannot help but think about what could happen. And—"

"What *could* happen is precisely the point." Madame put her needlework in her lap and met Gwen's gaze. "The gentleman who gave you this news, this Mr. Trumble—"

"Albert," Gwen said under her breath.

"He is the same man who told you that you were penniless after your father's death, is he not?"

Gwen nodded. "Yes."

"And his information was erroneous then, was it not?

"Yes. But—"

"But even should his vague comments prove to be accurate now, there will be time to determine a course of action short of running away. I would hate to see that happen again, and I am certain, should the situation warrant it, that we can find a much more suitable solution." Madame nodded at the sofa beside her chair. "Now, do sit down, Gwendolyn, you are making me dizzy."

Gwen sank onto the sofa. "I cannot lose them, Madame. They are my family. I am all they have. And they are all I have."

Madame raised a chastising brow. "And what of your husband? Is he not your family now?"

"Of course." Gwen picked at a thread on the arm of the sofa and avoided Madame's gaze. "But Marcus is . . . well . . ."

"Honorable and intelligent. And I suspect he has a

good heart." Madame studied her for a long moment. "When are you going to tell him about the girls?"

"Soon," Gwen hedged.

"And what, pray tell, is your definition of *soon*?"

"I don't know." Gwen huffed and got to her feet, took one look at Madame's frown, and promptly sat back down. "I don't know."

"My dear girl, I understand your fears. They make a great deal of sense. The men in your life, starting with your own father, have not proven themselves to be especially trustworthy."

"What if Marcus is no better?" Gwen hated to say it aloud but it had to be said. "What if the kindness and consideration he has shown me does not extend to my nieces? What if—"

"What if the moon was indeed made of cheese?" Madame shook her head in exasperation. "Gwendolyn, I realize trust does not come easy to you but you are an intelligent woman. Think about the kind of man you have married. He has done nothing whatsoever to earn your suspicion."

"I don't think he wants daughters," Gwen said under her breath.

"Not terribly surprising, most men don't. Did he actually say he didn't want daughters?"

"Not in those exact words," Gwen muttered. "Upon reflection, I suppose I could have read more into his comments than was warranted."

"You are his wife now, you could simply ask him."

"That would be the intelligent thing to do. But apparently I am not as intelligent as you seem to think."

Gwen folded her hands in her lap and stared at them. "I couldn't bear it if he didn't want them. I will not subject them to living where they are not wanted. And I would"—she tried not to choke on the words—"leave him rather than give them up."

"So if it came to a choice"—Madame's voice was gentle—"you would choose them over him?"

Gwen swallowed back the lump in her throat. "I would have no choice."

Madame studied her for a long, silent moment. "You love him, don't you?"

"No," Gwen said without thinking, then sighed. "I don't know. I thought I didn't until I considered living my life without him. And now"—she shook her head—"I don't know how I feel. I thought I was simply . . . well, you'll think it's silly."

"Perhaps."

Gwen drew a deep breath. "In lust with him."

"In lust?" Madame laughed. "I daresay I have never heard of being in lust before."

"Neither had I. But it seemed rather appropriate." Gwen thought for a moment. "He makes me feel as if I were completely unique and entirely special. As if I were the most important person in the world to him."

"When you are lying in his bed?"

"No." Gwen drew her brows together. "Well, then too, of course, but other times as well. All the time, really. He looks at me as if I were quite remarkable. As if he were the luckiest man in the world, and I feel equally lucky. More perhaps. And Madame . . ." Gwen leaned toward the older woman. "When his eyes meet mine, across a dining table or an entire room, I feel the oddest warmth, almost as though he has actually touched me. And he'll smile, this slightly wry, crooked, charming type of smile, and I know it's just for me. A secret shared between us." Gwen shook her head and settled back on the sofa, awe bringing a soft smile to her face. "It's quite remarkable."

"It is indeed."

For a long moment Gwen considered what she'd at last put into words. She hadn't realized until now just how important Marcus had become in her life. Even to her, it did indeed sound like love.

But it wasn't. She hardened her resolve. It might well be something more than lust, but it wasn't love. She simply would not permit it.

She lifted her chin and met Madame's gaze directly. "I will do whatever I must to keep my family. I will not let those girls grow up as I did. And I will not let anyone take them from me."

"We wouldn't go anyway." Charity's voice sounded from the doorway.

Madame frowned. "Have you been eavesdropping again?"

"It was an accident." Hope stepped into the room, her sisters close on her heels. "We didn't mean to over-hear. It just happened."

"You"—Patience pointed an accusing finger at Gwen—"were talking exceedingly loud."

"Was I?" Gwen said. "I hadn't thought so. Indeed, I thought my tone was quite discreet."

"Not at all." Hope shook her head. "Why, we barely had to strain the tiniest bit to hear every word."

Gwen lifted a brow. "Every word?"

"Not every word," Charity said quickly. "Just the last part about not letting anyone take us away."

"And the part about how Lord Pennington makes your heart pitter-pat." Patience gazed upward, fluttered her eyelashes, and clasped her hands over her heart.

Gwen gasped. "I most certainly never said anything of the kind."

"It sounded like that." Hope collapsed at Gwen's feet in a most unladylike manner.

"Well, it wasn't," Gwen said firmly.

"Why don't you like him?" Charity settled beside Gwen and studied her. "You did marry him."

"The matter of my marriage is neither here nor there." Gwen's voice was firm. "And I do like him."

"He gives her secret smiles." Patience heaved an overly dramatic, heartfelt sigh. "And when his eyes meet hers—"

"That's quite enough," Madame said firmly.

Patience grinned and sank down on the floor beside her younger sister.

"Why do you think he doesn't want us?" Charity said abruptly. "It because we're girls, isn't it? Miss Pickle-face said most people want sons not daughters."

"I don't know that he doesn't want you," Gwen said carefully.

"Then why haven't you told him about us?" Patience said, with the ability of a child to go immediately to the point.

Three pairs of eyes stared at her, a question in every gaze, a challenge on each face.

"I haven't told him because"—Gwen drew a deep breath—"as much as I hate to admit it, I'm scared."

"You?" Charity snickered. "I hadn't thought you were scared of much of anything."

Hope stared at her suspiciously. "You don't particularly look scared."

"And he didn't especially look scary." Patience shook her head.

"He can be quite firm," Gwen murmured.

Marcus could also be exceedingly cool and rather remote. She thought the truth of his nature was in those moments when it was just the two of them and he was open and candid. She suspected, or hoped, the controlled, unemotional façade he displayed publicly was completely at odds with his real self.

Still, she didn't yet know him well enough or have enough confidence in her own assessment of his character to abandon her fears regardless of how much she wanted to. She could very well be entirely wrong. Madame had advised patience, and it was as necessary in the decision of when to tell him about the girls as it was when, and if, she should take her nieces away entirely.

A thought struck her, and she studied Charity carefully. "Do you want to stay with me, then?"

"Yes." Hope nodded vigorously. "You aren't nearly as bad as we'd thought at first."

"Of course, that was before we knew you," Patience said quickly. "Now that we do, we think there is the distinct possibility we could learn to like you. Quite a lot."

Madame bent her head toward her needlework to hide her smile.

"Actually, you have grown on us." Hope drew her

brows together thoughtfully. "Rather like a wart. I had a wart once and it—"

"That's disgusting." Patience's tone was lofty.

"And what do you think?" Gwen turned to Charity.

"Oh, I think warts are disgusting too." Charity smirked then shrugged. "I think you're better than stowing away on board ship and being tossed into the sea or having to sleep in alleys with rats."

"And I suppose that is better than nothing," Gwen said under her breath, stifling a touch of disappointment.

What did she expect anyway? The girls had resented her from the moment they'd met, and Gwen had done little since then to change their minds. Certainly she got along better with these children than any of those she'd had in her charge during her ill-fated years as a governess, but still she'd not been able to spend nearly enough time with them as it would certainly take to forge a solid relationship, even possibly affection.

"However, in the interest of fairness"—Charity traded glances with her sisters—"we are of the joint opinion—"

"We voted," Hope said.

"—that anyone that Madame de Chabot and Madame Freneau like as much as they like you probably has qualities we simply haven't noticed yet."

Patience and Hope sported matching grins. Even Charity favored Gwen with a reluctant smile. "So we have further decided, no matter what might happen, we wish to stay with you."

"Because I'm better than"—Gwen grimaced— "rats?"

"We don't like rats." Hope's tone was firm.

"Very well, then. I suppose I shall have to take what I can and be grateful for that." Gwen smiled with relief. "In truth, even though I am apparently the least of any number of evils, I am still quite pleased."

Again the girls exchanged glances. "We do think you should know, however," Patience began in a patient manner, as if to make certain Gwen understood, "it isn't as if we liked you a great deal."

"Not yet, anyway," Hope said staunchly. "We feel it's entirely too soon to like you a great deal."

"However, we are willing"—Charity nodded at Madame—"to give you the benefit of the doubt based on Madame Freneau's recommendation."

Hope lowered her voice in a confidential manner. "We like her a great deal."

"And Madame de Chabot as well." Patience smiled wistfully. "She has the most wonderful stories about balls and castles and princes and all manner of exciting people and places."

"I see." Gwen's voice was weak. "I suppose I should thank them for championing my cause."

"Aunt Gwendolyn." Charity's nose wrinkled as if the title sounded as awkward to her ears as it did to Gwen's. "We simply wish to be a family again."

"We did like being a family." Patience sighed.

Hope sniffed. "We had a great deal of fun."

Charity slanted her sisters a quieting glance. "We know without Mama and Papa nothing will ever be the same, but we are all tired of not knowing what will happen to us next. We firmly believe that you—"

"And Lord Pennington," Patience said.

"Who didn't seem at all frightening. Rather like the kind of man who would get a girl a dog," Hope added.

"—are our best hope for . . ." Charity thought for a moment. "Salvation. Yes, that's it." For the first time since Gwen had met her, Charity cast her a genuine smile. "Salvation."

"If not here on earth then in the world to come," Hope intoned piously.

"One wonders what would have happened if they'd been found by pirates instead of missionaries," Madame said under her breath.

"I have never been anyone's salvation before, but I shall try to live up to it." Gwen studied the faces of the three girls for a long moment, then nodded and without further thought, spit on her finger.

All three sisters promptly followed suit. Nieces and aunt proceeded with the traditional ceremony and as one turned toward Madame. She smiled in resignation, spit, and mixed her "blood" with theirs.

"I know Colette will regret missing this," Madame murmured.

"We can certainly do it again when she arrives home." Patience grinned. "I suspect she would hate to miss a blood oath."

"Now we are even more bound together than before," Hope said somberly. "Every blood oath makes the one before it that much stronger, you know."

Patience nodded. "Bound together through all eternity."

"It means we will not leave you." Charity's gaze met Gwen's.

An odd sort of acknowledgment flashed between

them. There was a vow here far beyond the rubbing of wet fingers, regardless of whether they were moistened with blood or something far less pagan. Gwen realized she and Charity were more alike than dissimilar. Each had taken on the responsibilities of survival at a young age: Gwen for herself, Charity for her sisters.

And now, between them, there was a promise that from this moment forward, they would share that responsibility. That whatever happened they were indeed bound one to the other. And neither would bear the burden alone.

"Excellent." Gwen's gaze meshed with Charity's. "Because I have no intention of allowing you to leave. Nor will I ever permit anyone to take you from me." She held up her finger. "And I promise by all the blood in my veins that I shall never break this oath or else suffer the dire, horrible consequences." She lowered her voice dramatically, and in the back of her mind noted she'd never meant anything as much as she did this promise to these children. "Forever."

"You wish to go to the country," Gwen said slowly. "Now?"

"As soon as it can be arranged." Marcus leaned against the mantel, his arms crossed over his chest, in a manner that would be considered indolent if not for the tense line of his body. Gwen realized he was much more somber than the offhand nature of his words would indicate and wondered if there was something amiss. "I should think tomorrow at the very latest. It's but half a day's drive from London, and I do think you should see Holcroft Hall—"

"Holcroft Hall?" Gwen studied him thoughtfully. Perhaps he was simply concerned about her reaction to leaving town. "Your family seat? The family seat of the Earls of Pennington?"

"Precisely. As it has been since the first earl."

"Near the village of Pennington itself, then, I presume?" Gwen struggled to hide the note of excitement in her voice.

The house her father had left her was near Pennington. If Madame was agreeable to accompanying them, Gwen could move the girls there and continue her surreptitious visits. A sojourn in the country for her and her nieces would be nothing short of perfect. It wouldn't remove any possible threat, but it might make avoiding whatever problems might come a bit easier. If nothing else, it gave Gwen a welcome illusion of security and allowed her to actually do something rather than wait to see what might happen. She would send word to Madame later today, and with luck the girls would soon be safely in the country, at least for the moment. At once a weight lifted from Gwen's shoulders and her mood lightened.

"Of course"—Marcus shrugged—"the village itself is not very big, you understand, but the countryside is quite scenic, especially at this time of year, and—"

"And you can breathe freely and feel the earth beneath your feet."

An odd look crossed his face as if he were both embarrassed at having told her that and pleased she'd remembered.

"Something like that." He cleared his throat. "As I

was saying, it's an especially lovely time of year. Much nicer there than in London."

"Is it?" She tilted her head and studied him. "My dear Lord Pennington, are you trying to talk me into this?" She couldn't resist a teasing grin. He really was terribly endearing.

"Don't be absurd." His tone was aloof, and she didn't believe it for a moment. "I have interests that need attention at the estate, and I have already decided we shall leave as soon as possible."

She stared at him for a moment, then laughed.

His brows pulled together. "What is so funny?"

"You." She grinned. "You're quite amusing when you're being the cool, unemotional Lord Pennington who has firmly put his foot down and made an irrevocable decision."

"Am I?" His tone was unchanged, but there was a definite twinkle in his eye.

"Indeed you are. Especially when you adopt that pompous manner of yours."

"Pompous." His mouth dropped open. "Pompous?"

"You may say it as often as you wish, my lord, it does not change the fact of it."

"I am not pompous," he said in a decidedly pompous manner.

She raised a brow.

He frowned. "Am I?"

She nodded.

He thought for a moment. "Is it better than being cold and unemotional?"

She grinned. "I find it quite entertaining."

He narrowed his eyes and studied her for a long moment. "What precisely has happened to you, Gwen? You are . . . What's the word I'm thinking of?"

"Happy?" she said innocently.

"Yes, that's it." He stared in a suspicious manner. "You look exceedingly happy. Why?"

"I'm not entirely sure." She considered him thoughtfully. "This marriage of ours is working out far better than I had expected."

"Is it?"

She nodded. "You are far better than I had expected."

"Am I?"

"Yes, you are." She laughed. "Why do you seem so surprised? You've never struck me as a man not thoroughly aware of his own worth. In truth, didn't you tell me what an excellent catch you were?"

"I might have said something like that."

"You've certainly never seemed to lack confidence in yourself or in your attraction for women."

"Apparently marriage has changed me," he muttered. "You have changed me."

She stepped closer to him. "How could I possibly have changed you?"

"I don't know but you have." He narrowed his eyes. "I am not at all happy."

"Don't be absurd, Marcus," she scoffed. "You haven't anything to be unhappy about."

"Don't I?" His voice was soft.

"Of course not," she said firmly. "You've maintained your fortune. You've avoided marriage to someone completely unsuitable—"

"Have I?"

"Yes. I was handpicked by your father, and your mother likes me, as does your closest friend." She slipped her arms around his neck. "You are quite lucky, my lord."

His brows drew together. "What are you doing?"

She sighed. "You seem to ask that a great deal." She brought her lips to his and brushed them seductively across his mouth until he responded. He gathered her closer and kissed her with a fierce intensity that quite took her breath away.

The familiar sense of need rose within her, and she wondered how terribly improper it would be to make love here in the parlor in the middle of the afternoon.

His lips moved from hers to explore her neck and the base of her throat. "I am a fool, Lady Pennington."

Her head dropped back and she clutched at his arms. "Are you, Lord Pennington? Why?"

"It scarcely matters." His hands roamed eagerly down her back and over her derrière. "Suffice it to say, I have listened to my own ridiculous doubts based on nothing of substance instead of following what my head has told me."

She pressed closer against him to feel his arousal growing hard against her. "I daresay that's not your head speaking now."

He laughed. "No, it most assuredly is not." Without warning he scooped her up in his arms and carried her toward the door. "However, my head is saying the parlor is most definitely not the proper place to continue this discussion."

She kissed his neck. "Godfrey would be scandalized."

"To hell with Godfrey," Marcus muttered. He reached the door and stopped to gaze down at her, his look questioning. "Are you certain you wish to go to the country and leave London?"

"Well, not this very moment." She tugged at the knot of his cravat. "Tomorrow is soon enough."

"You shall miss a great number of parties, you know. Balls, routs, that sort of thing."

"I have missed them before." She frowned at his cravat. "I cannot get this blasted thing untied."

He chuckled. "Patience, my dear."

"Patience is a virtue I have never had in abundance." She sighed and gazed up at him. "I think the country sounds wonderful."

"Does it?"

"It does indeed. It's been years since I've spent any time at all in the English countryside. Even when I was a girl I was away at school far more often then I was at Townsend Park."

He stared down at her with a bemused smile. "You really do want to go?"

"I want to go anywhere as long as you are there," she said without thinking, then wished she could take back the words. It was an admission she wasn't ready to make. "Yes, of course. Spring in the country. Why, who would possibly not wish to go?"

"Why did you marry me, Gwen?" His tone was abruptly serious.

"What an odd question." She trailed her fingers over his shirt and marveled at the way his muscles tensed beneath the fabric. "You needed this marriage. Our fathers thought it was for the best. Beyond that"—she smiled up at him—"I suppose I married you for all the usual reasons. You, my lord, are an exceedingly good catch."

"And you, Lady Pennington"—he shifted her in his arms and pulled open the door, then proceeded toward the stairs—"are really quite extraordinary."

A subdued gasp sounded from the shadows and Marcus grinned. "Godfrey," he called to the unseen butler, "we shall leave for the country in the morning. Please see to the arrangements."

"Yes, my lord." Godfrey's voice rang with a subtle note of resignation.

Gwen giggled and buried her head against her husband's chest. "He still does not approve of me."

"Godfrey does not particularly approve of anyone. Besides, his approval is of no consequence." Marcus took the stairs two at a time. "You are the lady of the house and as such, he is in your service."

Marcus reached his bedchamber and pushed the door open. "He will approve the moment he realizes what I have discovered." He stepped into the room and kicked the door shut. His gaze, dark and green and promising, met hers. "I am indeed a lucky man."

Chapter Thirteen

*There is nothing more delightful
than a man in love. Unless of course
it is a wealthy man in love.*

Colette de Chabot

"You can see most of the estate from here." Marcus settled back in his saddle and studied the view he knew
even with his eyes closed. This rise on the very edge of
the estate, not a proper hill really but high enough to
suit, with its lone beech tree as a sort of sentinel, had
been one of his favorite spots since he'd been old
enough to sit a horse.

"It's a wonderful view." Gwen's gaze followed his
own.

He glanced at her and bit back a contented smile.

Gwen sat on her horse with a confidence that belied
her unease a scant five days ago when they'd arrived at
Holcroft Hall. It was understandable, of course; it had
been years since she'd ridden on a regular basis. Still,
the woman was a natural in the saddle and was on her

way to becoming an excellent horsewoman. Indeed, she'd been determined to master riding.

She and Marcus had ridden every morning since their arrival, and she'd set out on her own each afternoon. He'd been naturally concerned at first, but she'd refused to even consider allowing a groom to accompany her, pointing out the estate was her home and no harm would come to her there. He'd had work of his own to keep him busy: he'd not lied when he'd said there were estate matters that needed his attention. Still, he'd noted precisely when she'd ridden off each day and exactly when she'd return, well prepared to ride to her rescue if need be.

"I love it here," he said, still gazing off into the distance. "Over there is the road to the village and around that bend is the old dower house. In the distance you can just make out the lake, more a pond, really. I used to sit under that tree and stare for hours." He leaned toward her confidentially. "When I was a boy I had the lay of the land fixed in my mind and I would re-create every bit of it in the gardens by the north side of the hall as a battle-field for my toy soldiers." He chuckled. "I commanded some impressive battles there through the years."

She raised a brow. "And were you always victorious?"

He gasped with mock dismay. "I cannot believe you would ask such a thing. Why, I was the most decorated general in His Majesty's service." Marcus grinned. "Of course, I was also the only one on the battlefield over two inches tall."

"I can see the hall from here." She shielded her eyes with her hand.

"I'm surprised you haven't found this spot before

now," he said with a teasing note in his voice. "Given the vast amount of time you have spent wandering the grounds on horseback."

She cast him a chastising glance. "When one is concerned with staying in the saddle, one tends to miss much of the landscape."

He laughed with an ease he hadn't had since childhood.

Gwen hadn't needed rescuing, of course. Marcus had faced the fact that there was perhaps never a woman less in need of rescuing, or more independent than his Miss Townsend—Lady Pennington.

It was one of the things he loved about her.

That too was a fact he could no longer ignore. Here in the country, away from the distractions of London, he'd realized Reggie was right. His fears about another man in Gwen's life were unwarranted and nothing more than his own self-doubts. Doubts that had subtly plagued him for much of his adult life, unrecognized until now.

In recent days he'd come to several remarkable understandings about himself, late at night, with her lying by his side. She had her own rooms, of course, but he preferred having her in his bed, and she seemed to prefer it as well. He prayed she always would. He'd realized, in those contented moments, that his caution about truly caring for a woman, about love, was interwoven with his own odd doubts and the odder yet suspicion that perhaps he had never especially considered himself worthy of love. Ridiculous idea—he'd never thought himself anything but supremely confident—but present nonetheless.

Until her.

Gwen was everything he'd ever wanted in a woman.

Everything he'd ever wanted in a wife. She was clever and witty and had a fine intelligence that shone from her lovely blue eyes. Yet in spite of her independent nature, she was willing to do what was necessary to be the countess he needed, whether that was learn to sit a horse with grace or acknowledge yet another introduction with a genuine smile. She'd met his tenants and many of the people of Pennington and was unfailingly gracious and kind. He suspected they'd already taken her into their hearts.

As had he.

And if an odd shadow flickered in her eyes now and again, and if he caught her looking at him once or twice with a kind of unexplained sorrow, and if she fell silent on occasion as if she had retreated behind her own private wall, well, he could scarcely fault her for that. He had spent most of his life behind a wall: cool, amused, and aloof. Unemotional.

"The hall is quite impressive, you know. Far more so than Townsend Park." Gwen stared at the far-off house thoughtfully. "It's really rather intimidating."

He laughed. "I can't imagine you find anything intimidating."

"I find a great deal intimidating," she said wryly.

The hall was indeed grand, although Marcus had never particularly thought it such. It had occupied its spot in the center of the estate for nearly two centuries, a great stone entity softened by age and affection.

"It is a bit imposing perhaps." He took her hand and pulled it to his lips. "But it's home."

"Home." A smile tugged the corners of her mouth. "That has a lovely sound to it."

"It shall sound even better when the laughter of a dozen children fills its rooms."

She snatched her hand from his. "A dozen children?"

"Did I fail to mention that?" He grinned. "Or perhaps you've forgotten."

"I daresay I would have remembered a dozen children."

"I have always wanted a large family."

"But a dozen children." She shook her head. "Honestly, Marcus, that's—"

"Very well." He heaved an overly dramatic sigh. "Perhaps a dozen is a bit much. A half dozen will do."

"All boys, no doubt."

"In that, my darling Lady Pennington, you are completely mistaken."

Her brows drew together. "But you said—"

"Whatever I may or may not have said, in the admittedly awkward circumstances of our initial meetings, was not entirely what I intended." He met her gaze directly. "Gwen, I should quite like to have a son or two to carry on my family name—"

"I thought as much," she said under her breath.

"However"—his voice was firm—"that does not mean I would not welcome daughters. I should like nothing better than a small herd of red-haired, blue-eyed females squealing about the place."

She gazed at him with disbelief.

"I know that worries you because the future of women in this world is frequently difficult and their position often uncertain. I suspect you don't wish for daughters because of your own experiences. I wish I could turn back the clock and save you from the years following your father's death but I can't." He stared into her eyes with all the sincerity in his heart. "But I swear to you now, I shall make certain the future of any daughters we may have will not be dependent solely on their abilities to make a good match. I promise I shall do everything in my power to ensure they have financial security in the event of my demise."

Gwen stared as if she were in shock.

Marcus held his breath. What if he were wrong? What if her opposition to daughters had nothing to do with her background? What if she didn't want children at all? Or at least not as many as he did?

Unease settled in his stomach. "Aren't you going to say something?"

"I think . . ." She shook her head. "Girls do not come in herds." A slow smile spread across her face. "Flocks perhaps, or, I don't know, gatherings or groups or—"

He laughed with sheer relief. "You don't mind then? Having a large family? Even girls?"

"Not in the least. I have always wanted a large family myself." She paused as if considering her words. "And I owe you an apology. I took your words in a manner in which they were not intended. I suspect I may well have been looking for a meaning they did not have based more on my own experience than any true knowledge of you. I should have trusted you from the outset."

"Still, that's understandable," he said quickly. "We were thrust together by an odd set of circumstances—"

"Fate?" she said with a grin.

"Fate." He returned her smile. "For some of us, trust does not come easily."

"Perhaps, but trust is important. I have never truly trusted anyone before, aside from Colette and Madame, of course. You had given me no reason not to trust you. I should have known better than to paint all men with the same brush and base my conclusions on little more than my own fears."

"That seems to be something we have in common," he said under his breath.

She looked confused. "What?"

"It's of no consequence." He shrugged. "All that matters now is the future." He wagged his brows in a lascivious manner. "And we should begin work immediately on that large family."

She laughed again, and the sound rippled through his blood and into his soul. He wanted to tell her he loved her, but now was not the time. She might well be ready to trust him, but love might take a bit longer. Still, he was confident she cared about him and thought, or hoped, it might well be love. Her views on love were even odder than his, and she simply wasn't as ready to admit to the emotion as he was.

And if she did not love him now, she would eventually. He was confident about that as well, confidence sprung from the depths of his own feeling. In truth, at the moment, anything, including love, seemed not only possible but probable. He grinned to himself. Reggie was right: the flight was indeed magnificent.

They walked their horses in a leisurely manner until the dower house came into view.

"Blast it all." He reined his horse to a stop.

"What is it?"

"Look, down there, that's the dower house." He

squinted in an effort to more clearly make out what he was certain he was seeing. "Do you see it?"

"The house that resembles an overgrown cottage?" she said lightly. "I see it. It looks rather charming."

"Bloody hell, it looks like someone has moved in. Look, Gwen, there's a carriage and laundry drying and"—he peered closer—"is that a child?"

"One of a dozen, no doubt," she teased.

He shot her a quick glare. "This is not in the least bit amusing."

"No, of course not." She bit back a grin. "Well, if it's part of the estate, can't you simply demand they move?"

"No, damnation, it's part of the estate, or at least it should be, but I don't own it." He blew a long, frustrated breath. "I have been trying to get that piece of property back for years. My father sold it shortly before his death for some absurd reason. I've never been able to figure out why."

"Perhaps he thought you would never marry and therefore your mother would have no need of a dower house." An innocent note sounded in her voice, and he didn't believe it for a moment. She definitely found this amusing.

He ignored her. "I didn't even know it had been sold until last year."

"And the owner won't sell it back to you now?"

"I don't know who the owner is." He ran his hand through his hair. "Whiting handled the whole thing. He claims he's not at liberty to disclose the name of the owner. In truth, he was rather surprised to learn I was unaware of the sale."

"Apparently your father made any number of

arrangements he did not see fit to inform you of," she said mildly.

"So it would seem," he muttered. "Whiting has been trying to negotiate a purchase with the owner. The house has been empty for years, and I was under the impression that the owner had no particular plans for it."

"It does seem much easier to buy something no one wants." She shrugged. "However, now that the house is occupied—"

"Now that it's occupied I could bypass Whiting altogether and speak to the owner directly." He nodded thoughtfully. "That's exactly what I should do."

"Now?" she blurted.

"There is no time like the present, my dear. With any luck, I shall convince the man to sell this very day." He started his horse toward the house, then stopped and looked back. "Are you coming?"

"Of course, if that's what you wish." She sidled her horse up close to his and laid her hand on his arm. Her voice was low and decidedly seductive. "But I was under the impression you had other plans for the rest of the morning."

She caught her lower lip between her teeth and gazed up at him, her eyes wide, dark blue and inviting. He swallowed hard. "Other plans?"

"Something about work? For the future?" Her fingers trailed idly up his arm. "That needs immediate attention?"

"Of course," he said slowly. "This business can certainly wait."

"I thought perhaps it could." She smiled in a knowing manner, and he resisted the urge to pull her from her horse and make love to her right there on the grass. "Now then, Marcus, I think it's past time to show you just how well I have mastered the art of sitting a horse. I shall race you back to the hall."

"I never enter a race I do not intend to win. And I never race without knowing the stakes." His gaze roamed over her, and he shifted in his saddle to accommodate his abrupt discomfort. "What is my prize when I win?"

"Why, my dear Lord Pennington, *should* you win"— she smiled in an altogether too provocative manner— "anything you wish." She laughed and before he could say a word, took off.

He called after her. "And if you win?"

Her words trailed on the wind in her wake. "Anything I wish."

He dug in his heels and started after her. He didn't especially care if he beat her to the hall or not. Given the stakes, win or lose, he was indeed a lucky man.

"You certainly appear up to no good," a familiar wry voice broke into Marcus's thoughts.

He looked up from the ledgers and correspondence spread before him on the massive desk that had served his father and his father before him and grinned at Reggie leaning idly in the open doorway of the Holcroft Hall library. "I am."

"I thought as much." Reggie sauntered into the room and sank into an upholstered chair positioned in front of the desk. "Don't you have an estate manager for all of this?"

Marcus leaned back in his chair. "Of course. But he's

done his part, and now it's time for me to do mine, as you well know. You handle your estate precisely the same way."

Reggie shrugged, and something about his manner struck Marcus as odd, almost as if his casual air was forced.

"I thought you weren't coming until the end of the week?" Marcus studied his friend curiously.

"London was exceedingly dull. I'm not entirely sure why. Perhaps I have simply grown bored with it all. Besides, you are such a good example I decided there was much at Berkley Manor that needed attention. Beyond that," Reggie said pointedly, "it is the end of the week."

"Is it?" Marcus suspected the grin on his face was nothing short of ridiculous. "Already? Are you sure?"

"Quite." Reggie's expression was thoughtful, his words measured. "I see you are in better spirits now than at our last meeting."

"Reggie, what you see before you is a changed man." He laced his fingers behind his neck and tilted back his chair. "A man who is content with his lot in life. No, not merely content, but happy." He grinned. "Unreservedly, unabashedly, irrevocably happy."

"I see," Reggie said slowly. "And the cause of all this unreserved, unabashed, irrevocable happiness?"

"The cause? I should think you of all people would recognize the cause."

"I'm afraid I do."

Marcus thumped his chair back to the floor and leaned forward. "Then you should be happy for me as well."

"Of course," Reggie murmured. "Congratulations

are no doubt in order. And that calls for a drink in celebration."

He stood quickly and crossed the room to a cabinet
built into the wall between bookcases, designed to match
the fluted wood columns that marked one wide section of
bookshelves from the next around the walls of the library. Marcus had always considered it either an archi-
tectural masterpiece or a joke. Probably a bit of both.
While the columns in the room appeared at first glance to
be nothing more than decorative embellishments, nearly
half concealed such cabinets. Reggie pulled open the
door to the one that housed Marcus's brandy.

"Would you like a glass?" Reggie's voice was muffled
behind the cabinet door.

"No, but I do appreciate your generous offer," Marcus said wryly. "Especially as it is my brandy."

"I thought you would." Reggie returned to the desk,
two glasses in one hand, a decanter in the other.

Marcus raised a curious brow.

"It would be most impolite of you to let a guest drink
alone." Reggie set the glasses on the desk, a shade harder
than was necessary, and again Marcus noted Reggie's demeanor. He was preoccupied, as if something of importance weighed on his mind. It was not at all his usual
manner. "You wouldn't want to be rude."

"Wouldn't I?"

"Never." Reggie filled the glasses, pushed one across
the desk to Marcus, then took his seat. "Not you. You,
Marcus, have always been unfailingly polite."

"One of the rules one lives by," Marcus murmured
and watched his friend with growing concern.

Marcus knew the viscount as well as he knew himself, and there was definitely something amiss. Reggie studied the brandy in his glass silently, as if the amber liquid held the answer to whatever was plaguing him. His silence alone was worrisome.

Reggie was not the sort of man given to brooding or moodiness. His unrestrained nature never failed to recover from even the most devastating of circumstances. Marcus remembered when Reggie's father had died a good ten years or so ago. While the pain his friend suffered was obvious, Reggie had chosen to handle his grief by celebrating his father's life rather than mourning his loss. It was a lesson Marcus took to heart when his own father had died.

"Are you all right?" Marcus said.

Reggie paid him no heed.

Indeed, throughout their long years of friendship, Marcus could not recall an occasion when Reggie's basic enjoyment of life did not overcome whatever ill fortune had reared its head. Even while in the final throes of a disastrous love affair, and Marcus had long ago lost count of those, Reggie was typically overly dramatic, always boisterous and eventually philosophical. And always more than willing to freely discuss and, in truth, examine every word, every nuance, every minor aspect of whatever had led to the latest breaking of his heart.

"Reggie?"

But he was never, ever subdued or reserved or reticent. He was never quiet.

Marcus tried again. "I credit my current good humor to the fact that the sun was a remarkable shade of green today, which I cannot help but think will surely benefit the tenants in their quest for an excellent harvest this year."

Reggie's gaze jerked to Marcus's and his brow furrowed. "What?"

"That's what I want to know," Marcus said slowly. "What on earth is the matter with you?"

"Nothing." Reggie shook his head and took a long swallow of his brandy.

"Nothing?" Marcus snorted in disbelief. "You may be an excellent liar when it comes to telling a lady she is the loveliest thing you've ever seen, but you've never managed it especially well with me."

"You're not all that lovely." A slight smile tugged at Reggie's lips. "In point of fact, I don't find you the least bit att—"

"Come on, out with it," Marcus said firmly. "I have never seen you in such melancholy spirits. Why, you're positively . . ." Marcus searched for the right word, then grinned. "Poetic."

Reggie barked a short laugh. "Well, if my plan to attract the undying affections of the ladies by being dashing and dangerous doesn't work, I can certainly adopt the attitude of a brooding poet."

"You're doing it far too well, my friend." Marcus's voice sobered. "What's happened in the last few days to put you in such a state?"

Reggie blew a long breath. "I have discovered I may well have been wrong."

Marcus laughed with abrupt relief. "That's all? You've been wrong about any number of things before, and I daresay will be again."

"No doubt." Reggie shrugged dismissively.

"What, precisely, were you wrong about?"

Reggie hesitated, then drew a deep breath. "The nature of men and the honor of women."

Marcus narrowed his eyes. "Impressively philosophical but not much of an answer."

"You think not? I thought it was an excellent answer." Reggie swirled the brandy in his glass thoughtfully for a long moment. "I seem to find myself on the horns of a rather nasty dilemma."

"And?"

"And I fear whatever choice I make will have terrible repercussions." Reggie got to his feet and wandered toward the nearest bookshelf. "As I said, it is a nasty dilemma."

"That does sound dire." Marcus leaned back in his chair and watched him carefully, trying to ignore a growing sense of impending disaster on his friend's behalf. "Am I to gather, then, that in the scant few days since I left London, you've become embroiled in yet another affair of the heart?"

"Would that it were that simple," Reggie murmured, perusing the books as if to find an answer among their spines.

"Blast it all, Reggie," Marcus snapped. "You've never been the least bit reluctant to confide in me before, why are you so reticent to do so now?"

Reggie coolly pulled a book from the shelves and paged through it. "The stakes are much higher now."

"What stakes? Do stop going around in circles, old man, and come to the point. What are you talking about?"

Reggie snapped the book shut and shoved it back in its place on the shelf. "I gather from your manner when I arrived all is well with you? Between you and your wife, that is?"

Marcus heaved a sigh of frustration. "Yes, of course, we are bloody blissful together. My life is well in hand, it's yours that is of concern at the moment."

"Even so." Reggie folded his arms over his chest and leaned against the wall of books. "Correct me if I'm wrong, but I further assume you have at long last fallen over the precipice?"

"Yes, yes," Marcus said impatiently, "and I am quite enjoying the flight. Now what—"

"I was wrong, Marcus." Regret sounded in Reggie's voice.

"You've said that and I still don't understand. What are you talking about?"

"Everything." Reggie blew a long breath, and his gaze locked with Marcus's. "I was wrong and you were right."

For a long moment Marcus stared in confusion, then at once he understood exactly what Reggie couldn't bring himself to say. Realization slammed into Marcus with the force of a fist to his chest, stealing his breath and clawing at his soul. He got to his feet, braced his hands on the desk, and struggled to remain sane.

And distantly in the back of his mind, he noted the faint but unmistakable sound of something falling from a great height and crashing irrevocably to earth.

And knew it was his heart.

Chapter Fourteen

The only thing more lacking in intelligence
than a man in love is, regrettably, any man at all.

Helena Pennington

"You learned something in London, didn't you? About Gwen and this man you were so confident did not exist?"

"I am sorry, Marcus." Reggie shook his head and stepped closer. "I didn't want to tell you but I—"

"You didn't tell me!" Marcus grabbed his glass, tossed the brandy down his throat, then grabbed for the decanter, knowing it was that or his oldest friend's throat. "You haven't told me a bloody thing!"

"I know." Reggie shook his head. "This is exceedingly difficult for me."

"My apologies for making your life awkward!" Marcus drew a deep breath and tried to force a note of calm to his voice. "Tell me precisely what you have learned. Now."

"It's not what I learned." Reggie grimaced. "It's what I saw."

"What could you possibly have seen in London—"

"Not London, here."

"What?"

"I saw her, Marcus." Reggie winced. "With . . . him."

"From the beginning!"

Reggie drew a deep breath. "I was on my way here and I took a shortcut from the London road. You know, the one that cuts a good half an hour off the ride and goes past the old dower house." He cast Marcus a curious look. "Did you know it's occupied?"

"Yes!" Marcus clenched his teeth. "Go on."

"Very well. As I was passing, I saw a gentleman ride up and go into the house. I didn't recognize him. He was older than we are, obviously wealthy, and"—Reggie lowered his voice confidentially—"he had an air about him that said he didn't want to be seen."

"And then," Marcus prompted.

"I thought it was odd, of course, as no one has lived there for some time, and curious as well given the man's secretive manner. I would bet my fortune he had arranged an assignation of an amorous nature—"

"Reggie!"

"Sorry. Well, I was giving it no further thought, aside from a chuckle or two, as I have been in similar situations, when I saw your wife arrive." Reggie's forehead furrowed with concern. "She rode straight up to the house and didn't even bother to knock. Just went right in without a moment's hesitation."

"I see," Marcus said slowly, struggling to maintain his calm. "And?"

"And . . . that's it." Reggie frowned. "Isn't that enough?"

"No," Marcus said sharply. "It's not nearly enough."

He needed to consider this in a rational manner and ignore the thudding of his heart in his chest and the heavy weight in the pit of his stomach and the lump in his throat. At first glance, it did indeed seem as though Gwen was meeting someone in the old dower house. Reggie had seen her and some unknown gentleman, but there wasn't, in truth, any real evidence of anything untoward. There could be any number of excellent explanations as to precisely what Gwen was doing.

"Marcus?"

What she might well have been doing every afternoon since their arrival.

"Marcus, what are you thinking?"

"I'm thinking, Reggie"—Marcus forced a note of calm to his voice—"that you are just as prone to jump to erroneous conclusions as I am."

Reggie's mouth dropped open. "Erroneous conclusions? Come now. What I saw is much more damaging than anything you based your previous suspicions on. You had nothing whatsoever to go on. I have solid proof of something not quite right."

Marcus stared at his friend. "Thank you for putting it all in perspective."

"Sorry."

"I refuse to think the worst of her until I know the truth." Even as he said the words, Marcus knew they would be easier to say than to abide by.

"What are you going to do?"

"I don't know." Marcus ran his hand through his

hair. Hadn't he and Gwen talked about trust just that morning? How could he expect her to trust him if he didn't extend her the same courtesy? "I have come to know my wife rather well in recent days. Or at least I think I have. She has been on her own since her father's death, and it is unreasonable for me to expect her to change her nature as quickly as she changed her marital state. I must respect that she is an independent soul and private as well, and in many ways, I think, as cautious as I about emotion, but I do not doubt that she is an honorable person."

"Perhaps, but she's also a woman." Reggie shook his head mournfully. "They are a different breed entirely and, in my experience, not nearly as trustworthy as men."

"Gwen is," Marcus said stoutly, struggling to believe it.

"You're taking this far better than I thought you would."

"Am I?" Marcus laughed shortly. "It doesn't feel as if I am."

"Well, you are, and I quite appreciate it. Good God, this has been awful." Reggie downed the contents of his glass, stepped to the desk, and refilled it. "I want you to know, I did not come here straightaway. I rode for a long time, debating whether or not to tell you. You have no idea how difficult this has been for me."

"Again my apologies." Sarcasm dripped from Marcus's words.

"Accepted. I know you, Marcus. I knew once your heart was finally involved there would be no halfway measures for you." Reggie aimed his glass at Marcus.

"You've never been in love before. Love has always made me quite irrational, and frankly I expected a certain measure of insanity from you as well."

"Thank you for your vote of confidence, but I have always prided myself on remaining collected in the face of disaster."

"You're quite welcome. But you've never faced a disaster like this. Who knew how it might affect you? You might well have shot the messenger."

"I still might," Marcus muttered.

"I knew I was taking my life in my hands, worse still, risking our friendship, but ultimately I realized I had no choice but to tell you. I owe you that even if, in the end, you hated me." Reggie studied him carefully. "What are you going to do?"

"As I see it, I have several choices." Marcus sipped at his brandy, his mind churning with the possibilities. "I can do what I have always done and back away. Allow the lady in question to go her own way. Of course, this is not simply any lady, this is my wife. Or I could fight for her."

"And?"

"And I may well be fooling myself, but I am confident this can all be explained. I am confident as well Gwen cares for me; she might even love me. Furthermore, I don't believe what has passed between us since our marriage has been nothing more than an act on her part." He shrugged. "I could, of course, be wrong."

"But you don't think you are?"

"No, I don't. Or at least I hope I'm not. I doubt that she is that good an actress." Marcus turned and paced the room, trying to work through the assorted thoughts in his head. "In those instances in the past when I was involved with a woman, I always held back my emotions, rightly so as it turned out. Therefore, it was not especially difficult for me to do the honorable thing and yield my position to another man. Now, however, I have lost my heart to, of all people, my wife. I will not give her up." He stopped and met Reggie's gaze. "She is my life."

"Then . . ." Reggie drew the word out in a deliberate manner. "You choose to fight for her?"

"I cannot live without her," Marcus said simply, knowing it was nothing less than the truth.

Determination swept through him. He would not give her up. He was confident she had not betrayed him, but if by some slim chance he was wrong, he would start over. They would start over. He would court her and charm her and seduce her again and again if necessary. He would do anything to keep this woman he loved in his life, in his bed, and by his side for the rest of his days.

"I never thought I'd hear you say that." Reggie blew a long breath. "I'm really quite impressed."

"Thank you." Marcus strode to the desk, slapped his glass down, and started toward the door.

"Where are you going?"

"To the dower house. I'm going to get to the bottom of this. Mind you, I still believe there is an innocent explanation, or at least an explanation other than the conclusion you've reached, but Gwen is involved in something, and I want to know what it is."

"So much for respecting her independence and her privacy."

Marcus snorted. "You *believed* that?"

"It sounded good," Reggie murmured. "Wait for me."

Marcus glanced over his shoulder. "You're coming, then?"

"I wouldn't miss it." Reggie grinned, and Marcus noted his friend's usual nature was once again restored. "Marcus?"

"Yes?"

Reggie drew a deep breath. "I hope I'm wrong."

"I have no doubt of it," Marcus said with a confidence he didn't completely feel. "Besides"—Marcus grinned—"you have been wrong many times before and will be again."

And Marcus prayed this time was no different.

"That's his horse," Reggie said under his breath.

"Then he's still here." Marcus studied the scene thoughtfully.

There was a carriage parked to the side of the house. The dower house had no stables of its own, but no horses for the vehicle were in evidence. Nor was Gwen's horse to be seen, and Marcus was at once disappointed and relieved. Whatever was going on here, it would not involve a confrontation with his wife. At least not yet.

"Come on, then." Marcus directed his horse to the yard and dismounted. Reggie followed suit, and the pair started toward the door.

On the ride from the hall. Marcus had decided the best way to approach this was with total innocence. He had a legitimate interest in the purchase of the house. It was only natural that he come to present his offer in person.

Without warning, the door opened. A tall, distinguished gentleman stepped out, his figure blocking the face of the woman behind him.

Reggie nudged Marcus. "Isn't that the Duke of—"

"Indeed it is," Marcus said softly. Was this the owner of the property? He drew a deep breath and stepped forward. "Good day, Your Grace."

"Pennington? And Berkley." The duke laughed ruefully. "I should have known I might run into you two in this part of the world." He glanced back over his shoulder. "It seems, my dear, we have been found out."

Marcus's heart caught.

A vaguely familiar laugh sounded behind the duke, delightful and utterly feminine.

Madame de Chabot stepped into sight and extended her hand. "Lord Pennington, what a pleasant surprise."

"Madame." Relief choked Marcus's voice. He took her hand and raised it to his lips. "This is indeed a pleasant surprise." He turned to Reggie. "Lord Berkley, you remember Madame de Chabot? She is a dear friend of my wife's."

"Of course." Reggie's eyes widened with realization, and he grabbed her hand with unrestrained enthusiasm. "I could scarcely forget such a remarkably lovely creature."

The duke cleared his throat, and Reggie dropped her hand at once.

She laughed. "I could never forget you either, my lord."

"Pardon me, Madame," Marcus said slowly, "but am I to understand you are residing here?"

"For the moment," she said with an amused smile.

"Although in truth I am no more than a guest."

"I believe it's past time for explanations, my dear. Lord Pennington deserves to know precisely what is afoot here," the duke said firmly.

Madame's gaze met the duke's. "But it is not my secret to tell, *mon chér.*"

"Nonetheless, at this point you cannot leave him with the endless questions that he obviously has. And, as I believe Lord Berkley may well have been the gentleman I saw at a distance upon my arrival today"—he glanced at Reggie, who smiled weakly—"Lord Pennington's questions can no longer wait."

She lifted a shoulder in a delicate shrug. "If you think it's best."

"I do. And, as those questions for the most part do not involve me, and the day grows late, I shall take my leave." The duke took Madame's hand and lifted it to his lips. His gaze never left hers, and a look of such intensity passed between them, Marcus was compelled to avert his eyes, as if he watched something deeply intimate between the couple. He glanced at Reggie, who stared unabashedly. Marcus jabbed him with his elbow, and Reggie cast him an annoyed glare.

"I would be most appreciative, gentlemen"—the duke directed his words to Marcus and Reggie—"if you would keep my presence here to yourselves. I would not wish to sully Madame de Chabot's reputation with idle gossip."

"I do not care, Edward," she said fiercely, gazing up at him.

"But I do." He smiled down at her, and Marcus knew without a doubt that these two were deeply in love.

He knew the duke's circumstances, of course, no one

in England didn't. His Grace's wife was insane and had
been throughout the length of their marriage, a dozen
years or so, Marcus thought. The rumor was, she was
mad even before they wed and the duke was tricked into
the marriage, but his honor would not permit divorce.

"Of course, Your Grace," Marcus said. Reggie nodded his agreement.

"Thank you." The duke cast a last lingering glance
at Madame de Chabot, then mounted his horse and
rode off.

She watched him for a long moment and sighed. Then
she straightened her shoulders and cast Marcus a knowing smile. "You think your wife has betrayed you, no?"

"No, of course not," Marcus said quickly, knowing
full well she would not entirely believe him.

"*I* thought his wife had betrayed him." Reggie grimaced.

"You?" She raised an amused brow. "But you are so
charming, so lighthearted. I would not imagine you to
be so suspicious."

Reggie stared at the ground mournfully. "I was a
fool."

"Yes, you were." She laughed. "But you are a man,
and such things as foolishness cannot be completely
avoided."

"Madame." Marcus stepped forward. "Both Lord
Berkley and I have been guilty of reaching unsubstantiated conclusions. But I wish you to know I care a great
deal about Miss Townsend, Gwen, and—"

"He's in love with her," Reggie said in a smug whisper.

"How delightful." Madame de Chabot beamed.

"For the most part it is delightful." Marcus shook his

head. "However, it has also made me act in ways that are contrary to my nature. Indeed, there have been moments since I met her when I have found myself being, well, rather emotional and quite irrational."

"That is indeed love, my lord." She laughed, then sobered and considered him thoughtfully. "And with love comes acceptance of the one we care for, does it not?"

"I would think so," Marcus said.

"Acceptance of those things that are not anticipated but accompany each of us nonetheless. Those little pieces of, oh what am I trying to say"—she searched for the right word—"life, as it were. Unresolved situations from our past or irrational feelings we have not yet come to grips with or something more substantial like, oh, family obligations."

"Lady Pennington has no family. She's an orphan," Reggie pointed out.

Madame de Chabot heaved a sigh. "My dear Lord Berkley, you are indeed charming and I realize you are doing your best to be helpful, but perhaps, just for the moment, it would be best if you were to restrain from any further comment."

Reggie bristled with indignation. "I was simply trying—"

"Quiet, Reggie," Marcus said.

"*Merci.*" She cast Reggie a smile guaranteed to dissolve even the staunchest reserve. The duke was a very lucky man.

"Francesca," she called through the open doorway. "We have visitors."

"Madame Freneau is here too?" Marcus drew his

brows together. Perhaps the duke didn't own the house? Or he did but—

"Visitors?" Madame Freneau appeared in the doorway. Her eyes widened at the sight of Marcus. "Lord Pennington? What on earth are you doing here?"

"Precisely the question I was about to ask you," Marcus said wryly.

"Madame Freneau." Reggie stepped forward and took the lady's hand. "It is indeed a pleasure to see you again." Reggie raised her hand to his lips and murmured, "A very great pleasure."

Marcus stared at his friend and realized he had seen that look on Reggie's face before. And at the moment he could certainly understand it. Madame Freneau's appearance and her demeanor were substantially more casual and relaxed than he'd seen before. Her fair hair tumbled about her shoulders, and her checks were flushed. Marcus had known she was younger than he, but the maturity of her bearing had always made her seem older. He'd never realized how lovely she was. And judging by Reggie's reaction, he'd never realized it either.

She pulled her hand from Reggie's and favored him with a smile every bit as intoxicating as her sister-in-law's. "It is a pleasure to see you as well."

"I'm certain we are all pleased to see everyone," Marcus interrupted, "but I confess, I am thoroughly confused. Will someone please tell me what is going on here?"

"He is not at all pleasant when he's confused," Reggie said in a confidential aside to Madame Freneau.

"I can certainly see that." Madame Freneau shook her head. "Still, it is not my secret to tell."

Marcus ignored a rising sense of irritation. "I quite

frankly no longer care whose secret it is. I want answers and I want them now!"

Neither woman seemed especially impressed by his demand. They exchanged glances, then Madame Freneau drew a deep breath. "Very well, my lord. This is not how I imagined this particular moment. Indeed, I had not planned to be present at all."

"Nor had I." Madame de Chabot shrugged. "In truth, Gwendolyn agreed not an hour ago that she would confess all to you tonight. I believe she said you are usually in very good spirits"—the Frenchwoman gazed up at him innocently—"right before bed."

Reggie snickered. "No doubt."

"Quiet," Marcus snapped, then turned his attention back to the women. "Now then, ladies, if you please."

"I suppose it can no longer be avoided," Madame Freneau said with an air of resignation, her gaze slipping past him.

"Apparently not." Madame de Chabot too looked at something behind him.

Marcus glared. "What are you—"

Reggie laughed. "Turn around, Marcus. You should see this."

"I'm not sure I want to," Marcus muttered and turned. "Good Lord."

Three children, three *girls*, stood a scant few feet away and glared at him with all the defiant indignation of youth. They were of varying heights, with varying shades of red hair. Their appearance had the carefree dishevelment of a day spent in serious play out of doors. Indeed, the middle girl had a smudge of dirt on her cheek.

And each and every one bore a distinct resemblance to his wife.

"Who . . ." He stared in disbelief. "What . . ."

They stared right back. He amended his original assessment. It wasn't merely youthful indignation on their faces: it was feminine indignation.

Reggie cleared his throat. "Shouldn't someone say something?"

"Him first." The smallest pointed at Marcus.

"Who are you?" Marcus blurted.

"Marcus. Where are your manners?" Reggie rolled his gaze toward the sky. "That's not at all the way to greet three obviously accomplished young ladies." He stepped toward the children. "Allow me to introduce myself and my rather impolite friend. I am Viscount Berkley and this is the Earl of Pennington." Reggie swept a polished bow. "And you?"

The girls studied him suspiciously, then looked at one another and nodded. The tallest and obviously oldest stepped forward. "These are my sisters, Miss Patience Loring"—the girl with the smudge curtsied—"and Miss Hope Loring." The youngest bobbed. "I am Miss Charity Loring." The girl extended her hand. Reggie took it without hesitation and raised it to his lips.

"I am most pleased to meet you, Miss Loring," Reggie said in very much the same tone he'd used with Madame Freneau.

The girl's eyes widened and an expression of awe crossed her face.

"Are you pleased to meet me as well?" The next child in line, Patience, thrust out her hand.

"Indeed I am." Reggie's voice was serious. He took her hand, brushed a light kiss across it, then turned to the youngest.

"Oh, I don't want you to kiss my hand." The little girl firmly put her hand behind her back. Her tone was lofty. "A woman who is free with her favors will always come to no good."

One of the ladies behind Marcus coughed or perhaps choked.

Marcus bit back a grin and stepped forward. "Well done. You're absolutely right." He bent down in front of the youngest, Hope. "Now that we have been properly introduced, perhaps you could help me with a bit of a problem. I know your names but"—he lowered his voice in a confidential manner—"I don't know who you are. And I suspect that's very important, isn't it?"

"Perhaps." The child studied him carefully. "Do you like dogs?"

"Dogs?" It wasn't exactly what he expected. "Why, yes, I do like dogs."

"And do you like girls?" she continued.

"Indeed I do," he said somberly. "You may ask anyone if you don't believe me."

"I can vouch for that." Reggie grinned. "He's always been exceedingly fond of ladies."

"I don't mean ladies." Hope cast Reggie a look of definite reproof. "I mean little girls. Children. *Daughters.*"

"Absolutely." Marcus nodded. "I was just saying today that I should hope to have a very large family with a great number of daughters, little girls to run around my home."

"Really?" She stared at him with all the intensity of her young years.

"Really," he said firmly.

"Aunt Gwendolyn didn't think you would," Charity broke in.

Marcus stood. "*Aunt* Gwendolyn?" His gaze met Madame Freneau's. "Aunt Gwendolyn?"

"They are her sister's children," Madame said.

He drew his brows together. "The one eaten by cannibals?"

Patience snorted. "We just told her that."

"They really drowned," Hope said with a heartfelt sigh.

"I am sorry," he murmured.

"Aunt Gwen was afraid you wouldn't want us. And she didn't want us to live anyplace where we were not wanted," Patience added. "It was very nice of her. We haven't liked her very much but she is rather nice."

Hope tugged at his sleeve, leaned close, and lowered her voice. "We do like her a bit more now. But I don't think anyone liked her, or wanted her, when *she* was a girl."

"It's really rather sad when you think about it," Charity said with a thoughtful frown. "Do you want her?"

"Very much so." Marcus had never said truer words in his life.

Hope narrowed her eyes. "And do you want us?"

Marcus's gaze slipped from one girl to the next, and they seemed to hold a collective breath. At once he realized he was getting a glimpse of the future. His daughters would look a great deal like . . . his nieces.

He nodded and then grinned. "Very much so."

"You'll have to swear to it," Patience said firmly.

Hope grinned. "With blood."

Reggie choked back a laugh.

"We'll be inside if you need us," Madame Freneau said with a smile. A moment later the ladies had disappeared into the house.

Marcus raised a brow. "Blood?"

"Nothing else will do." Charity watched him carefully, and Marcus knew this was a test.

"Absolutely. What was I thinking?" Marcus grabbed Reggie and pulled him to his side. "And I know Lord Berkley will want to participate as well. We are as close as brothers. Closer even. Why, you can call him Uncle Reggie."

Reggie groaned. "Uncle Reggie?"

"Would you prefer Reginald?" Marcus said under his breath.

"Uncle Reggie it is." Reggie's tone was less than enthusiastic. "But I'm not overly fond of blood. Especially my own."

Hope planted her hands on her hips. "How old are you?"

"One and thirty," Reggie said cautiously. "Why?"

"I am only ten and blood doesn't bother me one bit." Hope smirked.

"You're obviously a braver man than I am," Reggie muttered.

"Come now, Reggie, we did the same sort of thing when we were boys." Marcus directed his words to the girls. "And I still have the scar on my elbow to prove it."

Patience's eyes widened. "Do you? Can I see it?"

"Some other time perhaps. Now then." Marcus looked eagerly around the group. "Who has the knife?"

"What knife?" Charity said uneasily

"Surely you have a knife?" Marcus's shocked voice belied his relief that they didn't conceal knives amid their skirts. "How can we draw blood without a knife?"

"We don't use blood." Patience shook her head.

Marcus gasped. "No blood?"

"No. We spit." Hope huffed and proceeded to match her action to her words. She held out her index finger. "See?"

Reggie's expression cleared. "Well, I'm certainly willing to do that."

"I don't know, Reggie." Marcus shook his head somberly. "Is it really a blood oath without blood? I mean, does it have the same meaning? The same authority? I have some serious reservations about this."

"We've always done it this way," Patience said firmly. "And it has always worked."

"It's still a sacred vow." Charity's eyes narrowed. "Of course, if you don't want to do it—"

"Oh, I'll certainly do it. Symbolic blood is probably better than no blood at all." Marcus spit on his finger. "Now what?"

Patience grinned. "Now we rub our fingers together and then we repeat the solemn words."

"I just knew there had to be solemn words," Reggie said under his breath and cheerfully spit on his finger.

A few moment later, after much spitting and rubbing, Hope raised her arms like a tiny pagan priestess. "And I promise by all the blood in my veins"—her voice was low and dramatic, and it was all Marcus could do to keep a straight face—"that I shall never break this oath or else suffer the dire, horrible consequences."

"I promise," Marcus vowed with all the sincerity the moment called for.

"Amen." Reggie's voice rang with enthusiasm and the girls giggled in unison. "Although I would like to know exactly what the dire, horrible consequences are should the oath be broken."

"They're bad." Patience shook her head mournfully. "Very, very bad."

"It scarcely matters since none of us has any intention of breaking the oath." Marcus grinned at the girls.

His remarkably good spirits had returned with a vengeance. The discovery of Gwen's nieces explained a good deal about his wife's attitude and behavior, possibly even why she had agreed to marry him in the first place. It hadn't been easy to trust her completely, and admittedly he had known a twinge of doubt. Now he was quite pleased with himself that he'd listened more to his heart than to his head.

"Now what?" Reggie said.

"Now, old man, ladies." Marcus's gaze slid from one to the next and his grin widened. "I believe it's time for all of us to go home."

Chapter Fifteen

*In spite of the faults of men, or perhaps
because of them, we cannot live without them.
And what woman would truly wish to?*

Francesca Freneau

There really isn't anything to worry about.

Gwen had repeated the assurance to herself over and
over until it became a refrain repeating incessantly in
her head. Marcus's comments on their ride today and
Gwen's own knowledge of his character had strengthened her resolve to tell him about the girls as soon as
possible. Madame Freneau had supported her decision
wholeheartedly, although Madame had made no secret
of the fact that Marcus should have been made aware of
Gwen's nieces long before now.

Gwen hadn't seen Marcus since her return from the
dower house. It had been rather odd being there when
Colette's visitor had arrived. And odder yet discovering
his identity. Their situation was terribly sad, and Gwen
wished she could do something to help, but apparently

there was nothing anyone could do for the couple. And Gwen had her own circumstances to worry about.

Marcus hadn't been home when she'd returned. Godfrey had said he and Lord Berkley had gone out. Odd, she'd thought Berkley wasn't expected so soon, although it scarcely mattered, she supposed. The viscount was obviously going to be around a great deal. Not that she minded—she quite liked the man—but perhaps it was time someone did something to help him find a wife of his own.

Gwen had tried to keep herself busy, going over her planned explanation to her husband a dozen times in her head, but had succumbed to a weariness brought on, no doubt, by worry, and had fallen asleep. Surely Marcus had returned by now, but he wasn't in his rooms. She headed for the library. When Marcus was in the house, he spent much of his time there and would likely be there now.

She'd dressed for dinner even though she was an hour or so early and was determined to find her husband and reveal everything, believing that she might as well get her ordeal over with. She'd originally thought dinner would be an excellent time to casually mention the girls over a cut of good roasted beef or a glass of wine and had considered as well telling him all right before bed, or better still, afterward, but she'd already put off this confrontation as long as possible. Not that it would be a confrontation, she reminded herself, even though, at the moment, she was certainly braced for something very much like a confrontation.

She descended the stairs in a sedate manner befitting the Countess of Pennington, although admittedly her manner was restrained more by apprehension than by any sense of propriety.

There really isn't anything to worry about.

Abruptly the thought struck her that regardless of his reaction, she could do precisely as she wished. She had her own money in a London account Mr. Whiting had arranged, as well as her own house. If Marcus didn't want to raise her nieces, she could certainly provide for them without his help. Madame Freneau might well agree to serve as a full-time governess, tutor, and companion. Gwen could find a house in the city for those times when she and Marcus resided in London, and she could continue to visit every day. It was not an ideal solution but it was an answer of sorts.

She reached the bottom of the stairs and started toward the library. A faint laugh sounded somewhere in the dim reaches of the house. No, not a laugh, more like a giggle. Probably a maid somewhere flirting with a footman. Gwen had seen any number of such flirtations in her years as a governess but had always rebuffed advances directed toward her. She was far too aware of the proper demeanor her position demanded. At once it struck her how terribly tired she was of being proper.

No, her momentary relief faded. If Marcus didn't want the girls he wouldn't be the man she thought he was. And how could Gwen live with a man like that? Even for a mere seven and a half years.

She reached the library door, drew a deep breath, straightened her shoulders, and adopted a pleasant smile.

There really isn't anything to worry about.

She started to knock, then decided this was as much her library as his, pushed the door open, and stepped into the room. The lamps were already lit against the encroaching sunset, and the room lay in that deep gold and blue shadowed state that marked the end of the day. A half-empty glass sat beside a decanter on the desk.

"Marcus?" She stepped farther into the library.

"He isn't here right now." Lord Berkley uncurled his long figure from a chair placed before the desk and got to his feet, his ever-present smile on his face. "But I expect him back any moment."

"Lord Berkley." She smiled in spite of a touch of annoyance at his presence. With the viscount here she couldn't possibly reveal all to Marcus. On the other hand, a third party did offer her a legitimate postponement. She held out her hand with renewed enthusiasm. "I thought you weren't coming until the end of the week?"

"It is the end of the week." He laughed and brushed his lips across the back of her hand. "You and your husband have a great deal in common."

"Do we?"

"You'd be surprised." He grinned, and she wondered exactly what he meant. Not that it really mattered. The viscount stepped to the desk and refilled the glass in his hand. "Would you care for something? I know where the clean glasses are kept."

"Then you know more than I." She shook her head. "I am still learning how to get from one room to another."

"Shall I, then? Your husband's brandy is excellent."

"No doubt." She shuddered at the memory of her last experience with brandy. "I think not, thank you."

"No?" He considered her thoughtfully, then nodded. "Sherry, then? Madeira? Something else to your liking, perhaps?"

She laughed. "My dear Lord Berkley, one would think you were trying to get me foxed."

"Why, Lady Pennington, I'm shocked that you would think that." Berkley's voice was indignant but amusement twinkled in his eye. "I would never attempt such a thing with a married woman." He paused. "At least not one married to a friend."

"I'm so glad to know you have certain moral standards."

"Oh, I do indeed."

"I should hate to think you are a bad influence on my husband."

"Nothing of the sort." He lowered his voice in a confidential manner. "If anything, he has always been a bad influence on me."

"Really?" She raised a brow.

"Well, perhaps not always." He grinned and took a sip of his brandy. "In truth, we have always been an equally bad influence on one another."

"Sherry."

"What?"

"If you are going to tell tales about my husband, perhaps they would go better with sherry."

"Excellent choice." He crossed the room to what looked like another of the decorative half columns that encircled the library and pulled open a door she never suspected existed. He returned to the desk with a bottle and a glass, poured the sherry, and handed it to her. "Marcus has excellent taste."

"Thank you." Gwen had the distinct impression the viscount wasn't merely referring to the wine.

"I must tell you, I quite approve of this match between the two of you."

"Do you?"

"I do indeed, although I am compelled to confess, I once harbored a vague hope he would turn his affections toward my sister and become, through marriage, my brother, but that was not to be."

"Really?" She ignored a definite twinge of jealousy toward this sister of the viscount. "Did your sister not care for Lord Pennington?"

"Oh, she has adored him always. Unfortunately, she adores her dogs and horses a great deal more." He grinned. "She is barely fifteen and Marcus has always viewed her with the same annoyance and affection as I have. As a little sister."

"I see." Gwen smiled and sipped the sherry. "So, my lord, why are you so approving of his marriage to me? This match was not entirely his choice."

"No, but I think it has turned out for the best." He studied her thoughtfully. "Marcus has always been reserved when it comes to his feelings. Much of the time, even I have not known precisely what he was thinking." He raised his glass to her. "You, my dear Lady Pennington, have broken down that reserve."

"Have I?"

"Indeed you have." He smiled ruefully. "With you he has found what he did not expect but has always wanted. From what I've seen thus far, you are very good for him. I never thought I'd admit such a thing, but I am exceedingly jealous of his good fortune."

His words warmed her heart. "That is perhaps the nicest thing anyone has ever said to me."

"Are you flirting with my wife again?" Marcus's voice sounded from the doorway.

"Again and always." Berkley clapped his hand over his heart. "You have caught me, old man, I was trying to convince her to toss you aside and run away with me."

"And was it working?" Marcus strode to her side and took her hands in his. His laughing gaze meshed with hers. "Are you about to abandon me and go off with this . . . this scoundrel?" He raised her hands to his lips. "I should not bear it, you know."

"Nor should I," she said softly, staring into his eyes. A faint voice in the back of her mind whispered softly. *Fate.*

Berkley groaned. "There you have it. Once again we are back to the crux of the problem. If I were a scoundrel, she'd be off with me in a moment."

She laughed and pulled her hands from her husband's. "Never, my lord."

Marcus grinned. "Reggie has a theory that women find irresistible those men who are no good for them."

"It's not a theory," Berkley said loftily. "I have given a great deal of thought and study to the question, and I believe it to be a fact. What do you think, my lady?"

She shook her head. "I think you need to give it substantially more thought."

"Actually," Marcus said slowly. "I think there is

some validity to the idea that a touch of those qualities that are perhaps less than sterling can be quite intriguing. Don't you agree, my dear?"

She pulled her brows together. "Most certainly not."

He continued as if he hadn't heard her. "And not just in terms of men but when it comes to women as well."

"There's nothing like a woman with a secret, I always say." Berkley nodded firmly. "It makes a lady mysterious and rather intoxicating."

"Taking your theory a step further then"—Marcus's brows drew together—"it would stand to reason that ladies we find, to use your term, *intoxicating*—"

"It's an excellent term," Berkley said smugly.

"Indeed it is." Marcus nodded. "The point is: if a lady is indeed *intoxicating* it would make sense that she would, of necessity, have a secret."

Gwen stared in disbelief. "That's absurd."

"Even if we didn't know she had a secret, there would still be something about her." Marcus's voice was thoughtful. "Some sort of air about her. Like a lingering perfume that you're always aware of or—"

"A tune that lurks in the back of your mind but you can't quite place," Berkley said.

"Exactly. She's a mystery you cannot seem to solve, probably because you haven't the faintest idea what questions to ask. Although, personally, I have always enjoyed a bit of a mystery." Marcus moved to the desk and picked up his glass. "Yes indeed, unraveling a mystery is an excellent exercise for one's mind."

"Is it?" Gwen had the uncomfortable feeling that the men were talking about something entirely different than their words would indicate. "I much prefer things to be entirely straightforward myself."

"Do you?" Marcus raised a brow.

"Yes I do." Her voice was firm, but unease settled in her stomach.

"I would never have thought that," Marcus murmured and sipped at his brandy. "Do you have secrets, Gwen?"

"Me?" Her voice came out in an odd squeak. She cleared her throat. "No." She paused. "Of course not." This would be the perfect time to tell him about the girls. "I suppose we all have some sort of minor secrets." But Berkley was here and she had no idea if that would work to her favor or her detriment. "I daresay mine are not at all significant." Still, it was probably better to tell her new husband he had a complete family in private. "But at the moment"—she smiled sweetly— "I can't think of a thing."

"Oh come now, my dear Gwendolyn." Marcus studied her curiously. "I'd wager you have at least one substantial secret."

"Perhaps even two," Berkley added helpfully.

Marcus nodded. "Or three."

"Ah, but if I were to tell you, it would take all the fun out of it, wouldn't it?" She took a quick sip of her sherry, for a moment wishing desperately it was brandy, and searched just as desperately for a less dangerous topic of conversation. After all, she hadn't blatantly lied to him thus far. And it did seem a shame to do so now when she was so close to telling him everything. "So, she said brightly, "Godfrey said the two of you had gone for a ride today. It was a lovely day. Did you have a pleasant time?"

"Very pleasant." Berkley grinned.

"More than pleasant," Marcus added. "It is the oddest thing, but even though I have spent much of my life here, I almost never fail to see something new and interesting, especially in the spring. Don't you agree, Reggie?"

"Absolutely."

"How nice," Gwen murmured. She had no particular interest in whatever newfound sights the season had brought, but as long as Marcus was no longer talking about secrets, spring on the estate was as good a topic as any.

"Not all of it is pleasant, of course," Marcus said. "Spring does tend to make you aware of repairs that need attention."

"Always." Berkley nodded.

Gwen sipped her sherry and feigned rapt attention.

"Indeed, even though I no longer own it, I did notice quite a bit of work needs to be done on"—he paused—"the dower house."

The dower house? Gwen choked on her wine. *When was he at the dower house?*

Marcus started toward her. "Are you all right?"

"A firm blow between the shoulder blades will help," Berkley offered.

Gwen held up her hand to stop them both and choked out the words. "No, thank you. I'm quite all right."

"Are you sure?" Marcus's tone was concerned but there was a twinkle of amusement in his eyes.

She blinked back tears, sniffed, and met her husband's gaze directly. She stared at him for a long moment. Marcus could barely keep the smile from his face. He had the look of a man who had the upper hand and well knew it. She glanced at Berkley, who had the grace to avert his eyes, but he too failed to hide his grin. Again her gaze returned to her husband.

At once she realized he knew all about the girls. Why, he'd probably even met them. And just as obviously, if he was this amused, he wasn't at all upset. Relief rushed through her, accompanied by more than a touch of annoyance. Why didn't he just tell her what he knew? What kind of cat-and-mouse game was he playing?

She crossed her arms over her chest and glared. "Well?"

"Well, what?" Marcus said cautiously.

"As this has nothing really to do with me . . ." Berkley edged toward the door. "And surely I'm needed elsewhere." He reached the door and slipped out.

She barely noticed. "Aren't you going to tell me what you've learned? Or ask me questions or something?"

Marcus studied her thoughtfully. "I don't think so."

She stared. "Why not?"

He shrugged. "There's no need. I know everything I need to know."

"Do you?" she said carefully.

"Indeed I do, and what I don't know precisely, I have managed to figure out. And probably quite accurately as well." He grinned in an annoyingly smug manner. "Shall I go on?"

"Please do."

"First of all, you agreed to marry me to get your inheritance so that you could provide for your nieces. Quite admirable really." He sipped his brandy. "You didn't tell me about them because you didn't trust me."

She started to protest, then stopped. After all, he was right.

"Granted, in the beginning you had no reason to trust me. You didn't even know me. You had no way of knowing whether I would welcome these children into my home or not." He shook his head. "I have given a great deal of thought to this and it is understandable. Until me, there hadn't been a single man in your life who had earned your trust."

She lifted her chin. "You needn't feel sorry for me."

"I don't," he said simply. "Or at least I don't now. I do, however, feel sorry for the child who grew up feeling unwanted. And for the girl who was told her father had left her penniless. And for the young woman who found herself the object of unwanted attentions by her employers and other men." He narrowed his eyes. "But I haven't the least bit of sympathy for the current Countess of Pennington, who has three little girls who, albeit somewhat reluctantly, have some affection for her, and a new mother-in-law who adores her, and a husband who"—he shrugged—"has discovered himself to be deeply in love with her."

Her breath caught. "You're in love with me?"

"Insane as it may sound." He set his glass down on the desk and smiled wryly. "I am."

"But"—she shook her head against the flurry of thoughts and emotions swirling in her head—"we agreed that you wouldn't."

"Yes, well, in that and that alone"—he started toward her—"you should not have trusted me."

"Don't come any closer," she said sharply.

"Why not?" He grinned wickedly and continued toward her. "This is the point at which I take you in my arms and we promise to love one another until the end of our days." He reached out to pull her into his embrace but she stepped away.

An odd sense of panic filled her. "I can't promise that, Marcus."

"Why not?" His brow furrowed. "We have no more secrets between us. I am more than willing to raise these girls as my own. In truth, I quite like them. Almost as much as I like their aunt."

"But"—she struggled for the right words—"I don't love you."

He studied her carefully, then grinned. "I don't believe you."

She gasped. "It's true. Granted, I feel a certain amount of affection for you. And I do like you a great deal. And admittedly I do feel"—she blurted the words—"lust for you."

He laughed and pulled her into his arms. "Lust?"

"Yes." She stared up at him defiantly. "I believe I am, well, in lust with you."

"In lust with me?" He laughed again, then bent to feather kisses along the side of her neck. "How delightful."

"You don't mind, then?" she said, struggling against the weakness in her knees his touch always triggered.

"Not in the least," he murmured. "I will take lust for the moment."

"What do you mean, for the moment?"

"My darling Lady Pennington." He raised his head and looked into her eyes, and she resisted the urge to melt against him. "It has taken me a very long time to find love. And I suspect it will take a fair amount of time for you to accept that I may be trusted. With your future and the future of your nieces and the future of our children. However, I believe you already trust me with your heart, whether you're willing to face that yet or not." His lips met hers, and he kissed her with a passion and desire that quite took her breath away. He drew his head back and grinned down at her. "You may call it lust all you wish but you love me, Gwen, and I shall spend every hour of the next seven and a half years in a concerted effort to make you admit it. Beginning right now."

She swallowed hard. "Here?"

"No, not here." He laughed. "At the moment we have a curious Berkley waiting, probably with his ear pressed against the door, as well as a new family that needs attention. I am more convinced than ever that it was fate that we should marry, and I am just as convinced I am destined to love you, as you are destined to love me."

"Really, why?"

"The three Fates in the garden decreed it, and there are three girls who will no doubt expect it." He kissed her again firmly. "Later I shall show you precisely what plan of attack I intend to use to convince you to accept your fate."

"Oh my." She breathed the words. "Regardless, Marcus." She pulled herself together and drew a deep breath. "Love is a trap for women and I shall not fall into it."

"My dear Lady Pennington." He grinned wickedly. "You already have."

Chapter Sixteen

*One can always count on uncles to set things right.
However, since uncles are men too, one cannot be as confident
that they recognize a problem in the first place.*

Charity Loring

"We wish to speak to you."

Marcus looked up from the desk to find himself confronted by three pairs of unblinking eyes. He was no longer surprised that the girls had managed to enter the library and line up before his desk without his notice. Indeed, while in the weeks since their arrival he had noticed they made a considerable amount of noise on occasion, they were also prone to stealth when they wished. And life was certainly no longer dull.

He leaned back in his chair and smiled. "What did you wish to speak to me about?"

The girls traded glances, then Charity squared her shoulders. "First of all, we want you to know we are quite happy here."

"We like our new family," Patience said.

"Especially Uncle Reggie and Grandmama Pennington," Hope added. "She is great fun for someone so old."

"She will be delighted to hear it, but I would suggest you not mention to her the old part." Marcus nodded somberly. "She is rather sensitive about her age."

His mother had arrived last week, a few days after Madames Freneau and de Chabot had returned to London, and was thrilled to discover the girls. They had become fast friends and, he'd been told, his mother didn't so much as hesitate to participate in the blood oath. Obviously a point in her favor in the eyes of his new nieces.

"This is all very good to know." He studied the faces before him. "But there's more, isn't there?"

Charity nodded. "We don't think Aunt Gwen is happy."

Hope leaned forward and lowered her voice confidentially. "We do like her now but she's really rather an odd sort of person, don't you think so?"

Marcus frowned. "What do you mean?"

"Well." Patience thought for moment. "She acts as if she's waiting for something to happen."

"Something horrible." Concern colored Charity's face. "Something dire."

"The end of the world when we shall all be judged," Hope intoned.

He bit back a grin. "Surely it's not that bad."

Again the girls exchanged looks. "It is that bad," Charity said firmly. "You just can't see it because you're a man and don't understand anything about women."

"Madame de Chabot says men are pleasant enough

creatures but not very, oh, what was it she said?" Patience hopped up to sit on the edge of his desk. "Perceptive. That's the word. She says they often don't see what's right under their noses."

"And is there something about my wife I'm not seeing?" he said slowly, wondering which was worse: the influence of the missionaries on these children or the influence of Madame de Chabot.

"Yes." Charity heaved a sigh. "And it's up to you to make it right."

He shook his head in confusion. "Make what right?"

"It's up to you to make her happy." Hope huffed.

"If she is unhappy, and frankly I don't know that she is"—he chose his words with care—"what would you suggest I do about it?"

"You have to give her what she wants more than anything else in the world," Hope said firmly. Her sisters nodded their agreement. "I think it's a dog."

"A dog?" He raised a brow.

Hope nodded. "A dog would make her happy. Extremely happy."

"Somehow I doubt that." He chuckled. "However, aside from a dog, what do the three of you think your aunt wants more than anything else in the world?"

"We don't know exactly but we have talked about it." Patience considered him for a moment. "Madame de Chabot says all a woman really wants is to love and be loved."

"Ah, but I do love her," he said with a smile. "Very much."

Hope's forehead furrowed. "And does she love you?"

"Of course she does." Patience rolled her gaze toward the ceiling. "She looks at him like he's a sweet she's dying to eat."

"But she won't because she's afraid of a stomachache." Charity gazed at him intently. "That's it, then, isn't it? She wants to love you but she won't or can't or something like that."

"That sounds stupid to me," Hope muttered. "I think what she really needs is a dog."

"Forgive me for pointing this out, ladies, and while I do appreciate your concern . . ." He paused. "The relationship between your aunt and myself isn't really your affair."

"We think it is." Patience cast him an innocent smile.

"Uncle Marcus," Charity began patiently, as if she were talking to a small child. "One of the things we quite like about you is that you don't treat us as if we are children."

"Even if you are," he said.

"That's not important right now." Charity waved in a dismissive gesture exactly like her aunt's. "For the first time since our parents, um, *left*, we feel as if we, well, belong somewhere and to someone."

"Aunt Gwen has never belonged anywhere," Patience said bluntly. "And she's never had a family. Not a real family."

"Or a dog," Hope murmured.

Charity crossed her arms over her chest. "Don't you think if you never had a family or never belonged anywhere or was never loved and then all of a sudden you had all these wonderful things, wouldn't you worry that maybe they'd all vanish as quickly as they'd appeared?"

"But a dog is always with you," Hope said under her breath.

"And sometimes, when you haven't had very good luck, you're afraid to say things out loud." Patience's heels thudded against the side of the desk. "Because you're afraid if you say how happy you are or how in love you are"—Patience shrugged—"the Fates will hear you and take it all away."

"You three certainly are an interesting mix of philosophies," Marcus murmured.

Patience grinned. "Thank you."

"So." Charity thought for a moment. "Perhaps all you really have to do is get her to admit how she feels about everything. Especially about you."

"And once she says it out loud and nothing happens"—Patience shrugged—"she'll be happy."

"We'll all be a lot happier with a dog in the house," Hope said.

"We'll see about the dog. As for the rest of it . . ." Marcus sat back and studied the trio.

They were exceptionally old for their ages. Of course, they had been through a great deal during their young lives. Their parents could well be faulted for bringing their children along on the adventurous life they had led before their deaths, but was that, in truth, worse than abandoning them to others to raise? Send them off to a school somewhere as Gwen had been sent away? At least these three never doubted they were wanted.

Were they right about Gwen? Was she indeed unhappy?

She'd been a bit moody since the girls had come to

live with them, but then she was a woman, and weren't such things to be expected of women? He'd always thought he knew a great deal about women but he had discovered, in the few short weeks since his marriage, what one knew of the gender from flirtations at public events or even intimate encounters had little to do with what one learned living day in and day out with a female. They were, or at least Gwen was, unique creatures and quite fascinating, even if they had a way of looking at the world that was completely foreign to him. Indeed, there were moments when the working of Gwen's mind completely escaped him and he wondered about not only her sanity but his own.

"It seems we are back to the crux of the matter," he said carefully. "If indeed your aunt is not happy, what do I do to make her so? And if she is, how do I get her to admit it?"

"You could give her a gift, I suppose. That might work." Charity's brow furrowed with thought.

"Madame de Chabot says there's nothing like a fine piece of jewelry from a man to improve a lady's spirits. I think it's a capital idea." Patience nodded her approval. "She mentioned that diamonds are especially effective."

"I would imagine," Marcus murmured.

"But Madame Freneau says a gift doesn't have to cost a great deal if it's from your heart." Charity considered him curiously. "What could you give her from your heart?"

He blew a long breath. "I haven't the vaguest idea."

"A dog would be . . ." Hope looked at the faces around her. "Well, it would," she muttered.

"I don't think a dog or diamonds is the right answer." Marcus shook his head. "But I don't know what the answer is."

"Well, you will surely think of something." Patience hopped off the desk with the satisfied air of one who has accomplished a critical mission. "We know you will."

"It may take some time though." Charity cast him a warning frown. "You can't expect her to immediately trust that everything she has now won't go away tomorrow. You probably have a bit of work ahead of you, but we have every confidence you will do what is necessary to make Aunt Gwen as content as we are." She met his gaze straight on. "We are most grateful for that, Uncle Marcus, and we don't want anything to muck it up. Do you understand?"

"Of course." He wasn't entirely certain, but he might have just been threatened.

Charity favored him with a brilliant smile, and abruptly he realized she would all too soon no longer be a child. It was a terrifying thought. "I thought you would."

The two older girls started toward the door. Hope hung back, her words low and intended for his ears alone. "I truly think a dog is an excellent idea, but if you don't think that is what will make Aunt Gwen happy, I shall understand. However, I do hope you will consider it on those occasions when you are trying to find a gift for someone else. I know *my* spirits would always be lifted by the presence of a dog."

"Thank you, Hope." His serious tone matched hers. "I shall indeed keep it in mind."

"Good." She grinned with obvious relief.

"Are you coming?" Patience called from the open door.

"Yes, of course." Hope scrambled after her sisters. Her voice drifted in from the hall. "I really do think a dog would . . ."

Marcus chuckled. A dog was certainly one problem he could solve without the least bit of effort. There were dogs at the stables, of course, but he wouldn't mind having some sort of more sedate creature for the girls. Nothing too fluffy or insipid. Something less than a working beast and more than an animal suited for nothing more than sitting in a lap and yapping indiscriminately.

The question of Gwen's state was a bit more difficult to solve.

Had he truly been so stupid, so dense, so smug in his own happiness that he hadn't noticed his wife was not? Apparently.

Charity was extremely clever for one so young. How could the girl see what he didn't? She was no doubt right about Gwen. Gwen did now have all those things she'd never really known before: family, home, and even love. Oh, there was fortune too, of course, but that certainly wasn't as important as those more intangible things. It made perfect sense that she would not be able to trust that it would not all vanish with the next stiff wind.

Marcus had always been cautious about his emotions and had recognized that same quality in Gwen. But he had never experienced the same kind of abrupt loss she'd faced in her life. He'd never known what it was to feel unwanted, as if you had no worth, as if you did not belong. How could anyone weather such emotional storms and emerge unscathed? Yet Gwen had survived remarkably well. She was strong and determined and . . . and apparently far too intelligent to accept her new life without question. It made a great deal of sense, and he was an arrogant, inconsiderate idiot not to have realized it.

Thanks to his nieces, he now understood.

Pity he hadn't the faintest idea what to do about it.

She was insane. There was simply no other answer.

Gwen slipped off her horse, ignoring the fact that getting back on the sidesaddle without help would be awkward if not impossible. But if she had to walk all the way back to the hall, leading the animal by the reins, so be it. A long walk would do her as much good as a long ride.

Marcus was right about this spot: it was indeed wonderful, especially late in the afternoon with the sun lingering low in the sky. In recent days she had found herself drawn here more and more often. It was the perfect place to think and attempt to sort out feelings that made absolutely no sense.

Gwen wandered over to the beech and sank down beneath its gnarled branches. She didn't particularly want to be insane, but it was the only answer that made even the least bit of sense.

For the first time she could remember, she wanted for nothing. Oh, not simply financially, although that was admittedly pleasant, but she had a place she could truly call home and people who wanted her around and a position of permanence. Even her fears about the girls had eased. She had heard nothing from Whiting and with each passing day Gwen was more and more confident that, once again, Albert had been mistaken.

She had, in truth, everything she'd ever wanted, everything that had been missing from her life, and more than she'd ever imagined.

She had Marcus.

She pulled her knees up in a most improper manner and wrapped her arms around them. What would he do when her insanity was discovered? Would he keep up a public image as the duke did and refuse to divorce her? Would he spend his life in a futureless liaison with a woman who could give him what his wife could not?

No, of course not. She heaved a heavy sigh. Marcus would never follow in the duke's footsteps because Marcus's wife was not truly insane. The madness that afflicted Gwen was nothing more than love.

She'd fallen in love with her husband, and she'd never faced anything more terrifying in her life. Not being penniless, not running away to take her first governess position or any of the ones that followed, absolutely nothing until now.

From the moment he'd admitted his own feelings, she'd had a horrible weight in the pit of her stomach. A dreadful feeling of apprehension that would not leave. A terrible sense that if she accepted all she now had, admitted she had done the one thing she'd promised herself she'd never do and fallen in love, something truly terrible would happen. The house of cards she had built would totter and finally crash. And destroy her in the process.

She rested her chin on her knees and stared unseeing

into the distance. She'd never thought of herself as being particularly cowardly, indeed, she'd considered herself rather courageous, the way she'd always been willing to seize control of her life. But lately she'd wondered if the greater courage wasn't in facing whatever confronted her head on instead of running from it. If true bravery didn't lie in facing down the panic that rose within her like her own personal demon. And if what she always thought was fearlessness was, in truth, the worst kind of lie. The kind you tell to yourself and never question.

She'd wondered about any number of things since Marcus had proclaimed his feelings. Had wondered and examined and given it all a great deal of careful thought and attention. And her own feelings and beliefs had changed, slowly, almost imperceptibly, from that point to this. Perhaps starting the very moment she'd met him, even if she hadn't wanted to acknowledge it before now.

There were worse things in the world than loving and being loved by someone like Marcus. She'd always blamed love for her mother's death in trying to give her father a son. Now she wondered if it was a choice her mother made gladly for the man she loved and perhaps for herself as well. It was love that lured her sister away from her family and ultimately led to her death in foreign lands far from home. Yet now Gwen wondered if the happiness her sister had obviously found with her unsuitable match, as well as the children they'd shared, wasn't well worth what she'd sacrificed.

As frightening as Gwen found her feelings about her husband, what was even worse was the realization that she would give up everything for him. She would gladly forfeit life or position or fortune or anything.

That was really what had her in such a state. The belief, deep down inside her, that accepting his love and loving him in return made her vulnerable in a way she'd never been before. And worse yet, the recognition that she no longer cared.

Maybe true courage lay in following your heart.

She blew a long, resigned breath. She loved him and he loved her, and no matter what happened in the world around them, that might well be all that truly mattered.

"I wondered if I'd find you here." Marcus's voice sounded from behind her.

"There you go again." She forced a light note into her voice. "Sneaking up on me."

He laughed and sat down on the ground beside her. "I was doing no such thing. Certainly I did approach your position in a somewhat roundabout manner, but it was entirely innocent on my part."

"Was it?"

"Perhaps not entirely." He grinned in an altogether wicked manner. "I rather enjoy that expression of outraged amusement you give me when I catch you unawares."

"Outraged amusement?" She raised a brow. "What kind of expression is that?"

"I suspect it is a look perfected by governesses and I doubt that I could ever truly duplicate it." He shook his head mournfully. "But only because you asked, mind you, I shall give it a try. It's something like this." He thought for a moment, then widened his eyes and pursed his lips.

She stared, then burst into laughter. "I don't look the least bit like that."

"Oh, but you do," he said in a slightly garbled manner dictated by the contorted position of his mouth.

"Stop it at once." She tried to smooth his expression, but he caught her hand and pulled it to his lips.

"I will, for a price."

Her gaze met his, and her heart skipped. "And what would that price be?"

"The truth." His gaze met hers. "Honesty."

"I have been honest with you for the most part," she said quickly. "Except for not telling you about my nieces and that may have been a . . . mistake on my part."

"A mistake?"

"Yes," she said firmly. "A simple error. Of judgment perhaps. I will give you that much but no more."

"From you, my dear Lady Pennington, I will always take what few morsels I can get. Especially when it comes to admitting that you could possibly have been wrong."

She shook her head and tried not to smile. "I don't believe I actually ever used the word *wrong*. Erroneous perhaps, misguided, even incorrect, but never specifically *wrong*."

"I see. Then it was obviously my own mistake to believe that you had. Admitted that you were wrong, that is."

"Absolutely." She grinned.

He laughed. "That's something, at any rate." He sobered, his expression abruptly intense. "Gwen, I . . ." He sighed as if he didn't know what to say. His gaze drifted to her hand in his. He turned it palm up and examined it as carefully as a Gypsy fortune-teller. At last his gaze returned to hers. "Are you happy?"

She smiled. "Of course I'm happy."

"Why?"

"Why?" She forced a light laugh. "Goodness, Marcus, I have everything any woman could ever want. Wealth, position, a lovely family. Why would I not be happy?"

He studied her intently. "I don't know exactly, but you have been acting in the oddest manner, and I wondered—"

"You needn't," she said quickly. "My manner is not the least bit odd. I am simply"—she thought for a moment—"female. Yes, that's it. I am a woman and you are not especially used to living in close proximity to a woman."

"That is what I thought too at first," he said under his breath.

"And now?"

"Now?" His gaze searched her face. "Now I am concerned. It has been brought to my attention that perhaps you are uneasy because of the suddenness with which your fortunes, your life, have changed. If you might fear that acknowledging this newfound happiness will cause it to vanish."

"That's ridiculous." She scrambled to her feet and stared down at him, ignoring the fact that, in part at least, he was right. "Wherever did you get such an absurd idea?"

He laced his fingers behind his neck and settled back against the tree. "A highly credible source, I assure you."

"Who?"

"Other women." A smug smile played over his lips. "Oh, they were rather shorter than you. Younger too. And a bit more outspoken, although I daresay that's hard to believe."

She narrowed her eyes and studied him. "You're talking about Charity, Patience, and Hope?"

He nodded.

"But they're children. You can't possibly—"

"I can and I do. These nieces of ours are wise beyond their years. Not surprising really. They have a great deal in common with their aunt." He considered her thoughtfully. "They think I simply need to convince you to admit that you love me, aloud I believe, or failing that, I have to give you what you want most in the world."

"And what exactly is that?"

"Hope thinks it's a dog."

"What do you think?"

"I think . . ." His eyes narrowed and a shiver ran down her spine. That particular look in his eye always made him appear just a bit dangerous and wickedly handsome. As if she were playing with fire. "I think I have given you all I have to give. My name, my home, my fortune, my heart."

She stared at him, and any last shred of resistance vanished. "What if I want more?"

He laughed. "Do you?"

"I don't think there could possibly *be* more."

"Nor do I. There is my life, of course, although that too is yours insofar as I can give it." He got to his feet in a slow and leisurely manner. "However, it does seem only fair I should expect something from you in return."

"I can't imagine what. You have kept your fortune because I married you."

"And you have kept possession of the money left to you by your father. You have retained the deed to the property I have wanted to purchase for years—"

"We may be able to come to an agreement on that."

"Damn decent of you." He stepped closer. "You have retained the independence of your manner."

"Come now, my lord, does a married woman truly retain any semblance of independence?"

"You seem to." He reached out with one arm and pulled her hard against him. The intensity of his green eyes belied the light note in his voice. "You are a cruel and heartless wench, Gwen. You have captured my very soul, yet you will not throw me so much as a mere morsel of affection."

Her breath caught. "I think the affection I have thrown you can scarcely be called mere."

"I'm not taking about that kind of affection but you're right. There is nothing *mere* about that." He bent to kiss the side of her neck. "Tell me you love me, Gwen."

"Very well, Marcus." Her voice was matter of fact. "I love you."

He raised his head and stared down at her suspiciously. "What did you say?"

She laughed and pulled out of his arms and backed away. "If you didn't hear—"

"I heard." He moved toward her. "However, I wish to hear it again."

"Why?"

"Because I have three smaller versions of you imply-
ing they shall do me great bodily harm if I do not do all
in my power to make you happy."

"Is that the only reason?"

"No, Lady Pennington, it isn't." He rolled his gaze
toward the heavens. "Gad, you are stubborn."

"I love you, Marcus. Are you happy now?"

"The question is, are you happy?"

Apparently the girls had been right. The very words
had lifted a weight off her shoulders.

She folded her arms over her chest and grinned.
"Yes, indeed I believe I am."

"Why?"

"Come now, Marcus, isn't my admission, aloud,
enough?"

He shook his head thoughtfully. "I don't think so."

"Very well." She heaved an overly dramatic sigh. "I
am happy because I have everything I could ever possibly want and more." Her voice caught. "I have you."

He studied her for a long moment. "Say it again."

"I love you."

"Say it like you mean it."

She laughed. "I do mean it."

He shook his head regretfully. "It didn't sound very
sincere to me."

"Marcus." She resisted the childish urge to stamp her
foot or to laugh again. "It was exceedingly sincere."

"I don't know." He sighed. "I thought it had a rather
halfhearted ring to it."

"You are so annoying." Abruptly she turned on her
heel and faced away from him, stretched her arms wide,

and yelled, "I love the Earl of Pennington! I love my husband! I love Marcus Aloysius Grenville Hamilton Holcroft!"

"And he loves you as well." Marcus's voice was low beside her ear. "Now, that did sound sincere." His arms wrapped around her. "And yet another instance where it is easier to confess one's true feelings when one is not face-to-face."

"Nonsense." She pulled away and turned toward him. "I think your so-called scientific inquiry into this matter needs further attention."

He chuckled and moved closer. "Do you?"

"I do indeed." She reached out and grabbed the edges of his jacket, then stepped backward, pulling him with her until she could rest her back against the tree. "In point of fact, I don't think your theory goes far enough."

"You don't?" He stepped closer.

"No." She met his gaze directly, and her stomach fluttered at the emotion she saw in his eyes. "I believe it is indeed easier to admit your thoughts and feelings when you're not looking at another person but only if you're unsure of your response or his." She rested her palms on his chest, the hard lines of his muscles tense beneath her touch. "Once you are confident, once you—"

"Trust?" He braced his hands on the tree on either side of her and stared down at her.

"I was going to say *know* but trust indeed plays a part." She drew a deep breath. "Once you realize that you can trust him with your feelings—"

"With your heart," he murmured.

She nodded and slid her hands up his jacket to curl against the back of his neck. "There is no need to avoid his eyes because you know precisely what you will find there."

"And what do you find in my eyes?" He moved to wrap his arms around her and pull her against him.

"My life," she said simply.

"Ah, Gwen." His lips met hers softly. "I never dreamed . . ."

"What?" she whispered.

"You." He drew her closer, and his lips pressed against hers. She opened her mouth in welcome and wondered if she would always feel this rush of passion in his arms. The ever-present fire that simmered just beneath the surface whenever he touched her flickered to life. She wanted him with her always, in the years to come and this very minute.

His kiss grew harder, her response more insistent. She pressed her body tighter against his, wanting, needing to feel the hardness of his arousal.

"Marcus." She pulled her lips from his. His mouth strayed to her throat, and her head dropped back against the tree.

"Yes?" he murmured.

"It would be highly improper . . ." She gasped. His hand moved to cup her breast, and she could feel the heat of his touch even through the fabric of her riding habit. "Wouldn't it?"

"Wouldn't what?" His hands roamed over her.

"If we were to . . . well . . . you know . . . here." Her fingers entwined in his hair.

"Yes." He shifted, one hand splayed across her back,

the other gathered the fabric of her gown until he could reach beneath it to run his hand up the length of her leg to her hips. "Highly improper."

"Still . . ." His fingers slipped between her legs and she sucked in a short breath. "We are married."

"Indeed we are."

She shifted to give him greater access. "And no one could see us here."

"Not a soul." His voice was low and a touch breathless.

"Then perhaps . . ." She ran her hand over the hard bulge in his trousers and was gratified by his sharp intake of breath.

His fingers slipped over her in a rhythm that thrummed from his touch upward to melt the very bones in her body.

"Good Lord, Gwen," he murmured against her neck. "This is . . ."

She gasped and tugged at his pants. "Indeed it is."

He fumbled to free himself from his trousers, then raised her leg to wrap around his hip. She gripped his shoulder and rested her back against the tree, and he slipped into her, the awkwardness of their position only increasing her arousal.

He moved within her, and she responded with the sheer delight she found in his touch and more, a bliss far beyond the excitement of their joining. It was indeed right and proper to be with this man, even here and now, under the setting sun, overlooking his world.

A primitive, animal desire drove her to meet his thrusts with a hard, fast urging of her own. To pull him deeper into her and push against him as if their very lives were at stake. The tense, hot wonder built within her with every stroke, every breath, every beat of his heart against hers. She wanted to scream with need, demand release and pure pleasure. And far too soon, her body convulsed around his and she did indeed scream softly, and she felt his shuddering release within her. For a moment neither moved, shocked by the intensity and the speed of their joining. At last he sagged against her.

"I have been thinking lately, Marcus"—she swallowed hard— "that I am terribly tired of being proper."

He made an odd sort of choking sound against her neck. "I daresay you needn't worry about that again."

Laughter bubbled up from somewhere deep inside her. He joined her and they clung together and laughed with a passion nearly as intense as their lovemaking. Laughter that came from a delightful sense of satisfaction and a joy she'd never imagined but now embraced in every fiber of her being.

He moved away just enough to allow her dress to fall back into place and give him room to recover his trousers. Then he pulled her back into his embrace.

"I fear you might be rather bruised tomorrow." He winced in sympathy. "I suspect this tree is not the most comfortable thing to make love against."

"I scarcely noticed, nor did I care. However"—she kissed him firmly—"next time you can be against the tree."

He lifted a brow. "And will there then be a next time?"

"Oh, I can almost guarantee it."

He laughed. "I think I shall quite enjoy having a wife

who is tired of being terribly proper as long as her improprieties are with me and me alone."

"Of course, my lord." She flashed him a wicked grin. "At least for the next seven and a half years."

His eyes narrowed. "Forever, Gwen."

"If I recall correctly, this condition about seven and a half years was your idea."

"That was before."

"Before?"

"Before I knew how incredibly lucky I was. Before I knew I had stumbled into the best thing to ever have happened to me. Before I realized seven and a half years, even a lifetime, with you will not be nearly enough." His gaze searched hers. "I promise you, Gwen, you can trust me. With your future and the future of your nieces and your children, our children."

She gazed at him and knew, with a surety she'd never known before, that she could indeed trust this man with the rest of her life. And her heart.

"Forever, Gwen," he growled. "Say it."

"Because if I say it aloud I'll be happy?" She couldn't help the teasing note in her voice.

"Because if you say it aloud we'll both be happy."

Her heart caught at the look in his eye.

"Very well, Lord Pennington." She smiled up at him and realized love wasn't at all a trap. "Forever."

It was a gift.

Chapter Seventeen

Even when a man has the best of intentions, it may be not
be enough, because in the end, he is but a mere mortal.
Some things even a good man cannot change.

Gwendolyn Pennington

Happiness was certainly not at all overrated.

Indeed, it was a kind of constant euphoria that underlaid her every step, her every breath, the very beat of her heart. She was inclined to laugh for no particular reason, even to giggle. It was suspiciously like the delightful sensation brought on by brandy without the unpleasant aftereffects.

Gwen sailed down the stairs to join her husband and Berkley in the enjoyable conversations, and often debates, that marked any evening Marcus's friend joined them for dinner.

It had been nearly a week since Gwen had admitted her love for her husband. Certainly, in a logical, rational part of her mind, she knew the intensity of her feelings would no doubt change with time, would ease and mellow, but she suspected that, like the patina on fine furniture, it would become even richer with the years.

Forever.

It had the loveliest sound to it.

The girls too were happy. They quite liked their new life and their new home and appeared at last to like their aunt as well. Gwen had just finished wishing them a good night, leaving them in the capable hands of their Grandmama Pennington, who took great delight in ending each day with a story. She too seemed content these days.

Gwen swept into the parlor and pulled up short. Marcus and Berkley and a stranger quickly got to their feet.

"Gwen." Marcus stepped toward her, an odd look on his face. "We have an unexpected guest."

"So I see." She cast the visitor a welcoming smile.

He was tall and rather attractive and struck her as vaguely familiar although she was certain they had never met.

"Allow me to present my wife, Lady Pennington. Gwen." Marcus's voice was controlled but there was an uneasy glint in his eyes. "This is Lord Townsend. Your cousin."

Shock stole her voice, and for a moment all she could do was stare. A myriad of intense emotions swirled through her, none of them logical. So this was the man who had taken her father's title and her home. She knew full well her reaction to his presence was irrational: her cousin had done nothing untoward, indeed, nothing whatsoever to deserve her enmity save be her father's only male heir. He was as much a victim of society's rules as she. Although it was hard to think of someone who had reaped nothing but benefits as a victim.

"Lady Pennington. Cousin." He stepped toward her, and she noted he had the decency to realize this meeting was not especially easy for her. "I regret that we have not had the chance to meet before now."

She drew a long, steadying breath, lifted her chin, and held out her hand. She managed to keep her voice calm and her hand steady. "As do I, my lord. It is good to meet you at last."

The room itself seemed to let out a sigh, as if it, along with its inhabitants, had held its breath in anticipation of her reaction.

Townsend took her hand and gazed into her eyes. "Please call me Adrian; we are family after all."

"Yes of course," she murmured. He bore a familial resemblance to his sister, but the features that were not the least bit attractive in a female were quite handsome in the masculine version. She withdrew her hand and cast him a pleasant smile. "I must say, your visit has taken me by surprise."

Berkley snorted, then coughed apologetically.

"I apologize for the lateness of the hour. I only returned to England recently and . . ." Townsend glanced at Marcus.

"Gwen," Marcus said coolly, "Lord Townsend is here about the girls."

Her heart stilled. "What about them?"

Marcus's expression was matter-of-fact, but concern showed in his eyes. "There is apparently a problem as to their guardianship."

She took her cue from her husband and forced a calm

note to her voice, ignoring the knowledge in the back of her mind that, for once, Albert had been right. "What sort of problem?"

"He seems to think he should be their guardian," Berkley blurted, then winced. "Sorry, I didn't mean . . ."

"I see." The level tone of her voice belied the churning in her stomach. "And why is that, my lord?"

"Adrian, please." Townsend had the good grace to look uncomfortable. "It has come to my attention, cousin—may I call you Gwendolyn?"

"You may not," she said without thinking, ignoring Marcus's warning glance.

"Very well." Townsend nodded. "Lady Pennington, when I returned home, my sister informed me you had taken charge of your nieces. At first I thought that was as it should be. You are their closest living relative."

"Indeed I am."

"However, information I did not have then has come to my attention, and I now believe it is in their best interests"—Townsend drew a deep breath—"that I take them into my keeping."

"No," she said without hesitation. "Absolutely not."

"What is this new information?" Marcus said quickly.

Townsend hesitated. "The Loring children are the beneficiaries of a substantial inheritance. As head of the family, I am in the best position to oversee their finances as well as provide the proper atmosphere for their upbringing."

"With you and your sister?" Gwen cast him a scathing glare. "She doesn't even like them. How can you possibly think growing up in a place where they aren't liked or truly wanted for that matter would be best for them? For anyone?"

"Gwen." Marcus placed a quieting hand on her arm and directed his attention to Townsend. "I am more than capable of overseeing whatever this inheritance amounts to. If you are concerned as to my honesty, you should understand my own finances are quite respectable and in order. However, I am more than willing to sign whatever legal documents you feel are appropriate to ensure their legacy remains intact for their future."

"I do appreciate that, my lord, but there's far more to all this than simply money." Townsend chose his words with care. "Paul Loring, the girls' father, was a friend of mine. In point of fact"—Townsend's gaze met hers—"I counseled him against running off with your sister."

"How very thoughtful of you." Sarcasm dripped from Gwen's words.

"Do not take my comment in a manner in which I did not intend, Lady Pennington." Townsend narrowed his eyes. "I had nothing against your sister. We had never met. At that time I had little specific knowledge of your branch of the family. As you are well aware, our connection is very distant. In truth, not until your father's death did I discover I was his only heir.

"Nonetheless, from what Loring told me of the matter, I did know your father was set against a match between him and your sister. Paul was my friend, and any marriage that did not have the blessing of family seemed to me ill-advised. Besides, he was but twenty years of age and far too young, in my opinion, to wed. Regardless, he paid no heed to my concerns."

Townsend's gaze met hers. "Do you know anything of your sister's husband?"

"No." Gwen clasped her hands together in an effort to stifle the panic building inside her. "I was but a child when Louisa married. I barely even remember her."

"I see." Townsend considered her thoughtfully. "Paul Loring was the youngest son of the Earl of Stokes. As such, he could not inherit the title, but he was the beneficiary of a substantial fortune through his mother's family. I don't remember the exact details, but I do recall it was rather unusual. At any rate, wealth, youth, and love can be a powerful combination. He and your sister were gone before anyone knew what they were about."

Berkley's brow furrowed. "I dimly recall hearing about this. It was quite a scandal, if I remember."

"As interesting as this is, Lord Townsend," Marcus said, "I do not see where it is pertinent to our current discussion. I concede that you were Mr. Loring's friend. But Lady Pennington is the children's aunt."

"Yes, of course. However . . ." Townsend pulled a folded paper from his waistcoat pocket. "I have recently come into possession of a letter from Paul—Mr. Loring—apparently written some years ago."

"And?" Fear gripped Gwen's heart.

"In it he requests that, if anything should happen to him or his wife, I should take custody of his children." Genuine regret shone on Townsend's face. "I am sorry." He handed the letter to Marcus.

"I don't believe a word of it." Gwen crossed her arms over her chest. "Even if I did, you cannot come into my home, announce you have my nieces' best interests at heart, wave a letter that may or may not be legitimate, and, oh yes, mention they have a considerable fortune you would be all too happy to mind for them, and expect me to simply say, 'Of course, cousin dear, you may have these children to do with as you please.'"

"That's enough, Gwen," Marcus murmured, his attention on the letter in his hand.

"It most certainly is not." She glared at him. Marcus ignored her. "It's not nearly enough." She turned her attention back to Townsend. "Well, you can't have them. I absolutely will not permit it."

"Nor will I." Berkley stepped to her side.

"Marcus?" Gwen snapped.

"In a moment." Marcus studied the letter. "I want to finish this."

"Lady Pennington. Cousin." Townsend stepped toward her. "Do understand, as you have said, you were a child when Paul and your sister married. How could you expect any man to entrust the future of his children to someone he had never met? He only wants what is best for them."

"As do I." Gwen's voice rose. "And what is best for them is to remain exactly where they are. They are well provided for here with people who care for them. Nor shall they want for anything in the future. And they are happy. Happiness, cousin, is a rare commodity in this world, particularly when it comes to those who have no say in the running of their own lives. Children, and more to the point, female children. I will not let you take that from them." She turned toward her husband. "Tell him, Marcus. Tell him he can't have them."

"I'm not sure I can right now." Marcus looked up and considered Townsend thoughtfully. "If this is genuine—"

"It is," Townsend said quickly.

"It appears fairly straightforward." Marcus glanced at the paper again, then at Townsend. "But surely you do not intend to take the girls with you tonight?"

Gwen gasped in horror. "Marcus! How can you—"

"It is at least a half day's ride from here to Townsend Park, probably longer in a carriage," her husband continued as if he hadn't heard her. "Indeed, there is no great hurry, is there?"

"No," Townsend said slowly. "I suppose not."

"Excellent." Marcus nodded. "Then you shall certainly stay the night."

"Marcus!" She couldn't believe her ears.

He ignored her again. "It would be best to break this news to the girls as gently as possible. Perhaps you could see your way clear to stay tomorrow as well."

"How can you possibly invite him to stay? You should be throwing him out. At once!" Gwen's control broke. "Don't you understand? He doesn't care about them. Not really. Maybe he has some sense of obligation because of their father's request but it's obvious he's only here because of their inheritance."

"That's quite enough, Gwen." Marcus's tone rang hard and firm, matching the look in his eye, and tore through her like a knife.

She sucked in a shocked breath.

He wasn't going to do anything?

"It may be easier for the girls if they had a day to get used to the idea of leaving." Marcus's manner was matter-of-fact. He turned toward Berkley. "Reggie, why don't you show Lord Townsend into the library. You know where the brandy is. I'm certain he could probably use a bit of refreshment right now."

He was going to let Townsend take the girls?

Berkley studied his friend for a moment, then nodded slowly. "Of course." He cast Gwen a quick smile of encouragement, then headed toward the door.

Maybe she should have married Berkley—Reggie—after all. At least he showed some concern about the situation. Dear, sweet Reggie. She clenched her fists by her sides. Marcus behaved as though this was no more than a minor inconvenience.

"I appreciate your attitude about all this, Lord Pennington," Townsend said. "It's damnably decent of you."

"Think nothing of it." Marcus shrugged and tossed the letter casually onto a side table as if it were of no importance. "We can continue our discussion in the morning. This is obviously a matter best decided by those of us who can remain rational and assess the situation with an unemotional eye."

"Rational?" Gwen choked on the word. "Rational?"

Reggie said something under his breath, and she wondered if it might have been a warning to her husband. Marcus certainly needed it. Reggie reached the door, jerked it open, and stepped aside to allow Townsend to precede him.

"I confess, I am somewhat confused by your obvious interest in all of this, Lord Berkley," Townsend said.

"I am not merely Lord Berkley," Reggie said loftily,

following the other man out of the parlor. "I am Uncle Reggie." He closed the door firmly behind him.

At once Gwen turned toward her husband. "Rational? Unemotional?"

"Yes," he snapped. "Bloody hell, Gwen, we have got to keep our wits about us."

"My wits are about me!"

"Then we are in a great deal of trouble!" He swiveled and paced the room. "You cannot handle a man like Townsend, who goes about waving papers that may or may not be legal, with sheer emotion. We have got to remain calm and collected."

"I don't want to be calm! I want to do something. I want you to do something. Beginning with removing him from this house! Immediately." She aimed an angry finger at him. "You're an earl. He's only a viscount. Can't you have him thrown in prison or hanged or something?"

"No, I can't. And even if I could, what would be the charge?"

"Abduction." She ticked the charges off on her fingers. "Theft. Fraud. Trespass—"

"I invited him to stay."

"Indeed you did." She fairly spat the words.

"Gwen." He drew a calming breath, moved to her, and took her hands. "I know how upset you are—"

"Do you?" She yanked her hands from his.

"Yes, I do. I too am concerned."

She jerked up her chin defiantly. "Are you?"

His jaw tightened. "Damnation, Gwen, of course I am. I have come to care for those girls as if they were my own."

"Well, you're certainly hiding it well."

"And you're not hiding it at all!"

For a long moment she glared at him, and he glared right back. She couldn't remember ever having been angrier with anyone even if a tiny voice in her head noted she was indeed somewhat irrational, and perhaps calmer heads should prevail. She paid it no heed.

He drew a deep breath. "Do try to consider the facts for a minute. Townsend's letter appears genuine, but whether or not it is, it may have no legal bearing on guardianship. We need to determine if indeed Townsend's demand carries any weight."

"And if it does?" She swallowed against the ache in her throat.

"I don't know." Marcus ran his hand through his hair. "However, I do know any number of influential people who may well be able to exert some sort of influence." Lines of worry creased his face.

At once she realized he was genuinely concerned. How could she have doubted it? Guilt rushed through her, for a moment washing aside her fear.

"I apologize, Marcus." She shook her head. "I was wrong to think, even for an instant, that you don't care about the girls. I am sorry."

"Well, that's something at any rate," he muttered.

"What are we going to do?" She hated the helpless note in her voice but she couldn't hide it.

"I have a plan, of sorts. I don't know if it will make any difference but . . ."

"What?"

"I asked Townsend to stay the night and hopefully tomorrow as well to give us a bit of time." Again he took her hands and gazed into her eyes. "I'm going to go to London, Gwen, to talk to Whiting about all this. You may not realize it, but he is an excellent solicitor. I have no idea if he is aware of this latest turn of events. Regardless, he will be able to advise us as to our standing in this situation, and hopefully provide us with options for keeping the girls as well."

"Do you really think so?" Her gaze searched his.

"I hope so." His voice was firm. "I'll leave for London at once."

"But it's late."

"I can be there by midnight. I'll get Whiting out of his bed for this. With luck I can be back by midmorning." Marcus squeezed her hands. "You must trust me, Gwen. I shall do all in my power to resolve this."

She didn't want to say it aloud but the words came of their own accord. "What if you can't?"

"I don't know." He blew a long, frustrated breath. "But I shall leave no stone unturned to keep the girls with us. They have become my children, and I love them almost as much as I love you."

"I am so scared." She blinked back a tear. "What if—"

"What if all works out for the best and all this emotion is wasted?" He brushed away an errant tear. "And if the worst happens, we can always follow your example."

She sniffed. "What do you mean?"

"Well"—he grinned—"we could all impulsively run off to America and become governesses."

She smiled weakly. "I cannot imagine you as a governess."

He widened his eyes with mock indignation. "I would be an excellent governess. Why, I have ready that look of outraged amusement of yours." He pursed his lips.

"Stop it." She laughed in spite of herself.

"In truth, I would probably make a better governess than you did. You may not have noticed, but I am excellent with children. The girls adore me."

"As does their aunt."

"Gwen." He pulled her into his arms. "I promised that you could trust me and you must trust me now. I will find an answer." His gazed bored into hers. "Do you trust me?"

"Of course," she said with a certainty she didn't entirely feel.

His eyes narrowed slightly, as if he'd heard something in her voice he didn't quite like. "Gwen?"

"I do love you, Marcus." She threw her arms around him and kissed him with a fierceness born of hope and fear and farewell. She drew back, swallowed the lump in her throat, and smiled up at him. "And I do trust you."

He studied her for a long moment. "I shall ask Reggie to stay the night as well. If you need anything—"

"I won't." She stepped back. "If you're going to London tonight, you'd best go now."

"I don't like to leave you like this."

"I'm fine. Perfectly calm and quite under control." She forced a smile. "Besides, Reggie is here and he has strict standards against the seduction of the wives of his friends."

"That's not what worries me," he murmured.

"What then?" she said lightly.

"I have the oddest feeling . . ." He shook his head. "I'm sure it's nothing." He started toward the door.

"Marcus?"

He turned. "Yes?"

"I . . ." An instant later she was in his arms again, clinging to him as if her very life depended on it. As it did.

He smoothed her hair. "It shall be all right, Gwen. I promise."

"I know," she whispered. She pulled away and stared up at him. "Apparently I am not quite as calm as I had thought."

"I was not fooled for a moment." The grin on his face belied the question in his eye.

"I'm being extraordinarily silly. It's not as if I will never see you again." The words caught at her heart. She stepped back and waved him toward the door. "Go now, before I become a complete fool. It's probably nothing more than the fact that we have never spent a night apart since we wed."

"And this shall be the last." He nodded firmly and stepped to the door, then turned back to her. "Forever, Gwen. Say it."

She raised her chin and smiled. "Forever, Marcus."

A moment later he was gone.

She stared at the door after him, for a minute or an hour or eternity. He was her heart, her soul, her life. Of course she trusted him to do the very best he could. But the chances were better than good that even Marcus could not resolve this problem.

He insisted on doing this all properly, talking to the

solicitor about legalities and options and any number of things Gwen had absolutely no confidence in. It was the world's legal rules that had taken her heritage from her in the first place, and she didn't doubt it would always take the side of a man over those of children and women.

She wasn't sure when she decided but at some point in the last few minutes she knew that, once again in her life, she had to take matters into her own hands.

In a scant two hours, Marcus would be halfway to London and there would be little chance of running into him at that point. She would rouse the girls then and they would sneak out of the house. They would travel by horseback instead of by carriage. It was faster and no doubt easier at night if perhaps somewhat dangerous. But the girls had grown rather good in the saddle since coming to the country. This moonlit dash across the countryside would be yet another adventure for them in their brief lives that had seen so many adventures already.

She would bring the girls to Colette and Madame long enough for her to arrange her finances. Her inheritance was safe in a London bank. It would be best to avoid Whiting but she could call on Albert to arrange things for her. Thank God she had insisted on keeping control of her funds.

Marcus's suggestion was excellent: they would indeed take the first ship to America. But this time Gwen had no need of employment. She had more than enough money now.

It had taken Whiting five years to find her. Even if Marcus came after her, it might well be years before he found them. By then the girls would be old enough to legally manage their own affairs. They would come into their inheritance and no one would be able to harm them. And they would have grown up happy and wanted and loved.

It was exceedingly odd; the panic that had always driven her in the past was absent tonight, replaced by an unrelenting determination and an absolute resolve. She had no idea if what she was doing was right. As right was judged by the world, it probably wasn't. Indeed, it might well be a dreadful mistake. But while she could trust Marcus to do his best, in this particular case she was not confident of success. It wasn't her husband she had no faith in: it was the rest of the world.

Right or wrong, she saw no other choice.

And if it was accompanied by an ache so intense it threatened to tear her apart, so be it. A hurt so deep, it was all she could do to stand upright; well, she would have to bear it. She had to accept as well the fact that she would probably never see Marcus again, hear his laughter, lie in his arms.

The least she could do was leave him a note. Explain exactly why she had no choice but to run. Again. Besides, she'd promised to love him forever. He should know she meant it. And know as well she would never stop loving him, not until the last breath left her body or the final beat of her heart.

He would never forgive her, of course. How could he? She would never forgive herself.

This would destroy him. His heart would snap in two much as hers was breaking at this very moment. He had avoided love as steadfastly as she had. And now . . .

She shook her head and slowly started toward the door. This was such a mess.

She had thought it took more courage to face a problem than to run from it. But this was different. This was not for herself. It took all the strength she had within her to follow the course she knew was best. To sacrifice one love for another.

Marcus would carry on, he had friends and family and people who cared about him. The girls had no one who truly cared about them. No one to make certain they would survive. Without her, they would grow up exactly as she had.

And that she could not permit.

Regardless of the price she had to pay.

Chapter Eighteen

*There is no power on earth that can
equal a man in love. He is a force that
even nature cannot conquer.*

Colette de Chabot

"Godfrey!"

Marcus strode into the foyer of Holcroft Hall, Whiting a step behind. It was already late morning, far later than he had hoped to return, yet it could not be helped. This whole matter was much more complicated than he had expected.

"Yes, my lord?" As always, Godfrey appeared out of nowhere.

"Get Mr. Whiting something to eat and drink and a bite for me as well. Have it brought to the library and have Lady Pennington and Lord Berkley join me there. At once."

"Lord Berkley is already in the library, sir, with Lord Townsend—"

"Excellent." Marcus started toward the library.

"Which Lady Pennington did you wish to see, my lord?"

"As many as you can find," Marcus said over his shoulder.

"Sir, I should tell you that might be a bit difficult," the butler called after him.

"Do what you can, Godfrey." Marcus threw open the library door and stepped aside, gesturing Whiting to enter before him. In truth, it might be somewhat easier to speak to Townsend without Gwen's presence or his mother's either, for that matter. She too adored the girls.

Townsend and Reggie sat in chairs facing one another, each with a glass of brandy in his hand, sharing what was obviously a strained silence. Marcus wondered how long they'd been alone in here together. Both men leaped to their feet at his appearance.

"Did you find them?" Reggie stepped forward, concern on his face.

Marcus pulled up short and stared. "Find who?"

Reggie and Townsend traded uneasy glances.

"Find who?" Marcus said again, fear pooling in the pit of his stomach.

Reggie winced. "You didn't get my message, then? I sent a servant after you the moment—"

"Find who?" Marcus snapped.

"My cousin and the children," Townsend said. "They have gone. Apparently they left sometime in the middle of the night."

"We didn't discover they were missing until an hour or so ago." Reggie shrugged helplessly. "We had no idea where they might have gone and thought it best to wait for your return before going after them."

"Bloody hell." Marcus grit his teeth. He wasn't surprised. Not in the least. He'd probably known last night that she'd had something like this in mind and simply hadn't wanted to accept it. Or perhaps he couldn't believe she would be that foolish.

"She left a note." Reggie nodded at the desk, his manner apologetic, as if this was somehow his fault.

Marcus stepped to the desk and snatched up the paper. He unfolded it and quickly scanned the message.

In a scant three lines Gwen explained that it wasn't him she didn't trust but the rest of the world. That she was doing what she truly thought was best. And that she would love him forever.

He stared at her perfect hand for a long moment. An odd sort of emptiness gripped him, and he was hard-pressed to focus on her words.

She had left him? Done what she'd always done when she could see no solution: run. Only this time she'd taken his heart with her.

Before he had so much as a twinge of regret or a modicum of sorrow or a sharp stab of pain, fierce determination swept through him.

"I don't think so, Miss Townsend." He crushed her note in his hand. He'd waited his entire life to find love. He'd be damned if he'd let it walk out on him now.

"Marcus?" Reggie stepped closer and laid his hand on his friend's arm. "Are you all right?"

"No. I am exceedingly tired, and the last thing I wish to do is chase across the country after my wife. But Reggie"—he met his friend's gaze directly—"I am about to do just that."

"Are you certain that's wise?" Reggie said carefully.

"She's left you, Marcus. It's difficult to face, but there you have it. It's the landing, old man. I know you're upset—"

"Upset?" Marcus's voice rang with anger. "I am bloody furious. From the moment I met that woman, absolutely everything has had to be her way and I have given in to her. She's kept her money, her house, and her independence. She has kept secrets from me—"

"Just three," Reggie murmured. "Not so bad really. I've known women—"

"I'm the one who was forced to first confess my feelings without the least bit of encouragement from her. Then I had to get her to admit hers so that she would stop moping and be happy. Happy! Can you believe that?" He shook his head. "She should have been bloody happy long before then."

"She is a woman, after all," Reggie said. "They are very odd creatures."

"She's led me around as if I've had a ring through my nose. I am the Earl of blasted Pennington and I've been acting like a smitten schoolboy!"

"Oh, it hasn't been that bad."

"No?" Marcus raised a brow. "On our wedding night, she had a list of what I was supposed to do and precisely when I was supposed to do it!"

"I wouldn't go around mentioning that if I were you," Reggie said under his breath. "It doesn't look at all good."

"There has not been the least bit of compromise in this relationship up to now, and I am damn tired of it." Marcus snatched the brandy from Reggie's hand and downed it in one swallow. "As soon as I catch up with her, things are going to be decidedly different."

"Well said, my lord." Townsend grinned.

Marcus had forgotten Gwen's cousin was in the room. There were matters right here that needed attending before he could follow his wife. Starting with this man.

He turned toward Townsend. "You lied to us."

Townsend's chin jerked up defiantly. "I wouldn't say lie, exactly."

"My God, it runs in the family." Marcus rolled his gaze toward the ceiling. "Would you prefer the term *deceive*?"

"As you apparently already know"—Townsend shrugged—"this was not exactly my choice. It was not how I would have done things."

"What is he talking about," Reggie said in an aside to Marcus.

A brisk knock sounded at the door, and at once it swung open. A maid carried in a tray bearing meats and breads and pitchers of what Marcus hoped was tea, or better yet coffee, strong and hot. His stomach growled at the sight. His mother followed a few steps behind the maid.

"Jeffrey." Her eyes widened with obvious delight.

Jeffrey?

Marcus's gaze followed his mother's.

Whiting nodded a greeting. "Helena." He cleared his throat. "Forgive me, Lady Pennington."

Helena's gaze shifted from the solicitor to her son and back. Her brow furrowed. "What are you doing here?"

"He's here because I asked him to come." Marcus

studied his mother. There was something decidedly odd about her manner.

"It seemed like a good idea at the time," Whiting said mildly.

"I see." Helena chose her words with care. "Why exactly is that?"

"Why?" Marcus glanced at the other men, then addressed his mother. "I gather you have no idea what's happened here."

Her eyes widened. "Something has happened?"

Marcus blew a long, exasperated breath.

"Allow me, Marcus." Reggie stepped forward. "It all began last night, my lady, with the arrival of this gentleman, Lord Townsend. He is the cousin of Lady Pennington—the young one—"

The older Lady Pennington raised an annoyed brow.

"What I mean is the current countess. Gwendolyn," Reggie said quickly.

"Delighted to meet you, Lady Pennington." Townsend smiled politely.

"As am I," she murmured.

Reggie continued. "He claimed he had the right, thanks to a letter from the girls' father—"

"My girls?" Indignation sounded in her voice.

"I thought that letter looked odd." Marcus glared at Townsend.

"—to guardianship of the children," Reggie finished. "Marcus rode to London—"

"To speak with me," Whiting cut in. Helena cast him a grateful smile. A bit too grateful and definitely too . . . personal.

"But my wife decided not to wait for my return."

Marcus grit his teeth. "She took matters into her own hands and left with the children."

"Left?" Helena shook her head in confusion. "What do you mean, left?"

"She's gone, Mother," Marcus snapped. "Fled in the middle of the night apparently."

"I don't believe it," Helena said staunchly.

"It's true, Lady Pennington," Townsend said. "My cousin was extremely overset last night. Quite frankly, I considered her to be rather irrational and somewhat unstable. Her actions bear that out. She is obviously not suited to be the guardian of defenseless children, and I understand she was not especially adequate as a governess either."

"Why you—" Reggie moved toward Townsend in a threatening manner.

"Not now," Marcus said coldly.

"Perhaps Gwendolyn was never suited to be a governess." Helena's tone matched her son's. "She was very young, and it's been my experience not all women are right for such positions. However, Gwendolyn and these children care for one another, and that, Lord Townsend, can neither be measured nor disregarded. As for the instability you seem to see in her . . ." Helena squared her shoulders. "I don't care if she's mad as a March hare, I like her a great deal. Indeed I have come to regard her with considerable affection.

"Marcus." She turned to her son. "I have done far too much to see it all end this way. Gwendolyn is the best thing to ever happen to you, and you would be a fool to let her get away."

"I have no intention of letting her get away,

Mother." He studied his mother carefully. "What do you mean: you have done far too much?"

"Did I say that?" A look of panic flitted through her eyes and her gaze slipped to Whiting. An amused smile curved his lips. "I suppose it scarcely matters now." She wrung her hands together. "Indeed, all has worked out so nicely. And it's really rather an interesting story, I should think. However, you probably should know"— she braced herself—"you never actually had to marry her."

"Of course I had—" Marcus narrowed his eyes. "Explain yourself, Mother."

"Jeffrey?" She cast another hopeful glance at the solicitor.

"This was not my idea," Whiting said firmly. "In truth, my dear Helena, I was as much an unwitting dupe in this as your son. And I shall not rescue you now."

My dear Helena?

"Very well." She heaved a resigned sigh. "Marcus, dear." She paused, obviously searching for the right words. It did not bode well.

"Do you remember how I used to assist your father in business matters? Most notably his correspondence?"

"Yes," Marcus drew the word out slowly.

"He had notoriously bad penmanship, almost illegible." She shook her head. "It was a shame really. He had a lovely way with words; they were simply impossible to read."

Marcus clenched his teeth. "Get on with it, Mother."

"You have to let me tell it my way or it will make no sense," she said with a huff. "As I was saying, even in the beginning of our marriage, I would assist him. Eventually, I took over virtually all his writing even"—she winced—"his signature."

"What are you trying to say?" Marcus held his breath.

"This is rather difficult . . ." She paused, apparently for courage. "The letter between your father and Gwendolyn's arranging your marriage, and the documents that accompanied it, well, I wrote them."

"What!" Marcus stared in shock.

"I signed your father's name and Lord Townsend's as well. I had Lord Townsend's signature on something, a bill of sale I believe, and I simply copied it." She glanced at Reggie. "It was exceedingly easy. The man's writing was scarcely better than a scrawl."

"That is interesting," Reggie murmured

"Oh, I'm certain he would have approved," she said quickly. "Indeed, he and Lord Townsend had spoken of such a match, and I do not doubt would have come to an agreement at some point. That was precisely why your father sold him the old dower house in the first place. Unfortunately, specific arrangements were never actually made before your father and then Lord Townsend died. And, well . . ."

"You're telling me," Marcus said slowly, trying to grasp the import of his mother's confession, "I did not need to marry Gwen to keep my fortune?"

"You could interpret it that way . . ." She gestured helplessly. "If you wish . . ."

Marcus's gaze met Whiting's. "There was never any threat to my finances? No deadline regarding my thirtieth birth date? No . . . anything?"

"Not to my knowledge," Whiting said.

"I thought the deadline was inspired," she murmured to Reggie.

"Excellent detail," Reggie said under his breath. "Added just the right touch."

"A great deal of this makes sense now. I thought it was absurd at first, particularly the timing. That nonsense about not being informed until three months before my birth date and everything else. Still." Marcus stared at his mother. "You seemed so shocked when I learned of this."

"I thought I did that part rather well," she said modestly. "I would have made an excellent actress."

"Positively inspired." Reggie grinned.

"Let me assure you," Whiting continued, "I had no idea the letter Lady Pennington presented to me was not legitimate. It was, after all, in the hand I had always known as your father's, and I had no reason to doubt Lord Townsend's signature. I was not made aware of this scheme of hers until after your marriage."

"And I begged him not to tell," Helena added. "Frankly, it seemed pointless. You and she got on so well together. Indeed, I thought it had quite become a love match. It seemed such a pity to muck it up."

Marcus rubbed his hand over his eyes. "I am extremely confused."

Reggie shoved a new glass of brandy into his hand. "This will help."

"I doubt it," Marcus muttered and drank anyway.

"I admit, it is a bit complex if you don't know all the details." Helena's brows pulled together. "You see, the idea only occurred to me after I discovered Jeffrey was searching for Gwendolyn. It seemed so perfect. Almost fated if you will. It was not until he actually located her that I put it into place." She cast the solicitor an apologetic smile. "I knew if I presented you with that letter too soon, there was a significant possibility you would learn it was not entirely legitimate."

Marcus raised a brow. "Entirely?"

"Thank you for your confidence," Whiting said wryly.

Marcus shifted his gaze from his mother to his solicitor and back. He struggled for the right words. "How did you . . . that is to say . . . with him and . . ."

"Jeffrey and I are quite close." Helena raised her chin and met her son's gaze directly. "We have been . . . close for some time. Several years in fact. And I fully intend to remain close with him for the foreseeable future."

"I've asked her to marry me any number of times but she won't hear of it," Whiting said matter-of-factly. "I am quite head over heels for the woman."

"Jeffrey." She cast him a most flirtatious grin.

"More interesting every minute," Reggie murmured.

"This is all . . ." Marcus shook his head. "I don't know what to say."

"You could try apologizing," Helena said.

"Apologize?" Marcus glared at her. "Whatever for?"

"If you had taken your responsibilities seriously and married long ago, I never would have been forced to take such steps." Her tone was lofty, her manner unrepentant. "You made it necessary for me to do something."

Marcus snorted in disbelief. "You're saying this is all my fault?"

"I believe I am, although it scarcely matters at this

point, dear. You have a wife you obviously care deeply for who returns your affection. Aside from today's minor difficulty, all has worked out beautifully." She cast him a satisfied smile. "I think you should thank me."

"Thank you? Thank you?" Marcus stared for a long moment, then reluctantly smiled. "Thank you, Mother."

"Think nothing of it, dear."

"I would prefer that you not meddle in my life in the future."

"I can try but . . ." She shook her head. "I certainly cannot make any promises."

"You can and you will," he said firmly, knowing full well his decree was futile. "We shall discuss it when I return from London. With my wife."

"You think that's where she's gone, then?" Reggie said.

"It's not her final destination, but yes, I'm certain that's where she's headed. With luck I can catch up to her today." Marcus shook his head wearily. "However, I shall follow her forever if need be."

"I'm coming with you, of course," Reggie said.

Marcus cast him a grateful smile. "Of course."

"Marcus," Helena laid her hand on his arm, "promise me you'll bring her back."

He smiled down at his mother, and a deep sense of gratitude flooded him. "Have no doubt of it."

"And the girls too," she insisted.

He glanced at Townsend. "That I cannot guarantee."

"I see." She drew a deep breath. "Do what you can."

"I shall do my best."

"Promise me," she said firmly.

He sighed. "Mother."

"Swear to it, Marcus." She crossed her arms over her chest. "Spit."

He groaned. "I daresay that's not necessary."

She fixed him with an unblinking gaze.

"Very well." He spit and held up his finger. "I promise by my very blood, so on and so forth, or face dire consequences."

"Amen," Reggie said firmly.

"Very good." Helena nodded with satisfaction. "Now I shall have something to eat wrapped up for you to take with you, and you may be on your way."

"I should probably come as well," Townsend said slowly.

"Probably." Marcus studied the other man carefully. "Whiting and I unraveled most of this puzzle this morning in London. However, I should like to hear more from you. We shall have a long talk about it on the way."

Marcus paused, then met the other man's gaze. "One more thing before we go, Townsend." Marcus smiled, fisted his hand and smashed it into Townsend's face. The sound of flesh crunching flesh resounded in the room. Townsend staggered back, tripped, and landed on his ass on the floor. The stunned look on his face was well worth the sting in Marcus's knuckles.

"Just so you understand, my wife is suited to do anything she sets her mind to. She is clever and courageous and I am damn lucky to have her, regardless of how it came about. And if she seemed to you either irrational or unstable, it's because she cares deeply for those children. As do I. Now . . ." He nodded at Reggie. "Help him up."

"Can't I plant him one too?" Reggie grinned.

"Later perhaps." Marcus returned his grin. "At the moment, we have more important things to do. Prime among them, finding my wife."

"You said London is not her final destination." Reggie's brow furrowed. "Then you think . . ."

"Without a doubt. But London is where her funds are and where her friends are. And given all that, it's also the best place to find transport"—Marcus blew a long breath and prayed he would not be too late—"to America."

Chapter Nineteen

*It is precisely when you have given
up hope that a good man will become a true hero.
It is why they are worth all the trouble.*

Gwendolyn Pennington

"I still don't understand why you insist on leaving to-night." Madame Freneau's words resounded in the darkness inside the duke's coach.

"I have told you over and over again," Gwen said with a calm she did not feel. "It's much better this way."

"Better or easier?"

"Both." Gwen's weary state echoed in the single word.

She and the girls had made it to London the night before without incident. It was the height of foolishness, and Gwen thanked the heavens they'd arrived unscathed. She'd known full well how dangerous a night-time ride across the country could be, especially for a woman and children unaccompanied by escort. Apparently the girls had understood as well. Hope had pointed out God was especially watchful over children and fools.

There was every possibility Gwen was indeed a fool. She'd been so certain when she'd left Marcus that she was doing what was best. That she'd had no choice. But with every mile put between them, her conviction faded. Still, it was too late to turn back now.

"You have everything, then?"

Gwen smiled in the dark. That too had been asked more than once. "Everything we shall need for the voyage."

They'd taken nothing with them when they'd left Holcroft Hall. But between the few purchases she'd made today and what Madame and Colette had managed to provide, she and the girls would make do until they reached America.

America. Gwen shook her head with disbelief. She'd never imagined she'd ever return to those foreign shores again.

A discreet knock sounded at the coach door.

"If you insist on going through with this, Gwendolyn," Madame said with a sigh in her voice, "it is apparently time.

The door swung open and one of the duke's servants offered a hand to help her out. She could already hear the girls' excited chatter outside the second coach.

Thanks to Colette, the duke had provided two vehicles to transport them all to the docks tonight, although he had not done so without adding his advice to that of the ladies. Absolutely no one save Gwen herself thought she was doing the right thing, and even she was having second thoughts.

Gwen glanced around the docks. The ship she had booked passage on would leave with the tide shortly after midnight. In spite of the lateness of the hour, the docks were well lit and a hive of activity. Waves of light spread outward from the ships and faded into the night and a deep fog.

"Aunt Gwen," Hope called and hurried toward her, a few steps in front of Patience, Charity, and Colette.

How could Gwen possibly be wrong? She knew these children would grow up exactly as she had and in the very same house, if she did not act. Marcus had the best of intentions but even the Earl of Pennington was not powerful enough to solve this dilemma.

She pushed aside any lingering doubts as well as an annoying voice in her head that refused to be silent and screamed she was making a horrendous mistake. She forced a bright note to her voice. "Are we ready then? For our grand adventure?"

"We are, of course, but . . ." Patience paused. "We want to know why we left the hall in the middle of the night."

"Without bringing along any of our things," Hope added. "We don't have a great deal but I would have liked to have brought along something."

"There is a blue dress I am quite fond of," Patience murmured.

"The point is, Aunt Gwen." Charity stepped forward. "We know something has happened. Something dreadful. We didn't ask you last night because you were rather harried. And today when we weren't sleeping, you were. Madames Freneau and de Chabot won't tell us anything."

Patience leaned forward and lowered her voice in a confidential manner. "Madame de Chabot just sighs, mumbles something in French, and proceeds to lose to us at cards. I don't think she's even trying."

"We deserve to know what has happened," Hope said firmly. "I know we're children, but we are quite mature for our years. Everyone says so."

Patience nodded. "Charity is nearly grown and I am barely two years younger and—"

"And I am more than capable of taking care of myself and oh, say, I know"—Hope grinned—"a dog."

"Oh, do stop talking about a dog, Hope." Charity leveled her sister an exasperated glare, then turned her attention back to Gwen. "What we are trying to say is that we are about to board a ship, to America from what we've heard, and we have no idea why. We think it's only fair that we know what precisely has happened."

"We do realize you've left Uncle Marcus." Patience shook her head. "And we think it's terrible."

"Which is why we are certain that whatever reason you have for taking us all so far away is probably an excellent one." Charity finished. "We simply want to know what it is."

"Yes, I suppose you're right." And hadn't Gwen always treated them a bit more like adults rather than mere children? At the start of a new life together, it was probably best to continue. "It is only fair." Gwen blew a long breath and chose her words carefully. "My cousin, Lord Townsend—"

"Pickleface's brother?" Hope asked.

Gwen didn't bother to correct her. "That's the one.

Because he is head of the family and you three apparently have a sizable inheritance, as well as the fact that years ago he knew your father, he feels that he should be your guardian. He wants you to return to Townsend Park to live."

"With Pickleface?" Patience shuddered. "What a horrid thought."

Charity frowned. "Can't Uncle Marcus do something?"

Gwen shook her head. "I fear it won't be enough. Which is why I think it would be best if we put as much distance between us and England, specifically Lord Townsend, as possible."

"But couldn't we take Uncle Marcus with us?" Hope asked. "He looks like he could use a bit of adventure."

"Of course we can't take him," Patience scoffed. "He's entirely too proper for an adventure of this sort."

"Aunt Gwen?" Charity studied her curiously. "Didn't you say running away never solved anyone's problems?"

Gwen winced to herself. "Yes, well, I might have said something along—"

"Oh no, you said it." Hope nodded. "I remember distinctly."

"It was when we were going to stow aboard a ship and go back to the Friendly Islands to live on the beach and eat fish," Patience added.

"Why was it not all right when we wanted to run off but it is all right now that you want to?" Charity's question was pointed.

Colette snorted.

"It's an excellent question, Gwendolyn," Madame said. "Perhaps you have an excellent answer?"

Hope nudged Patience, and both girls grinned. Charity's eyes widened and a smile broke on her face as well.

"I'm glad you all find this so amusing." Gwen's indignation covered her search for that excellent answer. "Of course I have an answer. I—"

"I should like to hear this as well." Marcus's voice sounded behind her.

Her heart thudded in her chest and a multitude of contrary emotions surged through her. He would stop them, of course, and that would lead to disaster, but part of her was never so grateful to hear anyone's voice as she was to hear his.

She turned to face him and resisted the urge to throw herself into his arms.

"Good evening, ladies." Marcus directed his greeting to the others, but his gaze stayed on her. "Wonderful night for a voyage, don't you think?"

"At last." Colette heaved a relieved sigh. "We wondered if you would make it in time."

"Everything today has taken longer than expected." He shrugged apologetically, as if he were explaining something of no more significance than a late arrival at dinner. "Although I did determine what, if any, ships would be leaving tonight for America and knew I had plenty of time to arrive here before its departure. You see, the moment we arrived in London—"

"We?" Gwen said sharply, her stomach twisting.

"Reggie, myself, and your cousin."

"You brought him with you?" An overwhelming

sense of defeat and betrayal washed through Gwen. "How could you?"

"I couldn't not bring him," Marcus said firmly. "Given what Whiting and I learned last night, or rather this morning, it seemed appropriate."

"Appropriate for what?" She glared at him. "For you to determine there is nothing you can do save abide by the rules and laws propagated for the benefit of those with power, men in particular, that disregard the needs and desires and happiness of the rest of us?"

"Now who is leaping to unsubstantiated conclusions?" Marcus's manner was relaxed, even casual.

She stared in stunned disbelief. What on earth was wrong with the man? He wasn't taking this nearly as seriously as he should. Didn't he realize the future of her nieces was at stake, not to mention their future? How could she ever forgive him for this?

"It's not at all what you think," Marcus said.

"It's exactly what I think," she snapped. "You're going to hand these children over to that man. My cousin"—the word left an unpleasant taste in her mouth—"who cares nothing for them and is only truly interested in getting his hands on their fortune."

"You do your cousin a grave disservice, Lady Pennington." A man's voice sounded behind her. "He was acting at my request."

Gwen whirled around. A tall, thin figure stepped forward from the shadows and the fog.

"Papa?" Charity's shocked whisper sounded behind Gwen.

Papa?

For a moment it was as if time itself stopped. The

stranger gazed with a hesitant smile and unabashed love at her nieces. *His . . . daughters?*

"Papa!" Hope screamed and hurled herself at him, followed immediately by her sisters. At once, all four were in one anothers' arms, laughing and weeping and promising each other that this was indeed real and not some specter formed by the night and the fog.

A shocked gasp sounded from Madame or Colette, Gwen wasn't sure, and she heard a sob of sheer emotion and realized it came from somewhere deep inside her.

"Gwen, this is Paul Loring." Marcus's arm slipped around her, and she sagged against him. "I told you it was appropriate."

"I don't understand." Gwen sniffed back against the tears that trickled down her face. "How can this . . ."

"It's a long story," Marcus murmured. "Fascinating though. I'm not entirely clear on all the details, but when their ship wrecked, Loring tossed the girls into a small boat along with a few others. He and your sister were washed away. He remembers very little about that but eventually woke up on an island somewhere. It was some time before he was rescued."

"And Louisa?" Gwen held her breath.

"She's gone, Gwen. I'm sorry." Marcus shook his head. "Loring searched for her for a long time to no avail. He did find the missionaries who had rescued the girls and knew they were safe and had been returned to England." Marcus paused. "He was headed home when he met up with your cousin. Townsend has been trying to locate Loring since he learned of his disappearance and the girls' survival."

It took a moment for Gwen to realize exactly what

Marcus was saying. "I have misjudged him, then, haven't I?"

"So it appears." Marcus chuckled. "However, he has misjudged you as well."

"I'm still confused." Gwen shook her head. "Didn't Mr. Whiting know about this?"

"Not entirely. He'd received some information, from Townsend's solicitor actually, but it was all quite vague and more an inquiry than anything else. It wasn't until I met with Whiting this morning that we managed to guess at the truth. You see, the letter Townsend showed us last night looked entirely too recent to my eye. However, we didn't know anything for certain until we went to Townsend's house here in London and discovered Loring himself."

"I'm afraid I still don't—" Gwen struggled to make sense of it all. "Why didn't he simply come to the hall with Townsend?"

"I thought it best not to appear without warning." Loring stepped closer, the girls still sobbing with joy and clinging to him as if they feared he would vanish if they let him go. "I see now it was probably a mistake."

Loring shook his head. "I know I have made a mess of this. I should have come forward the moment I returned to England with Adrian but, well, I'm not entirely certain how one returns from the dead. I thought it might be easier all around if I sent Adrian to fetch the girls with a paper giving him guardianship."

He gazed down at his children with unrestrained affection. "I was a bit of a coward. I was afraid. I feared telling them that I was alive while their mother . . ." A catch sounded in his voice.

"Oh, Papa." Charity sniffed. "We could never blame you for that."

"We know you did everything you could to save her." Patience choked back a sob. "You saved us."

"We love you, Papa." Hope sobbed. "And we have missed you terribly."

"But we are together now, my dear sweet girls." Loring's grip tightened around his children.

"This is so . . ." Colette's teary voice sounded behind Gwen.

"I know." Madame sniffed. "It's quite remarkable."

"Isn't it though?" Gwen struggled against a need to throw herself into Marcus's arms and weep. For happiness, of course, and for a terrible loss she was just now understanding.

Marcus drew her closer to his side. His voice was low, meant for her alone. "You have to give them up now, you know."

"I know." She forced a smile. "All I really ever wanted was for them to be with someone who cared about them. To be happy."

"Lady Pennington," Loring began.

"Gwen, please." She laughed weakly. "We are family."

"Of course, and you must call me Paul." He drew a deep breath. "I must apologize to you. Your husband has told me of all you went through after your father died. We had just learned of his death—news often travels exceedingly slow in less civilized parts of the world—and had decided to return to England when our ship was lost.

"You should understand as well that your sister cared for you a great deal." Paul shook his head. "She always assumed there would be time in the future for you to know one another."

Gwen's throat ached with tears, and she could do nothing more than nod.

"We shall miss living with you, Aunt Gwen." Hope's lower lip trembled.

"Oh, but we shall see you a great deal." Charity looked up at her father. "Won't we, Papa?"

"And Uncle Marcus and Uncle Reggie and Grand-mama Pennington. You'll like them, Papa, they're great fun." Patience grinned at her aunt. "We didn't like Aunt Gwen much in the beginning but we like her quite a bit now."

Gwen uttered something that might have been a cry or a laugh. "I have never had a finer compliment."

Marcus cleared his throat. "I imagine it could take a while for you to get your life in order, coming back from the dead and all that."

Paul laughed. "From what I have attempted thus far, it will be most awkward."

"You might wish to spend some time in the country. I have a dower house you are more than welcome to use. Even"—he sighed in resignation—"purchase if you wish."

"Marcus, how thoughtful of you." Gwen grinned. "Although, in truth, it is my dower house."

He bent low and spoke into her ear. "We shall be discussing that and a number of other matters."

"That's quite thoughtful of you both." Paul smiled at his daughters. "It's obvious from what I've heard and what I've seen tonight that there is a great deal of affection shared between all of you. I think staying in close proximity to your family—"

"Our family," Gwen said quickly.

Paul smiled. "I think it's an excellent idea. At least for now."

"But at this particular moment"—Madame stepped forward— "we should all return home. It's dank and dark and children should be in bed."

A flurry of arrangements followed and within moments, the group had divided into various vehicles for the trip back to Madame's. Gwen and Marcus were to take his carriage alone. They watched the duke's borrowed coaches roll away, then started toward their carriage.

"You have not lost them, you know," Marcus said softly. "Not really."

"I know. It's all for the best. They have their father back and . . ." She struggled against a fresh onslaught of tears. "And I, well, I have never been that good with children. It was an oddity really that they liked me at all."

Marcus laughed. "I predict our children will like you a great deal."

"Marcus." She drew a steadying breath. "About my actions, I—"

"Oh, we shall have a long discussion about your behavior, Miss Townsend—"

"Lady Pennington, if you please."

"A very long discussion. And in it we shall talk about such things as trust and independence and honesty and impulse and words like *forever*."

"Marcus." She stopped and stared up at him. "I said in my note that I would love you forever and I meant it."

"It would have done me no good if you had been half a world away." He pulled her sharply into his arms. "I would have followed you, you know. If it had taken the rest of my life, I would have found you."

The intensity of his vow left her breathless. "I did hope so."

He raised a brow. "Oh?"

"You must understand, it wasn't you I was leaving, it was the circumstances. I never wanted to leave you. After all"—she wrapped her arms around his neck— "we were brought together by the hand of fate."

"Helped along a bit by a more determined hand." He laughed. "Although it strikes me that the mother of the Fates is the Goddess of Necessity. Mothers doing what they feel necessary must be an eternal concept."

She narrowed her eyes in confusion. "What?"

"I'll explain later. For now . . ." He pulled her tighter against him. "It's enough to say from this moment forward, we shall allow nothing, not fate or its helpers, to come between us."

"Absolutely nothing." As the words left her lips, she knew she'd never said anything truer in her life. "Say it, Marcus."

He grinned. "Because if I say it aloud I'll be happy?"

"Because if you say it aloud we'll both be happy."

"Indeed we will, Lady Pennington." He bent to touch his lips to hers. "Forever, Gwen."

She melted against him and knew she'd found all she ever wanted with this arrogant, proper man and much, much more.

They would indeed, from this day forward, share their joys and their fears, every laugh and every tear, each hour and each day. There would be children who would grow safe and secure and never doubt they were well and truly loved.

And she knew as well, regardless of what they might have agreed to in a garden under the watchful eyes of the Fates themselves, seven and a half years would not be the end of what they'd found in each other.

"Forever, Marcus."

But merely the beginning.

Epilogue

Seven and a half years later

*Lord help me, I shall live a hundred years and never
understand the odd, annoying nature of men. And I should
live a thousand before I would do without them.*

Helena Pennington

"Odd time of year to have a party, don't you think?"
Lady Berkley said curiously. "Whatever possessed them
to do something like this in autumn?"

"Personally, Marian, I quite like this time of year. Besides, they said it was a celebration." Helena Pennington gazed out from the terrace over the wide lawns of
Holcroft Hall and the people milling about. So many
friends and family. "Of a promise, I believe."

Marian chuckled. "We have done well, Helena."

"Yes, we have." Helena nodded with satisfaction.
"Between our two sons we have six grandchildren now,
isn't it? No, seven. I do tend to count the twins as one.
Silly of me."

"Soon to be eight," Marian said smugly.

"The Loring girls have turned out nicely." Helena

nodded toward Charity and her new husband.

"Good breeding will tell." Marian nodded.

"As well as an exceptional stepmother. Their father married wisely."

"Indeed he did." An innocent note sounded in the other woman's voice. "And how is your Mr. Whiting?"

"My Mr. Whiting is delightful." Helena had refused his proposals of marriage on a regular basis but thought this year, perhaps, she'd accept. It might be rather a lot of fun and Lord knew it would cease those forbidding looks Marcus cast her whenever Jeffrey's name came up. "Quite delightful."

"I was thinking of getting a new solicitor myself." Marian flashed her a wicked grin, and both women laughed.

"Life has turned out exceptionally well, I think." Indeed, Helena could not remember being quite as content as she had these past seven and a half years.

"We have accomplished all we set out to do and a bit more. Still . . ." Marian sighed, "I do rather miss the Ladies' Society for the Betterment of the Future of Britain."

"Nonsense. It's just in something of a respite at the moment. All of us worked exceedingly hard for a time. And think of what fun we shall have when the next crop of offspring are ready for marriage."

"Surely they will not be as resistant as their parents to the bonds of wedlock?"

"But where would be the challenge then?" Lady Berkley's gaze met Helena's, and the two friends burst into laughter.

"The truly delightful thing"—Marian struggled to

regain her breath—"is that when the time comes we shall have the full support of their parents. Or at least their mothers."

"Indeed, I cannot foresee a time when a mother worth the name would not wish to see her offspring make a proper match."

"And with luck, find love as well." Marian chuckled. "We are romantics, Helena."

"Nonsense, Marian. In truth I think we are quite practical. I have no doubt there is little better in this life . . ." Her gaze drifted back to her future husband, and she smiled with the certain knowledge that all was right with the world. And even better, that she had had a hand in it.

"Than love with the proper husband."